Welcome to Mexico....

The three prisoners had the bags taken off their heads. Grant could see they were indeed, a woman and two children. The soldiers took out some speed cuffs and fastened their tied hands to the top strand of the fence.

"What are they going to do?" Bonneville asked again.

Grant didn't know. They looked like bait. He remained silent. One of the soldiers spoke English, and he called to Grant. "Hey, *Gringo,* you want them? Montoya is dead now. We don't need them anymore."

"Luke, what are they going to do?"

Before Grant could answer the soldiers stepped back from the fence and raised their weapons and fired into the backs of the prisoners. Then they fired at the US vehicle. Grant dropped to one knee and returned fire as he heard his windshield being blown out. He could hear Bonneville screaming something as she began firing. Two of the Mexicans went down. The others tried to drag them off, but Grant, or Bonneville, exploded one of their heads. The others gave up the effort and faded back into the brush. They fired a few more bursts before Grant heard an engine. He remembered that this was the area where an access road came almost to the fence at a sharp angle for the last few yards.

Other books by John Martin

Deployment

Recovery.

Overwatch
the Mexican Border

John F. Martin

iUniverse, Inc.
Bloomington

Overwatch
the Mexican Border

iUniverse books may be ordered through booksellers or by contacting:

iUniverse
1663 Liberty Drive
Bloomington, IN 47403
www.iuniverse.com
1-800-Authors (1-800-288-4677)

ISBN: 978-1-4620-2055-3 (sc)
ISBN: 978-1-4620-2056-0 (e)

Printed in the United States of America

iUniverse rev. date: 08/29/2011

Mexico has never been a particularly stable country. Since Hernando de Cortez first landed in the early 16th century, there has always been a war or rebellion brewing. Most of them were the home grown variety, ambitious generals, disgruntled politicians, fed-up peasants. Other than the Spanish, who started it all, none of the external invaders stayed very long. The Texans, the Americans (basically the same people, a generation apart), the French and the Americans (again) were diversions from the warlords, bandit leaders, charismatic priests, and native Indians who took pleasure in pillaging, raping and killing each other.

Oil revenues coming into the country had an effect on the standard of living, mainly for politicians, business tycoons and the old aristocracy who were still hanging on. Tourist dollars had a more direct impact on the peasants, but they had never seen anything like the rise of the drug gangs and the narco-terrorists. They were re-writing the rules of geo-political conflict, and local government, or just ignoring the rules and making it up as they went along. It was hard to tell if your standard of living was actually improving when your 16 year old had an AK-47 in his room and made more money in a week than you did all of last year.

It was either a civil war or a drug war, not that it mattered. War is war and the central government was losing either way. The army had been moved into the major cities to help control the situation. They were considered far more reliable than the federal or local police. They could be transferred away from their usual operational areas, and, just in case they were compromised, transferred out again. It was far from ideal, but it was the best plan they could come up with. Some unit officers were known to be under the influence of drug money. The real problem was how many and who.

The slide into anarchy wasn't clearly defined. There were parts of the country that hardly seemed affected by the daily executions. Then there were the areas that made Baghdad at the height of the Sunni revolt seem downright idyllic. The government just couldn't compete with the money and resources the drug cartels could put into the fight. The cartels had international tentacles, and some of the countries they came from were covertly providing support for the drug armies. Mexico, on the other hand, still had its own social programs and infrastructure to support. Fuel supplies had to be maintained, electricity generated and transmitted, water and sewerage provided, schools opened and a healthcare system to keep running. And this wasn't even a complete list of the basic services. The cartels didn't have that problem. Everything the government had was a legitimate target in their eyes. Every telephone pole, gas pump and civilian casualty was an expense for the government to fund. Safe areas, either through negotiations or extortion, were assets to be used and abused by the bad guys.

Mexico had other problems, but drugs were the worst. Diplomatically, they could plead for foreign aid from the rest of the world, especially from the thieves in the United Nations and the *gringos* north of the border. Neither one was a good option. The UN wanted to introduce their people, advisers and observers, into every level of the government, judiciary and military. And it came with conditions and concessions that only benefited the UN and gave power and safety to the cartels.

The United States had strings attached to its aid too. Not as onerous or costly, but almost as humiliating. The US had a list of conditions to be met and benchmarks to be reached. They also wanted observers and advisors, men and women who had their own agendas, but at least the *gringos* paid their own way. The real problem with the US aid was that Mexican politicians had long memories and strong prejudices. They also had sticky fingers. Corruption had been entrenched in both the legislature and the judiciary as long as anyone could remember. It was quietly accepted, primarily because there had been no other way. They were greedy, but they were Mexican, and as long as they prospered, they wouldn't do anything too extreme against the national interest. Drug money changed all that. Once you took that money, they owned you forever. The only way out was death. Even the ones that didn't take the money weren't immune. There was a long list of crusading officials and local politicians who gave a damn who were found dead and mutilated, if they were found at all. They had families too, and you couldn't protect them all.

That damned fence on the border didn't help. It had to be patrolled by the US to keep the problems to the south. That's where the Border Patrol came in, and there was one particular stretch in New Mexico that no one liked to spend much time in. It was called "the Dead Zone"; not for the fatalities, but for the lack of communications in and out of it. While the terrain was open to the Mexican side, it was boxed in by a horseshoe of features, from small, but inconveniently located hills, all the way back to the foot hills of the Continental Divide. It was a thirty mile stretch of fence and road where you were absolutely alone if anything happened. So far, nothing had happened. It almost seemed that even the illegal immigrants were avoiding the area. Nevertheless, experienced Border Patrol agents didn't like the communications blackout, and there was a running joke that it was the fastest stretch of jeep trail in the entire country.

It was Patrol Unit N-12's turn to run the Dead Zone. The patrols usually alternated between the Columbus and the Antelope Wells sector. It was Antelope Wells turn.

"Think we'll run into that *campesino* again?"

There had been reports of an old Mexican standing just inside the Mexican side about halfway up the Dead Zone, holding something low by his side. He was never doing anything, just standing there. During one of the infrequent coordination meetings with the Mexican *Federales,* they had asked if it would be possible for the US to provide them with a photo of the man. Since the request, every unit had carried a camera, but he hadn't been seen.

"I don't know, and I don't care. The old man stays on his side. He's not bothering me."

They were making good time up the jeep trail. It was a clear night, and the pot holes were easy to spot. The terrain was fairly constant, with a definite pitch downhill from left to right. On a clear night like tonight, you could see all the way to the lights of a small airfield at a place called *el Monumento*. There hadn't been any hard evidence, but it was suspected of being a transportation hub for the *Cuidad Juarez* cartels. They were coming over a small rise when the Mexican appeared off to their right.

"Hey, Matt! There's that Mexican again."

"What's he doing now?" Matt asked.

"You better look at this. I think he's carrying a rifle!"

"Dammit! We better check this out."

The driver stopped in the middle of the track and shut down the engine. The Sergeant rolled out of his seat and tossed his magazine on a dash. They had been by this spot often enough to know there wasn't much going on, and this Mexican had been what was called a "briefing item interest". Tonight it seemed as if he was trying to attract attention to himself. The senior agent leaned over the hood and picked up another pair of field glasses. There was nothing to be seen, and asked his partner where he had seen the Mexican.

"He was just a couple of yards over the border, Matt. I lost track of him when I called you."

Matt scanned the area one more time. There was still nothing to be seen. He turned to his partner just as a shot rang out. The other agent's head snapped back and he sprawled backwards on to the hood. What was happening didn't register with the senior agent at first. He stared blankly at the figure on the hood in front of him, watching the dark blood pool spread out from under the head, running down the front of the engine compartment. Suddenly, what was happening dawned on him. He turned to look back out at the border again.

He had the brief image of a flash in the distance. Then everything went dark.

Chapter 1

"The Americans are coming?" It was a question instead of a statement. They were words that the peasants in the north of Mexico have feared since the *gringo* General Blackjack Pershing chased Pancho Villa almost a century ago. It was feared as much as the phrase "the *federales* are coming."

"I know. It's nothing to worry about."

"Soldiers on the border will interfere with our routes. This area has been the most profitable for us and our partners. This will be a bad thing."

"*Carlito,* the soldiers they are sending us are being punished for what they did in Europe and Africa. They are not the best the gringos have to offer."

"*Si, Patron,* I understand that, but they have done a great deal of damage wherever they have been. They could be a problem."

"That is exactly why I do not feel they are to be feared. If you put a tame bull in a china shop he is still going to do damage. *Gringo* soldiers are no different. In Africa they took a lot of casualties. In Europe they ran afoul of the local security services and their own headquarters when they got a congressman killed. They were on the end of a very long chain of command and no one was supervising them. The American politicians do not like one of their own getting killed. They will be kept on a short leash here."

"I'm not so sure, *Patron*. If they decide to cause us trouble, I don't think they'll worry about a few politicians. After they got one killed they might have developed a taste for it. I know our soldiers do"

"We shall see, *Carlito,* we shall see. But it's not for you to worry about. After all, I am the *Commandante.*"

Carlito did not seem convinced. The *Commandante* shuffled some papers on his desk, giving his aide sidelong glances from time to time. He was still sulking.

"*Carlito*, if it will make you feel better you can accelerate some of the deliveries, but don't go too far. Killing those two agents may have been a mistake, but I'm glad you hid the bodies and their jeep. Too much attention can bring the Border Patrol down even harder. Everyone has worked to make this seem like a quiet sector. I have worked hard to make them believe we know nothing about their missing men. Let the *gringo* soldiers get settled into a routine. Once we take their measure, we will know how to proceed. They are only state militia, part time soldiers, coming to the end of their time. They will be gone soon and things can go back to normal."

The helicopters came in from the west, flying low and fast. The soldier shielded his eyes and followed them as they closed in on his position. They were Blackhawks, troop carriers. He could see one of them had a red cross in a white square on the nose, an air ambulance. We own the night, he thought, and we own the sky, where ever we go.

The unmarked chopper dropped back, and then drifted over to see who was watching, or more likely to check out what was going on in this long deserted section of the post. These were the old barracks that dated to World War II. They had been condemned as unlivable years ago, and if the budgets ever caught up with reality, they were to be torn down. Any activity here was certain to draw attention.

"Why are we in Texas?" That had been the question Sergeant First Class Jonah Price asked at every opportunity. It was also the question that couldn't be answered to anyone's satisfaction. His buddy, SFC Dave Sharp, who was filling the Operations NCO slot, could only repeat the briefing they had gotten before boarding the plane in Germany. "Price, stop asking me. I don't know any more. If the Sergeant Major knows anything else, he ain't saying, and the officers don't have a clue. They're sending us to the border. Maybe we're supposed to invade Mexico. We'll find out when we get there."

Price was never satisfied with the answer, and neither were the rest of the troops. It could have been a morale killer, if the move hadn't brought them this much closer to home. They had been getting shot at every where they went and Texas seemed like the safest place to be, even with a drug war going on right next door. The 289th Engineer Support Command had been activated to go to Iraq. Their orders had been changed to the Sudan, and after that assignment ended in a running gun fight out of the country, they were the unwanted step-children of NATO. The assignment to Moldova was supposed to be a chance to recover their strength, out of sight and out of mind. Too bad they forgot to tell the rag heads and the Russians. After saving the Russians' asses they were sent back to Germany, where they were too hot to send anywhere. The 289th wasn't about to become the Army's first choice for anything, but the feeling was that somehow, the Army would make an effort to regain control.

Nobody was ready for how it was all shaking out.

The alert had come in the middle of the night. At 0200 Captain Fischer, the acting Group Commander, had gotten the alert order. He called his staff together and showed them the message, and called a formation in their borrowed Motor Pool, ASAP. The Sergeant Major, noticing a distinct lack of detail in the message, managed to convince Fischer that everybody would be better off if he waited until morning. At least they'd have the benefit of daylight if there wasn't any more information coming. They all knew the Army was sending them somewhere. The European Union had been pressuring NATO to have them removed, but they all thought the orders would come through normal channels, and they would have time to process their equipment for an orderly transition. It wasn't to be.

The orders Fischer received called for them to be gone in 72 hours. Transportation had already been laid on, and they were to begin turning in all vehicles, sets, kits and organizational equipment immediately.

Packing out and clearing the country had been easy. They had been overrun by supply types who went through their paperwork and computers and whisked everything away. It only took a day and a half to strip them of any gear that could identify their type of unit.

While they were sitting on the tarmac waiting to board the aircraft, the staff had been pulled aside for an additional briefing. It wasn't much, and as soon as it started, CSM Grant recognized the smoke and mirrors. The information they were getting was a rehash of what was running on the 24 hour news channels. There was nothing about the new mission. Grant felt someone tap on his shoulder. A Sergeant Major he had never seen before told him to come into another room. Then the real briefing began.

"Sergeant Major Grant, what you are about to hear is classified. I won't bother you with how high, but it's enough to say that what you hear today cannot be passed on to anyone until your new commander clears it."

"So we're getting a new CO? Somebody fucked up enough to get us as a punishment?"

The briefer, a Colonel who Grant noticed wasn't wearing a name tape or any unit patches, had a cold look pass over his face for a few seconds. Then he took a deep breath and continued. "That's an unfortunate way to put it, Sergeant Major, but that's about the long and short of it. Lieutenant Colonel Kearney has proven himself a little too aggressive for his current assignment, but we feel he is a good fit for this unit."

Grant thought about that for a second. "We feel…?" Then it hit him. "Kearney? Daniel Kearney?"

"You've heard of him?" Everybody in the Army had heard of LTC Daniel Kearney. A rising star, and soon to be full Colonel, he had been given a composite Brigade to train up for Afghanistan. So far, they were the longest cycle at the National Training Center. None of the officers, save for Kearney, had deployed at all since 9/11, and it showed. In spite of widespread officer reliefs and constant shuffling of the experienced NCOs, the Brigade had not met any of its certification standards. The Brigade was currently being broken up and pieced out to other units, and many of the officers, Kearney excluded, were coming to the end of their careers. Kearney, a Regular Army Officer, had somehow managed to avoid getting any of the mud splashed on him. Some of the back channel chatter was that the Army was taking care of a 'dark green' over the 'light greens'.

"This is good for the 289th how?"

Another officer from the back of the room interrupted. This one, a General, didn't seem to be as understanding as the Colonel. "You're getting a new CO, Sergeant Major. That's the end of the discussion."

"All due respect, Sir, I have to work with him."

"That's incorrect, Sergeant Major. You have to work for him. He'll decide the scope of your duties. If that's unsatisfactory, you can decide to retire, and we'll find someone who's fucked up enough to replace you."

Grant knew a dressing down when he heard one. "Yes, Sir," was all he said.

The next twenty minutes were a rehash of what the staff was getting in the other room. Grant half listened as his attention was drawn to a series of maps taped to the wall. He wasn't close enough to make out any detail, but he could see that the maps were bisected. Half had detail, the rest was blank. The briefer finally moved to the maps. "This will be your new Area of Operations. Just to the west of El Paso, there's a section of the US and Mexican border that runs almost due north and south. The public mission, the one the rest of the staff is getting briefed on, will be that the 289th will be upgrading the jeep track that runs along the border for the Border Patrol, and maintain the fence that runs along it."

"The public mission?" Grant asked.

"Yes. The Mexican government is very sensitive about US troops on the border. They're very busy losing their drug war, and they worry about US intervention to stop smuggling and illegal immigration.

"We want to reassure them. There will be regular 'consultations' with the Mexicans so they can see the work your unit is doing. What they won't see is what a select group of you will be doing."

"Which is?"

The briefer started peeling away the white paper covering the Mexican side of the map. There were areas marked in red, all several kilometers from the border. "These are suspected human and narcotics smuggling hubs. Your task will be to neutralize them."

"Neutralize them? How?"

"The specifics will be detailed later. LTC Kearney is getting the same briefing as you. The operative plan is for it to look like the work of rival cartels, or in the extreme, rogue elements of the Mexican police or Army."

Grant pondered that for a moment. "You don't care if it causes more internal problems for the Mexicans?"

"Not at this time."

"And you think the 289th is capable of doing this?"

"No, Sergeant Major, we don't. What we believe is that you, and several of your fellow NCOs, are capable of selecting and training the right people to do this."

The General spoke again. "You did it in Darfur several times and then again in Moldova. We know you can repeat it."

"And since the press was so bad, if it all goes to shit in Mexico, you can blame it all on us, a bunch of over-the-hill thrill junkies."

"Very good, Sergeant Major. You catch on quickly."

"And our choices in the matter, if we have any?"

The General stood up and moved in front of Grant. "You really don't have any." He paused for a moment. "You do this, and we forgive and forget a lot of sins."

Grant sensed a bluff, or a load of bullshit, but he couldn't be sure. "Which sins do you think I need to have forgiven and forgotten?"

"Yours are simple, Sergeant Major. You have a relationship with Captain Bonneville that could be prosecuted. It would ruin both of your careers." There was another pause ever so slight, but noticeable. "Then there's always your three friends, Sharp, Price and Harrison."

"They aren't involved in that."

"No, but there's always illegal weapons, that highly irregular B-17 acquisition, and need I mention the reports of a substantial amount of cash and gold that was reported to be in the Janjaweed camp before your little outing?"

The two men stared at each other for a long, silent minute. "I can see you've done your homework on us. Will you be threatening them too?"

"Not for the moment. If you have any more questions, save them for when you see LTC Kearney."

The plane was a chartered Boeing 767. There was no ground crew, so they had to load their own baggage. Sharp and Price organized the bucket brigade that stowed everything in the lower bays, then waited for a crew member to come around and inspect it before they were closed up.

"At least they let us keep our personal gear."

"Price, will you shut the fuck up about that? They ain't gonna change their minds because your feelings are hurt. If we need any heavy stuff, they'll have to give it to us at Fort Bliss."

"Bliss has three things: Air Defense, Combat Brigades and the Sergeant Major Academy. All the engineers there belong to somebody. I checked. No heavy stuff we can get at. We're back to being infantry, Dave."

"Maybe you haven't noticed, but every place we go we always end up being infantry with a lot of heavy shit parked in the motor pool. At least this way we don't have to get our hopes up."

1SG Harrison had been listening to the bickering. He decided to intervene so he didn't have to listen to it all the way to Texas. "Were you two ass holes even listening? We're gonna upgrade a road and build 30 miles of fence."

"Yeah," Sharp answered. "And they're flying us 6,000 miles because we were the closest unemployed laborers."

Harrison shook his head. "Think what you want, but keep it to yourself. All you're doing now is looking for trouble."

The flight had been long, but not uncomfortable. There were only 120 of them, on a plane that could hold twice that. There was plenty of room to stretch and catch a decent nap. The food wasn't bad, the cabin crew friendly, and even though it was a military charter, meaning no booze service, the troops were experienced enough to bring some of their own stock. As long as they policed themselves and no one got terminally stupid, there would be no problems with the officers. They had their own supply up front anyway. Between Captain Fischer, the acting Group Commander, and Lieutenant Fuller, the new company commander, there was a lack of adult supervision.

Luke Grant and Ralph Harrison had placed themselves strategically on the plane, in between the officers up front and the enlisted out back. They took turns patrolling the aisles, making sure the NCOs were keeping a light hand on their soldiers. Occasionally, they had to play the part of "bad cop" when one of the junior officers felt a need to bond with the troops. In close confines with a little alcohol added, a young Lieutenant could quickly loose all hope of regaining control later on.

Captain Bonneville came back from time to time to sit with Grant. They could exchange pleasantries, trade small talk, even conduct some official military business. Their relationship was a poorly kept secret in the unit, but they made every effort to keep it in check in public and not give anyone cause for idle gossip. Fraternization rules were lax in the National Guard, but once a unit was activated the rules were stringent, and could bring a career or two to a crashing halt. Still, Bonneville wanted to spend some time with Grant. The rest of the staff was, well, boring. Grant decided that she didn't need to know about the take it or leave it offer the Army had just made. He'd work around the problem once they were on the ground and he could see the situation in Mexico up close.

The cabin lights came up when the pilot announced they were a half-hour out of Bangor, Maine. It was the primary customs clearing stop for most military transports coming from Europe and the Middle East. The drill was to un-ass the plane, grab all your gear and go through customs. The inspectors were used to troops coming through heavily armed. The military policy didn't allow for souvenirs, so the inspectors automatically assumed that visible weapons they carried were authorized. They didn't even open the rifle case Sharp carried his vintage Mauser sniper rifle in. The other soldiers who had broken down their trophy rifles didn't even have their duffel bags opened. Grant, Harrison, Sharp, Price, Bonneville and half a dozen others were carrying side-arms under their blouses. Grant had several of his Argentine Colt clones in his ruck sack. Those weren't checked either. Grant suspected their way had been greased by the powers that be. It was a very lax screening.

After the plane was cleared it was refueled and serviced for the flight to Fort Bliss. The 289th was able to spend the time in the terminal, making phone calls or enjoying some American made fast food or fresh domestic beer.

There had been a message waiting for Captain Fischer. After he read it he made arrangements for a conference room and called the staff together. "I've been informed that the new commander has been delayed, and won't join us for a week to ten days. We're to begin preparation for our assignment in the interim. There's a suggestion that we deal with the move to the field as an NCO training exercise, and let them deal with the details. I think that's an excellent idea. It'll give us more time to get ourselves organized without that distraction."

Captain Bonneville looked around the room and then interrupted him. "If you're going to follow through with that, shouldn't the Sergeant Major be here?"

"Captain, I'm certain CSM Grant is grateful you're looking out for his best interests, but this information only concerns the staff at this point." His smirk indicated a more subtle, off-color meaning. Bonneville ignored it. "The Sergeant Major is part of the staff, Captain Fischer, and since the sign out in front of any headquarters building we may have only has the Commander and Sergeant Major's names, I would say someone considers the position to be rather important in the overall scheme of things." There was a wave of chuckling in the room. Fischer's face reddened. She continued, "And if you think that making the exercise NCO driven, shouldn't he have the benefit of the advance notice?"

The bitch was right. "Very well, Captain. Why don't you go get him?"

Four hours later they were on the ground at Fort Bliss, Texas. There were buses and trucks waiting for them and their gear. There was an escort officer assigned to each bus, an armed escort officer, no less. Sharp tried to ask the one on his bus why. He was greeted with a cold "You don't need to know," and the officer turned his back on him. The rest of the soldiers watched the exchange wordlessly. It was a quiet ride to post. The buses dropped them at an older, deserted section, where the World War II dated buildings had not yet been replaced with new construction. The escorts pointed out an area that was assigned to them. The troops started to drift off to check out their surroundings, until First Sergeant Harrison stopped them. He put them in formation and told them to hold their position until things got organized.

"Where's Harte?" The Company Supply Sergeant raised his hand from the back of the formation. "Harte! Get your ass over there and sign for our buildings." He paused and looked around. "Price! Get a detail over to one of those trucks and get the gear unloaded. Then take the Motor Sergeant and some drivers with you and find a motor pool that will give us some vehicles. Don't come back without them."

"On it, Top." Price took his whole platoon with him to empty the trucks and told Mitchell, the Motor Sergeant, to bring some of his mechanics.

"Hold up, First Sergeant." It was the senior escort officer, a Major. He handed Harrison a sheaf of papers on a clip board. "I might as well give these to you, First Sergeant. You seem to be the only one thinking about what to do."

Harrison took the papers and flipped through them. Grant joined him and the two of them sorted through the pile and started calling out NCOs and giving them assignments. Sometimes, it looked like an officer was needed to complete a task. Grant took those and gave them to Captain Fischer to assign. Harrison smiled at him when he came back. "Just when everything was going so good."

"Yeah, I know. But he looked like he needed something to do."

The senior escort disappeared for a couple of hours, which Grant thought was a good thing for Captain Fischer. The acting commander was clearly out of his element on a strange post, with none of the usual support systems a politically connected officer could find at home station. He was frequently summoning the First Sergeant or Sergeant Major for advice, guidance or sometimes to just delegate a particularly onerous task.

After about an hour of this some of the junior NCOs came to Grant to ask his help. "Sergeant Major, we don't mean any disrespect, but these fucking officers are killing us."

Grant sympathized. "They're only trying to do their jobs. Bear with them for a bit longer."

"Hell, Sergeant Major, we don't mind helping them learn their jobs. Some of the Lieutenants are going out of their way to help us get shit done. But some of these staff officers are just asking stupid questions and arguing with us when they don't understand the answer." The soldier had a pleading look in his eyes. "Can you find something for them to do?"

There was something they could do. Grant went looking for Fischer and suggested he take the staff into what was apparently a headquarters building and have them organize. "Captain, if we're getting a new CO, maybe you and the staff should pull all the records and come up with a Unit Status Report for the new guy. You know that's the first thing he's going to ask for."

Fischer looked irritated. "Status? There is no status. We have no equipment, no weapons and damned little of anything else. What kind of a report will that be?"

Yup, Grant was convinced. Fischer had no clue at all. "Captain, that is the status. We've got the laptops and the programs. We need shit, a lot of it. All the staff needs to brief our shortages, prepare some requisitions and come up with a quick and dirty training schedule. You can't have it look like we got here and the only thing we have to do is lie around in the barracks."

"And where is all this information supposed to come from? I can't just pull it out of my ass!"

Grant was chewing on the inside of his cheek and it was starting to hurt. "You don't need to, Sir. You have a Table of Organization and Equipment, the TO&E, plus all the platoons have a Training and Evaluation Program. It's all on the computers." As an afterthought he added, "I'll have the First Sergeant send someone over to the Self Service Supply Center and pick up some office supplies. A few white boards and flip charts will give the staff something to work with."

The senior escort chose that moment to reappear. He handed Fischer a messenger envelope. "This is as good a time to tell you that the change of command may be moved up. This has a list of items you need to accomplish before a new commander arrives." Fischer looked down at the envelope, then over at the Sergeant Major. He smiled. "Major," he said to the escort, "this is just what we've been discussing."

The area was dark after sunset. There were no street lights. This was a forgotten section of Fort Bliss that was scheduled for demolition at some point. The fact that the buildings were still standing was a testament to budget priorities that didn't leave much for this area. Grant looked around and was trying to decide if he was just dissatisfied with conditions or royally pissed. He personally didn't care what the Army threw at him. He was used to it. These soldiers, on the other hand, had been doing everything that had been asked of them and more. They deserved better.

He stepped into the Company Headquarters building. It wasn't as large as what the staff had, but it was enough. Harrison had gathered the senior NCOs and was having his own briefing. Each platoon in turn went through their current status, what they were looking for in equipment, and what they hoped they could get on the training schedule. Harrison was getting it all down so he could give it to Lieutenant Fuller in the morning. Fuller was still new to the job, just getting it after the last CO, Captain Blackman, moved over to the staff. He had seen enough commanders come and go, and there was always a chance that Fuller could develop into a good officer. He showed promise. The new commander would probably ask what the company needed and expected. He wasn't about to leave his young Lieutenant twisting in the wind.

All things considered, they were in pretty good shape after only half a day of scurrying. The barracks were clean and in fairly good shape. The soldiers had bunks, linen and hot showers. Somewhere, Supply

Sergeant Harte had even found curtains for the female barracks. Now that he wasn't influenced by MSG Winder, he was getting his work done. Moura, the dining facility manager, had found a mobile kitchen trailer he could set up outside the mess hall for now, and he even drew some decent rations. There was a central dining facility about a mile away that Harrison was still working on getting access.

Sergeant Mitchell, true to form, had gotten access to the bone yard, and was able to pull out some salvageable vehicles and get authorization to cannibalize for parts. He promised four more vehicles over and above what Price and Lieutenant Stanley were able to draw from post. "All Blazers and Chevy Pick-ups, First Sergeant, but they'll run."

After everyone had left, Grant and Harrison settled in for a few drinks before they called it a day. "Just think, Luke. Yesterday morning we were forming up in Europe, fat, dumb and happy. Look at us now."

"Yeah. How many countries does that make that we've been run out of?" Grant asked.

"I prefer to ask what new adventures we have in store. As long as we're in the States, there's a good chance nobody's going to be shooting at us."

"I wouldn't bet on it!" Sharp was standing in the door. Price was right behind him. "I just ran into Captain Bonneville. Fischer let them in on what was in the magic envelope he got this afternoon. She'll be here in a minute."

Bonneville was right behind them. She smiled at Grant then sat next to the ever present beer cooler. She reached in and pulled one out. It wasn't a twist top, so Grant had to pop the cap for her. She took a long swallow, put the bottle down and pulled a note book out of her pocket. "Fischer tried to explain this, but didn't do a very good job. I'll just give you what he said." She looked up and paused as Price came in and grabbed a beer. Harrison motioned to him to stay and take a seat.

Bonneville continued. "After a short refit and train-up, we'll be leaving here."

Sharp interrupted. "How long do we have?"

"He didn't say. That'll probably be up to the new guy after he makes his assessment of us. Then we go to the border."

"We already knew that. But the border stretches for a couple of thousand miles." Harrison said. "Did they happen to mention where? That briefing in Germany left out a few details."

"New Mexico"

Everybody turned and looked at Grant.

"Well, that's more than we knew before. Have you been reading somebody's mail?"

"About thirty or forty miles west of here the border runs almost due north and south. That'll be our AO. We're going to be part of a Joint Task Force that's responsible for a long stretch of the border. We're going to be watching a stretch that needs a fence upgrade." Everybody was staring at him. "That's all I can say for now."

"So there's more?" Bonneville asked.

Grant leaned over and kissed her on the forehead. "That's good enough for now." He stood up. One thing I want you all to start thinking about is getting some recons of the area done. Fischer wants this move to be NCO driven, so, barring any unexpected problems, plan on some road trips this weekend."

"Will we have the vehicles for it?"

Grant thought about the General's comments in Germany. "We've got the corporate cards from the account Willa Harrison set up with the Janjaweed money. Use that to rent some."

Bonneville spoke up. "Are you going to tell the CO?"

The four Sergeants had a brief laugh, and Harrison spoke. "We should, but how long have you known us? If he doesn't think about it, we'll be ahead of the game."

They broke up to leave. Harrison sent them on ahead. He'd stay behind and wait for the duty NCO to get back from his shower. They said their good nights and went their separate ways, except for Grant and Bonneville. "I know you're going to walk me to my quarters, Sergeant Major."

The 289th had been assigned an area that usually housed a full battalion. When the area had first been laid out, the individual companies would surround their area. A row of these areas would constitute a regiment; the headquarters would be centered on the row, usually across the street. Behind a row of regimental headquarters would be an expansive parade ground, and opposite that, a divisional headquarters. That was all in the past. What hadn't been torn down was largely deserted, except for this little island.

They were quiet until they were halfway across the small drill field in the center of the battalion area they had been assigned. With all the buildings available, Fischer had spread everyone out. Officers were on one corner, senior NCOs on another, and the female officers and NCOs were at the extreme opposite end. Bonneville spoke first. "I wanted to do something this weekend, Like maybe go into town and get a room somewhere away from all this?"

Grant thought for a minute. So far, all the plans he had been making with Harrison, Sharp and Price had been tentative. They didn't have an operational plan yet, and no timetable. Once the new guy hit the ground, there may not be another opportunity to get away. Still, he wanted to be practical. Going into El Paso could have them running into other soldiers from the 289th. That would not be good for the discretion they still tried to practice. "I'm way ahead of you on that. Starting next week I have to spend some time at the Sergeant Major Academy. This weekend, I'm going to Mexico. Are you up for a road trip?"

"Why are you going to Mexico?"

"We need to get some idea of what's happening on the other side of the wire. I'm pretty sure that little tidbit won't be included in any briefing Fischer gets, and I'm damn sure he won't think to ask about it."

"I thought Mexico was off limits to soldiers because of the troubles?"

"It is. Pack an overnight bag and don't bring your military ID, just your passport and drivers license. We'll go over as tourists."

"What if we get caught?"

"What are they going to do with us? Send us to Fort Bliss?"

"Is it dangerous?"

"It shouldn't be. We'll just be tourists. We'll do some sightseeing, take a few pictures, and you can spend a small fortune buying souvenirs."

"I mean on the border."

"I tend to doubt it. Picking off a rancher or taking a shot at a Border Patrol agent is one thing. Even the cartels don't want a lot of attention paid to the outlying area. Quiet is good for business." He didn't want to tell her about the cross border plans until he absolutely had to.

They were at her billets. "Can you come in for a while?"

"Better not. Somebody might complain. Let's see how the neighbors are for a few days. If I get sent to the SMA I'll get a room at the visitor's center. It's set up like a motel." She slipped her arm around him and gave him a hug. "One more thing," he said. "Get your greens sent out, blues too, if you've got 'em."

"Why?"

"The Academy has regular formal functions and they know how make the most out of a formal occasion. Here," he wrote a string of numbers on the back of a card. "That's the shipping account number for Harrisons' company. Have your mother box them up and overnight them."

First Sergeant Harrison had the company formed in the parking lot before the staff showed up. He had them dress and cover, then put them at ease. He still wasn't sure why Fischer had called this formation. As far as he could tell, nothing had changed.

Two things caught his attention at the same time. The first was the staff casually strolling out of the headquarters building, stumbling to get sorted out. It was a far cry from the crisp, military ceremony they had when the unit was activated. The other was a small group, probably a platoon, marching in from the left of the formation. He heard SFC Sharp mumble in the background "Who the fuck is this group?"

"I don't know. They have their own guidon. Maybe it's a courtesy element from post."

Now it was Price's turn. "Can't be anybody special. These guys can't even stay in step." It was true. Although they were in formation and marching to a called cadence, they were far from in step. The platoon sergeant brought them to a halt, dressed them with the engineers, and put them at ease. Harrison made a half turn to find out who they were, but Captain Bonneville's voice rang out.

"Group, attention!"

The formation snapped to attention and the officers replaced the NCOs in front of the formation. Harrison looked over at the newcomers as he made his way to his new position to the rear. They were carrying an infantry guidon. The wind momentarily held it out so he could see the designation. They were a part of Delta Company, 4th Battalion, of the 711th Infantry. Harrison had never heard of it. They were probably a National Guard unit too. There was the usual flurry of movement among the staff as Fischer moved to the front. He put the formation at ease, and then made a short announcement. "There has been a slight change to our organization. The platoon to your left will be joining us. That's all. First Sergeant, take charge!" Harrison and Fischer exchanged salutes, then the First Sergeant did an about face and dismissed the formation, all except the new platoon.

In the midst of the milling around, Sharp and Price gathered around Harrison. "What the fuck was that all about?" Price asked.

"I don't know, Pricey. Seems like the good Captain is exercising his command prerogatives."

"What about these guys?"

"We'll find out pretty soon." Harrison looked over at the newcomers. The platoon leader, he could now see was a First Lieutenant, his platoon sergeant and two squad leaders were standing together looking at them. "They look lost."

"Yeah, Dave, that they do." Harrison motioned for them to come over. "Let's find out who they are."

They were a mixed bag of troops who had been living in another section of the old post waiting for assignment. The orders had come through that morning, and they were short and to the point: they were now assigned to the 289th. Harrison wasted no time with niceties. He informed their Lieutenant, a slightly overweight Signal Corps, type that they needed to vacate their current quarters and move in immediately. He pointed out which barracks were designated for the officers, but Lieutenant Johnson took one look at the old building and informed the First Sergeant he'd be keeping his BOQ over on the new post. That was about the time Captain Bonneville, with her personnel NCO SSG Gordon arrived with the Sergeant Major. She caught the tail end of the conversation and told Johnson he'd be moving. "All our officers live here," she told him.

"I'd rather stay where I am. I'm settled in and I'm authorized a quarters allowance."

Bonneville had no time to argue. "Get your stuff, you're moving here. Do you have any records for your people?"

"Back in my quarters."

"Good. We'll kill two birds with one stone. Sergeant Gordon will take you back and help you pack. Or would you prefer I go?" Without waiting for a response she turned to Harrison. "First Sergeant, get the enlisted men moved before lunch. I'll start processing them at 1300." With that, there was an exchange of salutes and she was gone. Lt. Johnson mumbled something about having a rental car, and Gordon told him they could pick it up after he was out of the BOQ, and they moved off. Sharp was looking back and forth between Grant and Harrison. "You've been teaching her some bad habits, Luke? That poor guy didn't have a chance!"

"Yeah, my bubbly personality is infectious."

Processing started on time. They were an Infantry platoon, and Sharp ran them everywhere they went. Their Platoon Sergeant, Callan, protested that they hadn't been acclimated to the hot Texas weather, but Sharp blew him off. "I've seen you guys over there since we've been here. You're as acclimated as we are. Get used to it."

Bonneville had her whole section, now expanded to 4 people, doing the processing. It didn't take long before they had made an unusual discovery, and sent for the Sergeant Major.

They were an Infantry platoon in name only. In fact, not one of them held the 11B MOS of an infantryman. Grant looked down the list and raised his eyebrows. There was a Spanish linguist, and an Arabic one, too; an intelligence analyst, two unmanned aerial surveillance drone operators, a computer specialist, several communicators, including a satellite guy, a legal specialist, a weapons repair specialist, some mechanics, a water purification team and a layering of combat engineers.

"What does this mean, Luke?"

Grant shook his head. "It looks like someone is fattening us up for the slaughter."

"What?"

"I can't say now, at least I'm not supposed to." He looked at the roster again. There was a meaning to these people. "How long has this group been together?"

Bonneville pulled a few records and checked dates. "From the looks of it, they started getting assigned a little over a month ago. Johnson said they gave him the guidon so no one would know what they were supposed to be, and they wouldn't tell him either."

A month ago was before they got thrown out of Europe. It looked like this operation they were involved with had been in the planning stages for quite a while before they got involved.

"Well," Grant started, "I'm a long way from being certain, but this looks a lot like the type of people you'd find backing up a special operations mission."

"Is there any word on the new commander?" Grant asked.

"He's supposed to be here next week. Why?"

"I need to do something, and I think time's running out. I'm going to set something up in the Mess Hall after supper. Come by and bring Gordon. I think I need to involve you in something you may not want to be in."

"Do I still get to go to Mexico with you?"

"Of course."

"Then I'll be there."

Everyone drifted into the Mess Hall after the cooks and contract

KPs had cleaned up for the night. One of the nice things about some posts was that they hired local civilians to do the Kitchen Police chores, freeing up the soldiers for actual training. The Mess Sergeant put on a pot of coffee and laid out some sandwiches he had made up for them. After asking Harrison to make sure everything was turned off and locked up, he excused himself.

Grant tacked his maps to the wall and had everyone put away their note books. He pointed out that anything they heard tonight was to stay between them for now. There were a few raised eyebrows, but everyone agreed.

He recapped the briefing he had gotten in Germany. The maps were all local purchase, and he had marked them up as best he could remember. Since he had damn little hard information about what they were, he didn't speculate, nor did he encourage guesswork. "When the time comes, we'll find out for ourselves."

"So what are we supposed to do, Luke?" Sharp asked.

"There's something out there we have to neutralize. I don't know what, but we have to make it look like the cartels are feeding off one another, or the Mexican army is moving in for a cut."

"Any support from the big Army?" This question from Price.

"I'll let Captain Bonneville answer that. She's seen the records on these new guys. I don't know if we can trust them, or if they know what we're supposed to do, but they were sent here for a reason."

Bonneville went over the specialties of the new platoon. It wasn't a combination that pointed to any particular function, but it was clear that, if they were provided with the equipment suited to their training, they would provide a local resource for surveillance, intelligence planning and discreet communications.

Harrison picked up on the communications. "I thought you said the area was pretty much blacked out for communications? How are the commo guys going to help?"

"It's blacked out from the outside. If you look at these features," he highlighted three areas with a yellow marker, "signals don't travel in or out, except here to the Mexican side. But being in that bowl, we should have excellent contact between units."

"What about cell phones?"

"Good question, Robinson. Once we're in there, we might be able to get a temporary cell tower, but I don't know if the Army will spring for it. As it turns out, we may not need it. The area seems to have pretty good coverage on the Mexican network."

"So we need Mexican cells? How do we get those?"

"No problem." Grant said. "Down by the border crossing there's a bunch of little strip malls that specialize in separating the day laborers and tourists from their money. One of them specializes in disposable pre-paid phones. I've got two cases of them to use as needed."

From there he went into the details of what he wanted for the weekend. He moved from map to map, handing out assignments. Sharp stopped him before he could get too far into the planning. "You'll have to count me out for this one. Fischer thinks I have too much time on my hands. He wants me to take the new guys out to the field over the weekend. He wants me to give him an assessment. We're going out Friday night."

Grant snorted. "Nice of him to let me know. You do realize that none of them are grunts?"

"Think that might be a problem, Boss?"

"Only if somebody plans on using them in a tactical role. Go easy on them, but find out what they're capable of and at least get them up to speed so they can survive if we happen to get involved with something."

"Do you think the new guy will know if they're Infantry or not? Or will he care?"

"If it's who I think it is it probably won't matter. He should have gotten even more of a briefing than I did. If not, we'll work around it." He didn't seem interested in saying more about that, and no one asked.

He turned back to the maps. "First problem and this is for you, Price. Our area starts south of this *Sierra Rica* range, about here," he pointed to a small spot about a kilometer inside the border."This place is called Border Wells. You need to see if we can get the heavy equipment in through there. If we can't, no problem. We'll move it out early and take a long detour. This place might be a good bivouac site for the heavy stuff. If not there, then try further south here." He pointed to a spot called Double Well, located in the Hatchita Valley."That's about a ten kilometer stretch, give or take. That'll be your AO to start."

"To start?"

"Yeah, you'll be working on the entire stretch of road. At some point you'll have to relocate so you're not burning up time and fuel commuting to work. All of you keep that in mind. You will relocate when Price has to move." He looked over to a young female Lieutenant who was sitting there quietly. "Lieutenant Stanley, I'm assuming a lot here. Do you have any problems with what we're doing?"

The officer shook her head and wrinkled her nose. "I get more involved when you do things than when the Group does it. If it's OK with Captain Bonneville, I guess I can share a jail cell with her." That got a laugh from the group.

"Let's hope we don't have to!" was Bonneville's comment.

Grant moved on. "We have about another 25 klicks of border here. I was planning on splitting it up three ways, but not having Sharp puts a kink into that. I wanted him to look at the extreme southern end."

Harrison spoke up. "What about me? I think I remember how to do a simple recon."

"I thought about that, Ralph, but I need somebody back here in case there's a problem. Robinson, I'll use you for the next section." Robinson moved closer to the front of the group. "Start here at Cabin Well," Grant pointed to another spot. It's on an access road from Double Well, so maybe you and Sergeant Price can work something out."

"Roger that!"

"From there I want you to check out about 12 klicks to grid 6590. There might be a dirt strip in that area. Nobody has mentioned it yet, but I'm pretty sure something like that in that area won't go unnoticed for long."

"Luke, can I make a suggestion?" Price asked.

Grant nodded.

"We've got two construction platoons," he gestured towards SFC

Powell and SFC Mason. "They're here, so let's use them. Mitchell too." Mitchell was the Motor Sergeant.

"You're right. We need to share the wealth. You guys have done everything you've had to. I need to include you more."

"No problem, Sergeant Major." Mason said. "I don't know about that shit they want done in Mexico, but we can back you up on this side if you need it. You've already turned most of my carpenters in snake eaters anyway."

That settled it. Grant gave Mason the top half of the area, from the supposed air strip to a place called Campbell Well. Powell got the rest, to the southern end of the AO, Corner Well.

"Give these areas a good look, and take a lot of pictures. We need to find a place to put headquarters, and I think somewhere in the area between Cabin and Double Well. That's about as centrally located we can get them without them being in the way, no offense intended to the S-1."

"You'll pay for that, Sergeant Major!"

"I'm sure I will."

Sharp wasn't finished yet. "You've got all the worker bees doing something this weekend. What's the king bee got planned?"

"Since you asked, I'm taking Captain Bonneville to Mexico. We're going to look at the red areas up close and personal."

From the look on Bonneville's face, Sharp knew looking at bad guys hadn't been part of her weekend plans.

Grant passed out Mexican cell phones to all the teams. "Activate them and swap numbers. Just use them to call each other, and don't gossip. Keep track of the air time. When you run low, see me for another one."

"What do we do with the old ones, Sergeant Major?"

"Either give it to me or burn it. Don't just break them up or throw them away. I want all memory to get destroyed so they can't be traced."

"Can we have maps?' That was Robinson.

"Not the marked ones. I have some clean ones for you. Take a couple so everyone with you has one."

Chapter 2

Grant and Bonneville had crossed the border on Friday night. There had been an all-wheel drive rental waiting for them on the Mexican side, as promised by the storekeeper he had bought the cell phones from. Almost as an afterthought, he let Captain Fischer know he'd be out of the Group area, although he was deliberately vague about where he'd be. Fischer made a comment about Grant seeing old friends on post, and Grant let him have that thought. He did leave his cell phone number, one of the disposables they bought by the box. Linda Bonneville signed out too, but her destination was simply "El Paso". When she told Luke Grant about it, she simply added, "Well, I didn't say how long I'd be there."

Fischer was generally in agreement that the company, with the exception of the infantry platoon and any duty people, could have time off as long as they didn't wander too far. Grant and Bonneville had checked into a high end hotel in what was considered the "safe" part of the central district of *Juarez*. He used the Swiss credit card that came with the account Harrisons' wife had set up for them with Arab money they had 'acquired' in Sudan. The Swiss card was accepted worldwide, and there wasn't any IRS reporting that would lead back to them. They arranged to pick up a picnic style lunch for early in the morning, had a good meal in the hotel restaurant and a few drinks in the bar, and then retired to their room.

Bonneville kept him up until past midnight. He hadn't expected her to be as fresh as she was at breakfast.

The map that came with the Jeep was lacking in detail, so he used a paste up from the maps he had used in his briefing, carefully marked up so it would appear he was looking for old landmarks from Pancho Villa's days. He hoped he wouldn't have to use that story. If they were stopped by the *federales* or the local police he really didn't have enough background to explain his story, but a thin story on short notice was better than none. Linda Bonneville's role, if she were called on to play one, would be that of the bored girlfriend who was humoring her sugar daddy boyfriend. It was also a thin cover story, but it didn't require much background.

They drove a little over an hour on a modern highway, heading to the southwest, until he estimated he was opposite the lower end of their Area of Operations. There had been a lot of side roads on the border side of the highway. Some of them looked well used, but his map didn't show any manmade objects. He made a mental note to get some satellite photos of the area. There had also been an occasional Mexican army truck rolling by. The soldiers didn't seem to be very alert to their surroundings. They must have considered this to be a quiet sector.

The AO stretched about 32 kilometers in a straight line; south to north, then the border took a 90 degree turn to the east. The closest border crossing, at Columbus, and main road, was about thirty miles from the international corner. He planned to pick up that road, head back to Juarez in time for a late afternoon drink and a *siesta*, or whatever else Bonneville had planned for him. While she had always been adventurous when they had been on deployment, it was mild compared to what she was like far away from the flag pole.

They had stopped to eat in a little grove after they had forded a small river at a cattle crossing. She made it clear what was on her mind if there hadn't been so many signs of activity in the area.

This part of the border had a pretty interesting history less than a century ago. Before the US got involved in World War I, Mexico had been wrapped up in one of its periodic revolutions. The government was pretty unpopular, and a bunch of patriots and bandits were setting up their own little states and challenging the army and the central government. This had been the operating area of Pancho Villa and his *Division del Norte*, one of the more popular of the patriot/bandit/

revolutionaries. He pretty much controlled this area, and made periodic trips into the US to steal cattle, rob banks and buy guns and supplies. There were even some Americans who supported him. One went as far as to make a movie about him.

Villa pretty much had the government by the ass, and there was little they could do about him. Success bred contempt, though, and Villa thought he was invincible. He decided to take on the *gringos del norte*, and in 1916 led a raid over the border to Columbus, New Mexico. His intelligence must have been faulty, because he failed to allow for a US cavalry troop that was stationed just outside of town. They gave his *Villistas* a bloody nose, and, the last thing he expected, the Mexican government gave the US permission to hunt him down. That led to the punitive expedition under General "Blackjack" Pershing, and his aide, George Patton. Pershing had a meteoric rise in the Army after the Spanish American War. Somehow, he was promoted over hundreds of senior officers from Captain to Brigadier General. It was almost like George Custer during the Civil War, and many of his contemporaries expected him to come to the same end. They never did catch Villa, but they disrupted his organization enough so that by the time the US troops were pulled out to go to war in Europe, Villa couldn't recover his initiative. He was assassinated by his own people a few years later.

After lunch they drove closer to the border, approaching the dirt strip at *el Monumento* from the south. There was a small plane sitting alone on the end of the runway. The only other activity was around a cluster of buildings on either side of the road. Grant slowed and told Bonneville to act like she was pissed off because he was lost. "Keep your eyes open and don't get out of the jeep. If anybody comes close, just keep ranting about how stupid I was to get lost."

Grant pulled up to the largest building. Through the open door he could make out a figure in the background, covering him with what looked like an M-16. There wasn't enough light to see if he was wearing a uniform. He pulled out his map, folded to show the area of the Columbus border crossing, and tried to mime he was lost.

"*Adonde esta?*" He hoped they would believe it was all the Spanish he knew. A man leaning against the building gave a rapid fire response, and then waved Grant off. Another man walked out. His faced looked well lived in, and there was the bump of a gun under his shirt tail. *"Que pasa, gringo?"*

"English? Does anyone speak English?" Behind him he could hear Bonneville muttering "Ask him where the fuck we are! I want to get out of this fucking desert!"

The lived in face said something to the man leaning against the building, and they both laughed. "Your wife is angry, no?"

"Jesus! She's been bitching at me for the last hour. Can you tell me how close I am to the border station?"

The man looked at his map and said something else in Spanish. There was more laughter, and two more men came out of the building. They circled around the jeep, seeing what was in the back, and especially checking out Bonneville. Her tight shorts and shirt, tied halter style, gave them plenty to look at. She continued to play her role. "Can one of you tell this genius how to get back to the US? He's been driving around here all day and I'm sick of it!" There were more comments in Spanish, and more laughter. The lived in face took the map from Grant and unfolded it. "You're about 45 kilometers from where you want to be, *senor.*" He pointed to the map, then off to his right. "You want to be on that road."

Grant looked at the map and then towards the road. "Forty five kilometers? That's what, about thirty miles?"

"Si, senor. Stay on that road."

Grant turned back to Bonneville. "See, hon? I knew we were on the right road." He walked back and got into the jeep. Lived in face followed him. He put his hand on the steering wheel as Grant thanked him.

"*De nada, senor.* You should drive and not stop. Take your angry wife back to the air conditioning. This is not a place you want to be in after dark."

"Who were they?"

"Some old *gringo* trying to impress his *puta.*" The Mexicans seemed to refer to every good looking *gringa* as a whore. It went along with their opinion of all women, except their wives and mothers.

"Keep an eye on them. No one ever comes down here without a reason."

"Don't worry, *Jefe,* he was practically begging his little whore not to be mad at him. That *viejo* isn't going to get any pussy tonight!"

Grant drove off and kept picking up speed until he thought he was out of rifle range. He rummaged around in his pack and pulled out a pair of field glasses. He handed them to Bonneville and told her to watch for a dust cloud from anybody following them. After a few more klicks with no pursuit, he slowed down.

"You did good back there, Linda."

"Those were not nice people. Did you see the one with the gun inside?"

"Yeah. This was not your local flying club. They didn't want us hanging around for some reason. I'll bet it had something to do with the plane parked there. From what he said, I'll bet there's a lot of activity in the area after dark. We'll need to get eyes on it somehow." He pulled over and took the glasses. A quick scan to the southwest showed a high spot a couple of clicks from the air strip that had enough elevation to keep it under observation. He pointed it out to Bonneville. "That's where we need to be."

"Right now?"

"No, I mean for an OP. If I had Sharp on the southern end of the road, he would have thought of it. He'll have to make it a priority after we get settled in."

Grant drove on. Over the next 20 klicks or so they passed through several seemingly abandoned villages. He slowed enough to look around, and could see the subtle signs of recent habitation. The villages were used, probably as smuggling way stations but not occupied full time. He stopped at the last one before the road angled off to the northeast. There was a trail leading straight to the border. He was tempted to follow it, but thought better. He didn't know what condition it would be in just a few hundred yards away, and he didn't want to get trapped in Mexico unarmed. Bonneville pointed out a dust cloud to him. "It looks like it might be on the other side of the fence." Grant checked with the glasses. It was. He could see two vehicles coming to a stop. Several figures got out. He could see Price looking at him through his glasses.

Grant opened his cell phone and was pleased to see he had service here in the desert. It was one of the disposables, one of many they had bought. He speed dialed Price. "Put that finger away before I shove it up your ass and pick your nose from the inside."

He could see Price pull the phone away from his ear and stare at it. He looked across the border and raised his glasses again. "That you, Luke? I thought it was some fucking wetback and his *chiquita* out for a ride. You must have better binoculars than I do."

"Next time buy the good stuff. We can afford it. Who's that with Robinson?"

"Kid named Sinclair, another one of Sharps' disciples."

"You see anything interesting yet?" They were about halfway up the AO. Meeting like this hadn't been planned, but it was fortuitous.

"Boss, whoever said this is a quiet section is a fucking liar. We've got so many trails running off the border trace I'm surprised they didn't put up street signs."

"Yeah, I've got a lot of activity on this side. Any Border Patrol in the area?"

Price was off the phone for a moment. Grant could hear him telling his companions who he was talking to. Then there were three sets of glasses on him. "They call themselves ICE now, Immigration and Customs Enforcement, but no, nothing around here. They were pretty heavy from the Columbus crossing to about five miles before the turn. They seemed to think we were wasting our time. They call this 'the Dead Zone', and I think they're afraid of it."

Grant found that interesting. "They know who you are?" He was distracted by a flash of light just short of where Price was. "Heads up. You got movement about 200 meters to your left front."

"Got 'em. Elko spotted them a while ago. They were trying to come across the wire. They scurried back when we drove up. They'll probably hide out and try again after we're gone."

He focused in on the flash again. It didn't look right. "Price, are you carrying?"

"Yeah, why?" A shot rang out and spider webbed the Jeep's windshield. Price and Elko went to ground. Grant could see Robinson drawing his own weapon and firing two quick shots in return. There were multiple sounds of engines revving up, then three motor bikes broke cover and headed south. Grant followed them while he called out to Price. "Everyone OK over there?"

"Yeah, we're fine," came the answer, "but I should have gotten the insurance on the rental."

Grant followed the rooster tails of dust to the south. You don't leave motor bikes and a rifle hidden if you're just trying to sneak into the States, he thought to himself. This meant something, but he wasn't sure what. Behind Price there was another cloud of dust. He could see them turn to look back.

"What do you have, Price?"

"Don't know. Sounds like another dirt bike. I think we may have interrupted a delivery. Think we inconvenienced the powers that be?"

Grant didn't think so. "Probably not. Only one bike on your side. Looks more like a small time bunch of opportunists looking for a quick score. The shooting might bring the big boys, that's why they got out so quick."

Quiet section my ass, Grant thought. The cowboys are riding motor cycles up to the border and shooting at anybody they see to scare them away. "If you got GPS, mark the location and tell the Feds on your way out. When we move in we'll have to do something around here. What have you got planned for the rest of the day?"

"We're gonna check in with the vertical people down south. They should be about done too. Then we're going into Columbus for something to eat. Think we should head back to Bliss?"

"No, take the night off. Get a couple of rooms and write up your notes, then kick back. If you head back tonight there you'll get in too late, and there'll be too much going on to get your maps marked."

The rest of the day had been generally uneventful. While Grant kept watching west towards the border, he noticed there were a few large buildings to the east, usually sitting on high ground with a good view towards the US. One site in particular caught his attention. There was a tower on one end of the main building. When he looked at it through the glasses, he could make out someone looking back. There was another someone watching through a scoped rifle. Grant gauged the distance to be close to three quarters of a mile. Sharp could probably make the shot, but this guy either didn't think he could, or didn't think they were worth the bullet. Whichever was the case, Grant got Bonneville back into the Jeep and moved off. He had Bonneville mark the spot.

The tower had been watching for Grant with interest. The airfield to the south had alerted them to the presence of the *gringo viejo* and his *puta*. They had been tracking the dust tail since they heard the faint shots from the southwest earlier. The senior man had the control room check their stations to see who was responsible. Their only report was of a couple of motorcycles in the desert. They were either out hunting jack rabbits, target shooting, or they were some coyotes who decided it was too hot today to walk across the border and decided to execute their migrants. That was bad for everyone's business, but it happened.

"Keep an eye out for vultures. We'll have to send out somebody to bury the bodies if there are any."

"Why don't those fucking *coyotes* take their people to the border before they kill them? Let the *gringo* Border Patrol clean them up."

"You're still mad because you had to clean up the last batch." He went back to his binoculars. "I see a jeep coming up from the south. It must be the *gringo* and his *puta* from the airfield."

The other man slid his rifle up to its stand and tracked the jeep through the scope. The jeep had stopped and the man had gotten out. He was a big bastard. He tried to zoom in on the *puta* who stayed in the jeep, but his scope didn't have the magnification. He could tell she had big teats, the kind he like to play with, but other than that she was too skinny for his tastes.

"He's curious."

"He was curious. I think he saw you and your rifle. He's getting back in the Jeep and getting out of here. He probably doesn't want the *puta* to know he's ready to shit his pants."

They both got a good laugh out of that.

When they reached the main north-south road, Grant turned left towards the US. Bonneville, who had been starting to nap, woke and realized what he was doing. "Where are you going? I thought we had another night in Juarez. I left all my stuff in the room! You promised!"

He reached over and squeezed her knee. "Relax. There's a town called *Palomas* just south of the border. There should be a *bodega* or something close to the outskirts. We're running low on water." He didn't bother to add that he also wanted to see what was going on close to the border, or more accurately, who was in charge.

They didn't have to travel far before they came on to the outskirts of *Palomas.* There was a scattering of houses, mostly concrete block structures. Most had the mandatory skinny burro and dog in the fenced yard. Some had a cow, and almost all had a small satellite dish. There was a little traffic, but less than he expected. He also noticed a lack of police or military checkpoints that had lined the roads around Juarez. This was either a quiet area, or the government didn't have the resources to spend here. Grant suspected the latter. He pulled into what looked like a fairly modern and clean *bodega.* There were a few scattered cars in the parking lot; most prominent was a red extended cab pick-up with chrome wheels. A couple of drug store type cowboys, mirrored sunglasses, fancy plaid shirts, big belt buckles and silver toed boots were leaning against the grill. They were giving Grant the eye. He looked over to Bonneville and suddenly realized who they were leering at. Bonneville was a well built woman. She had unbuttoned her shirt and tied it around her midriff. She had been sweating, and her light colored blouse was sticking to her in all the right places, and it was very obvious she wasn't wearing a bra. She saw Grant give the Mexicans the once over. "Trouble?"

"I don't think so. Homer and Gomer over there are probably wondering what the hot chick sees in the old *gringo*." He handed her a wad of *pesos*. "Why don't you go in and get us some ice and drinks for the cooler."

"What are you going to do?"

"Hopefully, nothing, but our friends are slithering over. Probably better that I make nice to them than you."

"Why don't we both go in?"

"Because it might come down to them wanting something more than we want to keep it. You'll be safe inside, and I can watch the Jeep."

"There are two of them!"

"Correction, there are only two of them. Now get your pretty ass into the store before the boys get close enough to see how really good you look in that blouse. And check the seals on the water bottles. Make sure they haven't been refilled" She gave him a dirty look as she got out and walked away. Grant watched her, and then looked at Homer and Gomer. They were watching her too, but they decided to start with Grant. They could get the *puta* later.

Grant slid out of the driver's seat and planted his feet on the ground. Homer was saying something in rapid fire Spanish. Grant just smiled. "*No hablo, amigo*." Homer came closer and stood directly in front of him. Gomer was just off to the right.

Homer smiled, and showed a diamond imbedded in his front tooth. "*Gringo*, I said I want your Jeep and your *puta*." He pulled his shirt tail up so Grant could see the butt of a pistol jammed in his waist. It looked like a stainless steel Beretta 92. Gomer smiled too. His teeth weren't as pretty. And he pulled his shirt up to show his gun, another stainless Beretta. Damn, Grant thought. A lowlife must make a pretty good living down here. He put both hands up chest high. The key ring was around the middle finger of his left hand. Homer and Gomer were both looking at it, probably thinking they were having a really good day. They were getting a new Jeep, and a *gringa puta* to fuck on a Saturday night. Homer was still smiling when Grant drove the heel of his left hand into his chest, reaching out and pulling the Beretta as Homer fell on his ass. Grant racked the slide, just in case this ass hole didn't keep it loaded, ejected a round and fed a fresh bullet into the chamber. Gomer was still watching his *amigo* land on the ground while Grant tapped him on the chest with the gun barrel. He just shook his head no to stop Gomer from making any stupid moves, then reached down and grabbed the other gun and stuffed it in his back pocket. He motioned for Homer to stand up and made both cowboys turn around. Grant ignored whatever the hell they were muttering in Spanish and gave them a quick pat down. Both of them had little designer sheath knives on their belts, as well as spare magazines. Grant took them, too.

He prodded them in the back and walked them back to their truck. As they passed the passenger side, he reached down and drove a knife into the tire. He did the same on the driver's side. Homer didn't like that and took a swing at Grant. He rapped him on the bridge of his nose, and Homer was down on his ass again. Gomer put his hands a little higher and backed up.

"You look familiar, *Gringo*."

The comment took Grant by surprise. What the hell does that mean, he thought. Keeping an eye on both of them, Grant checked the cab and recovered a folding stock AK-47 and more magazines. These were some serious players. He slung the assault rifle over his shoulder, and then poked a hole in the rear tire. He motioned for Gomer to help Homer up, then motioned with the Beretta and spoke for the first time. "Run" was all he said. It was all he had to say. They took off down the street.

Bonneville came out with ice and a bag of drinks. Grant had the AK laying between the seats and the spare Beretta on the passenger seat. Bonneville looked at them and shook her head. "You must have put on quite a show. The old couple in there wouldn't take my money." She handed the wad of *pesos* back to Grant. He opened the cooler and put in the drinks and poured the ice. "Run in and give them the money anyway. Just leave it on the counter. It might help them forget they can identify us, just in case."

He backed out and headed down the road as soon as Bonneville came back. "What are we going to do with the guns?" she asked.

"The AK you can strip down and start throwing the parts away. We'll keep the pistols until we're ready to cross back into the US tomorrow."

"Just in case?" She was smiling.

"Yes, Linda, just in case."

They got back to the hotel just as the sun was going down. Grant and Bonneville both had the start of sunburn, so she took a long soak in the whirlpool tub in their suite, then had Grant rub lotion into her pinkish skin. She responded to his touch, and the two of them were naked on the floor. They both had to take showers before going down to dinner.

The hotel had a first class restaurant, with an extensive menu. Linda tried the fish, while Grant stuck to the tried and true prime rib. It was all washed down with an excellent California Cabernet, followed by dessert and several shots of tequila. Grant enjoyed coming to Mexico. There were so many brands of tequila that just weren't available in the States, and he suspected that the brands that were exported were watered down anyway. The *anejos* always seemed to taste better. Bonneville was just past tipsy by the time they got back to their room, and tipsy always made her feel sexy and adventurous. She proceeded to show Grant why she wanted to get away with him, and he was truly grateful.

Linda Bonneville woke to the sound of automatic fire coming from not very far away. She laid there and listened. They were on the tenth floor. Why did it sound so close? She reached over for Grant. But his space was empty. She sat up and looked around the room. The slider to the balcony was open. The curtains were hanging straight down, no sign of a breeze. She could see Grant outlined by the railing, looking down. She found her sleep shirt and slipped it over her head, pulling it on as she went to stand beside him. She slipped an arm through his and looked out to where she could see lines of tracer fire going back and forth about a block away. "What is it?" she asked.

Grant handed her the field glasses. She took them and focused on a low building. She could see flames licking out of some of the windows, and uniformed bodies sprawled on the pavement on the street side. There was firing coming out, and return fire coming from a line of open trucks across the street. "It looks like the bad guys decided to take out the neighborhood police station." Grant reached and took the glasses back. "There's an army check point a couple of blocks down the street, but they don't seem too interested in getting involved." He looked back to the police station. There was less return fire. "It looks like the cops are losing." An RPG shot across the street and exploded inside. After a few seconds of silence, Grant could hear shouts from inside. Then the police started to come out, hands high, some supporting injured comrades. The attackers swarmed around them, lining them up on the edge of the sidewalk. Suddenly, the gunmen fired into the group and continued until there was no movement. One industrious shooter clipped in a fresh magazine, then walked from body to body, delivering a head shot.

No one moved at the army check point, even though they had a clear view of the scene. Grant could feel fingernails digging into his upper arm. "Why aren't those bastards doing anything to help? They're just standing there!"

"I don't know," was all Grant could say. It did provide an important lesson though. In this little war, you couldn't trust anybody. He would have to impress that on his soldiers who might come across a Mexican unit while patrolling a remote stretch of border.

Grant led Bonneville back inside, but left the slider open. He poured two drinks and handed her one. She gulped it down, but refused another. "Is it safe to stay here tonight?"

"I think it will be." He took the two shiny pistols from his bag and checked to make sure they were both loaded. Then he put one on each night stand. "Make damn sure you wake me up before you start shooting anybody though. We old *gringos* sometimes get up in the middle of the night to use *el bano* over there. I don't want any surprises."

The rest of the night was quiet, but neither of them got much sleep.

"Now what?" Elko asked. The road was blocked by a police cordon. Up ahead he could see a straggly line of marchers waving Mexican flags and placards.

"I don't know. I'm new in town," Price responded. He saw a space and pulled in. 'Let's find a place to get a drink," he said as he got out. He looked in the back at Robinson. "You coming, or are you gonna sit out here in the hot sun?"

"I just thought you'd want somebody to stay with the vehicles."

Price and Elko looked at each other and laughed. "Why? They're rentals." Price said.

"Yeah," Elko added, "and he put them on the Sergeant Major's credit card."

They wandered down a side street, following the noise and looking for someplace out of the sun. Robinson pointed to a patio style restaurant across the street. It was right off the sidewalk, and it was partially shaded from the sun by, of all things, a vine covered pergola. Even better, it looked like it was half-empty. "Would that do for you, Sergeant Price?"

Price thought a moment. He looked at the thin crowd down the street. It looked like whatever was going to happen was starting up a few blocks down. On his other side, there was a flat bed trailer draped with red, white and green bunting, and had a couple of Mexican flags stuck in holders at either end. There was a Mariachi band tuning up between them. "That'll be perfect. We can keep an eye on what's shaking out here and maybe learn something."

They crossed over and walked past the sign that told them to seat themselves. A dark haired beauty brought menus and offered drinks. Robinson asked for a soda.

"You want a beer, Eddie?" Price asked.

"I thought we were on duty."

"We are, sort of, but I'm having one anyway. I'm pretty sure nobody is going to report you."

Elko smiled. "I'm not driving so I'm having a couple, maybe more."

Price held up four fingers, and the waitress just smiled and told them she'd be right back. Price turned around and watched the marchers form. They were loud, but seemed to be good-natured. The lack of *gringo* faces stood out. When the girl brought their beers they ordered burgers all around, then he asked her what was going on. "It's a counter protest."

"Counter protest? Against what?"

The girl looked out toward the crowd and exhaled loudly. "Last week we had one of those border militias here. They made a lot of noise, beat up some illegals they caught on the fence, then left. Now these people are showing up. They'll probably make a lot of noise, get drunk, start a few fights then leave a lot of bad feelings."

"You don't seem like you care for either side." Price said.

"I don't. Neither side is doing any good. They all need to go away and let the Border Patrol get the fence built. Then maybe the druggies and the army will go away." "The army's been a problem?" Price asked. "I didn't think there had been any soldiers around here."

"I'm not talking about the US Army, I mean the Mexicans. They've been running rings around the Border Patrol. You never know when you're going to run into a group of Mexicans carrying machine guns."

"What do you mean? The Mexican army is operating on our side of the line? That doesn't sound right."

"It may not be right, but they aren't anywhere near where they should be. We keep hearing that our soldiers are gonna be here soon. When they come, there'll be trouble."

When the waitress was gone, Robinson asked Price, "What do you think, Sergeant Price? There gonna be trouble?"

"Drop the rank. I don't know, Eddie. Mexican army has enough problems on their side of the line. I don't know why they'd be up here."

"They probably weren't soldiers."

A lightly accented voice spoke up from the next table. Two casually dressed Mexicans were finishing up their meal. The older one was balling up his napkin and putting it by his plate. The Americans turned as one to look at him. The speaker was a middle aged man, light skinned and obviously fit. His companion was younger, darker and fitter. He repeated himself. "They probably weren't soldiers. In fact, I can almost guarantee they weren't Mexican soldiers. They were smugglers protecting their routes."

"You said almost guarantee. Not 100%." Elko said.

"You are very perceptive, young lady. Or should I say Sergeant? You are all military, are you not?"

Price held up his hand before anyone could answer. "Two Mexicans," he gestured, "both armed, asking questions. You're law enforcement, military or the smugglers. Which would it be?"

"Relax, Sergeant Price. We are not *la policia*, the American army, or the smugglers. We are simply tourists having lunch and some conversation."

Price finished his beer and looked for the waitress. When he got her attention he signaled for another round. He pointed to the other table to include them. "I say again, armed, and you made a point of saying the 'American' army. That would lead me to believe you are Mexican army. Would I be close?"

The beers arrived. "Close enough, Sergeant, and thank you *por las cervezas*. If you are going to be operating in this area we will probably be seeing more of each other in the coming days and weeks. I have a meeting with some people at Fort Bliss next week. Perhaps you will be there." He took a sip of his beer, stood, dropped a few bills on the table and walked to the door. The second man drank his beer straight down and stood. "*Mi Commandante* insists on paying for your lunch." Then he was gone too.

Grant insisted on going to the restaurant for breakfast. Room service would have been nice, but he wanted to get a feel for the mood in town. It was pretty tense. Over omelets and coffee they discussed heading back to the border. They had seen enough the night before, and now the military had a heavy presence in the hotel district. He didn't want to spend the day passing through check points and answering stupid questions. They would drive back to the border crossing, dump the guns before they crossed over and think about having lunch in El Paso. Bonneville was resigned to the new plan. "So much for spending a small fortune on souvenirs."

"You'll get another chance. There are plenty of rip-off shops by the crossing. They'll be happy to take your money."

The desk clerk tried to reassure them that the area was safe now that the army was present. Grant just grunted. The clerk didn't see how responsive the army had been the night before, and Grant didn't want to be the ugly American and tell him. He made an excuse, blaming *la senorita* for being so nervous. While they were waiting for the valet to bring the jeep around his phone buzzed. It was Harrison.

"You coming back pretty soon, Luke?"

"We're on our way out the door right now, why?"

"We heard what happened down there last night. You weren't involved in any way, were you?"

"We stayed far away from that. Why are you calling?"

"Well, surprise, surprise, the new Group Commander showed up about mid-morning yesterday and promptly went looking for his staff. You can tell Captain Bonneville that you and she are the only ones who bothered to sign out, so he's only slightly pissed at you two. He is however, very pissed off at the rest of the staff, so you can probably score some points if you show up first. That's just a suggestion, mind you."

"Where are you now?"

"I'm sitting here having breakfast in El Paso. Things were slow so I thought maybe you'd like a ride back to post instead of another long cab ride. When are you going to be there?"

"Maybe ten, fifteen minutes. Make it fifteen minutes. I have a few things I was going to toss, but if I can I'd like to bring back with me. Can you make friends down at the border crossing and help me out?"

Harrison knew he meant guns. "Anything good?" Grant gave him a roundabout description of what happened in *Palomas.* Harrison stopped him. "Sequential serial numbers might mean something. Try to hide them in the bottom of your bags. I'll use my charm and run some interference for you. I understand there's a little *tequiliera* near the

Mexican gate. Pick up some good *anejo* for yourself and the lady, and maybe a bottle or two of the cheap stuff for the *federales*. You never know when you might have to grease the skids. See you in a few."

Grant dropped his jeep off just down from the border crossing. The owner was surprised about three things. First, he got it back at all. Second, he got it back early, and third, it was all in one piece. Grant handed him a wad of pesos for a tip. Then he went into a tequila shop that was in a strip mall next door to the customs station. Bonneville wandered into another shop that specialized in silver. Grant thought to himself that ought to take care of some of the disappointment. He found a couple of expensive brands that he knew he couldn't get in the States, and had Bonneville pick up two bottles of less expensive brand names. When they came out there was a lull in the tourist lines trying to get back north. Grant would have preferred a crowd, but that was what the extra booze was for. It turned out he didn't need it. Harrison and a Border Patrol officer were standing by the counter in the Mexican station.

"There's my daughter and son-in-law!" Harrison shouted. "I was so worried about you two!" He looked at the Mexican official. "We just found out she was pregnant with my first grandchild. Her mother and I were so worried when we heard about the trouble last night." He hugged Bonneville and gave her a wet kiss on the forehead. Bonneville squirmed out of his grasp. "Dad, please! You're embarrassing me." He grabbed Grant and repeated the hug and kiss. Grant could feel his cheeks getting red.

They passed their passports over to the official who stamped them and waved them on their way. All the Mexicans were smiling at them, enjoying his discomfort. Bonneville reached into her back pack and pulled out a bottle of tequila and placed it on the counter. "Please excuse *mi padre*. He's a silly old man."

The Mexican laughed. "*Si, esta loco.*" Then he slid the bottle into a drawer.

The Border Patrol agent dropped back a few steps. "You didn't have to do that. Your father here already gave them a couple of bottles." He ushered them through the US side and scanned their passports. "Welcome back to the United States, Captain, and Sergeant Major. Your father has been a pain in the ass. I hope it was worth the embarrassment."

"What was that all about, Ralph? "

"When you told me what you picked up, I thought you might need a good story. The Border Patrol was very helpful after I explained who you were and you might have been compromised. They seem to have gotten a pretty good briefing about us being in New Mexico, and they're going to try to make sure we get some good liaison"

"Did he really think you're my father?" Bonneville asked?

"Oh, absolutely. The National Guard seems to have the same heritage all over the country. He said he was in a unit 20 years ago that had three generations of an extended family. There were so many with the same family name that roll call was a real challenge. His Sergeant Major started out as a company clerk in headquarters and did thirty five years without a transfer. You don't see that anymore. He really thinks you're pregnant, by the way. That was the little detail that made the story believable."

"That's not good, Ralph. He does an incident report on two soldiers sneaking through Mexican Customs; we could be in deep shit. He scanned our passports."

"Don't worry. No incident report. He heard about us last week and he thinks he can probably put in to be our liaison. Now, let me tell you about Price."

Harrison laid out the information Price had brought back from his part of the recon. Grant made him repeat the story about the Mexicans in the restaurant twice. That bothered him. He expected they would run into drug smugglers. With only a wire fence and reduced Border Patrol presence, it must have been the cartels dream. The armed bands of soldiers wandering around openly, however, were a problem they hadn't been briefed on. It was either a big secret, or the story had been dismissed as gossip and wishful thinking. He'd put Sharp onto looking into it deeper once they were on line.

Grant told Harrison about the assault on the police station. The part about the executions was disturbing enough, but the army being so close and not helping sounded like collusion, or the situation was deteriorating far out of the government's control.

"Those drug fuckers are ballsy, Luke. It sounds like they bought themselves a piece of the army."

Grant agreed. "They already owned part of the police at the local and federal level. There had to be a few people in the army who wanted a piece of the pie, and it looks like they got it. I've got something else for you to check out." He pulled the Berettas out of his pack. Harrison glanced at them. "My, my, aren't they pretty. I didn't know you liked that street punk glitter."

Grant told him the story of Homer and Gomer at the *bodega* in *Palomas*. He handed him a slip of paper with the serial numbers written down. "I thought it was just a gang thing with them both having shiny guns. Having numbers one digit apart was too much of a coincidence. Maybe you can track who ordered them."

Chapter 3

Monday morning started with an explosion of activity. It seems the Army finally got around to paying attention to the 289th. Military and civilian visitors began streaming in and out of headquarters while the troops were still in PT formation. When they got back from a modest 2 mile run, the parking lot behind the HQ building, or the "hack shack", as the troops began calling it, was full, and the staff duty NCO was trying to round up the staff officers. The only one who had actually shown up for PT, Captain Bonneville, quickly directed him over to the officer billets. The staff sections had returned to their old ways of avoiding anything to do with the line platoons. LTC Kearney, who didn't have quarters in the area yet, had arrived just as 1SG Harrison had been rousting the troops out of the barracks. He had seen the S-1 and his Command Sergeant Major in their PT uniforms, and evidently thought all was well in the world. He explained that he had been warned about the visitors over the weekend, but he would be joining them for PT the next morning.

Harrison was going through some cool down exercises and stretches as the staff began trickling by to report to the Commander. The 1SG could sense the ripple going through the formation and called "At Ease!" before the hoots could begin. SFC Price, never one to be shy, announced just loud enough for the passing officers to hear, "Can you believe these fucking people? They're actually wearing PT gear. Like the Colonel's gonna be fooled!" He was rewarded with some dirty looks, but most tried to avoid the stares of the troops. Price didn't care one way or another. Those people did not display any professionalism or loyalty to the unit. He saluted them because they wore the rank, which was all he felt he was required to do.

After breakfast there was a work formation. The troops were held in place while platoon leaders and Sergeants got marching orders in the "hack shack". All the platoons were to draw unit sets, and there was some, but not much, heavy equipment available to draw. There would be organic vehicles too, and nothing was said about the old equipment rescued from the scrap yard. Sergeant Mitchell looked towards the CSM with questioning eyes. Grant just shook his head. The extra stuff would come in handy. Besides, this unit did some of its best work with the off-the-books equipment they usually acquired.

There was also another staff call announced for 1000.

Sharp picked this moment to bring his worn out platoon into the area. They looked dirty and tired. Sleep had not been on the training schedule. What was surprising was that there were no stragglers in the formation, and they were singing a ribald airborne ditty. Sharp wheeled them into position in front of the Mess Hall and gave them a quick pep talk. The Mess Sergeant appeared at the door and gave Sharp thumbs up. Sharp waved in return, and then told his platoon to grab some breakfast, get cleaned up, get into fresh uniforms, and report back by 0930. He had more plans for them. They gave a loud "Hooah!" when he dismissed them. Grant and Harrison walked over.

"Those boys are awfully cheerful. What did you do, bivouac by a cat house?" Harrison asked.

"I love you too, First Sergeant. I had about sixty hours to figure out who they were and motivate them."

"Dave," Grant said, "it looks like you did. What are your plans for them now?"

"Can we get some coffee? I'll tell you while I have my breakfast. I'm getting too fucking old to live on MREs every day"

Grant and Harrison grabbed cups by the urn and found a table away from the troops. Sharp went through the line and came back with his tray. They let him wolf down about half his food before they started to question him. He ignored their question and took out his note book.

"I spent a lot of time talking to them, and let me tell you, they don't have a happy story. You're looking at a group of soldiers who got collectively fucked by the big green machine." He swallowed some more food, and then continued. "When they were activated, they got pulled as fillers from units all over their state. Not one of them has an Infantry MOS. The closest they come is a couple of Combat Engineers and some Artillery. The rest are mechanics, finance clerks, equipment operators, and a bunch of different jobs. See that red-headed kid over there?" He pointed at a happy looking troop laughing with his friends. "He's got a degree in computer science and was an info tech specialist. He's used to keeping a Brigade's worth of computers working together. The kid he's talking to? He's an Intel Specialist. He was an honor grad from the course here at Bliss."

"What are we going to do with them, Dave?" Harrison asked as he finished his coffee.

He pulled a couple of folded sheets of paper from his pocket and slid them over. It was a list of personnel swaps he wanted to do in the company. Harrison pointed out one entry to Grant. Sharp wanted to trade positions with Callan. "Is this your idea of a stealth entry, Dave?"

"No, Luke. It only makes sense. Callan says he was an ops NCO in a Fires Brigade." That was the new term for an artillery brigade. "I'm a grunt, he's not. We get some round pegs into round holes for a change, and all of a sudden a lot of people who got screwed will be happy." He stood up and took his tray. "I need a shower. Think about it for a minute. The right people doing the right job, at the right time. What a fucking concept."

"What about the support platoon we were getting? You start doing all these swaps and the headquarters platoon gets fatter and the line platoons shrink." Harrison said.

"You really think this bunch was intended to be a platoon of grunts backing us up? If they were, somebody is bankrolling us to fall flat on our faces. Move these guys around, don't rebuild the support platoon, stick me over in S-2 and let me have an under strength recon section. It'll make more sense than having over committed platoons on the line. I can be your tactical reserve."

They were quiet as Sharp walked away to dump his tray and went to find his own shower. When he was gone Harrison and Grant discussed the list. "I hate to say it," Harrison opined, "but it looks like the moron could be on to something here."

Grant thought of the disruption that forty personnel moves would cause just before they went to the field. Then he stopped himself. Before they went to the field would be the best time. Some of the new people would actually know what they would need for a change. "I hate to admit it, Ralph. He's right. We never had this luxury before. I'll run it by the S-1 and the CO as soon as I have a chance. Is this going to fuck up your duty rosters?"

Harrison shook his head. "I'll make it work."

The staff call was actually a briefing from a group of officers from Joint Task Force Southwest Border, or JTF-SB. This was the organization the 289th was about to join. The briefers had prepared maps along one side of the room that encompassed the entire Mexican border, from San Diego on the Pacific coast, to El Paso. The maps were heavily annotated, with pictures, charts and statistics connected to specific points by string. In front of the room was a very large scale map of the sector that ran from Antelope Wells to Columbus. They would be assigned to the only part of the entire border that ran true north and south.

After a few introductory remarks, the briefing began with an overview of the situation along the entire border, section by section. The briefers, each with his own area of specialty, took turns giving their part. It was a long, slow listing of miles of fence completed, planned and under construction. There were statistics on linear footage covered by seismic sensors, video, infra-red and night vision cameras. There were details on tunneling activity, fence breaches, and outright sabotage by the fence crews. Grant's ass was starting to fall asleep, and many of the others in the room were fidgeting. He also noticed that there was a distinct aversion to answering questions. After a couple of hours Kearney decided to call a break for lunch. Grant took this opportunity to bring Captain Bonneville with him to present the proposed changes.

Kearney approved the personnel changes without any objections. "You trust this SFC Sharp, Sergeant Major?"

"Colonel, let me just say that we take turns carrying each other out of bad places. By my reckoning, it's his turn to do the carrying next."

"Good enough for me." He turned to Captain Bonneville. "Is this going to put a burden on your section? That's a lot of changes."

Bonneville smiled at the Colonel. "Not a bit, Sir. My personnel NCO is very good at what she does, and I pick up another personnel clerk in all these moves." Kearney dismissed Bonneville, but asked Grant to stay a few minutes.

"Good to see you again, Sergeant Major."

"I'm hoping I can say the same thing to you, Colonel. You seemed to have become another one of those urban legends the Army is full of."

Kearney smiled. "I'll tell you about that, but not now. A lot of time and effort went into what they want us to do. I'll talk to you after the dog and pony show."

Sharp and Price were grousing over their lunches. It was hard to believe they had endured two hours and had learned nothing of their sector yet. When they saw Grant and Bonneville come in they got up to join them at their table. They asked questions about the briefing, but Grant didn't have any answers for them. Bonneville added, "This has been so boring. I don't know what the point of it is yet."

Harrison came over. He tossed a folder onto the table as he sat down with his tray. "Gifts from the gods, Gentlemen and Lady. I have made a friend over at the intelligence school, and he has provided me with satellite photos, aerial recon photos and interpretations, Mexican army and police orders of battle and organization in the area, and, drum roll please, a shit load of info and pictures of the powers that be in the cartels in the Juarez area as of," he made a show of looking at his watch, "thirty-six hours ago."

Grant slid them over and flipped open a folder. "This is great, Ralph. How did you get it?"

"I went over and asked what they had. Seems they know all about us moving into the area. They've been collecting this info for months as part of the Intel course. They've been offering it to anyone they talked to, but haven't had any takers. I think I made friends just by asking for it."

Sharp picked through a few photos. "If this is what a school can come up with, the big boys must have some really good stuff for us. Has the Colonel seen this?"

"Not yet. I figured Luke could pass it to him when the time was right. No sense stealing the JTF thunder." He finished a few bites of his salad. Harrison had been eating lighter and working out more. He was trying to drop some of the extra weight he had picked up living large in Germany. He stood up to leave. "By the way, pass the word. Kearney wants either the platoon leader or their Sergeant to attend the rest of the brief. I guess the good stuff will be coming this afternoon."

Sharp pointed to the envelope Harrison hadn't put on the table. It was fatter than the rest. "What's in that one? The Colonel's secret recipe?"

Harrison sat back down. "I was saving this for later. The Robinson boys just gave it to me. They wondered if you'd be okay with this." He opened the envelope and slid out a framed picture. There were actually two photos. The top one was a still from an old western film. In it, the four main characters were walking down a street in a Mexican town, side by side, all heavily armed. Across the top was the legend 'The Wild Bunch'. Under the movie picture was the word 'Then'. Below it was another photo, taken the morning after the action at the Russian chemical compound. The sun was just rising and there was smoke and flame in the background. It was the four of them, Grant, Sharp, Price and Harrison, all heavily armed and dirty. They were carrying their weapons in almost the same positions as the actors were. Under the picture was one word. 'Now'.

Price was the first to speak. "I like it. Can I get a copy?"

"That's what the boys were wondering, Pricey. They have one for each of us. Just in time, too."

"What do you mean?"

"In their youthful enthusiasm, they let one of their bonehead friends post this on a Military web site on the Internet. It's already been downloaded a couple of thousand times."

Grant picked up the picture and looked at it quietly. "Anybody here remember that movie?"

Price did. "Yeah, I do. A bunch of over the hill gunfighters took on the Mexican army to rescue their friend. They kicked some serious ass!"

"Remember how it ended?"

Everyone got quiet. Grant looked at each of them, waiting for a response. There was none coming. He handed the frame back to Harrison. "It's a great picture, Ralph. Thank the Gold Dust twins for me. Try not to remind them that everybody dies in the end."

The afternoon session dealt exclusively with their sector, and Grant found it disappointing. Other than a physical description of the landscape, they had no real info. It had been described as a quiet area, and there had been few intelligence resources dedicated to it. Grant studied some of the photos of the Mexican side, trying to locate the large building with the watch tower. He couldn't. Then he noticed that the photos were all at least several years old. He was getting the feeling that most of the information they were getting on this area was way out of date. Some of the Mexican situation was more up to date, but it sounded as if it had been taken out of newspaper reports. There seemed to be little hard intelligence that someone had actually verified. Grant decided to keep his own counsel for now. There would be time after this briefing to give the Colonel his information and let him rattle some cages with it.

The briefers concluded by telling them that the next day would be filled by interagency briefings. When Kearney asked what that meant, the chief briefer gave a laundry list of alphabetical agencies that had a stake in what the 289th would be doing. Kearney again pressed for details.

"Well, Colonel, everyone has a piece of this pie. The DEA is interested in the smuggling aspect. Homeland Security wants to keep an eye out for terrorists and weapons. The FBI is looking for human traffickers. The Border Patrol is the lead agency out here, and they're concerned with the integrity of the fence line and the condition of the border trace. The General Services Administration has a dirt strip they want you to look at. The Bureau of Land Management controls and administers a lot of these areas, and they have a project or two for you. And last but not least, the Interior Department wants to make sure you don't mess with any tribal lands or upset the Native Americans. Like I said, everybody has a piece of this pie."

"Are they all going to be looking over our shoulders?"

"To begin with, they probably will. But remember, this is only a small slice of the border. It gets ignored by both sides pretty much. As long as it stays quiet, they'll probably lose interest and leave you be in short order."

Kearney faced down the briefer. "Here's something you better take back to all those people. We didn't fuck up the situation; we're just here to fix it." He paused for effect. "My position on them all is that they will at best be advisory to us. My chain of command runs up through the JTF. Anything they want once I hit the ground they can bring to my CP as a formal request, and we'll look at it."

"I don't think that'll be possible, Colonel. The stake holders won't want to give up control."

"The stake holders won't be out on their asses living in tents and sucking up the high desert 24/7. We will control the AO."

"What do you mean? What kind of info are they leaving out?" Grant handed the folder to Kearney and told him to flip through a few of the photos and compare them to what JTF-SW had left on their briefing boards. "That crap they gave us is out of date. I don't know if it's by design, or they just don't know any better, but this info is up to date." Kearney shuffled some of the aerials, found the one with the watch tower compound and checked the grid coordinates. He found the matching spot on the wall and held it up. Grant was right. The briefing photos were out of date.

"I hate to ask, but how did you know that compound was there?"

"I saw it. There was a guy in the tower watching me, and another guy with a scoped rifle aimed at me."

"This looks like it's almost a mile and a half, maybe more, on the Mexican side. How did you pick out that detail?"

"I was a little closer, maybe three quarters of a mile."

Kearney looked at Grant, put the photos back in the folder and took a seat. He took a deep breath then began. "Sergeant Major, this would be a good time to let your commander know what the fuck you've been doing behind his back."

"It wasn't behind your back. It wasn't even behind Fishers' back. The NCOs were given a mission. We got no guidance, no supervision and no follow-up. Fischer wants to be a Major. He's only interested if we make him look bad, and he's been around long enough to know that we can do our jobs better than he can do his."

"Is that the assessment of a CSM to his commander, or sour grapes?"

"When you took over, you became the boss. Until then, we did what needed to be done, and it was all within the law, for the most part."

Grant started with their arrival in Texas and the cluster fuck that was their welcome to Fort Bliss. He continued through the briefing and their collective decision to get ready for whatever the Army had in store for them. "As soon as we found out where we'd be going we laid out a couple of hasty recons. They were all planned before you arrived. It was all done on our own time and didn't involve anything official. It all fell under the heading of Sergeant's Business. That's what we get paid for."

"No officers were involved?"

"Not really. The NCOs did all the planning and execution. Some of the Platoon Leaders are interested enough in what's going on to want to learn. We tried to teach them."

"'Not really' means 'yes' then. Are you gonna tell me who?"

Grant did. Kearney was not a big fan of female leaders in line platoons, and he said so. "Don't sell these women short, Sir. Stanley backed us up pretty good and got a Combat Action Badge in Europe.

She earned it. Powers comes from a long line of contractors and knows her shit. More important, they both know how to lead, and the troops trust them to be right." Then he went into the general details the trip down the border trace. He included the story about meeting Price on the trail and him getting shot at. He left out the part about Robinson returning fire. He also mentioned that someone had been on the US side, and Price had evidently interrupted something. Kearney asked a couple of general questions, and then let Grant continue. He reported on the meeting in Columbus at the restaurant, with what Price believed was a Mexican Army officer doing his own recon.

"Did Price submit a report?"

"No, Sir. He wrote it up, and it's in the background packet, if anyone gets interested enough to look at it, but it was all unofficial. He went for a joy ride and got his window smashed. That was all."

"He didn't think getting shot at was important enough to report?"

"Colonel, Price has been shot at and hit too often to worry about the misses."

Kearney let that pass. He hadn't been shot at enough to consider it routine, and hoped he never would. He told Grant to tell about his part of the trip. After he was finished the Colonel asked who was with him. "I know you didn't drive around northern Mexico and stay in a swanky hotel room alone. Why are you trying to protect Captain Bonneville?"

"Captain Bonneville?"

"I went looking for her on Saturday. The only answer I could get was she went into El Paso. When I asked about you, nobody knew anything. Before you start explaining, I know about you two."

"She volunteered. I thought it would make a good cover."

"Bullshit, but I'll let that pass for now. I was warned last week that you were considered a loose cannon. What else have you been up to?"

"That's all, Colonel. We jumped the gun, and we would have told you earlier if you had been here. We just got overcome by events."

"What about all this," he pointed to the folder Grant had given him.

"Serendipity, pure and simple. The First Sergeant went looking for some resources and the Intel School welcomed him with open arms. He just got this stuff today. He gave it to me at lunch. You wouldn't have had time to digest any of this before the JTF people came back, so I waited and gave it to you now."

"There any copies of this?"

"Negative, you got it all."

"How about the other one?"

"What other one, Sir?"

"'The Wild Bunch'? When were you going to let me in on that one?"

"Christ, I saw it for the first time today. You've already got a copy?"

"Don't let this 'Wild Bunch' shit go to your head, and don't let your troops spread it around anymore. It's going to bite you in the ass. You're dismissed." Grant got up to leave. Kearney stopped him. "I need time to think about all this. I have the staff coming in for a quick planning session. Stay in the area."

Grant skipped supper and went to his quarters. After a hot shower, he decided to sample one of the $200 bottles of tequila he had brought back. The stuff was surprisingly smooth. He had a second glass, then decided it was really too good to be drinking alone. That was what the cheap stuff was for. He recapped the bottle and gathered his PT gear. A good run on a hot evening would help clear his head. As he headed out the door he had a thought. One of these days, booze, old age and the heat was going to catch up with him, and somebody would find his body in a ditch at the end of a very long road, just an old man who had run one mile too many. But, fuck it, as long as it was quick.

One mile led to two, then three. He was circumnavigating the parade field in the dark. Technically, he wasn't in the area, as Kearney had directed him, but it was close enough, and he had left a note on his door saying he was out for a run. Maybe someone would have been observant enough to see him in the moonlight.

He finally decided to hang it up and returned to his room. The door was open, and there were voices inside, loud voices. He nudged the door open and saw Harrison, Sharp and Price, all with their feet up on his furniture, drinking his booze. One of the expensive bottles was empty, lying on its side, and a second one was down by half. Everyone seemed to be in a good mood. He walked over and grabbed the bottle from Price before he could do any more damage to it, and poured himself a shot.

Price waved his glass. "Damn, Boss, you got good taste in booze. Where'd you find this stuff? I never heard of it before."

"Like you barbarians understand good booze."

"Lighten up, Luke. They're celebrating."

"Celebrating what?"

Sharp told him. "My new best buddy, Callan, went over to the shop to familiarize himself with the AO we're getting. While he was there, Fischer decided he needed a gopher, and Callan got elected. So while he's passing coffee around. . ."

"Wait!" Grant interrupted. "An E-7 passing coffee and Kearney didn't say anything?"

"Not a word. Anyway, Kearney asks for suggestions for border dispositions, and the staff just gives him the slack jawed look. They still don't have a clue. Kearney got tired of waiting, so he asked Callan for his thoughts, from the NCO perspective."

Harrison spoke up. "Callan has a subtle edge on us. Nobody knows him, and he hasn't been here long enough for us to drag him to the dark side."

Grant let that go. "What did he say to Kearney?"

"He walked over to the big map and started pointing out platoon areas, equipment staging sites and patrol zones. Kearney thought about it for a minute, and then told Bonneville that her changes were a good call. She passed the credit over to you and me. You're about halfway out of the dog house."

"He'll be all the way out once you all get out of here and leave us alone." They looked towards the voice at the door. Captain Bonneville was standing there in her PT uniform, day pack slung over her shoulder. "I have some details to discuss with the Sergeant Major, and it's not for general consumption."

There was a flurry of "Yes. Ma'ams" as they gathered their debris and headed out the door. Price made a grab for the half empty bottle, but Bonneville took it back from him as he passed her. She closed the door behind them, and then snapped the lock. She was peeling off her shirt as she turned around. "You have the only room with its own shower in the area. I'm tired of sharing one with four other women at a time." She walked past Grant, running her fingers over his chest. "Are you just going to stand there? Or are you going to come soap me up?"

"You do know that the walls here aren't very thick?"

"Then you'll just have to try not to be a loud soaper."

The civilian agencies didn't provide a briefing. It was more of a conference, with JTF-SB assigning priorities to a long wish list of projects. It was a long list. The four biggest were restringing a barbed wire fence along the entire length of their sector, re-grading the road, patrolling and, interestingly enough, rendering an old dirt strip unusable. That would be the strip Price had looked at. It was essentially a very wide straight section of a desert road, with some old buildings off to the side. Sitting in the back of the room, Sharp mumbled to Grant "Another fucking air strip. Those always mean trouble."

"No planes this time, Dave. Just plow it up and get out."

"Yeah, I'll bet. Somebody won't like the idea."

The biggest bone of contention had been the Rules of Engagement, or ROE. Nobody wanted the Army involved in confrontations with illegals. One opinion was that they shouldn't be armed. Kearney and the JTF representative nixed that quickly. There were too many guns on the other side for the soldiers to be weaponless. There was a quick concession. The troops could carry their weapons, but ammunition would be kept separate from the weapons. Another proposal was no fixed positions in sight of the border. That was vetoed. If they couldn't watch likely crossing areas, why be there at all? The last objection raised was by a pencil neck geek who was a political advisor to the governor. He said the Mexicans objected to any "ostentatious displays" of the US flag on the border. The NCOs in the back of the room raised a loud grumble. Kearney silenced them, then told the advisor that if the Mexicans didn't like the US flag, they shouldn't look over the border. "It's still our country, and my soldiers serve under its flag."

"The Governor will have something to say about that!"

"As long as he's not in my chain of command, I don't care what he has to say."

After the briefing Grant, Sharp and Price went through the area taking their own inventory of the gear they were getting. Other than an expanded allotment of vehicles, there was an amazing array of new and interesting toys for them to play with. There were two suit case sized carrying cases that contained an RQ-11B Unmanned Aerial Surveillance system. It consisted of three 4.5 pound, battery operated aircraft that could be hand launched and recovered, and utilized a variety of active and passive surveillance systems. Being small and battery operated, it was a quiet system. One trade off was that it had a limited range and mission time, but it was more than adequate for their needs. It would supplement another system that Harrison had been promised as support from the Intelligence School. The classes were always looking for field training exercise scenarios, and they could help cover the several hundred square kilometers of US territory.

There was a case of Unattended Acoustic Sensors. Sharp picked up a manual and quickly flipped through it. "These might be more trouble than they're worth," he said, unless we can use them far enough out to get an early warning."

"How far? " Price asked.

"Maybe a klick out."

"We can do that."

The night vision devices were a disappointment. Sharp did a quick count and determined they were short by half. "We'll have to give priority to the line platoons and the recon section. Headquarters weenies are shit out of luck!" Grant pointed out that they would also be issued some, but probably not enough, weapons mounted NV systems, for each of the line platoons. Price pointed out the need for somebody to run the numbers on all the gear issued. "You know damn well, some of it's going to disappear into the staff sections. They won't want to join us on the border, but they sure as hell will want to dress up for the camera phones."

Grant reassured him: "Harrison's already on it. He got the Colonel to put out the word to Gaston. All the gear goes out to the line, except for enough to equip a guard mount every night. They're already lining up to plead their cases about who should be exempt from duty." Nobody would be satisfied. First Sergeant Harrison was ruthless with a duty roster.

Next to them were the platoon radios. The PRC-126 handheld tactical radios only had a range of three kilometers, and maybe more in the open terrain, but they were supplemental to the PRC-77 and the VRC-12 systems, so they should suffice. Each platoon area would also have a signal booster mast centrally located. It wasn't an ideal situation, but Grant reminded them that somebody would always be listening to radio traffic: that was one of the reasons he had bought the throw away phones. The Humvees would all be equipped with secure tactical radios. It would do.

The next pile Grant had saved for last. There was one very large hard case, and four slightly smaller cases. "I saved these just for you, Sergeant Sharp," Grant said as he pulled one of the smaller cases over and opened it up. It was the M-110 Semi Automatic Sniper System. The rifle was a 7.62mm killer, with a 3.5x10 scope and a suppressor. And there were four of them. Sharp took it out of the case and inspected it closely. Price crowded in over his shoulder.

"I'll bet that fucker can shoot rings around the M-14s you were using in Africa!"

Sharp nodded his head. "This baby is capable of thousand meter hits." He turned to look at Grant. "When can I zero it?"

The Sergeant Major didn't say anything. He just opened the last case. "This one you can't suppress. So don't get too close to your target."

It was an M-107 .50 caliber Long Range Sniper System, capable of hits out to 2,000 meters. "There won't be any time to get to a long enough range before we move out. I'll get you a couple of days to find a spot out in the desert. Pick your marksmen carefully, and then put the rifles out of sight."

"Out of sight? Why?"

"You can't be flashing a long range precision weapons system close to the border. The locals might get a little sensitive about something like that."

"Then why did we get them?"

"Somebody up there likes you. Treat these like your 'Sunday-go-to-meeting' clothes. They only come out for special occasions."

Grant went looking for Kearney, and found him in the headquarters building speaking with some of his staff. Grant went into his own office and shuffled papers for a few minutes until he heard the meeting break up. He stood in his doorway, waiting for the room to empty out, and went to sit near Kearney. "When do we get the bad news?"

"What bad news?"

Grant squinted at Kearney. He couldn't tell if he was serious or not, so he moved on carefully. "When we talk about the build-up for this little nature walk, are we coming from the same angle?"

Kearney had a blank look. "What are you talking about, CSM?"

"What are our responsibilities when it comes to border crossings? Do we have to wait for someone else to give us a priority list and then get a green light? I only have a rough idea of the target areas from the briefing I got in Germany."

"Until we get the word to the contrary, our job will be to prevent crossings, plain and simple."

"What about our objectives on the Mexican side?"

"CSM, we don't want to be referring to them as objectives. Pass the word to anybody who might be talking about it. Other than to try not to destabilize the area, we haven't really gotten a go ahead for anything. We treat anything on the border with a firm hand and a big smile, but the mess on the other side is their mess, not ours. That is the official line."

Fuck me, thought Grant. He didn't get the same story I did. "Colonel, that's not the briefing I got before we left Germany. And I was under the impression you were supposed to be on board with it."

"I know. I got the same briefing initially, but mine seems to have some subtle differences from yours."

"How so?"

"Sergeant Major, I have a different stake in these operations. It appears that someone thought this would be best if conducted as an NCO driven operation."

"Meaning unsanctioned?"

"You're getting the point. What happened with my Stryker Brigade train-up wasn't under my control. I'm pretty certain I was set up to fail there, then come down here and fail even worse with this group. I don't intend to let that happen. I intend to be as hard ass as I can on the US side, but they're looking for scapegoats in case something goes wrong. Let me tell you, with the way this has been laid out and resourced, I think they thought they found one."

"That doesn't let us off the hook, Colonel. There's going to be a bunch of people with stars coming down to send us on our merry way. When that happens, it'll be a little too late for me to start telling them my conscience is bothering me."

"You do what you have to, Grant. I've already let you know what my guidance is. I have no intention of facing a board of inquiry or a Congressional Committee with dirty hands. When the word to execute comes down, I'll keep the staff off your back if I can, but my part ends at that triple strand fence." Kearney got up and walked to the door.

"Oh, and, Sergeant Major? This conversation never happened."

The next two days were given over to configuring individual march elements of the convoy to the AO. Because of the added work projects, there was a reorganization of the heavy equipment. Stanley and Price would each take a section, Price at the airfield and Stanley on the border. The airfield wasn't expected to take more than a few days, and then they would regroup. There were some buildings to be dismantled, so Price got a squad of carpenters. They would belong to Price as long as the heavy equipment was working. Once he was done, SFC Mason would assume control of the project and regain his people. Their part of the project wasn't expected to run more than a couple of days longer. Contracts had already been signed for construction dumpsters to haul away any building debris. Once they were done, all that would remain of the site would be a large, cleared, broken field and tire tracks where the road was left.

Traffic control points were established along the route. Once Columbus was passed, they would be following the border trace. Side roads leading to assembly areas would be identified and marked by the advance parties. The plan was to have the sites established and secured before the main body left. The convoy march elements would leave according to who had the furthest to go, another one of Callan's ideas. It simplified control and eliminated congestion at the turns. The layout of each platoon position would be up to the platoon leader, based on guidance from Captain Fischer and the S-3. That meant SFC Callan. Observation post positions would also be left to the platoons, along with the mounted patrol schedules in individual sectors. Once in position there was a generous 72 hour window for them to get situated, organized and active. Communications weren't as generous as they had been in Sudan, but more than adequate for the area they were in.

Harrison was extra busy. Food, water, sanitation, shower points, fueling points, maintenance, resupply and personnel accountability would all pass through him at some point. Not that he would be directly responsible for it all, but there always came a point where someone would want information, and the response would be, "Ask the First Sergeant." So Harrison asked, meddled, interjected and suggested. It didn't endear him to the staff sections who should have been handling it, but it made them think, made them plan and, hopefully, made them get it right.

Two nights before move out came the treat Grant had promised Bonneville. The Sergeants Major Academy was hosting a dining in, a military way of describing a formal dinner, with music and dancing.

Grant cleared it with Kearney and any officer or enlisted who wanted to attend, and had the necessary uniform, could go as the CSMs guest. No ACUs were permitted. Grant was surprised at the number of soldiers who actually had a Class 'A' uniform with them, but he gladly paid for their meals. He also arranged for them to sit together, and arranged for wine to be available for the toasts. Many are surprised at their first experience with a formal military meal. There are many off the cuff speeches, and many more toasts. Grant also arranged for a room at the Post Guest House so he and Bonneville could spend the night together without looking over their shoulders.

It had been a good evening. Grant could tell that the younger enlisted men and women had enjoyed themselves, and the officers learned a few things about the NCO culture. The food was excellent, the stories were good, and only slightly off color, and the band played a good selection of dance music. As Harrison said later, "Even the old geezers could get up and move around." And since many of the SMA students had invited members of their own units, no one paid much attention when Grant led Bonneville out on the dance floor several times.

Yeah, he thought, it was a good night all around.

The day after they returned Grant found Harrison sitting in front of his orderly room. The equipment had been loaded and the convoys were lined up in the company area. A guard mount had been posted, and the area was settling down to small parties celebrating their last night out of the field for a while. After this, time off would be spent under canvas out on the border. They would periodically have access to the local towns, what there were of them, but overnight passes would not be a regular happening.

"Deep in thought, Top?"

"Just hoping I haven't left something out. These short notice moves are starting to come awfully close together."

"Ralph, I want you to know that I think you've been doing an absolutely magnificent job as First Sergeant. We all do, and I don't know if you hear that enough."

"Stop it. You're going to drive me to tears, and it won't be a pretty sight."

Grant shrugged. "Fair enough. Now, tell me, why are you sitting out here all by yourself? If it ain't done, it'll keep until tomorrow."

Harrison stood up and stretched. "I am out here, Sergeant Major, because I'm tired." He sat back down.

"We're all tired, Ralph. It's been a busy few days. Things will lighten up once we get set up out there." He made a vague gesture with his arm.

Harrison shook his head. "That's not what I mean. I'm just getting tired. I was happy retired, Luke, I signed on with you for a trip to Africa because I thought I needed it. We were supposed to help, and that didn't work out so well."

"You're right about that."

"I know I am. Look where we are now. Do you realize we've been thrown out of four countries on two continents in less than a year? And we're supposed to be the good guys! Now we've got another shit job that nobody wants, and everybody's worried that we'll fuck it up." He stood up again. "No, I've had it. After this is over I'm going back to being retired. I got a boot-legged bomber I can play with and probably only a few years to enjoy it. This is a young man's Army now. I go to a Post NCO call, and even the Sergeant Majors are twenty years younger than me, and a lot of them are women to boot. It's time to pack it in." He picked up a stone from the ground and looked at it. He turned it over in his fingers a few times, and threw it away. "But don't worry about me, Luke. You got handed a shitty deal here. Whatever you need for support, you'll get it from me. I won't leave your ass hanging in some little *pueblo* on the other side of the line."

Grant gave him an abbreviated version of the conversation he had with the Colonel. "I don't know what the build up for him was, but it looks like he wants it both ways. If we're a hit, he looks like the next George Patton. If we screw the pooch, he can say he went on record against it."

"Like I said, Luke, I'm getting too old for this shit." He stood up and brushed some imaginary dust from his trousers. "And from where I stand, so are you."

Grant couldn't think of anything to say. When he looked up, his friend was gone. The worst of it was, he knew he was right.

Sharp and Price had spent the previous day and night shepherding the advance parties out to their sites and getting them set up to receive the main body. They were back because they had to be. Kearney wanted the leaders to experience the agony of a slow convoy roll. There was a Mexican officer standing with Kearney, watching the 289th mount their trucks and roll out. "That's the guy who bought us lunch in Columbus," Price said. "I knew he was a Mexican officer. And he said he'd see me again. I thought it would be over some rifle sights."

"It could happen yet." Sharp replied. "We tend to run short of that good old 'international cooperation' real quick wherever we go." He stuck out his hand. "I'll come by and see you on the airstrip in a couple of days." Price grabbed it and shook. "You might want to hurry. I don't plan on being there long. It's a shit job. All we're doing is hauling somebody else's trash."

Grant had noticed him too. The Mexican was discussing something with the Colonel, who called Grant over. "Sergeant Major, this is Major Apuesta from the Mexican Army." Grant rendered a hand salute, which was returned. Then the Major offered his hand. "A pleasure, Sergeant Major. I was hoping to meet the leader of the famous 'Wild Bunch'. Perhaps next time I will be able to bring my senior NCO. He has an interest in you."

"Major, that picture was a bad joke by some of the troops that got out of hand. I hope you and your people can accept it as that, nothing more."

"You're too modest, Sergeant Major. Every soldier I know wishes he had a reputation like the one you have built up. Don't you consider it something to be proud of?"

"You can tell anyone who wishes that to be careful of what they wish for. Someday, they might get it."

"I will pass that on, but I would still like you to meet my Sergeant. This type of cooperation is best done at a lower level."

"Cooperation?"

Kearney answered. "We hope to be able to coordinate efforts with the Major's battalion on the border. He has general security duties in the district and will try to free up some of his assets to patrol his side of the line."

Major Apuesta smiled. "Your Sergeant Major looks skeptical, Colonel."

"No, Major, I'm not skeptical. A little cooperation is always good."

LTC Kearney interrupted. "Is there a problem, Sergeant Major Grant?"

Grant gave a little chuckle. "No problems, Sir. I was just thinking. The last senior NCO I got to 'cooperate' with turned out to be a Senior Colonel in the Moldovan Internal Security Service. It didn't have a happy ending."

It was Apuesta's turn to laugh. "I will tell my Sergeant Cardozo of your concerns. After all I've subjected him to over the years, he might be happy to know there is a chance he is actually my superior!" Now all three men laughed. "I will be riding with your Colonel as far as the crossing at Columbus. I have a vehicle waiting for me in *Palomas*. Will you be riding with us?"

"Sadly, no, Major. I seem to have run afoul of somebody and need to speak with an Inspector General. After that, I'll be spending my day visiting our field locations. Perhaps next time." Grant glanced down at Apuesta's belt. There was an empty holster on his hip. "What do you normally carry, Major?"

Apuesta placed his hand on the empty holster. "Like your Army, we carry the Beretta 92. You call it the M-9. My headquarters carries the stainless model. We find it gives better service in this climate."

The IG was setup in Kearney's old office. He had several manila folders opened on the desk, and was making notes on a yellow legal pad. Grant didn't bother to report. He just walked in and took a seat in front of the desk. The Inspector glanced up over his glasses, made a mental note of the lapse of military courtesy, and then continued writing for a few seconds. Then he put his pen down and started in.

"Sergeant Major, I'll get right to the point. I know you're busy. There are several serious complaints by members of the 289th regarding your review and recommendation for combat awards for both the Sudanese and Moldovan actions. Two soldiers in particular are complaining they were denied, while the Mess Section got decorated for delivering coffee."

Grant took the offered seat. "I'll be glad to help, Colonel, but there weren't any irregularities. Every soldier who was recommended for an award who deserved one got it. We even checked all the after action reports to make sure nobody was left out. It was a very fair review."

"Sergeant Sullivan claims his awards were twice denied because of the personal animosity of another NCO you support, and Lieutenant Sage claims his combat awards were denied because he's gay"

"This I've got to hear!"

"This is no laughing matter, Sergeant Major. Sergeant Sullivan claims that he was denied awards because he reported Sergeant Price for stealing ammunition from a qualification range at the mobilization station. He claims the charges were ignored because you came to Sergeant Price's defense, and the investigating officer was, in his words, 'afraid of you'. Can you comment on that?"

Grant leaned back, took a sip of his coffee, and then looked directly at the IG. "Sergeant Sullivan, to say the least, is a liar. His problem is that in spite of his appearance and bluster, he's a lousy soldier and a worse NCO. His trouble with Price started when Price caught him falsifying his score on a PT test. They continued when the entire unit had to go through weapons qualification as part of the mobilization drill. Sullivan was supposed to run the ammo point, but wasn't anywhere to be found on the line. He was in the armorer's trailer drinking coffee. Price organized the ammo point, then went and found Sullivan and hustled his little ass back to where he belonged. At the end of the day, Price caught him trying to get another NCO to certify his score as an expert rifleman."

"What was wrong with that?" the IG asked.

"On the surface, nothing, except the NCO he was trying to get to sign off for him hadn't been on the line all day, and Sullivan never fired his weapon either. He started telling the stolen ammo story in Moldova, after he had been turned down for a Combat Action Badge and a 'V' device on an Army Achievement Medal." There are several awards that can be for either valor or merit. When it's for valor, a 'V' device is mentioned in the award line to differentiate.

"Why were they turned down?"

"To get a CAB or a 'V', you have to be a participant, not a distant observer. Sullivan did not take part in any of the actions in the Sudan. He never fired his weapon in anger. In fact, he never fired it at all. He was present during an air strike that caused no casualties, and he was on the lead element of a convoy that wasn't affected by an ambush. The AAM seemed to have been recommended for everyone on that vehicle by the officer in charge because they drove out of Sudan at night and didn't have any breakdowns. Probably good work, but not valorous."

"How about his award for actions in Moldova?"

"More of the same. He got someone, I forget who, to recommend him for a Bronze Star with 'V' for bringing up fuel and ammo during the fight at the Russian chemical compound."

The IG put down his pen. "Now that sounded legitimate. Why was it rejected?"

"Again, Sir, it would have been a brave act, if it had happened. That night we didn't have any fuel or ammo brought forward. The First Sergeant arranged for some extra security at the aid station, and the Mess Sergeant brought up food with his assistant. They got involved in the fight at the aid station, which is why their awards were approved. SFC Moura even earned a Purple Heart in that action. Sullivan never left the compound that night."

"How can you be certain? Sounds like there was a lot of activity to keep track of."

"Yes, Sir, it was. That was why I insist that every NCO keep rosters of their people at all times, and everyone was accounted for immediately after the actions. I still have those rosters. You'll find Sullivan's name on the Logistics Rear roster Sergeant Harte maintained. None of his people left the compound."

"Can I see those rosters?"

"I'll get them. Grant left the room. He returned in less than five minutes with a couple of folders. Each labeled for a particular action. "These are copies of all the after action reports and the rosters."

"Where are the originals?"

"The S-1, Captain Bonneville, maintains them in the unit historical file."

The Colonel picked through several rosters, made some notes, and then asked "Can I keep these?"

Grant said he could.

"Now I want to ask you about Lieutenant Sage."

"Colonel, can I interrupt? I had no idea that he's gay. I take 'Don't Ask, Don't Tell' a step farther. I don't know and don't care. A man, or woman, can lead their own life off duty. As long as it's not illegal and doesn't affect his or her duty performance, or that of the section or company, I don't need or want to know about it."

"You had no idea he was gay?"

"Not until you said it. Sage was denied combat awards for the same reason as Sullivan. You have to be there to earn them. He wasn't."

The Colonel gathered up his notes and the folders Grant had given him. He slid them into his brief case, snapped it shut and stood up. He offered his hand to Grant. "Sergeant Major, thanks for your cooperation. Once I write up my report that should be the end of it. It'll be up to LTC Kearney if he wants to pursue disciplinary action against Sullivan."

"And Lieutenant Sage?"

"His fate was sealed when he made his assertion of homosexuality. I've already had orders cut relieving him of all duties and being administratively attached to post headquarters. He'll be out of the Army in a few days. If he had kept his mouth shut he could have probably lasted until they changed the policy. I guess he thought being a phony hero was more important."

"That's too bad, Colonel. I think he could have been a good officer with some platoon experience. Next time somebody feels like they really need a medal I hope they come to me first. Sometimes it isn't quite worth what they have to risk getting it."

"You regret some of your awards, Sergeant Major?"

"No, Sir. I'm glad I have every one of them. I just wish some of them hadn't been so painful."

"And the mystique?"

"Mystique?"

"The 'Wild Bunch'?"

"Would you believe, Colonel, that it seems the entire world knew about that picture before I saw it?"

"I would, Sergeant Major. I've already spoken to your commander about it. He's satisfied you knew nothing about it. Still, it's an item of interest up the chain of command. Try not to let it spread anymore."

"I'll try my best, Sir, but it's the enlisted men who have taken a shine to the concept, but I'll put out the word. Is there anything else?"

There was, and Grant was blind-sided by it. "How do you know a Colonel Kosavich, Sergeant Major?"

That was a loaded question. "I met him when he was a Senior Sergeant in the Moldovan Army. He turned out to be a Senior Colonel in their intelligence services."

"Why would he send you a tank?"

A shipping container had come through the Port of New York full of diplomatic tags. That in itself wasn't unusual, except the destination was listed as the home of record, a private residence, of a senior American enlisted man. All the paperwork had been properly vetted by the State Department, and all licenses had been duly granted by the Bureau of Alcohol, Tobacco, Firearms and Explosives. It seemed it was a complete tank. It did raise questions.

"The morning after the fight at the Russian compound, Kosavich told me that one of his Stuart tanks had been destroyed. He had at least three present that night, and one had broken down early on. I made the off-hand comment that I had wanted to take it home. He must have taken me seriously."

Apuesta got out of the HUMMV just shy of the Columbus border crossing and saluted Colonel Kearney. “I hope our soldiers are able to work together very closely, Colonel.”

Kearney returned his salute. “I hope so too, Major. I look forward to our weekly meetings. Is your driver close by?”

Apuesta looked over his shoulder at the crossing. There was a Mexican HUMMV parked just beyond the customs station. “I can see my loyal Sergeant Major waiting patiently for me on the other side of the fence. Unfortunately, your Border Patrol is not as cooperative as your Army. He also carries a diplomatic passport, but they will not pass a military vehicle. Perhaps we can make that change too.”

“We shall see, Major.” With that he signaled his driver to move out.

The Mexican officer watched his American counterpart drive off, then turned and walked to the pedestrian crossing point. He brusquely and forcefully brushed past tourists and his own countrymen returning to Mexico. He was not concerned with niceties anymore. The American soldiers were out of sight, and the Border Patrol didn’t like him or his men anyway. The people in line, well, they were nothing to him. He held up his diplomatic passport and waved it in front of the agent. He knew what was coming, it always happened. The agent snapped at him to come back and took his passport from him, taking great pains to study it. Apuesta knew there was nothing wrong. The inspection was about the only way these shit heads could harass him. Anything more and they would be subject to a diplomatic protest and disciplinary action. Apuesta didn’t mind baiting them. If they tried to protest, his own country would brush it off, and the appeasement minded American politicians would fall over themselves trying to apologize. His Sergeant Major saw the apparent slight and was out of the vehicle and coming over. Sergeant Major Cardozo was short tempered and very protective of his *Commandante.* It would be very easy for Cardozo to cross over to American territory with his unholstered weapon and really create an incident. Apuesta lifted his hand to about waist level and waved him off. He could tell his man was not assuaged. Somewhere tonight some *gringo tourista* would pay for the Border Patrol’s insolence. Knowing Cardozo, it would probably be some drunken young college girl, and she would not enjoy the experience. He waited while the agent went through his harassing ritual with his hand out impatiently. It was soon over and he had his passport and was sitting besides Cardozo.

"Some day, *mi Commandante,* they are going to push you too far, and I will have the pleasure of leading a platoon to wipe that border post off the map."

Apuesta smiled and put his hand on his Sergeant's soldier. "*Esteban*, you must learn to take these little insults with a grain of salt. The Americans know they are powerless, and this is their pitiful way of trying to gain some sort of moral equivalence. It means nothing."

"All the same, *Commandante*, what they try to do to you is insulting to you, to the Army and to Mexico. Someday I will make them pay."

It was a familiar dialogue. Cardozo had the same rant every time Apuesta had to cross the border. Someday he would find one of the agents on the Mexican side of the border and make him pay, very slowly and very painfully, but for now it would be the tourists that suffered. Apuesta changed the subject. "Do we have any more information on the people who assaulted my two lieutenants?" He was referring to the two men Grant had relieved of their pistols and an AK-47. It was embarrassing for his men to have to admit they were bested by anyone, especially in their own territory. If it hadn't been for the fact that they both lost their issued stainless steel Berretta 92s, they probably would have said nothing. As it was, they embellished their story to make it look like they had been surprised by a much larger and better armed group who wanted to send a message, and a challenge, to Apuesta by insulting his men. The fact that they didn't identify themselves as any particular cartel was not surprising to Apuesta: every group thought they were well known and fearsome enough to not need an introduction.

"No, *mi Commandante*. We are continuing our inquiries." That meant they were grabbing known and suspected cartel members off the street and torturing them for any information they could provide. So far they had not had any luck. Not knowing it was a lone American who had bested his men hampered his investigation.

"Don't worry too much about it, *Esteban*. Those shiny pistols are trophies they will find it hard to not flash around. Once they surface, we will know about it."

"I hope so, *Commandante.* I don't like anybody getting an advantage on us."

Apuesta kept his own council about the story. He hadn't heard of any of the cartels being brazen enough to assault two of his officers and not kill them. There was something wrong with the story that he would eventually figure out. For now, it made for an interesting exercise and gave his men an additional reason to hunt down the opposition. Cardozo interrupted his thoughts with another question, this time about the Americans.

"What did you think of the American soldiers they are placing opposite us? Will they be a problem?"

Apuesta didn't think so. "They have several well known enlisted men. One of them has their Medal of Honor. I think you should make an effort to meet him at their Sergeant Major School at Fort Bliss. It will be very instructive."

"What about the rest of them?"

The Major gave a wave of his hand. "They are all part time soldiers, far away from home and anxious for their time in uniform to end. They will not be a problem."

"Those part time soldiers seemed to have given a good account of themselves in Africa and Europe."

"Propaganda, *Esteban,* nothing more. They were forced out of Africa with their tails between their legs, and in Europe they had to bring in tanks to get them out of trouble. Can you imagine, *Esteban,* tanks! And all they were fighting were some rebels who were traveling in a gypsy caravan! Don't worry about them, they are nothing."

Cardozo didn't say anything. The propaganda stories were coming out of both sides. The truth had to be somewhere in the middle, or at least he hoped it would be. He had some friends at the Sergeant Major Academy he could try to get some information from. Apuesta had the opinion that the American NCOs were exactly like the Mexican NCOs: worthless without a good officer. Cardozo knew the truth was something else entirely. The Americans put a lot of time and effort into training their sergeants, and once they were trained, they put a lot of faith into their judgment and initiative.

Time would tell.

For most of the 289th the move went as planned. Advance units had established traffic control and laid out bivouacs. There was a site plan for each platoon, and it was followed in almost all locations. The only area where no arrangements were made was at the Headquarters area. SFC Mitchell had sent out part of his Motor Pool to erect the maintenance tent and establish a motor park and maintenance area, but Lieutenant Fuller, going against Harrison's recommendation, decided that since they were in such a small area, a junior NCO could be trusted with the job of advance party. Unfortunately, the NCO he selected for the job was not up to the task.

The junior S-4 NCO, Sergeant Sullivan, was one of those soldiers who always looked good at someone else's expense. While his job skills were barely adequate, he managed, somehow, to exploit and accentuate failings in his section to his own advantage. It worked in his section, but once he wandered from his comfort zone he was quickly revealed to be a fraud. Two events happened when he had occasion to come to Sergeant Price's attention, during the PT exam, and again during weapons qualification. It was enough to make Sullivan avoid any contact with Price that he could. Once they were deployed he had been fairly successful at it.

Sullivan volunteered for the advance party, wanting to make certain his comforts were cared for without the demands of any other duties interfering. Instead of laying out tentage according to plan, and assigning troops to start erecting them, he had them dumped in a central pile, then selected one for his section and had it erected on a slight rise in the center of the site. Then he took the section vehicle and returned to his traffic control point, giving his assistant a folder and telling him to hold on to it, otherwise leaving his detail leaderless and without direction. Once his segment of the convoy passed, he informed the S-4 that he was going to follow the back trail and make sure nothing had been lost by the convoy. The S-4 complimented him on his foresight and sent him on his way. The fiasco at the bivouac fell squarely on his assistants' shoulders, and by default, onto Lieutenant Fullers'.

Sullivan and his driver rode back to Columbus, found an out of the way restaurant, and relaxed with a few beers. A Latino girl caught his eye, and he wasted more time trying to impress her with his importance, not realizing that the bar he was in was controlled by one of the cartels, and the girl, her name was Rosita, was one of the working girls. Everything he told her was duly noted, and she passed it on to her *patron* behind the bar. "You say his name was Sullivan?"

"*Si, Patron.* He acted like he was very important, that's why he was able to come here for a drink with his driver."

"If he comes back, Rosita, treat him very well. You may have to fuck this *gringo por nada*, but you will be rewarded for it." He waved a little plastic packet in front of her eyes. Cocaine. She smiled and took it from him.

"The *gringo* comes back I'll make him think he's the greatest lover in the world!"

"That's good, Rosita, and it won't hurt if you can get him to try some of your favorite candy."

"*No esta un problemo!*" I rub a little in the right place and get him to lick it off, he'll want more."

"No details. Just do what I tell you."

The bartender went to the back room to report on this new find. His *patron* was skeptical. "A sergeant? I know enough about the *gringo* army to know a mere three stripe sergeant isn't important enough to know much."

"No," the bar tender responded, "but I'll bet he's high enough to be able to get information he shouldn't have. If Rosita does her job well, we'll be able to get it from him."

The *patron* was unconvinced. "If the *gringo* does come back you can try, but don't waste too much time on him. We need to find out about how the *Norte Americanos* are going to shut down our best routes. Let me contact *el Commandante*. He's been spending some time with their Colonel."

Five minutes later he had his answer. "The *Commandante* seems to share your opinion. He doesn't think they will be too organized for a few days, so he wants us to fly a load in tonight. It might be the last until we can see what they're doing." Almost as an afterthought he added "And throw in some of the special cargo our hook nosed friend wants us to carry."

When Sullivan returned, the bivouac was almost sorted out, and he made a show of producing an unissued carpenters set from the back of his truck, proof that the line platoons were incompetent, and that he had gone over and above his duties once again. It was always good to be noticed at the beginning of a promotion cycle.

First Sergeant Harrison wasn't impressed. "You think you're pretty slick, Sullivan. Don't think you got away with anything."

"I don't know what you mean, Top."

"You call me 'First Sergeant'. You haven't earned the right. Where did you go?"

"Like I told Captain Gaston, I was on the convoy route looking for lost equipment. And I found some."

"You're full of shit, Sullivan. Maintenance was the last vehicle in line. They didn't see any equipment on the road, and I was with them, and we didn't see you pass us going the wrong way. You want to try again?"

Gaston had seen the two talking and came over to see what was going on. He heard the last part of the exchange and quickly interrupted. "That's enough, First Sergeant. Sullivan works for me and I'm satisfied with his explanation."

"With all due respect then, Captain, I need the line number off that 'lost' set and a copy of the hand receipt so I can make sure the right platoon sergeant recovers it and he gets his ass chewed a little for losing it." With that he pulled out his ever present notebook and wrote down the numbers stenciled on the box.

Gaston flustered. "Property accountability is my domain, First Sergeant. I'll handle it."

"Yes, Sir, I'm sure you will. But NCOs losing equipment is my business, and occasionally, I like my pound of flesh!"

Sullivan began thinking about ways to make the First Sergeant look bad.

There were two representatives from the General Services Administration waiting for Price at the airfield. They had folders of plans and copies of contracts for the dismantling of the half dozen structures clustered on one side. They were all in various stages of disrepair, except for a steel Quonset hut. This was to be dismantled and saved. The GSA guys said it was of some historical significance. Price doubted that. He had seen them all over the world. The only difference between them all was the layers of paint and rust.

None of the construction dumpsters were in place yet. There was a rented crane and flat bed to load the Quonset sections, and the all-important portable toilets. Somehow, the small water tower and its pumps were still working. Price put a few of his soldiers to work setting up showers. "What about tents?" one of them asked. "Put up one," he looked around and pointed to a clear spot off to the side. "Then find out which building the carpenters are going to pull down last. We'll use the buildings while we can."

"How about light discipline?"

"Yeah, why not. Until we get the word to the contrary, let's enforce noise and light discipline at night." And almost as an afterthought, "Set up a CQ and a guard rotation between the two sections for tonight, just in case we get some cross border traffic."

He set his men to organizing their bivouac while he took a tour with the civilians. There wasn't much to see in the buildings, most had been stripped of their fixtures a long time ago. The Quonset hut, on the other hand, had a substantial set of locks on the door. The GSA didn't have any keys, so they did a quick walk around. There were some shuttered windows high up, but they seemed to be secured from the inside. There wasn't a back door. They returned to the front and speculated on what was inside. The locks were rusted. One of the GSA guys said that this had been an emergency military strip at one time. "The history, as far as I know, was that it was an emergency field for bomber training, mostly B-17s and B-24s. It got reactivated in the 60's, and rumor had it that it had provided air support for the Bay of Pigs in Cuba. It might have been a refueling stop for planes going to Central America during the 80s, but nobody really talks about that too much."

"Looks to be in pretty good shape."

"Yeah, since then, it's been used by the Border Patrol and the Interior Department as an emergency strip, but there are better facilities now."

"How come it's not marked on the maps?"

"We're the government. We make the maps, and I guess we didn't want it shown."

All it seemed to be used for now was a sometime drag strip for the locals, and probably for drug smuggling flights from Mexico. The latter was the reason it was to be plowed under. Price called for one of his operators to bring over some chains. They would pull the door off. The GSA wanted to know what was inside. Price drew his Beretta, cleared it, and changed magazines. "Shot shells," he explained, "in case of snakes." With the chains hooked to a tow pintle, one tug took the lock off.

The door pulled open easy enough. Flashlights were produced, and they followed Price in. "You have the gun." There were no snakes seen. Both sides of the hut were lined with shelves. They were about half filled with boxes and mechanical parts, all covered with a heavy coat of dust. The GSA guys picked through some of them, read labels on boxes, and conferred. Price picked up a manual and read the cover. It was an air frame manual for a B-17. Under it was another manual for flight controls. Harrison, he thought, would want this. He walked through and looked at more boxes and parts. It was slowly dawning on him that this was probably the maintenance supply hut, and most of this junk would probably be aircraft parts. If the manuals were any indication, there were probably a bunch of parts Harrison could use in restoring the 'Wicked Witch', the B-17 they had recovered from Sudan.

How Harrison had ended up with the wrecked bomber was an almost funny story. They had arranged for the Air Force to back haul the plane, figuring it would end up in an Air Force museum somewhere. Once it got to the States, the crew had just dumped the pallets it was loaded on off to the side of a hanger. The base commander, a notorious neat freak, chanced by and went ballistic at the thought of all this "junk" littering his flight line. Unfortunately, or fortunately, as it turned out, no one could find the manifests. The crew chief remembered the name of the Army First Sergeant who seemed to be calling the shots. The base commander did some calling to the Army, and then ordered the wreckage loaded onto a flat bed and delivered to Harrison's home of record, with a bill for air freight, by the pound.

Harrison's wife also went ballistic, but quickly found out what a B-17 carcass was worth. She got a lawyer involved, paid all the charges, and got title to the plane before the government or anyone else could change their minds. Then she started a non-profit, of which Harrison, Grant, Price and Sharp were all directors and co-owners, and commenced to fund raise and restore the plane to flying condition.

"Hey," Price called, "what do you want to happen to all this junk?"

The two GSA guys conferred. One of them spoke. "We hadn't counted on this. I don't know if we can get another Dumpster. Can you find a way to dispose of it? If you can find a guy to haul it off for scrap, you can use it for beer money."

Chapter 4

Despite having two days to get established on the ground before active patrolling was scheduled to start, the line platoons were better organized than the Headquarters believed. Sharp and his Recon section, eager to get out from under the watch of Captain Menklin, the S-2, put his first patrols out starting at midnight. The rest of the platoons were taking the first night for themselves and were going to start in the morning. Sharp's efforts paid off almost at once.

They had just turned onto the jeep trail, as the border road was called on the maps, and crested a small rise. As they came down their night vision goggles (Sharp insisted on his troops getting used to driving totally blacked out at night) picked up a group huddled along the road on the US side of the border. They had obviously heard the Hummer coming, as it wasn't a stealthy vehicle. They could see two figures, both carrying rifles, motion the group to their feet, then one of the armed men waved. Sharps' driver, SPC Sinclair, said "I thought the Border Patrol wasn't working this area?"

"That's what I thought too. They're not in any border uniform I've been briefed on." Sinclair asked what he wanted to do.

"It almost looks like they're expecting us. Hit 'em with your headlights." In the bright glare they could see maybe twenty people. Most were clutching some sort of bag, suitcase or backpack. The two armed men were their escorts, and they definitely didn't look like border agents. As the HUMMV rolled closer, the man on Sharp's side slung his rifle and walked right up to his door, yelling something in Spanish. The other one was coming to the driver's side.

"Guns up, Sinclair. Take the one on your side." They were both out their doors and onto the strangers. Sharp used his rifle to drive his target down to the ground. Sinclair was subtler. He had a high intensity flashlight with a pressure switch mounted under his barrel. He pointed the muzzle into his man's face and hit the switch. The Mexican was momentarily blinded, and then recognized what he was looking at. His hands went up. Sinclair spun him onto the hood and took his weapon. Then he pulled him around to the front of the Hummer and put him on the ground. The Mexican knew enough to keep his hands on his head.

Sharp's playmate tried to resist. He made an effort to unsling his rifle, but Sharp stopped him with thrust of his barrel into the man's forehead. His reaction was to bring both his hands up to cover the bleeding, and Sharp used his free hand to flip him over and take his weapon. Then he dragged him out front to join his friend.

Sinclair motioned with his rifle to the rest of the group, some of whom scrambling back to the Mexican side through a cut in the wire. "What about them, Sarge?"

"Let 'em go. Keep your rifle on these two." Sharp knelt over them and searched. He came up with spare rifle magazines, knives and a hand held radio. He picked up one of their rifles and worked the action, chambering a fresh round. "Get the speed cuffs out of my bag and secure these two. Then familiarize yourself with the other rifle." There was chatter on the radio that Sharp didn't understand. He could hear another engine approaching and there was a glow of headlights from the rise they had just crested. Another vehicle had them locked in its headlights. There was some more yelling, and then an automatic weapon cut loose on the back of the Hummer. Sharp reacted instantly, firing single shots above the headlights into where he thought the windshield would be. He called out to Sinclair to take out the lights. There was a long burst from that side, and the lights went out. As soon as it was dark Sinclair stopped shooting, and Sharp closed on the truck, keeping up his fire. The rifle clicked empty, and he realized he had been firing the FN-FAL he had taken from the Mexican, and the spare magazines were still on the bumper of the Hummer. He reversed direction and ran to reload. The two Mexicans were gone. Sinclair was on the far side of the Hummer, out of sight.

"Sinclair! You OK?"

"I'm good!"

"Where are the Mexicans?"

"Don't know. I was watching the truck!"

Shit, Sharp thought, two more problems running around in the dark. "Keep an eye out for them. I'm going back to the truck." He approached slowly, keeping his rifle up and pointed at the cab. There were no sounds, no movement. He got close enough to open the driver's door. A figure slumped out, a rifle clattering after it. Sharp swept it aside with his foot and looked into the cab. There was somebody else in there, and from the looks of him by the dashboard lights, he was dead too.

He yelled back to his driver, "Get the head shed on the radio!"

"No go, Boss, looks like the radio is shot up pretty good!"

He fished into one of his cargo pockets and pulled out a cell phone. Two bars. Great, he thought. All this and lousy cell service too. He hit Grant's speed dial number anyway. He heard a ringing on the far end.

Kearney was storming through the bivouac shaking up his staff. When Grant woke him up to tell him about Sharp, he pulled on his boots and ran to the commo tent before Grant could stop him. When he found the commo crew all asleep, he went from zero to ballistic in .05 seconds. There was no radio watch in his tactical operations center, and no one there, either. The only person awake was the staff duty NCO, and he was reading a book. Commo hadn't run any of the lines into the First Sergeant's office tent yet.

The Colonel shouted out orders as they came to mind. Grant already had a HUMMV and driver ready. He had gone to the S-4 tent to draw some ammo to bring out to the field and had his own battle with the Supply Officer. Captain Gaston initially refused to release any ammo without authority from the CO. "The CO said only the guard mount was to get ammo in the Headquarters area." When Kearney's voice could be heard bellowing through the area, Grant just smiled at him and said, "Hang on. I'll get him." After Gaston's eyes returned to their normal size, he decided that the Sergeant Major's word would be good enough for him.

Grant loaded the ammo cans in the back seat of the Hummer, first taking out a couple of boxes to charge some magazines. He wasn't really surprised to see that it was boxed ammo. It would have been too easy if the S-4 section had ordered ammo on stripper clips in bandoleers.

Kearney was approaching the HUMMV, finally ready to go. He was telling him how he had told Fischer to call the border station in Columbus, when Grant's phone rang again. "Now what?" was all he said as Grant listened without interrupting. Finally he said "Keep your people safe. I'll be there as fast as I can with some ammo."

"What was that about? Sharp again?"

"No, Sir. That was Price. He just had a plane land at the air strip."

The heavy equipment section had pulled their vehicles in close behind the buildings on the strip, and got settled in for the night. Price set the security detail, and made sure they had loaded their magazines. They had been disappointed that the ammo had been packed in 20 round boxes instead of bandoleers and stripper clips. Price was never one to go anywhere unprepared, and he made a mental note to somehow get the right ammo. His most important instruction was "Unless they're shooting up the area, get me up before you do anything!"

"And if they are shooting us up, Sarge?"

"Hopefully I'll hear them."

He had just made his last round of the area. The guards had decided that the old control tower with its 360-degree view would be perfect for them, and Price agreed. The relief sentries could get some sleep while the duty guy kept an eye out with the night vision goggles. He was at the foot of the stairs when he got called back up.

"Hey, Sergeant Price! We got some activity up to the north. Looks like a couple of vehicles pulling onto the end of the strip. What do you want to do?" Price climbed back up and picked up a spare set of goggles. He could make out four, no, five vehicles, stopped at the end of the strip. Two of them peeled off and headed down the center of the strip. He watched them go past. At the southern end, they reversed direction and put their high beams on the runway. Two vehicles up north did the same, while the fifth pulled off to the side. The resolution in the goggles was pretty good, and he could make out three figures get out and huddle by the rear of last vehicle.

"What do you think they're doing, Sarge?"

"I don't know," Price answered as he reached down and picked up a loaded magazine and slipped it in his M-4, "but you better get your buddies on their feet, then get the others up. Tell them to keep quiet, and no lights." The soldier acknowledged and went off. Price gave the rest of the detail instructions, and then he heard another sound. It was faint, and it was coming from the south. It sounded like a small plane. He scanned the skies, and then picked it up in his goggles. It was a small, high winged single engine craft. It was flying with no navigation lights, but the cockpit instrument glow made it look like there was a searchlight inside. It was losing altitude, and it was definitely coming in for a landing.

Price raced down the stairs and jumped into his vehicle. The noise it made when he started it was partially drowned out by the plane coming down the runway. He pulled it out front, pointing it in the direction that he believed the plane would stop, and got out. He heard another soldier come up beside him.

"What's the plan, Sergeant?"

"Plan? What makes you think I have a plan? Keep behind something solid and watch the ones to the south."

"Who do you think they are?"

"Gotta be smugglers. That's probably why the Feds want us to tear this place up."

The plane taxied to a stop and swung around to face in the direction it came from. The engine RPM's dropped, but not quite into an idle. Price had seen enough "hot" landings under fire to know that this pilot was planning on a quick getaway. He watched through his goggles as the men on the ground ran to the plane and started pulling containers from the cargo compartment. They were piling them up to the side when Price pushed his NVGs aside and pulled the switch on his headlights. The bright light caught the men off guard, but only momentarily. One of them raised an AK-47 and sent a long burst at Price. One of the Hummer headlights shattered as the plane engine accelerated and it sped past on its take-off roll. He let a long burst rip down the side of the plane, then he started laying down controlled short bursts at the people who were firing at him. He saw one go down before his other headlight was shot out. He quickly repositioned his NVGs and resumed fire. He saw another figure go down. The two vehicles that had been illuminating the strip from the south came roaring by, another automatic rifle putting rounds into his HUMMV as it went by. Price swapped out his empty magazine and chased them with a long burst. When he looked back to the north, the casualties were being unceremoniously tossed into the back of one of the vehicles. One figure made a move to the baggage piles, but Price dissuaded him with a well-placed burst. He could hear shouting now, and all the figures boarded their vehicles and sped off. Price emptied his magazine after them, and then switched to his last magazine. He called for someone, anyone, to bring another vehicle and ammo up, and then called out to check on casualties among his troops. There were none. He looked over to his partner.

"How's your ammo?"

"I'm out." Price noticed he didn't have his gear on either. They hadn't been expecting anything to happen so quickly. He laid his 9mm on the central platform and told the soldier to take it. Then he switched on the radio and tried to raise the net. The radio sat high up in the cab, above the line of the windshield. It had taken several hits. Fortunately, he had a hand held in his cargo pocket. Group didn't answer. He got Sharp instead. "Use your cell phone. The bastards at the rear aren't up! Need help?" Price gave him a quick rundown on what had happened to him, and Sharp relayed his tale of woe.

"Call Luke. This'll make his night!"

Price made the call as they walked over to the baggage pile. He had the driver stop short and keep it illuminated. He got out and approached slowly, sweeping the area with his rifle. To one side he could see dark spots on the ground, bloodstains from the two he had hit. He turned his attention to the bags. The first he opened was no surprise. It was full of taped up plastic bags. These had to be drugs. He tossed a few similar sized bags aside, and then opened one that looked bigger and heavier. It was full of RPG launchers. Another bag held tubes that Price recognized as shipping containers for the rockets. This was some serious shit. There were two Ak-47s lying near the bloodstains. Price retrieved them and checked the magazines. They were about half full. He called his driver over and handed him one of the rifles, then sent him back to roust the rest of the troops.

"You think any of them are still in the rack, Sarge?"

"Probably not, but make sure anyway. Get them organized into a defensive perimeter and give that" he pointed at the AK, "to Sergeant Monson, then come back here with the Hummer. And don't bring anyone with you."

"What about ammo?"

"Yeah, bring some back."

He could hear the starter turning over on the HUMMV, but the engine wasn't catching. First day out of the gate and he was already breaking the equipment. "Never mind that. Run back and pick up another vehicle. Then get on the radio and call the rear. Tell them we're going to need a mechanic."

"I thought Sergeant Sharp said the net wasn't up?"

"Yeah, I know. Just have the RTO keep trying. If Sharp talked to the CSM, the net will be up real fucking soon."

CSM Grant decided to take a medic with him. Kearney had gone on ahead to meet Sharp, and had told Grant to check on Price. If his situation was secure Grant was to bring extra people to the fence line. His rationale was that Sharp had bodies, Price didn't, and that made Sharp the man of the hour. Sergeant Abbott was up and ready, so despite Doctor Carlson's objection, she was the one to go.

"Grab a change of clothes Abbott. You may be out there for a few days."

"Way ahead of you, Sergeant Major. I've got a set in my assault pack."

Abbott was grateful for the chance to get out of the rear area. "Sergeant Major, you would not believe how whacked these people are back here. They've totally forgotten everything we learned in the Sudan. I'd rather be out with the platoons."

"So would I, Sergeant. So would I."

Grant headed towards straight to the airstrip. There were a series of trails and roads that ran back from the border that he had been studying on his maps. He planned to spend some time learning all the back roads, and this was as good a time as any to start. Later he could find the quicker cross-country routes. He had Abbott concentrate on loading magazines. He was pissed off that the morons in supply hadn't requisitioned combat loaded ammo. Loading stripper clips would have been faster than ripping open cardboard boxes and loading bullets one by one. He found the route and sped up. A quick glance at his map showed him he'd be passing close behind Sharps position before he turned west again and headed to the strip. He slowed and watched the terrain to his left. Abbott noticed and asked what was up.

"Nothing, I hope, but we're close enough to Sergeant Sharp that anybody that ran off may have headed this way instead of back into Mexico. Why don't you get into the gun hatch and keep an eye out." He handed her a portable spotlight. The rest of the ride was uneventful. They made good time getting out to Price. Just shy of the airstrip, Grant could see a glow in the sky. It looked like Price had erected his light sets, trailer mounted light poles that had their own generators. He stopped and made contact on the radio. "Let Sergeant Price know I'm coming in." He waited a few moments to let the message be relayed. There was an all clear given and he drove into where Price and a few of his soldiers had set up a hasty perimeter around the baggage pile. Price gave him a quick situation report, or sit-rep, and waited for questions. Grant had none about the action. He handed over the ammo can. Price made a face.

"More of the loose shit? We on a tight budget, or are those pukes back in the rear saving the easy to load stuff to sell at a flea market?"

"That's all I've got for now. Head shed went on the cheap. They didn't expect anything like this. We'll have to requisition the right stuff."

"Yeah, but for now," he looked at the can as he passed it to another

NCO, "840 rounds barely is about 2 magazines each. Almost half hour to load and about a minute to shoot up in a good fire fight."

"Try not to have another one." Grant motioned to the pile. "What's in the bags?"

"Some have drugs. The rest I don't know yet. We haven't looked in all of them. With all the blood puddles over there, I thought I better leave it for the Border Patrol guys. They coming?"

"Damned if I know. The liaison agent hasn't shown up yet, and probably won't until morning."

"You didn't call anyone?"

"Not my job, Jonah. I've got a commander who makes those calls. When I was in the real Army I used to count on my O-5s to know what to do. I hope this one doesn't let me down too bad. Come on. Let's take a look."

They walked over and stood by the baggage. Two of the cases were obviously RPGs. The rest were all unmarked hard sided cases. Grant called Sergeant Abbott over.

"Got enough latex gloves to loan us a few?"

"Sure thing, Sergeant Major," she answered as she rummaged through her pack. "I always keep a box handy."

Grant and Price pulled the gloves on. Grant opened the first case. It was full of plastic wrapped packages. He closed it back up and put it to one side. He indicated a similar case to Price. He opened it and found the same packages. There were six bags packed with what Grant guessed were drugs. "Stack 'em up, and put a guard on them. I don't think we need anybody touching them until the feds get here."

There were three more bags of different sizes. Two were packed with AK-47s. Price picked one out and held it to the light. "This ain't good."

"What is it?"

"All full auto, and made in Venezuela."

"Fuck me!" was Grant's first response. "Now I know why Chavez needed his own AK factory. OK, check them all for serial numbers, make a list, then pack them back up and put them off to the side. I don't think we need to be turning those in."

Price had a puzzled look on his face. "Why not?"

"If they're going to be shooting at us, whoever sent us here will be anxious for us to do something about it, and we'll have to take it home to them pretty soon. I'd rather operate on their side with stuff that can't be traced to us." Grant waited while Price made his list, and helped him stack the cases. Then they turned their attention to the last case. It was loaded with sealed ammo cans for the AKs. Price pulled out an odd looking one. "Whoops! Got something here!" It was a GI can marked '5.56mm – 800 rounds in bandoleers'. Price worked the lever and opened it. "Looky here, Luke. It's full of .223"

"Put that with the rifles. Use the loose stuff to load your magazines for now. Save that for back-up. Give me a box of that 7.62x39."

Grant opened the box. "All Russian. I guess Hugo hasn't got his ammo plant up and running yet. What about the rest of it?"

"All 7.62 for the AK."

Grant thought for a minute, and then took the can from Price. "Rearrange that shit so it looks like there's nothing missing, and stash this. We'll find a place for it out of sight." Price passed the can to another soldier.

"And, Pricey, make sure your people know they don't know anything."

Grant looked over to the eastern horizon. Dawn was still a few hours off, and there was a lot of work to do. The first order of business was moving the weapons and ammo. The Border Patrol could have the RPGs and try to find out who supplied them. The small arms would be kept for future operations. They could have the drugs, too. Grant was hoping they could avoid having to store any of that. There was a lot of money represented by those plastic wrapped bags, a lot of money and a lot of temptation. He would rather not test the will power of his soldiers, and he really didn't want to attract efforts by the drug gangs to get their product back. The Border Patrol or the DEA could haul it off, the sooner the better.

Price's HUMMV was pretty shot up. None of the vehicles they drew from Bliss were armored. There had been no expectation they would need them, so they were all soft tops or, like Grant's, fiberglass topped. The engine compartment on this one had all the peripherals shattered, but the block was probably intact. SFC Mitchell would have his first challenge of the exercise.

"Can I get a loaner?"

"Pricey, I can probably get you a Blazer for now. HUMMVs are pretty scarce."

"Get one from the staff pukes."

"Kearney's already got them sharing. Mine and his are about the only exclusives, and no, you can't have mine." He looked around the area. I'll need to take a detail over to where Sharp is. While they're getting organized give me a quick tour." The two made the rounds of the area. Price took him into the Quonset hut to show him what was on the shelves."GSA guy said to get rid of it. He didn't care how," Price said.

"It's a gray area, Price. Might be illegal."

"And the Arab money and the crates of guns are what, misunderstandings? Luke, the guy said sell it for scrap and use it for beer money. I don't need beer money."

"All right, all right. I'll tell Harrison. He can load it up and bring it back to the rear detachment at Bliss. His wife can sic the lawyers on it to make sure it's all legal."

"Seems like it's a long way around just to get rid of scrap."

"Scrap?" Grant nudged a stack of wooden crates. "These are superchargers for the engines so they can operate at 30,000 feet. One of these pieces of 'scrap' would keep you in beer for a few years. Don't get stupid on me." They stepped outside of the hut and Grant looked around for his vehicle. He saw Abbott coming out of the base of the control tower and signaled her over. He told her to get the HUMMV and they would be off to the other site.

"Can I stay here for a while, Sergeant Major, just in case something else pops up?"

Grant shook his head. "Sergeant Sharp has a couple of bodies, and he said there were a lot of illegals in the area when the shooting started. There may be some collateral damage in the brush he won't find until the sun comes up."

It didn't take long to get to Sharps position. As they turned onto the jeep track, Grant could see a fire glowing in the distance. A quick check of his map showed that it was probably in the area of the airstrip he had driven through on his 'Mexican weekend', as he liked to call it. His best guess was that the light plane Price had fired out may not have been able to land safely. As he crested the small rise he had his driver slow down. There was a glow from the vehicle lights ahead. The first vehicle he saw was an open bed one- ton stake truck, the one that had come up behind Sharp and started shooting him up. He could see the puddle left by one of the now dead shooters. Driving to the front, the stake body's headlights were still on, illuminating five bodies: three were laid out in front of the truck, and another two were a little distance away. Sharp was sitting on the back of his obviously shot up HUMMV writing on a yellow legal pad. Kearney was a little further down the track, his vehicle angled across the road. He was standing in the open door, radio handset in hand. Grant glanced at his own radio and turned up the volume, but there was nothing coming over the frequency. He called in a quick commo check to 'any station' and once he got a response was satisfied there was no problem with his set, but Kearney was still talking to someone. He checked his Communications Electronic Operating Instructions booklet, the CEOI, and found the alternate frequency for the day and adjusted to it. There was still nothing but silence. Whoever Kearney was speaking to wasn't on the same network as the rest of them.

He had his driver stop and spoke to Sharp until Kearney finished his conversation. He could sense rather than see that there was a light security screen thrown up around the area. Two more vehicles were parked past the commanders' vehicle. The rest of the recon section probably. Sharp gave him a brief replay of what happened, then put down his legal pad and took Grant to where the bodies were laid out. He nudged the first two with his boot. They were partly lying on their sides. Grant could see the ends of the speed cuffs sticking out. "These guys were the escort for the group. The way they walked up to us, they must have thought we were their ride. Me and Sinclair were able to take them right out." They walked to the other group. "These guys came over the hill and hit their brakes. Whoever was in charge must have sized up the situation and decided to cut his losses."

"What happened to those two?"

"As soon as the shooting started they up and hot footed it for the break in the wire. One of the gomers in the truck must have thought they weren't worth rescuing."

"And the illegals?"

"They all beat the feet too. I don't know if any of them headed west, but I think most of them tried to go back to Mexico."

"Tried?"

"Yeah." Sharp took out a flashlight and shined it in the direction of a clump of bushes on the Mexican side. "There are a couple of bodies clustered around that scrub brush. I guess nobody wanted them talking about what happened."

Grant gave him a quizzical look. Sharp knew what he wanted. "Yeah, I went over and checked on them. They're all dead. Six of them. Looks like the rest kept running. They dropped their packs and kept going. I took a look, and left it all over there."

"What did they have?"

"I'm no chemist and I don't do drugs, but I'd have to guess either heroin or cocaine. They were doing double duty, sneaking into the US and working as mules. Looks like a bad career choice."

Grant tapped the legal pad. "Was this your idea?"

"Nope. The Colonel got here, gave me the third degree, and told me to write it all down to cover my ass."

"Did you mention checking out the bodies over there?"

"Didn't tell him, not writing it down. I'm stupid about a lot of things. This isn't one of them."

Kearney was finished with his conversation and came over. "You up to speed, Sergeant Major?"

He answered "Yes, Sir," then launched into a recap of what happened with Price, leaving out the AKs and the ammo. Kearney thought for a moment, "They probably thought we wouldn't be well organized yet and decided to keep sending their people across. There were probably a bunch of penetrations tonight."

Grant nodded. "I've got to agree with you. We'll probably find a bunch of fresh breaks in the wire when the sun comes up. Good news/ bad news is now we'll have a location for some of the major crossings. We'll know where to deploy our sensor line to begin with."

"They won't do you much good right on the border."

Grant didn't say they were planning on placing them a kilometer inside Mexico.

"No, but if we get a reading, maybe we can track them with the drones and figure out where they're heading on our side."

They could hear a helicopter in the distance. There were navigation lights approaching from the east. It circled a few times and settled down on what must have been a clearing several hundred yards away.

"That'll be Major Apuesta." Kearney said.

"He made good time." Sharp opined.

Kearney gave him a scowl. "Never mind how fast he got here! I called him from back at headquarters." He looked at Grant. "Let's not forget we're supposed to be cooperating with the Mexican authorities." Grant remained silent. Sharp asked, "What about the Border Patrol?"

"They'll be here at first light."

Kearney walked back to the break in the wire and waved his flashlight at the group he could see coming towards him with their own lanterns.

Grant put his hand on his friends' shoulder. "Keep cool, Dave. You aren't in any trouble here. This was a good takedown. You've got the weapons to prove it." It was true. Sharp had policed up the weapons from the five 'bandits', and ended up with two Argentine FN-FALs, a German G-3, a Spanish Cetme, which was a close relative of the G-3 and another Venezuelan AK-47. "Let Kearney handle the Mexicans. It's officially over our pay grade now."

Kearney greeted Major Apuesta at the break in the border fence. Grant could hear pieces of the conversation, enough to know that the Mexican Army Major had first stopped at the airfield to investigate the fire on the runway. The gist of it seemed to be that the place was deserted; even the body of the pilot was gone. Grant had a quick question for himself: how did Apuesta know that the pilot was dead?

The next shocker was when Kearney led Apuesta and his escorts on to the American side and led them to the bodies that were laid out. Sharp started to push past him, but Grant grabbed his arm to restrain him. "Let it play out, Dave. He's calling the shots." The Mexicans shined their lights on the faces of each one, and had a brief conversation. One of them stepped away from the bodies and made a radio call. There was the sound of another helicopter spooling up. The navigation lights appeared in the direction of the airstrip. The Mexican with the radio kept talking as he walked over to the top of the rise and broke open a glow stick. He was guiding the helicopter in for a landing on the US side. Now Grant thought it would be a good time to intervene. He walked over to Kearney and Apuesta and began to speak. One of the escorts chose that time to turn around, and in the glow of the flashlight he recognized him. The Mexican squinted, and Grant could see the wheels clicking in his head. The Mexican thought he recognized Grant too. Grant spoke first.

"Ever get those tires fixed?"

The eyes went wide. Now he knew where he had seen this *gringo* before. He put his hand on his flap holster and started to unsnap it, when he heard Sharp grunt at him. He looked past Grant and could see Dave Sharp, SFC, US Army, with his M-4 carbine leveled at his waist. Sharp just shook his head and the Mexican let his hand drop. Apuesta heard Grants comment, but Sharp was out of his line of sight. "You two have met before?"

"Yeah, Major, we've met. He was broken down with a couple of flat tires not too long ago. I offered to help, but he and his *amigo* seemed to have the situation well in hand." Grant took a half a step in. "Is that your buddy landing the chopper?" The Mexicans hands were balled up. He was getting ready to swing at Grant when Apuesta stepped between them and faced his subordinate. There was a rapid exchange of Spanish and Grant heard the term *gringo* tossed back and forth. The Mexican turned on his heel and headed back to the Mexican side. Apuesta put up his hands and gave a broad smile.

"My apologies, Sergeant Major, my soldier is very hot tempered. The flat tires were very embarrassing to him, and his friends had fun with it at his expense. I sent him back to cool down. The next time you meet, he will apologize."

The second helicopter was on the ground, and two sets of litter bearers came running over to retrieve the bodies. Grant tried to get Kearney to reconsider. He refused. "Major Apuesta and his men recognized them as members of one of the cartels from *Juarez.* It's better he take them so we don't have to get involved with a shooting investigation."

"Colonel, they were killed on our side."

"Sergeant Major, I think we can agree that their associates kept Sergeant Sharp and his driver pinned down while the pulled the bodies over to the Mexican side."

"What about their truck and weapons?"

"Lose them somewhere. Do you want Apuesta to take them?"

Grant thought a moment. "No. We'll dump them." He gave a quick salute and turned away. Kearney called after him. "Oh, and Sergeant Major? Make sure Sharp and his driver, what's his name?"

"Sinclair"

"Make sure Sharp and Sinclair understand what the official story is. Will that be a problem?"

"No, Colonel, no problem."

After the Mexican helicopter left with the bodies, Grant asked Apuesta if he was going to take care of the pile the Sharp had pointed out on the Mexican side. Apuesta sent his escorts to check them out, and took his leave. "Don't worry about them, Sergeant Major. We will handle it." He paused as if he had a thought stuck in his head. "I wasn't aware you had visited my country. Next time you come let me know, and I will arrange a suitable escort." He walked to where the bodies were and collected his men without glancing at his dead countrymen. Grant and Sharp watched him leave. "Well, that told us something," Grant said.

"Yeah, I'll bet those poor bastards will be lying there until the vultures get them."

"That's not what I meant, but there's nothing we can do about them, Dave. I don't want you policing up bodies on their side."

Sharp asked, 'What did you mean?"

"There's a helicopter LZ just over there, and a pretty clearly defined trail system. Get the drone people to run a series of pictures going out that way. Then make this your first sensor area."

"Still want them a kilometer out?"

"At least that, probably more like a klick and a half."

"I'll get on it tonight."

"No you won't. You have people. Let them do it. I've got other plans for you tonight." Grant told him about his plans for *Sierra el Indio.*

Kearney interrupted their plans. "Sergeant Major, give your vehicle to Sergeant Sharp. He'll need it more than you."

"Yes sir. I'll get one of the Blazers for now."

Kearney laughed. "You old guys like that outdated equipment, don't you?"

"It's only outdated if it doesn't work, Colonel."

"Well, be that as it may, you would have been losing the Hummer anyway. You'll be heading back to Bliss tomorrow for a few days."

"Tomorrow? Why?" Grant didn't like the sound of that.

"I should have told you sooner. I've known about it for a few days. The Sergeant Major Academy has been tasked with setting up a third world NCO program, and somebody wants your input."

"That'll be a waste of my time and theirs. "

Kearney broke into a broad smile. "You're wrong about that, CSM. This course is going to be for the Sudanese Peoples Liberation Army. You've got some experience in that part of the world, or so I hear." Kearney was chuckling as he turned and walked away. He called back over his shoulder, "You better hop in with me if you want to get back to the CP."

Grant waved him off. "I want to help Sharp break down these rifles and scatter the parts. I'll catch a ride back with the maintenance team."

Kearney didn't respond. He just got in his vehicle and drove off. Cresting the hill he passed a maintenance truck. Mitchell was driving, and he was a little pissed off. As he pulled up he was shouting out the window, "I can't believe you and Price wiped out two of my vehicles already! Where am I supposed to get parts out here?"

Grant answered him. "Just make a list of what you need. The funding for parts comes out of the JTF. Whatever you do, don't let them go back to Bliss. We'll never get replacements."

"Well, all I have are tow bars right now. I don't bring the wrecker for HUMMVs. Can you pull that pile of parts back to the maintenance tent? It'll save me from making two trips."

Mitchell had his mechanics hook Sharps shot up vehicle behind Grants, and then he went off to find Price.

"What do you want me to do with the rifles?" Sharp asked.

Grant motioned to the rear of the Hummer. "Stuff them in back and cover them with gear. After you dump us off, go see Price. He's got some more stuff we shouldn't have. Pick out something for me, you and maybe two others. Then get the drones up and make a run over *el Indio* for good measure. We'll go over at last light tonight and try to be back by midnight. I've got a big day tomorrow."

Back at the headquarters bivouac, Grant checked in with the CP to see if anything else was going on, then headed to his tent to catch a couple of hours sleep. Most Commanders and their Sergeant Majors bunk in together in the field. Grant would, if Kearney insisted on it, but he found having his own tent more convenient. It allowed him to come and go without disturbing anyone, or raising eyebrows, and it gave him his own planning space. He had the carpenters put up tack boards across the top of the tent walls so he could hang up a set of maps of the area. He made overlays with details of the area nobody needed to know about and kept them with him. It was convenient. Everyone was working off the same scale maps, so if he needed to update anything, he could do it to scale on the spot. He also had a set that he had trimmed the borders off and taped them together, then folded them so he could quickly change the view in his map case. That way, he was always oriented on the ground. Most of the vehicles were equipped with GPS, and Grant considered it a useful tool, but he didn't depend on it.

Batteries died and equipment malfunctioned, but a map and compass had one moving part.

He took a look at the approaches to *el Indio* before he turned in. It looked like a covered approach, with no more than two klicks in, mostly uphill, and two klicks out, mostly downhill, of walking in a couple of hours. It should be bright enough for them to scan the whole valley from up there, and get back before midnight. The drone pictures would tell him more, but he was satisfied he had a good plan. It was time to sleep. Or so he thought.

Captain Bonneville called to him from outside. There was a certain standard of decorum they had to meet in the field, especially in broad daylight. He pulled the flaps back and brought two folding chairs to the opening.

"What's up, Captain?"

She had a puzzled look on her face. "Kearney just told me I had to go back to Bliss tonight, something about a classified briefing on a new personnel computer program we'll be getting. I'm riding in with a supply run to the rear."

"Is that a problem?"

"It is. As far as I know there are no new personnel programs. We just did an update before we came to the field."

"If it's classified, how would you know about it?"

"I wouldn't, but it also wouldn't take them," she looked at her notes, "up to three days to complete the briefing. Something's going on."

Grant discreetly put his hand on her knee that was furthest from the door. "Don't worry about it. We'll get rooms at the guest house and you can tell me about it when you get back."

She gave him another puzzled look. ""We'll get rooms? Do you think Colonel Kearney is going to let you come back to hold my hand?"

He squeezed her knee."Not to hold your hand. I have to go back to the Academy for three days. They want my input on a new program."

"Your input?"

"Yeah, when you're in the Hall of Fame at the SMA, they seem to think your pretty hot shit. I think I have my picture in three or four museums right now, not to mention uncounted post offices. They think I know what I'm talking about."

"Can you come with me tonight? I really don't want to make that ride with Gaston and his people. It's bad enough we have to 'coordinate' our use of one truck."

"Wish I could, but I have a date with Sharp and his people tonight."

She wrinkled her nose. "More boy scout stuff?"

He told her about the shootings the night before. She had gotten a quick briefing on them from the duty NCO. "Does this have anything to do with that?"

"I hope not. Tonight I want to be swift, silent and unnoticed. We may need a good long range OP, and this may be the best place for it."

"Can't Dave Sharp handle it on his own?"

"He can, but Sharp has a habit of taking it all on himself. I told him to start letting his people do more and I told him to bring a couple of them with us tonight. I want to make sure he starts letting them do their jobs."

"When are you going to let Sharp do his own job?"

"That's why I'm going, so I can make sure he is. Then I'm going to go out of my way to make sure I never cross the Mexican border again." He paused. "That is, unless I'm taking you to another nice hotel for a getaway."

They were hunkered down in the brush on the Mexican side of the border. Grant, Sharp and two of Sharps NCOs were all wearing unmarked OD mechanics coveralls provided by SFC Mitchell. They were carrying AK-47s, with spare magazines stuffed into load bearing equipment Sharp had taken off the bodies the night before. They were all wearing hydration packs. Since they were off the shelf items and not marked 'US', Grant was willing to risk them. Even the Mexican army probably used them. Two of the dead Mexicans from the night before were wearing them. They were more convenient than a canteen.

Sharp had a security element move in earlier in the afternoon, just to keep an eye on things. They would stay on the US side unless they were needed. The two NCOs who would accompany them were with the security team. Sharp didn't want to be trying to move any more people than necessary when it was time to go. He and Grant were dropped off a good kilometer to the west of the border, and they followed a natural defile up to the fence. The drone photos had shown that there was nothing other than scrub on *el Indio.* Grant had been concerned that there might be sheep or goat herds, and trails running all over, but it looked like this was a dead corner as far as the world was concerned. The route had been marked on an overlay, and the point man moved off, followed by Sharp, Grant and the trail guard.

El Indio had three peaks arranged in a triangle. The highest was to the north, with a slightly lower point directly to the south. The lowest peak formed the point of the triangle, directly centered to the east. They were following a covered defile leading up between the two westerly peaks, the northern one being their objective for the night. The climb was steep in places, but not difficult, and they made better time than Grant had allowed for. Things were looking good for getting back and getting some sleep tonight. At the ridge connecting the two closest peaks they turned north. The ground dropped off to the east before rising again for the third peak.. The brush was sparser, but rock outcroppings gave them good cover from every direction except overhead. That would be a concern they could deal with once a semi-permanent position was established. The crest of the hill ran roughly northwest to southeast. There was some brush on the summit, but more importantly, more rock formations, and some of them provided overhangs that were deep enough to provide shade and cover for all daylight hours. Taking out his field glasses, Grant had an unobstructed view of the airstrip. The crashed plane had already been loaded on a flat bed trailer and was sitting by the roadside waiting to be driven off. While he was watching, there was a puff of black smoke from the exhaust stacks and the trailer moved off to the north. Sharp was standing next to him, watching the same scene.

"I wonder who's paying for that?" Sharp asked.

"I don't know, but I'll bet he's not happy about losing that toy."

Grant divided the summit into three areas and had the rest of the team each take a section and start preparing range cards. There was a full moon and a clear sky. While they were doing that, he moved down the saddle to examine the approaches from the Mexican side. He was satisfied that they were slightly more broken, and could be used to channel anyone approaching into a sensor array. That would give a small team ample warning for a quick getaway. When he got back to the top the range cards were finished. Sharp pointed out that there was an awful lot of activity in an area full of desert scrub and deserted villages. There were specks of light scattered through the valley, either stationary in the abandoned buildings, or scurrying along the roads in between. In his cynical way, Sharp spoke what everyone was thinking: "If this place was so quiet, how do you suppose they missed all these people running around?" Sharp wanted to leave his people on the summit to keep watch. Grant vetoed the idea. They weren't organized or equipped to leave a semi-permanent OP up here right now.

"I'll give you three days to organize something. When I get back from Bliss you can run it by me, then we'll decide, but don't do anything until then. We need a lot more overheads. I'll have Harrison bug his new friends at the Intel School. In the meantime, start getting a sensor line out there on the likely avenues of approach. We need to know what's out there before we go stumbling around in the dark."

They made a quick check of the area to make certain they hadn't left any traces, and then they moved back to the US side in reverse order of how they went up. The security element reported all had been quiet. The hike back to the pick-up point was likewise uneventful.

Back at the CP Grant checked in with the duty NCO in the operations tent to see how the rest of the AO had been. Just about every platoon was reporting activity to their front, but it all seemed to be well inside Mexican territory. Night OPs were being established at points that indicated activity in the past, and motorized patrols were making random passes on the jeep trail. "Is the Colonel aware of all this?"

"Yeah, Sergeant Major, he told me to relay the word that he didn't want everybody up all night. He said 30% would be a good alert status."

Grant agreed. The cartels and whoever else were out there had more people to keep awake all night. If they planned it right, they could keep the GIs hopping 24 hours a day long enough to wear everybody out, then waltz across wherever they wanted. Grant hoped they weren't that smart. Next he went by the motor pool. The two shot-up HUMMVs were in the maintenance tent, already stripped down with the shot up parts laid out on folding tables. One of the mechanics had a wiring harness stretched out and was comparing it to a wiring diagram. "Think you can salvage that, Dana?"

"Oh, hi, Sergeant Major. Yeah, I think I can get it back up. Sergeant Mitchell says it'll take a few days to get all the parts we need, so I figured I'd try to salvage what I could, just in case."

"Don't you have to exchange the old parts?"

"We do, but if they're not available, I want to be ready."

He left the motor pool and made a couple of stops on his way to his tent. Harrison had already turned in, which was always a good sign if the First Sergeant felt he could get a night of uninterrupted sleep. SSG Gordon was working late in the S-1 tent. She told Grant that Bonneville had left a couple of hours ago, and had already called back with her contact information at the guest house. She gave a copy of it to Grant. "The Captain said she was able to reserve the room next to hers for you," she said with a smile. Grant took the paper and thanked her. His last stop was Kearney's tent. There was a light on, so he announced himself. Kearney was sitting inside, looking through a folder, a glass of amber liquid on the table. Grant could see the bottle on another table in back. Kearney offered him a drink, and Grant accepted. They exchanged ideas about the number of people who should be on duty after dark, and agreed that a quarter to a third, at most, would be best unless there was information to indicate otherwise. Grant said he believed the Mexicans would keep up a pattern of noise, light and movement activity for a few nights. "They'll try to feel us out for a bit. They got their ass spanked pretty good the first time they fucked with us. I think they'll be more careful from here on in."

Kearney grunted. Grant could tell that this wasn't his first drink of the night. "Where did you go tonight?"

"Sergeant Sharp and I went looking for a high place to set up an OP."

"Find one?"

No sense lying about it. "Sort of, but I don't know if it'll work. I told Sharp to think about it for a few days and I check in with him when I get back from Bliss."

Kearney was studying his folder again. Grant said his good nights and rose to leave. "Enjoy your time away from the Group, Sergeant Major." He looked up. "I noticed from your records you don't take much in the way of leave time. That's not good for a man of your age and responsibilities."

"I relax when I can, Sir."

"See you when you get back."

Grant entered his dark tent and pulled the zippered door shut behind him. When they erected this tent, someone had attached the insulated liner for him. It helped keep the heat of the day out, but the temperatures regularly fell into the forties here in the high desert and without a heat source, it didn't do much. It did, however, help keep out some of the background noise. He dropped his load carrying vest with its porcelain inserts with a thud in one corner, and started stripping off his boots and uniform in the dark. He became aware of a rustling sound a few feet away. He cocked his arm back with a boot in his hand, ready to throw if there was a snake in here with him, then reached up and flicked the light switch that was mounted to the center pole. As soon as the light came on he dropped the boot. Sitting up on his bunk in his half zipped sleeping bag was Major Sylvia Carson, the Group doctor. From what he could see, she was naked.

"I was wondering when you were coming back tonight. I've been waiting for you."

Grant sat down in a folding chair. "I didn't know you were here."

"I could tell. Don't you turn on the light when you come in?"

"That's not what I meant. I thought you were still at Bliss."

Major Carson had been temporarily assigned to the post hospital when they arrived back in the States. There had been a shortage of her specialty, and the Army was quick to take advantage of her presence.

"They cut me loose yesterday. It took me a while to find out where everybody was and arrange a ride. I finally got a ride with that sleazy little Sergeant Sullivan in the S-4. That was an experience." Some of the junior enlisted female soldiers felt the same way about Sullivan, and went out of their way to avoid him. "Are you just going to sit there, or are you going to come over here and show me how happy you are to see me?" She swung her legs out of the sleeping bag and sat on the edge of the bunk. Grant could see that the rest of her was naked too. Her clothes were neatly folded on a chair at the foot of the cot. Her body was having the desired effect on him, and she knew.

"I am very happy to see you, Major, but I've got to warn you, I haven't had a shower in a couple of days."

She got a big smile on her face and stood to walk over to him. She knelt down with her arms resting on his thighs. "All the better," was all she said, and dropped her head. Her wet lips made Grants whole body shudder. The woman knew what she liked, and she was good at it. After a few minutes she spoke again. "I've been waiting a long time for this."

"You know, I'm going to hell," he said to her.

She stood up and led him to the cot. "I know. I am too."

She pushed him down on his back and slowly straddled him. For the briefest of moments Grant wondered if the aluminum GI cot could take the combined weight and her gyrations. Then she lowered herself onto him and rapidly brought herself to a climax, rested a moment, then started again. When she was done she smiled down at him. "Do you need a little rest?"

"You know, I am an old man, can we talk for a bit?"

She arched her body and brushed an erect nipple across his lips. "You talk, I want to play, and she slid down to work on Grant to get him ready again. When he was he rolled her over so that he was on top. She muffled her moans into his chest.

After a bit she snuggled up to Grant. "That's the old man that I remember, and that's the one I missed."

"I would have thought that by now you would have recruited

another officer for this so you wouldn't have to sneak around with me."

"What makes you think I haven't?"

"That was not sex with a woman who's been getting satisfied on a regular basis. If you have got a guy, you better see if he has a brother, because I don't think he's doing it for you."

She slapped at him playfully. "There isn't another guy yet, at least not a regular one. There's something about the thought of doing it with you that just curls my toes. I don't even mind sharing you with your little S-1."

"You know I'll be back at Bliss with her for the next few days."

"I know, and one of these days I'll get to arrange one of those little trips to be with you. Now shut up and fuck me!"

She was fit, energetic and put a lot of her body into her love making. At some point Grant noticed that he had to make very little effort. She knew what she wanted and how to get it. And she was multi-orgasmic, which had its own effect on him. Grant finally lost track of time. He had no idea what time she finally let him go to sleep.

When he woke in the morning, she was gone.

Meanwhile, Sergeant Sullivan, who had spent the previous day driving back and forth to Fort Bliss, was waking up from his own little R&R. After driving in for supplies, then driving back with Major Carson, (who he thought was a bitch, no matter how hot she was) and ferrying Captain Bonneville, (who he also thought was hot and approachable, but the Sergeant Major was tapping that) back to post, he felt he was entitled to a little of his own fun. Captain Gaston had given him permission to stay on post for the night, since he had already racked up so many miles. Besides, the parts maintenance had ordered for the two shot up Hummers would be ready in the morning.

Sullivan's first thought was to head to the little bar he had found in Columbus. That hot little Mexican barmaid Rosita seemed to go for him, and if he could find a place to stash his HUMMV overnight, he might be able to persuade her to spend the night with him.

He was surprised when the bartender let him park in the alley out back, even suggested it. He was even more surprised when, after only a couple of beers, it was Rosita who suggested he spend the night in her room upstairs from the bar. The sex was really great. He could tell this girl was really into him.

And the powder she was rubbing on his penis before they had sex really made him feel good. He slept like a baby when they were finished. In the morning she brought him coffee and a breakfast *burrito,* or some kind of Mexican roll-up. He asked her what the stuff was that she had rubbed on him the night before. She just sat in his lap and rubbed her breasts in his face. She hadn't put on a bra yet, and her nipples felt hard.

"You liked that?" She asked. He wasn't sure if she meant the powder or the face rub, but he liked them both.

"You know I do. Will you do it again?"

This time she didn't know whether he meant the powder or the face rub, so she pulled his face into her chest again. "Of course I will *carito.* I just want to make you happy."

Sullivan looked over at the clock on the microwave. It was getting late, but he decided, fuck it; this is too good to leave so soon. He took the chubby little ball of fire back to bed. Maintenance's parts could wait.

Downstairs the bartender and his *patron* were listening in and watching on a computer monitor. Rosita's room was wired for sound and video. You never knew when a horny *gringo* would oblige them with a little hush money to keep his indiscretions quiet. This *gringo* was different though.

He might have information that would help them get their product over the border with American military protection.

Chapter 5

Grant got an early start even though he didn't have to be at the academy until 1300. He decided to have a cup of coffee in the mess tent before he hit the road. He still had trouble referring to it as a dining facility; old habits die hard. He planned to stop somewhere in Columbus and have a somewhat normal breakfast. He didn't have a problem with Army chow; he just wanted to eat off something besides paper plates. He packed light. His uniforms were starting to show the wear and tear from extended periods in the field and some of them could stand replacement. Reservists and National Guardsmen were authorized to turn in worn uniforms for new items, but Grant felt that at his pay grade he should be able to afford to dress himself. The clothing sales store was close enough to the academy grounds to stop on his way in and pick up four or five new sets. His patrol cap was a little threadbare too. It got a lot of wear. Grant preferred it to the beret when he was in fatigues, another old term that was hard to erase from his vocabulary. It brought back memories of his first days in the Army, when olive drab was the color of choice, all the patches and chevrons were sewn on and in full color, and the US Army name tape was gold and black. You could tell what rank was approaching long before you had to salute. There wasn't any of that squinting at the flash on the beret or the inch and a half Velcro patch in the middle of the chest.

And then there was the old pleasure of 'breaking starch', a ritual few soldiers still on active duty remembered.

He passed two of the motorized patrols on his way out of the area. Everyone reported an active night on the Mexican side, lights and engine sounds, but nothing too close. The soldiers on patrol were of the opinion that the Mexicans were just trying to screw with their heads, but it didn't work.

The trip into Columbus was uneventful. There was one Border Patrol vehicle parked off to the side just before he got to the town. Grant slowed and waved, and they waved back. There was no other traffic, but there wasn't much of a reason for anyone to be on the jeep trail at this hour. Not a legal reason, anyway. He turned off the trail just before the border crossing station and headed down a couple of side streets looking for a diner, something other than a fast food chain. He found one in a slightly seedy part of town, but it looked clean from the outside, and it had off street parking. He had his choice of booths and picked one at the end with a view of the street and the front door. Several of the locals came in. They either nodded or said 'good morning' but nobody tried to engage him in conversation. That suited Grant fine.

After he finished his bacon, eggs and home fries he was enjoying a refill of what turned out to be some pretty damned good coffee, when a movement across the street and down the block caught his eye. There was a HUMMV pulling out of the alley next to a bar. He tried to make out who was driving, but it had the soft top up and the plastic windows on the door distorted the drivers' features. He could make out the engineer castle painted on the rear quarter. Kearney had ordered it painted on all the unit vehicles, so Grant knew it belonged to the 289th, but it was too far away to make out the bumper markings. Somebody was sneaking out with a vehicle to spend the night in town. Grant made a mental note to check on who was authorized to be out with a vehicle the night before. He doubted it would be one of the line platoon troops.

A voice from the bar asked "One of yours?"

Grant looked over at a middle aged man dressed in an old field jacket, right down to the black and gold US Army tag. "Why would he be one of mine?"

"The way you looked at the vehicle. You recognized something on it." He walked over and motioned to the seat opposite. "Mind if I join you?" Grant waved his hand at the empty bench. Without preamble the man continued. "I figured he's one of yours. Because we don't get too many soldiers spending the night here, and that particular one drives through town on a regular basis. And he's got a honey in that bar."

Grant just looked at him. "Who are you?" The man smiled. "How rude of me." He pulled out a wallet and flipped it open to show his badge and ID. "Mel Braga, New Mexico State Police." Grant took a quick look and grunted. "I say again, why would he be one of mine?"

"You're all part of that group spread up and down the Big Hatchet. Right now there's nothing out there but drug runners, illegals, and you guys. Oh, and a couple of missing Border Patrol agents."

"I hadn't heard about them."

"No surprise. It's a big secret. They think one of the cartels snatched them and are holding them for some kind of swap. But I digress. He talks about you."

"Who?"

"Your soldier buddy."

"We haven't established he's one of mine yet. How do you know he talks about me?"

The cop waved for a refill of their mugs. Once it came he continued. "People tell me things. When it happens over there, I pay attention."

"OK, I'll bite. What's he saying about me?"

"That Grant is a big fucking jerk who couldn't find his ass with both hands."

Grant nodded. "That's a pretty direct quote. Are you sure that's what he said?"

"Oh, I'm pretty sure. After a few beers he says quite a bit. He doesn't like you, but I don't get to hear as much from him anymore."

"Why not?"

"Like I said, he's got a honey over there, a crack whore named Rosita, a chubby little thing that probably had a future once. He doesn't have to bother with the preliminaries anymore. Just grab a quick beer and straight upstairs to bump uglies."

"Preliminaries?"

"Yeah, you know, get himself liquored up, buy her a few drinks, drop a few bucks with the bartender. He just comes in, waves, grabs a beer and they head right upstairs."

"Where's he hiding the Hummer?"

"You haven't asked if I know his name."

"I figure you'll blurt it out pretty soon, but I'm pretty sure I know who it is already?"

"How so?"

"Only a couple of people have any reason to come by here on official business on a regular basis. Somebody heading out with a Hummer without a reason would get noticed."

"But you said you know who. That sounded like a couple of possibilities."

"Well, one of them is a Captain, but he likes to be driven. Something about his image as a leader. That leaves his driver, who only goes with the Captain, and one other bright spot that really doesn't seem to like me anymore."

"You know your people, Sergeant Major."

"Why do you know them, or at least this one?"

Braga drained his cup and pointed at Grants. Grant shook his head and waited for an answer. "The place is one of several in town owned by either the Mexican Army, one of the cartels, or a joint venture."

"Distribution?"

"So far they're not doing anything except running a couple of girls. That bothers me more than if I knew they were doing something. Are you going to talk to your boy?"

"Do you want me to?"

"I'd prefer you didn't. I know they're trying to turn him, I may not know the next guy."

"Do they know you're watching them?"

"So far, I don't think so."

Grant considered his options. "I won't say anything to him for now, but I'll arrange for his time to get squeezed a little so it's harder for him to get here."

"Then what?"

"I've got things I need to do. Having him tell tales out of school might help."

"It could get dangerous for him."

Grant shook his head in agreement. "Yeah, but he's a big boy, and being a soldier can be a dangerous lifestyle. With any luck he'll know what he's getting himself into."

"And if he doesn't?"

"I guess he's pretty well fucked."

"That sounds pretty cold blooded."

"It is. I've got enough people trying to do their job without him trying to fuck it all up for a piece of ass. If he sees the light I'll welcome him back into the family. If he doesn't, well, I can probably replace him with an empty sand bag."

They exchanged cell phones and input each other's numbers. Grant offered to pay for breakfast, but Braga declined. His family owned the restaurant. "Just make sure you leave the waitress a good tip."

Grant arrived at the Bliss mid-morning. His first stop was the Group rear area where he had left his leased truck. He would be less conspicuous driving a new Ford than he would an almost 30 year old Blazer. From there he headed off to the Guest House. If you went into this place anywhere else besides a military base, you would think you were checking into a civilian chain hotel or motel. It was a far cry from the old days when they would remodel a couple of old barracks buildings. There were still bachelor NCO and officers quarters on base, and some of them were quite nice, but Grant had taken a liking to the Guest House. He chalked it up to a sign of getting old. The clerk, a civilian in a blue blazer with a nametag that said 'Zach', read his registration card, welcomed him back and asked if the rest of his party was on the way.

"I am the rest of my party. Why?"

The clerk was apologetic. "I'm sorry, Sergeant Major, Captain Bonneville said that there would be a Lieutenant Colonel Kearney and a First Sergeant Harrison would be with you."

Grant thought about that for a moment before he answered. Why would she say Kearney and Harrison were coming? There must have been some rule about how many had to be in the party before she could reserve a block of rooms. They were of sufficient rank to warrant special consideration, guaranteeing the rooms would be adjoining. That was one bright Captain he had there. It was a big enough group to avoid suspicion.

"I guess it's my turn to apologize, Zach. I didn't realize you were expecting them. I wasn't involved in making arrangements for this trip. The Colonel and First Sergeant won't be coming. Their deployment responsibilities required them to change their plans."

"No problem, Sergeant Major. It happens all the time."

His room was on an upper floor, with a view of the back of another building. He dumped his bag into a bureau drawer and looked around the room. There was a small safe tucked into the back of the closet. Grant read the instructions, then got his Argentine .45 and spare magazines out of his bag and locked them up. He had left the two stainless Berettas with Harrison. Satisfied they were secure, he headed back out. His first stop was the clothing sales store. He got what was on his shopping list, and looked around for items of opportunity. There was a display for a company that produced the challenge coins. Challenge coins had a quarter century history in the US Armed Forces. There were many stories told about how they came into being, most of them fanciful. Their original intent was to encourage soldiers to be better than they thought they could be. Their next use was to recognize soldiers for a variety of reasons, usually superior performance. Now they seemed to be passed out like candy, and even sold in Army-Navy stores.

Their actual creation came out of a tragedy. Sometime in the early 1980s the 101st Airborne Division was tasked with manning observation posts in the Sinai Desert to supervise the cease-fire between Egypt and Israel. One particular rotation had been awarded their Multi-national Force Observers Medals prior to getting on the plane to return to Fort Campbell, Kentucky. The plane crashed after taking off from a refueling stop in Gander, Newfoundland. When they recovered the bodies and their effects, a number of the medals were found, their suspension ribbons burnt off. The medals were polished up, and, in an emotional ceremony, were awarded to select junior enlisted men of the Division to 'challenge' them to continue the traditions of the 101st Airborne Division and honor the men who died. It was too good an idea to be a one-time happening, and it quickly spread.

Grant filled out an order for 200. The design he chose was the Medal of Honor superimposed with Command Sergeant Majors stripes surrounded by the words 'Sudan – Moldova – Mexican Border' on the reverse. The front would have the 289th Engineer Distinctive Unit Insignia surrounded by the unit designation, 289th Engineer Support Group, and the year. This would probably be the last assignment for the 289th, and it would make a nice souvenir for the troops, even the ones who didn't earn it. Two hundred was the minimum order. The clerk was reluctant to accept the order. The Medal of Honor logo was regulated by law, and it couldn't be used without some justification. Fortunately, the clerk was able to access a data base listing that had Grants' name and image on it. With an added detail of his name etched ever so small under the medal and stripe design, she added an official approval and accepted the order. He even got a 10% discount.

Next stop was the Class VI store, the military version of a liquor store. In some locations the selection was a little better than what you would find on the local economy and the reduced federal taxes made it a good buy. Being close to Mexico, the Fort Bliss store didn't disappoint. There were several brands of tequila that Grant was familiar with that weren't available in the United States. Not knowing when he'd get another opportunity, he picked out what bottles they had on the shelf.

The clerk wouldn't make the sale."Sorry, Sergeant Major." He pointed to a sign on the wall behind the register:

NO SALES TO PERSONNEL IN FIELD
UNIFORM DURING DUTY HOURS

Grant had forgotten about that rule. It had been around since the old frontier days in an effort to cut down on alcoholism in the frontier posts. Not that it ever seemed to work, but it was still in effect on about every military post in the country, except maybe the Pentagon and Washington DC area in general. There was a corollary rule in the Commissary store that allowed personnel in uniform to go to the head of the checkout line at lunch time, but this wasn't the same as buying groceries.

"OK, Son. I forgot about that, it's been a long time since I've been around the real Army. I'd hate to lose out on these though. Do you have more in stock, or can you hold it for me until 1600?"

The clerk checked his inventory on the computer. "Those are the last ones, Sergeant Major, but I guess I can hold them for you if you pay for them now. I'll box them up, but you'll have to pick them before 1700. That's when my shift ends." Grant paid and told him it was no problem. Then he went to grab a quick lunch at the local fast food place. The NCO Club would have been better, but it was located close to the Academy and his portrait was one of many hanging in the lobby. It was always embarrassing when someone pointed that out. One would have thought it would have been more convenient to have them hanging around the Great Hall instead, but that wasn't how it worked.

The presentation started precisely at 1300. Classes, lectures and seminars always started on time at the Sergeants Major Academy. Guest instructors, regardless of rank, honored that rule. In the place that set the standard for all enlisted training, standards were scrupulously observed. The topic was 'Establishment of a Senior NCO Course for the Sudanese Liberation Army'. Grant knew why they wanted him here. When the subject first came up some months ago they sought him out in Moldova for his opinions and ideas. The memory of the raid on Al Fashir and the ambush on the exfiltration from the country were still too fresh, and his opinions were neither appreciated nor welcomed. He hadn't changed his mind since then, and if they asked, he would repeat them.

The presenter did an admirable job of laying out the rationale, philosophy and suggested curriculum for the Sudanese. He mentioned several times that he had only been in country once, but he had gained a favorable impression of the NCOs he had met. Grant was willing to bet that any amiable NCOs were either under orders to be amiable, or Sudanese Majors or Colonels under orders to be amiable. His experience didn't scream friendship for their own people, let alone any foreign military. The country's president was under indictment by the International Court in The Hague for crimes against humanity for ethnic cleansing of his own people. There were three factions in the country fighting for control, and even if there had been a ceasefire agreement, they were still regularly killing off peace keepers from the African Union. The Janjaweed militias were still getting government support for their reign of terror in the Darfur region, even if it wasn't being reported with the gusto of past years, and nothing was being done to clean up the refugee camps on both sides of the Chad-Sudan border.

At the end of the two hour presentation the presenter opened up the floor to questions. There were several, and a lively give and take followed. The audience was generally supportive, but Grant could tell from the glances sent his way that everyone was waiting to hear his opinion. He hoped they would just accept his silence and let it go at that. It wasn't meant to be. "What do you think of the plan, Sergeant Major Grant? You have some experience in that part of the world."

"My experience doesn't support your plan. I don't think they're ready for a senior class. You'd be better off starting with a Primary Leadership Development Course for the junior NCOs and building on that. The senior NCOs will be too vested in their system and too co-opted by their politics to change."

The room went silent. That wasn't what they wanted to hear. "You don't think they're capable of changing?"

"I don't think they want to change. Senior NCOs got that way by lasting long enough to be trusted by the officer corps and the government. You start pouring money into that tier of leadership and you'll have problems down the road. They'll set up the criteria for entrance, and only politically reliable, and in that part of the world, religiously reliable candidates will be accepted. You have to remember that all through Africa that the shakier governments spent so much time watching the senior officers planning coups that they ignored the smarter senior NCOs who ended up carrying them out."

"You can't be serious."

"Look at history. How many NCOs took over their country?" There was silence. "You don't know, do you?" Grant went to the wall where there was a graphic of Africa on an easel. He picked up a black marker and started writing. "Mobutu in the Congo, Idi Amin in Uganda, Samuel Doe in Liberia. . ." The chief facilitator interrupted.

"Thank you, Sergeant Major. You've made your point. If there are no other questions, I think this would be a good point to end on."

There was a general commotion as the assembled NCOs gathered up their notes to leave. Grant tried to head right out, but he was intercepted by the facilitator. Grant knew him. They had attended this course together. He wasn't smiling, and he didn't offer his hand. "Luke Grant. I guess it's true what they say."

"And what would that be, Oscar?"

"That you're too old and too set in your ways to accept new ideas. You fucked up in Iraq, you fucked up in Sudan, you fucked up in Eastern Europe and now you'll probably fuck up in New Mexico. Why don't you just retire?"

"I don't retire because I still have to outlast people like you. You've never gotten your hands dirty, so you don't have a clue what happens that last two hundred meters beyond the wire. Now get out of my fucking way before I show you what happens, or do you think I'm too old and set in my ways to move you?"

He stepped out of the way. "I don't think you'll be back here, Grant we don't need you."

"You won't get your wish. It seems I have to be here tomorrow morning to hear a Mexican Sergeant Major explain how they're not winning their war with the drug cartels. Think they'll have another question and answer session?" For good measure Grant put his hand flat on the other mans' chest and pushed him back against the wall. Then he smiled and walked out. He looked at his watch. It was almost 1600. He could sit in the parking lot of the Class VI store and wait for his booze. Maybe Bonneville would be done with her conference by the time he got back to the Guest House. They would definitely be having dinner in El Paso tonight. He had had enough of the Army for one day.

His booze safely in hand, he returned to his room and selected one bottle and slipped it into the small ruck he used as a day bag. After a trip to the ice machine, he settled in for his first drink, when there was a knock on the connecting door to Bonneville's room. She was still in uniform, and gave him a big kiss. He waved at the bottle and asked if she wanted a drink.

"That would be delicious. Today has been a complete waste of my time. I've been to the same conference three times now." She took a couple of sips of her drink. "I still have one more day to put up with it. How about you?"

He gave her a quick rundown on what he thought would be a mistaken policy, then told her about his meeting with Mel Braga, the New Mexican State Trooper. She asked who he thought the GI at the bar could be. Grant was pretty sure it was Sullivan. Bonneville wasn't surprised. "None of the women like being around him. He's a little snake. He's careful enough with what he says that there's always a double meaning, just in case somebody complains. But there's no mistaking that smug leer. You just know what he's thinking when he looks at you. I never want to ride with him again."

"Well, for now, you don't have to. I think it'll be too late to head back tomorrow, so we'll spend another night and get an early start the next day. That OK with you?"

She gave a Marilyn Monroe type squeal and brought her shoulders together. If she had been wearing something low cut it would have really accented her cleavage. "I'll show you how OK it is." She came over and sat in his lap. There was a big wet kiss, and Grant felt himself stirring. Damn, she could get his motor racing fast. "First things first. I want to get out of here for a while. Do you have anything you can wear into town? I'll take you someplace nice for dinner. She did. She had gone to the PX at lunch and bought a few things. He always kept a change of clothes handy in his truck and had brought them in.

"Let me get a little soak in the tub before we go."She reached for the bottle and poured herself another hefty shot. "This'll make the rest of the day go away."

"Go easy on that. I don't want you falling asleep during dessert."

She gave a wicked grin. "Don't worry about that. I have my own dessert planned for you." She went back to her room, leaving the connecting door ajar. Grant decided to finish his drink, and then get a quick shower. He had gotten his boots off when there was a knock on his door. Just to be discreet, he closed the connecting door on his way to answer the knock. It was the General who had briefed him in Germany. There was a different soldier with him.

"Good evening, Sergeant Major. Got a few minutes?"

Grant glanced over at the other door. He was hoping Bonneville would take a long soak. He could hear the tub running through the walls. The General heard it too. "Don't worry about her; we'll be gone before she's finished." He walked over to the couch and sat, opening up the folder he was carrying. "These are your target folders. I hope you've had an opportunity to look over your AO."

Grant picked up the loose photos and flipped through them. They were better than anything they had been able to get so far, and he said so.

"How old are these?"

"They're all date stamped on the reverse. None of them are more than a few days old. In fact," he reached over and took one from the bottom of the pile, "here's an interesting shot of a hill top to the south. It would seem the Mexicans have a lookout up there. That might impact your operations."

Grant looked and recognized *el Indio.* "Don't worry about them." He handed the picture back. "See that one guy off to the southeast?" The General picked up a small magnifier and looked. "Oh yeah, I see him. What about him?"

"That was me."

"You've already been over the border?"

"Yeah, twice. I've driven the length of the Mexican side, from south of the airfield back up to the border, then this trip to check out an OP."

"And?"

"And nothing. Until I know what you want, I don't have anything to add."

"These folders will give you detailed instructions. Don't make any copies, and make sure they're destroyed after you finish your mission." He got up, and his silent companion moved to the door. Grant stopped him. "There is one more thing. I don't think Kearney is on board with any of this."

The General nodded. "Kearney has his own set of problems that he's only aggravating. I'll be going out to Double Wells tomorrow to brief him personally. I think he'll be more enthusiastic the next time you see him."

"And if he isn't?"

"At least he won't be disruptive." He held out his hand. "I'll see you again soon, Sergeant Major."

At that moment the connecting door opened. Linda Bonneville came in, looking towards the couch. She was in her underwear, just a bra and skimpy panties. She was holding an outfit on a hanger in one hand. "Do you think this will be OK to wear to dinner?" She stopped when she didn't see Grant sitting there. She turned to look towards the bathroom door and saw the three men standing there. She focused on the star in the center of one uniform. She was wearing one of the close-in-the-front bras that Grant liked so much. The clasp was undone and it was barely cupping her breasts by friction. Her eyes went wide and her mouth clamped shut. She dropped the hanger and reached up to cover her breasts as the General said "And this must be Captain Bonneville?" She turned and ran back into her room, slamming the door behind her. The General gave a little snicker. "Tell her that her little secret is safe with me, Sergeant Major. I'll be seeing both of you again."

"You're not really a General, are you?"

"Why do you say that?"

"Both times I've seen you, you've needed a haircut. Today you need a shave. If you are a one star, you're setting a poor example."

He smiled. "At ease, Sergeant Major. Let's not forget who's setting what kind of an example." He stepped out the door, and then put his hand up to hold it open. "And you might want to let the good Captain know that she's coming up on the next Major's list. There's still a chance she could have a good career."

As soon as the door was closed Grant went into Bonneville's' room. Her bra was tossed onto the bed with the outfit she had been displaying. The bathroom door was closed. He knocked softly. "Are you OK?"

"Go away!"

He tried the knob and found the door unlocked. He pushed it open and saw her in the tub. The panties were on the counter. She was covered up in bubbles. "Don't worry about them. They won't be a problem."

"Easy for you to say. You're not the one flashing a one star in a hotel room!" She threw a wet face cloth at him. "Why the hell didn't you warn me they were here?"

"Warn you? You were supposed to be taking a bath! I pushed the door shut. I didn't think you were going to come running back in looking like a lingerie model!"

She sank back into the tub. "Did I look that good?"

"Hell, yeah! If there hadn't been somebody else in the room your bra and panties would still be balled up on the floor in there."

"What are we going to do about them?"

"Don't worry. They already know about us. He's using it as leverage to get me to do that stuff on the Mexican side."

"Leverage?"

"Yeah, no big deal. I'm pretty sure he's not even a general. Probably some alphabet agency type trying to look important."

"What did he say?"

"Well, you made an impression. He said you're on the 0-4 list coming out. A little more skin and you could have made 0-5."

"Oh God!"

"Relax. Enjoy your soak. I'm going to grab a shower, then we can head out. Remember, you promised me dessert!"

Bonneville had calmed down by the time they went out for supper, and she was true to her word about dessert. She even woke him up in the middle of the night for an encore. He was still tired when they went their separate ways after breakfast, and he was pretty certain she was too.

There was a Mexican Sergeant Major Cardozo doing the lecture this morning, just as advertised. He had a well worn face and wore a variation of the old American Battle Dress Uniform with full colored Mexican insignia. His English was heavily accented, but he spoke clearly enough to be understood. The first hour or so was a history of foreign interventions in Mexico. He started with the *conquistadores* vicious treatment of the natives, then moved seamlessly as he spoke about later native uprisings against what he called 'the legitimate Spanish government'. French assistance in the Mexican Revolution that brought independence and Santa Anna to power seemed to be all right, but the Texas Revolution and their victory was a foreign intervention of the worst kind. The subsequent Mexican American War, which Mexico lost badly, was another bad thing. He railed against the theft of California and most of the land stretching east to the Louisiana Purchase through the Treaty of *Guadeloupe Hidalgo*, and felt the subsequent Gadsden Purchase was a similar swindle. Somehow, the US was to blame for the French occupation during the 1860's. He nicely avoided the fact that the US was wrapped up in its own Civil War, and it was US support that got the French to withdraw their troops. The point seemed to be don't spoil a good story with too many facts.

The next fifty years of revolution and counter-revolution was OK with Cardozo, but that seemed to be because it was all internal. Pancho Villas' raid on Columbus, New Mexico was a cultural high point for him, and Blackjack Pershings' Punitive Expedition that it caused was a *yanqui gringo* over-reaction. Grant looked around the room, wondering if someone was going to object to any of this, and was almost amazed that many of the attendees were taking notes. If there was going to be a test on all of this, Grant was certain he would fail.

By the time he got to the era of the drug problems Grant had tuned most of it out. It was all the fault of the US getting involved in Honduras and Nicaragua during the 1980s, causing the narco-terrorists to become armed with more sophisticated weaponry. The subsequent invasion of the southern tier of Mexico appeared to be the justification for the movement of so many illegals across the US border. US efforts to stem the tide, deport the illegals, and make border crossings so difficult were an insult to Mexican integrity, and the drug trade was the fault of the US because we were the biggest end user. Things would all be better if the border was opened and the cartels could move all of their operations to the US where they belonged, and Mexico could return to peace and prosperity. He described the operations his own battalion had been conducting to control the flow of migrants and drugs in the sector the engineers were working in. Theirs was a noble effort by loyal Mexicans to make the area safe for both counties.

Grant looked at his watch. It was almost time for a lunch break. The speaker was winding down, calling the armed presence of US soldiers on the border a provocation that could only end in shame and dishonor for the US Army. Grant noticed that some of the audience was starting to look at him as if it were his entire fault. There was a call for questions. Grant was first.

"I just have two questions, Sergeant Major, if you don't mind. You seem to be advocating for open US borders, but your country prosecutes anyone coming across your southern border, and I understand you have some harsh penalties."

"We're talking about US policy, not Mexican policy. The two situations are different."

"I don't think they're different at all, but since you aren't going to address it, I'll move to my other question." The Mexican was glaring at him now.

"You say that the cartels, using Venezuelan weapons, importing and processing Columbian cocaine and Indo-Chinese opium are all the US's fault? Doesn't Mexican greed have something to do with it?"

"None of the problems would exist if it wasn't for the American appetite for narcotics."

"That's convenient, but the cartels are wholly a Mexican creation, and they're the ones who are bribing the police and some of the army, and executing your own citizens. Don't you have a responsibility to solve some of your home grown problems?"

The facilitator, the same one Grant had the run in with the day before, stepped in to end the back and forth. "Time for a lunch break. Sergeant Major Cardozo will be back this afternoon for a round table on Mexican and US military cooperation. You are all welcome back for it." As the room began to clear out he called Grants name. "A moment, Sergeant Major."

Grant waited while he made his way over with the Mexican. "This conference was set up to foster a better understanding between our two countries. Just because you're pissed off because you drew a shitty assignment on the border doesn't give you any right to try to sabotage it." The Mexican wasn't saying anything.

"Listen, ass hole, you need to spend a day or two out there watching what goes on first, so keep your fucking opinions to yourself. There's no nobility out there. This guy," he waved his thumb in Cardozo's direction, "knows as well as I do parts of his army are as dirty as the cartels."

Cardozo spoke. "Can you prove that?"

"You know a Colonel Apuesta?"

"*Si*, he is my *Commandante*." That brought Grant back a step. Apuesta had mentioned his Sergeant Majors' name, but Grant wasn't paying that much attention.

"So you're part of the unit that uses stainless steel Berettas?"

"*Si*."

Grant took out his note book and copied two numbers on a fresh page. He ripped it out and handed to Cardozo. "When you get back, you run these numbers through your arms room and see who was issued them and where they are now. If they belong to one of two greasy little fucks with a big red pickup, ask them about the big *gringo* and his lady who flattened his tires and walked off with an AK."

"What will that prove?"

"Come over to the fence where my men are working and ask for me. They'll know how to find me. Then you can tell me how fucking noble and loyal your army is."

Grant was convinced that these past few days had been a waste of his time. If he didn't have his portrait hanging in all the right places here, he was pretty damn sure he would have been declared *persona non grata*. These fucking people were taking political correctness to all the wrong places. The idea behind the Sergeants Major Academy was to push the students to think outside the box, develop their abilities and make them even more professional than their military education and experiences had already made them. The product he had seen over these two days was a big disappointment.

"Sergeant Major Grant?"

He turned to see the Academy Commandant, another senior Command Sergeant Major. "Not what you expected was it?"

"No, not at all. What the fuck are you people trying to do here? Listening to people who haven't thought through their plan or just sit quietly while some second rate army's representative run the country down is bullshit."

"Politics, Sergeant Major. It's all politics. But don't you worry. This 'International Outreach' was thrust upon us by people who don't have a clue as to what policy is supposed to be. Core curriculum is safe. This other stuff is eyewash. I've got a whole section dedicated to blowing smoke up your ass. You would have never seen any of it if we hadn't gotten a request from those who prefer to remain nameless to get you in here so they could have an off the record talk. I hope that happened."

"Yeah, I think it did."

"Then my job is done. Good hunting." He walked off.

Grant and Bonneville had one more night on Bliss, and they elected to spend as much of it as possible off post. They had the time, and Grant had the resources, to get an expensive room in an up-scale hotel. He made a few calls before they checked out of the Guest House to make a reservation, and headed into El Paso. As they passed a mall, Grant had a thought and pulled in. He drove around until he spotted a store name he recognized and found a parking spot. Bonneville looked puzzled. "What do you need here?" she asked.

"I don't need anything. You, on the other hand, need something classy for a night out." He took a credit card out of his wallet and gave it to her. "Let's try this little shop. Find something you like and don't worry about what it costs."

"You know this place sells Vera Wang."

"Who's that?"

She smiled. "Never mind. I'll find something you'll like. Why don't you find yourself a sports coat?"

Inside they went their separate ways. It didn't take Grant long to find an off-the-rack jacket. Almost as an afterthought he picked out a dress shirt and a tie. What the hell. If Linda was going to look good, he could make an effort to clean up his act. He wandered back over to the women's section, but didn't see Linda. A sales lady saw him looking around and offered to help. He described Bonneville to her, and she pointed to the dressing rooms. "She has a couple of outfits in there. She should be out soon."

She was right. Bonneville came out of the dressing rooms with an arm full of clothes. She wouldn't let him see which one she had picked out. "Why don't you go wait in the truck. I have some more shopping to do before I'm ready."

He wasn't waiting long before she came out with an arm full of bags. He could tell some of the labels were pricey, to say the least. Oh well, he thought: she was worth it.

And she didn't disappoint. They checked into their hotel, and Grant made a reservation for their restaurant. Bonneville insisted he take the first shower, and when he came out she went in, taking all her bags with her. She was in there for what seemed like an hour, but when she came out the wait had been worth it. He didn't know how much that little red number cost him, not to mention shoes and whatever she had on underneath, and he probably never would, since Willa Harrison, the First Sergeants wife handled paying the credit card expenses for them. She may wrinkle her nose and complain about what they were spending, but she never commented on how much. Grant was glad he didn't have to do the bookkeeping.

Dinner was excellent, and so was the wine. They finished a bottle, and Grant had another one sent up to their room. After a light dessert, they took a short walk through the hotel garden, and went up to the room. The wine had been opened, and there was a tray of fruit. After another two glasses of wine, Bonneville started to dance around the room, doing a slow strip tease for Grant. Whatever she had spent on the dress, it was definitely worth it, but in no way compared to the value of her undergarments. He had never seen anybody as sexy as she was tonight. He was pleased with himself for his decision to spend the night in El Paso. She was pleased with him too, and spent most of the night showing him.

Morning came early. After a quick trip to pick up the Blazer in the rear area, Bonneville decided to store her new clothes in Grants' truck. It was under overhead cover, so things wouldn't broil. Grant had added some solar fans to the windows to keep a circulation going, and was able to extend the solar collectors to catch a little morning sun, just enough to keep the air from getting too stale. Then he checked with the Specialist who was holding down the fort to find out if anybody had been spending the night in the area. The Specialist said no, but checked his logs anyway. That interested Grant. "You keep logs on who comes and goes?"

"Yes, Sergeant Major. I've been getting dinged for not being here when the S-4 representative comes in to pick up parts. I'm here every day from 0700 until 1700. If I leave for chow I put up a sign, and if I go anywhere after hours I leave my cell number. Whoever is pissing and moaning must be sneaking in after hours."

"I've got no complaints with you, son. Can I see your log?" Grant took a quick look at it. "You have a computer here?"

"I do."

"Internet access?"

"Got that too, Sergeant Major. What do you need?"

Grant called Captain Bonneville in. "Can you give this soldier an e-mail address to send stuff to?"

Bonneville looked puzzled. "Sure. Why?"

He turned back to the Specialist. "Son, can you send me a copy of your log close of business every day? You can send it through the Captain."

"Will do, Sergeant Major. Anything else?"

"Keep me informed of anything unusual happening."

"Like Sergeant Sullivan bringing a couple of civilians with him on his runs?"

"Civilians?"

"Yeah. Day before yesterday he had some civilian girl with him. She looked Mexican. Yesterday it was the same girl, and he brought some hard looking Mexican guy with him. Should I say something to him?"

Grant mulled that over. Sullivan was up to something he shouldn't have been. Trooper Mel Braga could be on to something. "Don't say anything for now, but if you can, without causing a ruckus, get me some pictures of his company."

"Hooah! Will do, and Sergeant Major?"

"What?"

"Can you get me back to the field? This place sucks. I've got maybe an hour of work a day. I'd rather be digging trenches for Sergeant Price."

"I'll see what I can do about getting the S-4 to start rotating people."

Bonneville waited until they were on the road before asking questions. "What was that all about?"

"Maybe nothing. I just have a bad feeling about Sullivan riding around with the Mexicans."

"What are you going to do with pictures?"

"I might know a guy who can ID them for me. He might have some insight."

After that she made small talk until they got back to the area. Just before they came up to the heavy equipment work area, she reached out and touched his hand. "Thank you for last night. It's been a long time since we were able to spend time like that together. I hope it won't be another eternity before we can do it again."

Grant smiled. "We'll do it again, but I don't know if it'll be as plush as that place was. "

"A sleeping bag in the desert can work wonders for a girls' attitude sometimes."

"I'm going to remember you said that!"

The road project was going smoothly. Lieutenant Stanley had her equipment operating in a sequence that made for good progress. She figured on less than a week before she'd be ready to swap areas with one of the vertical platoons. She was even making progress on restringing the barbed wire fence, even though that had not been one of her responsibilities. Grant asked her about 'other' projects.

"We've been getting good information about the terrain over there," she waved her hand vaguely to the east, "and I've taken a couple of teams across to plant sensors in some likely avenues of approach." She pulled an overlay out of her map case and showed Grant. He made notes on one of his own overlays and told her she had done a good job. She smiled. "When do we start operating for real?"

"Soon I hope. Lieutenant, I don't want to hurt your feelings, but I really want to wait until Price is done with that airfield project before you go looking for trouble."

She said her feelings weren't hurt. "I've still got a few things to learn from Sergeant Price, but he says I'm almost ready to start hurting people and breaking things on my own."

"I'm sure you are. Lieutenant, but don't be in a hurry to go over to the dark side. Some days it's a tough trip back."

"I know, Sergeant Major. Price tells me that all the time, and I believe him. He's supposed to be coming by this morning to arrange a back haul of his equipment. He's just about done down there. You might pass him on the road."

"If I don't, give him my regards, and tell him to stop by the CP on his way home."

"I think he's up on the net."

"I'd rather not broadcast more than we have to. The Mexican army uses some of our equipment."

She pointed to the east. "Like those guys?" She pointed to a small group watching them through binoculars.

"I saw them when we pulled up. Are they regulars?"

"Sure are. Every day."

"How about at night?"

"No. I think they come over and inspect our work after we've gone, but when we move, they move. I've taken to waving hello and goodbye to them. I don't think they appreciate it. Think you can get commo to hijack their frequency? I've been learning the words to *la Cucaracha*. I'd really like to serenade them some morning."

"Don't try to piss them off too much. Is there anything else going on?"

"Random gunshots at night. I think somebody's trying to rattle us, but it isn't working. Somebody tried to get into my equipment laager a couple of nights ago, but my sentry scared him off. I think it might have been an illegal. He ran into my wire and left most of his sweatshirt hanging there."

They didn't run into Price on the road, just a roving patrol close to the CP access road. Bonneville went to the S-1 tent, and Grant headed to the Tactical Operations Center to check in with the Colonel. He was out on the road, but Callan was able to give him a briefing. He repeated the story about the random gunfire up and down the border. It didn't seem to be directed at the soldiers or the patrols, but the Colonel had ordered everyone on the border at night to wear Kevlar and body armor, just in case. As far as the areas of interest he had asked the drones to cover, there had been intermittent activity, but nothing particularly notable. "Looks like they've been sending out housekeeping people, nothing more."

"How about the Mexican Army?"

Callan pulled another log over. "They're pretty visible during the day, but they seem to disappear at night. The teams planting the sensors never see them."

"Is there anything out there at night?"

"Some illegals trying to cross over, but the patrols keep turning them back. We probably aren't getting them all yet, but we're doing pretty well in the sensor areas. I estimate about four more nights and we'll have all the known routes covered, then we'll have to sit back and wait until we find the new ones."

Grant went through a couple of folders and logs. Callan had done a good job organizing the TOC, and Grant told him so. Before he left, Grant had one more question.

"Has anybody been interested in what we're doing?"

"How do you mean, Sergeant Major?"

"Anybody out of the ordinary asking more than curiosity-type questions?"

"Not really. The S-4 Sergeant likes to pop in and hang around from time to time, but he says he's trying to get a feel of things to help plan logistics shit."

That piqued Grant's interest. "What in particular?"

"Oh, schedules, patrol routes, Ops, the usual stuff. Why."

"I don't know why, but start getting the word out to change all that periodically. It'll be good practice, and better security."

"And if he asks again?"

"Lie to him."

Chapter 6

Sergeant Price was heading north on the jeep trail in a good mood. He had finished tearing up the air strip ahead of schedule without having another drug plane try to land. His equipment hadn't suffered any breakdowns, and there hadn't been any injuries. Even the construction people were moving ahead with dismantling the buildings and getting the old Quonset hut ready for shipment. First Sergeant Harrison had taken responsibility for removing and shipping the aircraft parts that had been left behind, relieving Price of that burden. It was a good thing too, because Harrison had the presence of mind to arrange for the General Services Administration to sign a release declaring the contents of the building to be scrap and to be disposed of 'as he saw fit'. The lawyers for the 'Wicked Witch Foundation' the umbrella company founded to oversee the restoration of the B-17 were less than happy with the document. While it was 'legally sufficient' to avoid later charges of illegality, they were afraid the government could at some point press for payment of what were potentially some expensive surplus parts. Harrison had another lawyer look over the document, and he rendered an opinion that since the items were considered scrap, Harrison should get a final weight of the shipping container. Any claims on value would have to be decided on the scrap value of several tons of metal and wood packing.

Price tried not to think of the problem. He was anxious to get back on the main job of upgrading the border road, and, more importantly, to start carrying out their other 'assignments' on the Mexican side.

All the briefings he had gotten over the past week indicated that things wee going well. The platoons had been getting their sensor zones installed a kilometer to the east on the main avenues of approach, and it had already been paying dividends. Having the thirty to forty five minute warning had allowed the patrols to stop the migrants and their *coyote* guides at the fence and turn them back. Price knew they probably just went to a different area to try again, but they had to work harder at it. The whole plan would come together better if the damn Mexican army would do their part and patrol aggressively at night, but it seemed like all they were interested in was watching the *gringos* build their road and repair their fence during the day, then going back to only God knew where their bivouacs were. So far none of the drones had passed over any concentrations of soldiers in the border areas. They just drove in after first light, and disappeared after the work areas were secured. International cooperation was a very elusive animal.

He was running his field glasses over the terrain to see what was out there, when his driver slowed, then stopped. "What's up, Bobby. Need a piss break?"

Bobby was backing up now. "I thought I saw something in the brush back there," Price looked over his shoulder in time to see a camouflaged figure break from the brush and run across the road. He stopped momentarily at the fence and looked at the HUMMV, then slid between the strands of wire and disappeared into Mexico. Price was able to make out the rifle he was carrying was an FN-FAL. "That looks like one the patrols let slip last night," Bobby said. He parked by the wire and asked if Price wanted him to call it in. "No, not yet. Let's see what else is out here first."

The two men grabbed their weapons and slowly walked up and down both sides of the road. "Think he might have been the cause of some of that shooting we hear at night?"

"Could be, Bobby, could be. That FALs' muzzle blast would carry a long way."

"How do you think he got passed the sensors?"

"I don't know. They might be getting smart and leaving a stay behind group to wait until the patrol moves off. They can't stay stupid forever. The problem would go away if there was somebody on the ground on the other side of the wire." Price stopped and peered into the brush on the US side. He could see something blue a couple of dozen meters off. He told his driver to wait while he went to check. It was a beat up cooler lying on its side. It was empty, and had a bullet hole through it. There were tracks moving off into the interior.

He called back to the road. "Bobby, get some back up out here. I've got a trail leading off. I'm going to follow it for a bit."

"You got a radio?"

"Yeah," he answered, "I've got a hand held. I'll keep in touch."

Price was following a pretty distinct trail of foot prints on the ground for about 300 meters, when he started to see cast off belongings. There were small packs, empty water bottles, and clothing. He was wondering what it meant when he came upon his first body. It was a woman. She was laying face down, head towards the border. The blood stain on her blouse showed where she had been shot in the back. He started to take out his radio to report it, when he noticed more shapes lying up ahead. He slipped off the safety on his M-4 and crept up as quietly as he could. In a small clearing there were three more bodies. They all looked like they had been shot where they were sitting, execution style. More debris led off into the brush to the west. Price slipped out his radio and keyed the mike.

"Bobby, you better get Group on the line and tell them I've got bodies out here."

Bobby, acknowledged, and Price began to follow the trail again. He was coming up on another body when his radio hissed. "Group wants to know who and how many."

"Tell them it looks like illegals. There are five so far, and I think there may be more up ahead." He moved a little further on. He stopped to examine a back pack that was off to the side. You didn't need to be a genius to know that the plastic packages it held were probably full of drugs. This was starting to look like a drug and human smuggling operation gone terribly wrong. There was a low murmuring up ahead. Price got down low to look under the brush. He could see people sitting on the ground ahead. He wasn't certain, but it looked like someone was walking among them. He crept forward.

The brush started to thin out, and he could see about ten people sitting in a circle in a clearing. There was somebody walking back and forth in the middle of their circle. The son of a bitch was wearing the same camouflage uniform, and was holding same type of rifle as the guy they saw hightail it back over the border. He was keeping the muzzle pointed at the people on the ground. Price looked closer, and he could see the gunman was wearing a full set of load bearing equipment, and he could make out military style patches on the uniform. He looked like he was Mexican Army. The problem was, what the fuck was he doing here? Did he track them and was holding them until his partner got help to bring them back to Mexico, or was he the one who brought them here in the first place?

He waited until the soldier had his back turned to him, then stepped into the clearing. In his best Castilian Spanish he ordered the soldier to drop his weapon and put his hands on his head. Price knew at once it wasn't going to end the way he hoped. The Mexican glanced over his shoulders, first one, then the other. He started to turn in the direction of the rifle barrel, slowly trying to line it up on the American. "You better stop right there, *amigo*, or I will *mata lo*!" Price could see a stupid grin form on the on the Mexicans face over his rifle sight. The bastard was still turning towards him, a little faster now. Price didn't hesitate any longer. Fuck the rules of engagement. He ripped a three round burst into the back of the Mexican. The 5.56mm rounds tore through the man's' hydration pack and into his back, adding a clear cascade to the pink cloud that erupted from his chest. His spine must have been severed, because his rifle dropped from both hands as his knees buckled. Price kept his rifle aimed at his face, just in case. The Mexicans expression never changed as he flopped onto the ground. He still had that stupid grin on his face.

All of a sudden the small group threw themselves on the ground and started wailing. Price made sure the fallen soldiers rifle was secured and tried to calm the group. He kept saying over and over that he was an American soldier, and that they were safe. The fact that he didn't shoot them must have reassured them more than his words, and they slowly calmed down. He got back on the radio and answered Bobby's calls to him. He gave his location and a situation report, and estimated his position. "I'm pretty sure I'm due west of you, just about a hundred yards short of the parallel road, so have them come in that way. I'm gonna need medics and some Border Patrol to sort these people out. I think some of them are carrying a drug shipment."

As an after though he told his driver to keep an eye on the border, "That other mother fucker might come back to help his friend!"

The call back to the TOC arrived as Grant was having coffee with SFC Callan, going over the previous nights reports. Once he clarified that there were no US casualties he made arrangements for other elements to secure the border road and the parallel road. Sharp was called on his disposable phone while he was going to brief the colonel and get the medical section on the road. Sharp was told to take control of any units on the border. Grant added that the Mexicans had been in uniform, and the one who got back over the border might come back with help.

He saw Kearney coming out of the medical tent. He signaled him back inside and brief him and Major Carson. The doctor rattled off the names of three medics and told them to load the ambulance with a triage kit and take the ambulance to the site. One of them was Sergeant Abbott, who by now was pretty familiar with the road net in the area. Grant told her to drive. Carson grabbed a large medic bag and asked for a ride to the location while her medics were packing. The Colonel told her to go with Grant, and he would follow after he arranged for the Border Patrol and any local law enforcement to come to the scene. Carson was muttering to herself as the dashed across the bivouac area. "Damn, I should have anticipated this." She stopped and called back to Abbott to load plenty of bottled water. "Those people are probably dehydrated!"

She was quiet on the ride out, which was quick due to Grants' driving. She busied herself inventorying her bag and calling back lists of equipment she thought they might need to bring. Grant finally reached over and took the microphone away from her. "All you're doing now is confusing them, let them do their jobs." Then he radioed back for the medics to bring what they thought they would need. "They're good troops, Major. They'll bring what you need."

The Border Patrol and the New Mexico State Police both took close to an hour to arrive. By then Major Carson and her medics had a temporary shelter erected and was treating the survivors. They were all women with children and a couple of old men. Grant figured they must have been docile enough for two armed soldiers to handle. Price had been talking to them, in between translating for the medics. He gave the Colonel a detailed report, for a change leaving out none of the little details. Kearney judged it to be covered by their rules of engagement, and had SFC Callan search the body of the dead Mexican gunman. It had been determined that he was a soldier. He was carrying an ID card, a mixed bag of military documents in his wallet and pockets, and was wearing dog tags. He also had an annotated map of the area that he passed to Grant without comment.

Grant had pocketed the map after a quick examination. He followed the back trail until he came to the border, where Sharp had the area under control. From the north and west there were several helicopters in-bound, most likely law enforcement. Sharp pointed to the east, where several more were coming in. "Word travels fast," he said.

"I'd be willing to bet the one that made it back already made his report. This will either be some politician denying any involvement, or damage control accusing us of killing those people."

"You get an ID on the dead guy?"

"Callan's pretty sure he's Mexican army. He has all the right bells and whistles, plus this." Grant handed Sharp the map. He took his own map case out and pulled out an overlay. Once he laid it on the Mexicans' map the markings matched up exactly. "He had a damn good idea of the location of our sensor line out there. Where'd he get that from?"

"I've got a good idea. I'll tell you later."

The Mexican helicopters had landed some distance away, and there was a line of soldiers, all armed, making their way to the fence. The first two pulled out wire cutters and were preparing to snip the wire when Grant and Sharp both grabbed the cutters from them. Both Mexicans stepped back and started to raise their weapons. They stopped when one of Sharp's men fired a burst into the air. The situation, Grant thought, was about to get out of hand.

A flurry of orders in Spanish had the two men stepping back. Grant felt a moment of relief until Major Apuesta emerged from the brush, flanked by the two aides Grant had disarmed in Mexico. Things got tense again. Apuesta started by demanding access to the site. Grant tried to diplomatically tell him that would not be possible. It was now a matter for US authorities to deal with.

"I understand there is a Mexican soldier involved. I demand his immediate return!"

"Major, I believe that is way above both our pay grades now, but if you care to wait, I'll have Colonel Kearney come by as soon as the situation permits."

Apuesta started to come over the wire, but Grant held up his hand. "You'll have to wait on your own side, Major. Might I suggest you return to the shade of you helicopter and leave one of these people," people came out like a sneer, "to fetch you when my Colonel arrives." More US vehicles had arrived by this time. Apuesta looked around and realized any tactical advantage was held by the Americans. He spat out a few words to one of his aides and walked away.

"Keep an eye on the area, Dave. Nobody comes across. I'll try to get a Border agent over here to back that up so Kearney can't invite him in."

"You got it, Boss."

Grant went back to the triage site. The bodies of the civilians had been brought up, bagged, and place together on the parallel road. The State Police were going to evacuate them. There was a pile of back packs and plastic packs of drugs piled near them. The body of the soldier still lay where it fell. The feds and the state were arguing over custody. There were also vehicles arriving to take custody of the survivors. Price was talking to a State Trooper; Grant could see it was Mel Braga. Price was still carrying his rifle, and Grant took that as a good sign. Before he walked over to join them he let Kearney know that Apuesta was waiting for him on the border. "He's pissed off and getting insistent."

"Is he coming over here?"

"No. I didn't let him cross the line. I didn't think it would be a good idea to let an armed Mexican soldier come so far into US territory. Besides they" he waved his arm towards the Border Patrol and State Police, "might have other ideas about him being here."

"Yes, you're right, you're right. I'll go see him as soon as we're done here."

He got a quick recap of what the civilians had been saying from Braga. Their journey had started several days before, in one of the abandoned villages on the Mexican side. They had to wait because the soldiers, *soldado coyotes* they called them, were waiting for a map of the new route into *los Estados Unidos.* They had each paid the equivalent of $2.000 for the privilege of a safe passage across the border, where they would meet up with the rest of their families. The women claimed they had all been raped multiple times while they waited, by more than just the soldiers who came across with them. Their food and water ran out, and the *soldado coyotes* would not give them any. They were all very weak before they crossed the border, and they were made to leave their own belongings behind and carry packs full of drugs. Braga explained that that was a common practice among the *coyotes* that brought the illegals across. Once they got their money, they were just mules. The Mexican army escorting them, however, was a new twist that they had only recently been getting intelligence on.

"You'll be interested to know that the bar in Columbus is a wholly owned subsidiary of Major Domingo Apuesta of the Mexican army. When they aren't busy killing their fellow Mexicans and raping the illegals, his two primary aides double as bouncers. Your friend Sullivan seems to be quite friendly with them."

"How did that little fuck Sullivan get involved in this?" Price asked.

"Seems he's banging a fat little crack whore over there. He's probably passing information, too." Grant responded.

"How do you know that?"

Grant showed him the map. "Now we'll have to do something about that, sooner than later." Braga looked at him with wide eyes, but didn't comment on it. Instead, he continued with the story of the illegals. They were tired and thirsty, and they shot the first one while they were still in Mexico as an example. One of the American Army trucks had stopped right by where they were planning to cross, so they had to wait until they moved off. By then, the sky was starting to lighten up, and the soldiers were getting antsy. They shot a couple of more to try to hurry the group up, but it didn't do any good .Their radio was dead and they couldn't arrange a closer pickup, so they decided to hide out for the day while one of them went back to make contact with their ride. "That's about where Sergeant Price here got mixed up in all this."

"Am I in the clear for the shooting?"

"Oh, hell yeah. I've got ten witnesses who all agree you saved their lives. They don't think the ride would have been for them, just the drugs."

Grant indicated the body. "What about him?"

Braga smiled. "It's a game we play. That body is going to be one hell of a diplomatic headache for somebody, not to mention the paperwork nightmare. The State of New Mexico sure doesn't want it, and as far as I can tell, the Feds probably still have jurisdiction over this part of the country. I'll play nice and let them have him."

"Why don't you let the Border guys know Apuesta is waiting for Kearney back there. They might want to be in on what information gets passed on, especially if Apuesta is working both sides of the room." Braga thought it was a good idea and did just that. One of the agents separated himself from the group and drove off, most likely to be on the wire before Kearney got there.

The agent had already briefed Sharp by the time Kearney arrived. There was no way in hell any Mexican, soldier, cop, politician or migrant, was to cross the border anywhere but at the designated crossing points. Sharp described the scene at his first shootout, with the Mexicans policing up the bodies with Kearney's permission. "You didn't hear that from me," Sharp added.

"No problem," the agent said. He looked at the Mexican glaring at them from the other side of the wire. "I know this piece of shit. He and his buddies like to wait in *las Palomas* for the day trippers to come back from work on payday and shake them down. The bastard's got an official passport so he can cross the border and spend the money on our side. Let's see what he's got to say." The agent walked over to the fence. "Hey, fuck head! You think you're getting your buddy back like you did the other night?"

The Mexican snarled back. "One of these nights, *gringo*, we'll meet when you aren't surrounded by your friends. Then we'll talk."

The agent stepped closer and leaned over the fence. He brought his hand up to his temple in a mock salute. The quick move startled the Mexican. He stepped back quickly, stumbling as he did. The US soldiers watching laughed at him. So did the agent. "Not as easy when you don't have your *coyote* friends, is it. We'll meet, fuck head, and maybe I won't be wearing a badge then."

Before the situation could deteriorate any further, Kearny's vehicle could be seen down the road. Sharp called over, "Hey, you better get your master now. The adults need to talk." He looked back to the agent. "You two seemed to be old friends."

"Yeah, you noticed how he complained that he wanted us to turn over the body and any evidence, like your Colonel did the other night?"

"Did he say all that?"

"Well, that's what'll be in my report."

Kearny called a staff meeting after supper. Grant had been eager to get back into the field. They had made plans to do several recons over the border, preparatory to starting their raids to destroy the smugglers assets, and a long staff meeting would only delay their jumping off.

He had gotten his ass reamed late in the afternoon by the Joint Task Force commander. The Border Patrol had reported that statements from a Mexican officer indicated that Kearney had allowed the Mexican army access to a shooting scene and didn't report it up the chain of command. When Kearney tried to explain it in terms that made it look like a brilliant stroke of international cooperation, the commander cut him off. He was given a direct order that his responsibilities did not include that level of cooperation. He was also informed that his operations to deny safe havens to the smugglers needed to be implemented as soon as possible, but he was to avoid any contact with planned *Policia Federale* operations in the area.

"I don't know what the *Federales* have planned for this area."

That wasn't a problem. Sources in the Mexican government had provided a short list of raids planned for that night opposite their AO. Kearney was to observe from a safe distance.

The staff meeting was to inform the staff to keep their people off the border that night. Gaston protested. "I have Sergeant Sullivan scheduled to make a run in tonight so he can pick up parts for the motor pool first thing in the morning,"

Grant interrupted. "I didn't know we had any more critical equipment down that needed parts. I don't think it will be a good idea."

"Sergeant Sullivan said that there are some back orders that will be up tomorrow. He wants to get them in hand."

Kearney cut in. "I'm going to agree with the CSM. Captain Gaston, just inform him to head right back to his bunk. Maybe he can get an early start in the morning. The Mexicans will be operating around," he checked his notes, "*el Camello* and *el Monumento.* They're both close enough to the border for stray gunfire. With that in mind, Sergeant Major, make sure any night patrol activity stays out of the way and everybody outside our bivouac areas need to be in body armor and Kevlar."

"I'll see to it. I was planning on spending the night with SFC Mason's platoon, but I can get there on the parallel road and avoid the jeep trail entirely." Good God, Grant thought, Gaston doesn't have a clue as to what his golden boy is up to. Last thing we need is for him to tell Sullivan where the *Federales* are targeting.

"I have something better for you. General?" All heads turned as a general officer entered the tent. The room sprang to attention. "This is General Vaughn, Deputy Chief of Staff of the JTF. His people are setting up in the operations tent so we can watch the Mexican operations unfold in real time." Vaughn waved everyone into their seats. Kearney stepped away from the head of the tent.

"I guess this would be as good a time as any to let you know what the Colonel and Sergeant Major have known for some time." He launched into a brief recap of the original purpose of the border mission, including the cross border operations. There was some murmuring around the table, and he waited for it to die down before he continued.

"For some reason, there was a breach of operational security at the political level. It seems like some congressman or one of his staffers with a grudge, decided to give the Mexican government a copy of the original warning order. While it didn't specifically mention cross border operations, there were a few paragraphs of 'what ifs' that were to be considered. We've been denying the shit out of everything, but we have decided to scale back. Tonight's operations are designed to show us that they have a handle on their own problems." There was a rustle in the back of the room as Sullivan came in to ask Gaston when he could leave. There seemed to be a brief argument building when Grant decided to intervene. Grant took Sullivan by the elbow, applied 'a sufficient amount of pressure to insure compliance' and led him to the tent door. "You've been told, now shut up and go back to your rack."

"I have things to do."

"That's not a decision you make at your pay grade, Sergeant, now go do what you're told."

"This isn't over, Sergeant Major. SFC Mitchell needs those parts."

"What parts?" It was Mitchell. Grant spun Sullivan around. "Sullivan here says he has to get some back ordered parts for you."

Mitchell laughed. "This clown hasn't gone out of his way for me since we've been out here. In fact, every time I ask for something, he tells me I have to send my own parts guy back to post, he only does the routine shit." He stepped closer to Sullivan. "If you're going to lie about someone, try not to do it in front of them." Sullivan pulled his arm away and sulked off. "He's gonna be a problem, Sergeant Major."

"I know. Do me a favor and don't let him go anywhere alone with a vehicle, and definitely not one of the HUMMVs." He saw one of the Robinsons walking by and called to him. "Are you going with us tonight?"

"Yes, Sergeant Major. I'm with Sergeant Sharp. My brother will be with Sergeant Price."

"Anybody left here you can trust?"

When Robinson nodded, he told the young Sergeant to have his buddy keep an eye on Sullivan, and went back in the meeting. He stopped himself and turned back to Mitchell. "You're never even close to this area. What brings you here tonight?"

"Just wanted to let you know that all our vehicles are back up. Tell Price and Sharp to try to not break them before they get the tires dirty."

Grant was loading his gear when General Vaughn caught up with him. "Not staying for the show?"

"I'll be watching it, but from a better vantage point."

"You know, Grant, this could be an out for all of us. Mexico doesn't want us here, the Army's not thrilled with having the 289th here, and there sure in hell is somebody up on Capitol Hill who doesn't want us here. The Mexicans pull off their raids tonight and secure the area the way they're supposed to, and maybe we can all go home."

Grant heaved the last of his gear into the back seat of the Blazer and closed the door. "Do you believe any of that bullshit?"

"What do you mean?"

"Exactly what I said. You've got more scum bags out there with a piece of this action than I've got soldiers to hold them off. The drug and people routes in this area are controlled by the Mexican army. They own bars, safe houses and distribution centers over in Columbus. They're even trying to turn one of our supply types into a mule."

"Bribing a soldier isn't all that much. We can control that. The main thing is that this whole episode comes to an end in our favor. They prove they can control their territory, we can all go someplace else."

Grant shook his head. "Two points. First, look at Panama. Did Noriega control his territory? Yeah, he did. There was just too much money to be had to let it go."

"You're talking about a third world dictator who was a thug from the get go."

"I know. He was a thug. You can even call him our thug, but the leader of a country had his hands in the drug trade so deep we had to invade his country to get rid of him. We won't do that again."

"You said two things."

"The Mexicans already control the border. There isn't anything happening that they don't know about."

"If they controlled it we wouldn't be having these problems."

"That, General, is only because it's the wrong Mexicans who control it."

"Have it your way, Grant, for now. Just don't go out and get involved in whatever is happening." He held up a little blue velvet box. "Before you go, come back to the TOC for a few minutes."

Grant looked at the box. "Are you asking me to marry you? I guess 'don't ask, don't tell' is really going away."

"Don't be a smart ass. Bonneville makes Major tonight. I thought you'd like to be there when Kearney pins her."

"You don't pin the ACU."

"OK. Kearney can do the Velcro tab on her hat. You can do the one on her chest."

It was a traditional military ceremony. General Vaughn did the honors reading the orders while Kearney and Grant flanked Bonneville. Kearney took her patrol cap and replaced the two bars of a Captain with the embroidered gold leaf of a Major. Grant, with exaggerated delicacy, peeled off the square Velcro tab between the slash pockets of her blouse and replaced it with the new insignia of rank. There were a few brief words of congratulation, and Vaughn produced a cooler of beer and soda, and waved to a selection of hard liquor bottles on a side table. Grant decided on one quick drink to help Bonneville celebrate, then he would be on the road. He brought his glass over to her and whispered his congratulations. She looked up and smiled and took his offered hand. "It would be nice if we could go someplace and celebrate this the right way."

He knew what she meant. "We will. It'll just have to keep for now." He waved his glass around the tent at the new equipment and monitors that had been set up. "This is all smoke and mirrors. Whatever is going to happen tonight isn't what you'll be seeing here."

"How can you be sure?"

"No time tonight, but make plans to visit the platoons over the next few days. You can do that now that you'll be the XO."

"I will be?"

"You will until they bring in a branch qualified engineer. Kearney may not like it, but Vaughn is going to tie his hands. It seems the new General likes the new Major."

That puzzled Bonneville. "Why? I don't think we've ever met." Vaughn walked up at that moment and offered his congratulations, and verified what Grant had said about her being the new XO. "You might have to double hat it for a bit, but you're the new heir to the throne."

She stared at his face. Somewhere in the back of her mind she could recall parts of his face, but not from where. He recognized her confusion, and clarified it for her. "We met back at Fort Bliss." She still didn't understand, so Grant helped her. "You were only in the room for a moment." Both men could see the veil of confusion lift from her face, only to be replaced by a deepening red flush. Vaughn put up his hand before she could stammer anything out. "Don't worry, Major. As an officer and a gentleman we shall never speak of it again." After he walked away she turned on him. "You knew?"

"Yeah, but I never got a chance to say anything. This is the first time he's ever had a name tape on."

"We'll talk about this later." It was a statement of fact, almost an order. Grant nodded his head. "Yes, Ma'am!"

The northwest corner of the Mexican state of Chihuahua is shaped like a bowl. Between the two dominant features, the *Sierra Rica* in the north and *el Indio* in the south, the land gradually slopes, almost flows, steadily to the south and east until it comes to a large dry lake bed known as *Laguna los Moscos.* At one time, probably many thousands of years ago, it was the center of a fertile agricultural valley. Now it was little better than baked, flat desert surrounded by scrub brush. Rainfall was scant. The contour of the land once assured the lake would always be full, but that turned out to be one of nature's little jokes on man. The winds shifted, the rains went away, and all that remained were the traces of gullies that drained into *los Moscos*. The only real water was on the US side, and very little of it made its way to the poor farmers of *Chihuahua*. Hundreds of years of hard scrabble farming were evident all over the valley. The landscape is dotted with the remains of one and two room adobe houses. Here and there a cluster of buildings mark what used to be a small *pueblo*. "Abandoned" is usually the word marked under the old name on the map.

The twentieth century brought attempts at economic development. There are two packed dirt airstrips in the valley. The northern most one is similar to the dirt strip the American engineers recently destroyed. It was a wide spot in the road that was straight enough for someone to consider landing a light plane, and, over the years, it probably saw its share of one and two engine aircraft. The southern one was more deliberate. The runway angled with the direction of the prevailing winds. Heavy equipment or a lot of peasant powered hand tools widened it enough to have a taxiway on one side. There was a wide parking apron fronting a hanger and several outbuildings, all well maintained although not always occupied. The main power source in the valley came from generators. There was never any money in the Mexican budget for rural electrification this far out. The Americans patrolling the border knew that when there was activity in the valley, the generators would wail through the night.

The road net was minimal, a primarily north and south road that had branch roads angling off towards the US, and, infrequently, a road heading toward the east around *Laguna los Moscos*. Nothing went through the dry lake bed. It was flat but hot, and could be a long deadly walk if you broke down. Triple A didn't make road calls here.

The benefit to the Americans was its shape. The terrain offered excellent views across the valley on a clear night, especially from their semi-permanent OP on top of *el Indio*. A moonlit night made it easy to see distant activity without electronic amplification. You could identify exactly where any set of headlights was in the valley. A moonless night made it perfect for what the US Army was famous for: they owned the night, and possessed the most advanced night vision and thermal imaging technology on the planet.

Tonight was perfect, with no moon and a heavy cloud cover. If the Mexicans were going to use night vision, it would probably be of the infra-red variety. That would make them stand out to the American passive systems. The bad guys, if you could figure out who the bad guys were in this cast of characters, would hopefully feel safe enough in their own back yard to be using white light. The OP atop *el Indio*, now called 'the U-boat' which rotated according to a convoluted 72 hour schedule agreed to by all the platoons, was currently manned by elements of the 2nd Vertical Construction platoon. The line platoons seemed to enjoy the enforced inactivity on the OP, as opposed to the relatively boring task of stringing countless miles of three and four strand barded wire fencing. Only a few select people were assigned to the more exposed missions of sensor planting, or the even more risky missions of 'surveying and mapping' potential 'construction sites', the terms they were using to hide the fact that they were reconning future targets for destruction. You could talk openly about a construction site anywhere in an engineer outfit, and most within earshot with drown out the conversation as background chatter. Mention targets and objectives and somebody might start to wonder and pay attention. Not everyone was in on the secret, and everyone who was hoped it would stay that way.

The assignments tonight were all to be handled by three and four man teams with strict orders not to get involved in anything, just to observe and report. Each of these teams was backed up by an equally sized support element which would laager down roughly halfway from the border to the objective. They were not to approach any closer unless their primary team got into trouble and needed help getting out. There were eight assigned areas to cover, which left almost nothing as a reaction force. Grant had rolled the dice and stretched himself very thin. He had chosen the supposedly abandoned northern dirt strip for himself. There was a small cluster of buildings around a cross roads at the northeast end of the strip. It appeared to be the northern traffic choke point for the valley, situated between *los Moscos* and the border. He really wanted to go to the walled compound further north. Instinctively he knew it was important, and he felt that if push came to shove it was probably the key to neutralizing the area, but for now it was too far east of the border for an easy overnight mission on foot, and it was way too exposed to leave a patrol hiding out for two days and three nights. He doubted the Mexican army would cooperate with aviation support.

All the teams moved out at dusk. The U-boat advised there weren't any lights at all in the valley, and no movement. It seemed strange, but the drones confirmed it. The longest any team had to travel was about 7 kilometers as the crow flies, probably ten if the crow had to walk and hump thirty or forty pounds of gear. They were all wearing generic OD mechanics coveralls, Mexican army patrol caps and what looked like former East German web gear. They were all armed with captured AK-47s and grenades of dubious parentage. Side arms were limited to any non-US made they preferred. Grant had his Argentine Colt clone. The rest, a mix of com-bloc cast offs. Grant indulged himself by carrying a German made FAL. He liked the heft and the .308 cartridge. For the same reason, Sharp had selected a CETME. Neither would ordinarily select a weapon that didn't interchange with the rest of the unit, but none of the AKs had the optics or the reliability if they needed to do any long range engagement. The FAL and the CETME were both equipped with inexpensive but very serviceable East European optics.

Everybody was in position by midnight. The *federales* were supposed to begin their raid at 0200, and Grant wanted to allow plenty of wiggle room if there had been an over abundance of activity. So far, it seemed, he had planned on the safe side. There hadn't been any reports of activity anywhere in the valley. No vehicles, no lights, no generators and no casual movement by any of the objectives. It was very strange for any night. The *federales* would be hitting a dry hole tonight. He looked back towards the west and could make out the glow from his own headquarters bivouac on the near horizon. Everything else was dark.

He got reports from all his elements. The commo repeater the new

Signal Lieutenant had acquired had enabled their hand held radios to function the entire length of the valley, so they had left the disposable phones in the rear. The radios were the only piece of US identified equipment they were carrying. The damn phones had too much of a light signature at night. The fucking things lit up like a disco ball. After going back and forth with his NCOs, Grant decided to hold in place until after the *federales* came and went. They would at least know if they had come expecting a fight, or came in knowing they were hitting a dry hole.

They had just settled in when the U-boat reported road movement, a lot of road movement. Mexican army trucks pulled into three of the targets, the two airfields and a little no-horse village in between identified as *Las Archinas* on the map. It was the closest point to the border. The teams at all three sites reported smaller elements heading off to the west and taking up some kind of position about a klick from the border. In every case they were in the sensor belts. The rest seemed to be securing the buildings in their immediate areas. Grant continued to get situation reports as well as questions he couldn't answer. First and foremost was why the Mexican army was setting up where the *federales* were supposed to be raiding?

Next, there were reports of vehicles unloading what looked like civilians. They were all herded out of sight into the buildings. Sharp, who was obviously closer to his target than he should have been, reported that he had what looked like a mix of adult men and women, and they all looked shackled. "What do you think it means, Boss?"

"I've got no idea. I wish we could have planned for this. There was nothing about this on the army frequencies."

There was a crackle of static as Price cut in. "I'll take care of it." There were several minutes of silence, and Price was back on the air. "They set up a position not too far away from me. It's a real old air-cooled machine gun. I guess they're worried some stupid *gringo* might want to come over and play tonight. One of them was tired of lugging an old PRC-77 around and dumped it with their equipment pile. I just borrowed the frequency. I'll let you know what I hear."

"Give Callan the freq. You need to stay on our net. Callan can pass on anything he hears."

"Roger that!" Callan's voice cut in.

The net was quiet for the next few minutes. Grant spent his time asking for and receiving status reports from his teams. He had the U-boat alert for any signs of activity, like convoys in the distance, or helicopters, but they kept reporting "Negative." Then they came in with a report: "We've got vehicle traffic to the north. Looks like they're heading to Sergeant Masons area."

There was a report from Mason's team. "The Army just dumped off some people here." He was at *los Moscos,* the little abandoned village about 3 klicks north-west of Grant. "About half a dozen, and they look shackled too."

Grant tried to imagine scenarios why the Army would be bringing prisoners out here. The best he could come up with is that they were seeding the area to make the raid look better than it was.

Mason came back up on the air. "One of them is wearing a vest with *policia* across the back."

"One of the soldiers?"

"Negative. One of the prisoners. Want me to get closer to check it out?"

"Negative. We don't know what's going on, and I don't want anybody getting mixed up in it until we do." He paused. "Callan, anything?"

"Mexican traffic just reported that the evidence has been delivered."

"What evidence?"

"Didn't say."

Grant called all his teams. "Anybody see anything that looked like evidence being brought in?"

The reports were all the same. The only thing anyone had seen was the shackled prisoners. Sharp reported that the prisoners, or whatever the hell they were supposed to be, were being split up and spaced around the area. He noted that they were all under some kind of overhead cover. "They're probably worried about aerial surveillance. If somebody spilled the beans about the sensors, they must know about our drones by now too." Callan came up with his own report. "Negative on the drones. None of ours are up, but the bigwigs have a satellite display of the area."

"Anything we should know about?"

"Negative. The RFIDs you guys are wearing are showing up nice and bright. Mexicans are a little darker, but I can pick them out pretty good. Looks like everybody has good separation except Sergeant Sharp."

That was no surprise to Grant. If anybody was going to get in too close, Sharp would be on the top of the list, followed closely by Price. He called Sharp to back off. Sharp put him off. "There's something going on with these guys. I just want to get a better look." Grant knew it would be pointless, and, for Sharp, dangerous to push the point. He settled back to wait for another update.

The U-boat came up and reported air traffic inbound. There were two formations of helicopters heading in, one north and the other south. At that moment, the machine guns opened up. Callan was back on the radio. "CP hears a lot of shooting. Are you involved?" There was a flurry of reports assuring the CP all the teams weren't involved. The U-boat reported that they could see tracers arcing up into the sky from three separate locations, mainly paralleling the border. Then Mason reported gunshots at his location. Moments later, Sharp did too. Sharp had an edge to his voice. "It looks like they're shooting the prisoners! What do you want me to do?"

The Mexicans were positioning the prisoners in doorways and at windows, and then raking them with automatic fire. One body, wearing a *policia* vest, was dragged feet first halfway out a door. Once they had been shot, empty shell casings were strewn around them, and a matching caliber rifles placed near the bodies. They were being staged to look like they died in an intense gun fight.

Mason made the same report. The sound of the helicopters was loud now. They were close to setting down. Grant warned his soldiers off. "Stay under cover. You stick your head out now you'll be in the middle of a shit storm."

An unidentified voice reported "Hey, those are Army choppers."

"Say again?"

"Army choppers. I thought we were waiting for the *federales*?"

"The same thing is happening here." Grant recognized Sharps voice. "The ground troops are loading up and getting out of the area. They're just leaving the bodies."

"Stay clear of them. They could still be bait."

"I don't think so, Boss. Bait doesn't jerk like that when it's shot with a blank."

Before anybody could respond to that the helicopters were circling their target areas. Armed men sitting in the doors were firing into the buildings. One chopper would orbit, its occupants emptying their magazines. It moved off so they could reload while the second repeated the ballet. It looked like a well rehearsed maneuver. This went on for a few minutes at both locations. One chopper landed at *los Moscos* while the other went to join the other element. It discharged its troops, who charged into the buildings shooting. As soon as they got close the firing ceased, and the soldiers commenced to mill around, as if they didn't know what else to do. The other chopper landed on the runway several hundred yards from Grant and just sat there. This one, Grant noticed, was wearing *Policia Federale* markings. Everyone, except for one body Grant could see laying in the passenger bay, un-assed the bird, leaving the rotors turning slowly. The former occupants moved away towards the buildings at the crossroad. One of them turned and fired a burst at it from his assault rifle. The chopper went up in a flash. The body they left behind must have been window dressing.

Sharp was reporting the same type of assault from his location. All three choppers were down on the apron in front of the hanger. The dismounted assault force made their run into the target, then ceased firing. This group went into the hanger and started photographing the bodies where they lay before dragging them out.

Now the ground troops who had left before the attack returned, this time with lights blazing. There seemed to be a camera crew intent on recording every aspect of the victims of the raid. Callan was reporting a lot of radio traffic. The machine gun positions ceased fire. There were reports that they were breaking down their weapons and rejoining their comrades.

"There's a report that the raid was a success," Callan radioed. "The general tone is that they've eliminated the bandits and secured the area." There was a pause. "Now somebody is saying it's time to let the *gringos* know their help isn't needed here any more. I guess that means they want us to go home."

Grant didn't want to stay around to figure out what was going on. They could do that back on their own side of the border. He ordered his troops to begin exfiltrating the area. He waited until they all reported they were back, and was starting to lead his team up the gully that led to the border when Callan interrupted.

"I'm getting some chatter, and I think it's from your location. They're asking if they should move the trophy vehicle."

Grant moved back to his old position and scanned the area with his glasses. "I don't know what they're talking about. There aren't any vehicles in this area." He continued to scan until he saw some movement at an outlying building. It was about the size of a large shed or a small garage. There were men coming in and out. A truck was approaching from the south, and Callan radioed that they had been told to leave it. They could come back and make a show of it if nobody else found it. "Whoever it was said to leave it where it is, somebody would be along to collect it tomorrow or the day after. He said to leave the door unlocked."

"Okay, I've got a lot of interest in one of the out buildings. I'll wait a bit to see if they leave the area, then go check it out."

"The one star here says that's not a good idea."

"One star is there, not here, give him my regards."

Price came up on the air. "I'm not too far out. Want some back-up? I can be there in about 15."

"No, head for the barn. It looks like everyone is going to one of the other parties. As soon as they're a safe distance away I'll go in and check."

Grant had counted heads as the Mexicans got off the chopper, and he could see well enough to count them again as they got on the truck. He gave the area a few minutes to see if he had missed any stay behinds, then called Callan for a satellite check. "Can the bird see any movement?"

"Only you and your team. All eyes are on you."

"Let me know if that changes."

Grant directed his team by hand signals. Two men were to provide overwatch while he went in with the last man. He circled around in the brush until he was close to the shed, constantly checking the area for movement. Finally, directing his wing man to stay put, he dashed across the open space and pulled up tight to the side of the building. A quick check around the outside brought him to the other side of the door. He could see the hasp hanging open. Since there weren't any windows, he fished out a compact flashlight and held it to the side of his rifles hand guards. He slipped into the shed and hit the push button at the base of the light. Sitting in front of him, fully marked, was a United States Border Patrol truck. He checked the building to make certain he was alone: he was, so he called his team, asking if anyone had brought a camera. One voice responded he had, and Grant told him to hustle to his location. Callan kept cutting in and asking him what he found. Grant ignored him. He took the camera from the soldier and told him to search the vehicle. "What am I looking for?"

"Anything loose, Son, anything loose. Pretend you just broke into it and you're stealing anything you can find. Make sure you grab the license plates too." Grant got pictures of the license plates, vehicle data plate, and as best he could, the markings on the truck. There wasn't much room to move, and he didn't want to risk opening the door and let everyone see the flash. He found a black trash bag on a small work bench and passed it in to the soldier. "Put anything you find in here." He went back to the ID plate and pried it up with his knife. Instead of putting it in the bag he slipped it into his pocket. A few minutes later they were done.

"What are we going to do with the truck?"

"Burn it!"

"Won't that attract attention?"

Grant thought for a moment. "Let's hope they think it's the chopper flaring up again. I'm not leaving this for those people to play with."

Grant took his combat knife and slid under the truck. He found the gas line leading out of the tank. There was a flexible line connecting it to the rigid line leading to the engine. He cut it, and opened the gas cap to break the vacuum. The gas rapidly formed a puddle around the vehicle. There were a couple of quart bottles of oil on the work bench. He opened them up and poured them into the spreading pool of gas to make it burn longer. "Got any matches?" Neither of them was carrying any. Grant longed for the good old days when he was a pack a day smoker and always had matches or a disposable lighter. He had one in a survival pack he kept clipped to his MOLLE vest, but he hadn't thought to bring it with him tonight.

"Check the cab. See if there's a cigarette lighter."

Sure enough, there was one. Grant pushed it in and waited until it popped, then held it to a crumpled newspaper that he had dipped in gas. It glowed, and erupted in flames. Both soldiers backed out of the shed, and Grant threw the burning paper on the ground under the truck. He heard the *whoosh* of the gas igniting as he pressed the door shut and slipped a screw driver into the hasp.

They were halfway down the airstrip before the fire burned through the roof. They could still see the flames after they had crossed the border. Callan was calling again.

"We see another fireball at your location."

"Roger that. Some unfinished business."

"Somebody's looking for a sitrep."

Grant scowled. They never want to come along, but they damn sure want to know what's going on. "Negative. Not over the air." That got everyone's attention.

There was another voice on the radio. "We're all friends here. What do you have?" It was Vaughn. Grant had a choice to make, and he made it. "I think this one is 'need-to-know'. I'll keep it until we get back." There were no more transmissions from the CP. Grant did another quick one eighty to check on his soldiers. They were all with him. His point man was looking back at him, so Grant pointed and pumped his fist up and down, the signal for 'double time'. He saw the point nod, and pick up the pace back to the border. It was uphill all the way, but they made good time. They picked up their support element and crossed back into US territory dead on their pick up vehicle. There was a cooler in the back full of cold soft drinks and beers. Grant looked at his watch. He'd be having breakfast in another hour. He grabbed a cold beer and sucked it down. The driver was monitoring the radios inside, so he stripped off his harness and commo gear and told the soldier to let him know if anything came up. His vehicle was the rally point for all elements, so he lay down on the side of the road and took a quick nap. Getting old, he decided, was definitely starting to suck.

He hadn't even gotten comfortable when his radio operator called him. "I think there's a problem, Sergeant Major!" Grant was up and leaning in the truck in seconds. His harness and commo gear were in his hands, being hurriedly thrown on.

"What's going on, Son?"

"I think Sergeant Sharp brought a wounded Mexican back with him. He's calling for a medic, and he's saying it's not for a friendly."

Grant looked down the road to where Sharp would be coming from. That's fucking great, he thought to himself. Why couldn't he just let the bastard die and come home?

Grant didn't see any reason to go to where Sharp was since he was the rally point. The CP was on the air asking for more information, but Sharp was staying off the air. They queried Grant, but all he could do was claim ignorance. The net went quiet while everyone waited. Sharp was about 6 or 7 miles to the south. Give the medic some time to stabilize whoever the casualty was, and he estimated his wait to be about another half hour. He picked up a cell phone from the truck and looked at his RTO. He was still wearing the coveralls they used over the border. He told the soldier to change, and put out a message for everyone to make sure they were in proper uniform. He could hear helicopters to the east, and the U-boat was reporting a lot of vehicle traffic. The last thing he heeded was a nosy Mexican soldier catching sight of them in their 'black ops' outfits. He was slipping out of his and pulling on his ACUs while he speed dialed Sharp. To his surprise, somebody answered, but it wasn't Sharp.

"What's going on?"

"We're on our way, Sergeant Major. Sergeant Sharp said he'd brief you as soon as he got there."

"Can he give me a hint?"

Grant could hear Sharp in the background. "Tell him I didn't fucking plan on this. I was moving out when this bastard grabbed me by the ankle. He's shot up pretty good, but he was wearing Mexican cop shit, so I thought he might be one of the good guys."

"I heard him, put this on speaker!" He paused a few seconds. "Sharp, does he know who you are?"

"I doubt it, Boss. One of his holes is in the side of his head. I think he was one of the bodies they were salting the area with. Fucking amateurs can't even kill somebody right."

"Who's working on him?"

"Elko."

Well, that was a plus, Grant thought. Elko had been around with them long enough to know not to talk about it. He could see a line of trucks coming up from the south. For a change, all of them had their headlights on. When they pulled in he was gratified to see that all of them had switched uniforms. Shaarp gave him a quick rundown. Grant signaled the driver to step out for a moment. "You know the story?"

"We found him dangling on the wire on our side when we were coming back to the barn."

"That all you know?"

"I already gave them the story, Luke."

"OK, Son. Take him and the medic to the aid station at HQ. Try to stay on the road."

They watched as the truck sped to the north.

"I couldn't leave him, Luke. I don't know who all those people were, but it was murder, pure and simple."

"That's what they do in Mexico. You should have known better. He could complicate things."

Chapter 7

Major Carson did her best to stabilize the wounded Mexican while the medevac chopper was inbound. It took Callan some arguing, but a military chopper was dispatched to pick him up. He'd be transported to Columbus, where the Border Patrol would take him to a civilian hospital. The situation was already getting ugly. Mexican TV was reporting on the make-believe raid, calling it a great victory for the army and the government. Callan had captured the raw feed in the CP, and had somehow gotten the system to run the translation across the bottom of the screen. Most of it was so much canned commentary to describe the scenes of the raid. The camera lingered on the burnt out helicopter, and did a quick pan of bodies of supposed 'narco-terrorists' laid out at the different sites. There were also piles of weapons and packets of drugs being proudly displayed.

"This has been running in a loop for a couple of hours now," Callan was telling them. "The Mexicans seem pretty proud of what they did last night."

Sharp was nursing a cup of coffee, pissed off that it wasn't something stronger. He kept mumbling "Fucking liars" under his breath. Grant snapped at him "Give it a break, Dave, we've got enough problems without you editorializing!" He looked at Callan, but Major Bonneville cut in. "Where do they talk about their friendly casualties?"

Callan picked up a CD and slipped it into a laptop. "That's not on the air any more, Ma'am. They dropped all mention of it about an hour or so ago. I figure that was about the same time somebody was calling the *federales* and telling them we had picked up one of their boys. I recorded this when it first came on the air."

The report scrolled through what looked like the same images as was on the live feed, until it came to a shot of a podium with Mexican flags in the background with a portrait of a young looking Mexican police officer. The portrait was draped in black bunting. "This is what they cut out." The sub-titles read that they were mourning the loss of one of their officers, a supervisor on the drug task force named Emilio Montoya. A succession of speakers described what a good family man he had been before cutting over to a distraught looking *policia* who described how his friend had approached one of the buildings when the *narcos* were pretending to surrender, only to be brutally shot down by them. The *policia* described how he held his *amigo* as he died, and how he asked him to look after his family.

"And how is that a problem?" Grant asked. There was a stir in the back of the tent as Kearney and Vaughn entered. "Keep your seats" Vaughn said. "Continue, Sergeant Callan. We want to hear this too."

Callan waited until they took the seats in front that Sharp and Price abandoned. "The problem comes up here, Sir." He hit some keys on another laptop, and a series of pictures came up. They were of the casualty Price had rescued. There was also an image of a Mexican *Policia Federale* ID card identifying Emilio Montoya. "According to the news feed, Montoya was taken to a military hospital in *Cuidad Juarez* where they made super human efforts to save him. I can imagine the massive ass-chewings when somebody from the Border Patrol station in Columbus called up and told them who they had in the hospital. It couldn't have been pretty."

"It wasn't," Vaughn said. "There was a quick meeting of all the alphabet agencies to figure out what to do. The Mexicans asked for a news blackout on the raid on our side until they can come up with their version of events, but they seem to be having trouble controlling their own reporters."

"Where do we stand, General?" Grant asked.

"Right now, Sergeant Major, we're trying to minimize your involvement. That story you came up with is holding for the moment.

It's simple enough to be believable, and it'll stay that way, unless somebody decides to get creative. Is that going to happen?"

Sharp stood up in the back. He took a slow sip from his cup and put it down before he walked to the front of the group. "General, all my guys know their parts. I weeded it down that the crew I took in were the only ones present when I found Emilio, dangling from the wire. Everybody else showed up when I called for the medic."

"That story going to hold up?"

"I know my guys, and I trust them."

Grant interrupted. "There is one smaller problem."

"What's that?"

He had Callan run the CD again. "Watch the buildings. Callan, slow it down." They all watched then looked at Grant. "None of that footage was shot this morning. Once they found out there was a problem with a survivor they're reporting dead, somebody must have noticed what I did."

"Which is?"

Sharp burst out first. "Son of a bitch! Why didn't I see that before?" Price chimed in. He could see it now too. "Somebody down there fucked up!"

Vaughn was getting impatient. He snapped at them, "You want to let me in on the secret, or do I have to guess?"

Officers, Grant thought. Even the obvious has to be highlighted. "Look at the shadows."

"What about them?"

"Callan, scroll back to the shot of the shed with the double doors." Callan ran his fingers over the touch pad and froze the scene at the building Grant wanted. "Right there."

"I don't see any shadow."

"Exactly. Those doors face the border. If that was taken this morning they'd be in shadow. Those are brightly lit. Late afternoon sun."

Kearney looked hard. "Well now that they've changed the pictures on the feed, that doesn't prove anything."

"Sure it does, Colonel. Has anybody noticed any pictures of that particular building since they've done the editing?"

"Well, no, but it doesn't mean anything."

"The hell it doesn't, Sir. I burned that fucking building down last night!"

Vaughn looked at him. "And why would you do something like that?"

Grant reached down to the bag by his side, pulled out the license plates they had taken off the Border Patrol vehicle and tossed them on the table. Then he told Callan to run the pictures he had taken the night before. "When they started talking about the 'trophy vehicle', that's what they were talking about. I didn't see any point in letting them try to pin an accessory charge on the Border Patrol."

"Where did they get that?"

"Some time ago, two agents and their vehicle disappeared in this part of the border. Up until now it's all been speculation on what happened to them."

"What did happen to them? It looks like they could have gone over to the Mexican cartels."

"They could have, but if they're calling it a trophy, I'd say those two agents are dead. They probably smoked them on the road and buried them somewhere out there."

Kearney and Vaughn stepped out to confer. It was silent in the tent while they were out. Grant was conscious of Bonneville's leg up against his as they sat in the uncomfortable folding chairs. He looked at her and smiled, and let his mind wander to a place it shouldn't have been. She was giving him the same look. "We need to go for a walk later," she whispered.

"Better yet, if we can, let's go visit a line platoon or two. The farther away we get from this place the better."

Kearney and Vaughn came back in. "There's probably going to be a bunch of nosy people around here pretty soon. Where can you put all your people so they aren't available for a day or two?"

Sharp spoke up. "I've got a land navigation course laid out on the western end of the Game Preserve," he was talking about the Big Hatchet. "A couple of teams without GPS and a couple of dead radio batteries would keep them out of sight for a little bit."

"A helicopter could find them."

"OK, how about a survival, escape and evasion map reading course. They could always say they thought they were supposed to avoid being found."

Kearney and Vaughn both agreed that story would work, at least for a day or two, until the situation either stabilized or went completely to shit. They did, however, insist that one of the staff officers accompany them. Price and Sharp were both vocal in their protests, claiming senior NCOs could be trusted to keep their troops in line. Kearney disagreed, adding that his problem always seemed to be with the NCOs getting out of hand. "You gentlemen always seem to be at the dirty end of the stick. I would prefer a couple of days of you doing exactly what we expect from you."

Bonneville interrupted to ask who they would be sending just as Major Carson walked in with a status report on the Mexican survivor. Vaughn indicated she should give her report.

"Well, the good news is that he's still alive, even though I don't really feel that's good for him. He has some massive trauma to his back, with some spinal damage. He'll never walk again."

"At least he'll be alive."

"That's debatable. He's got some pretty serious bone splintering on his scalp. I'm not sure how bad it is, but there has to be some brain damage."

Kearney asked, "Will he be able to give any information?"

"Colonel, I doubt he'll ever do more than drool and blink his eyes. The hospital told me that to be on the safe side they put him into an artificial coma to keep him from trying anything on his own. The Mexicans sent a consular officer from their office in El Paso to try to question him. They got the impression the poor bastard was staying alive on purpose, just to screw with them."

Vaughn thanked her and asked her to stay. He and Kearney put their heads together for a few moments. Kearney asked if she thought she could be spared from the infirmary for a few days. Carson asked what they meant. They described the situation for her. She thought about it for a few moments, but declined. "As much as I'd like to take a vacation in one of the line platoon paradises," everyone recognized the sarcasm, "with all the heavy equipment moving around, and the way the soldiers keep finding illegals for me to take care of, it wouldn't be a good idea. As soon as I got out of the area Murphy's Law would kick in."

Kearney agreed with her. "Looks like it'll be you, Major," he said to Bonneville. She started to protest, claiming she had things to do, thinking about a road trip with Grant. It took her halfway through her recital of the piles of work she had in the S-1 tent before she realized Kearney would be sending her with Grant for a few days, exactly what she was hoping for. On reflection, she thought to herself, it was a better deal. She changed her tack, and admitted SSG Gordon, her section NCO, could probably manage the section and the workload with just a little guidance. Vaughn said he wanted them out the gate before noon, and dismissed the group. Bonneville flashed a little smile at Grant on her way out of the tent.

Outside the tent Grant looked across the little compound and saw Sullivan sitting outside of the S-4 tent. Sharp saw what he was looking at. "What about him, Luke? Who's gonna keep an eye on him while we're gone?"

"I have no idea, Dave. He's going to be a problem. We'll have to work on it when we get back. I'll have Callan keep him out of the TOC, and hope he hasn't learned anything else to pass on to his little crack whore."

"Maybe when we get back we can take a side trip into Columbus work something out? It's been a while since we all got together and trashed a bar."

"Sounds like the start of a plan." He looked around and called Callan over. "Make sure he," Grant said pointing at Sullivan, "doesn't get access to anything in the TOC. And try to get somebody to keep an eye on him while we're gone. He's too cozy with the Mexicans in Columbus."

Callan nodded. "I'll pass the word to the shift OICs. They're a good group. But as far as keeping an eye on him, I think he comes with a built in watchdog."

"What do you mean?"

Callan pointed into the tent behind Sullivan. There was another soldier sitting there. Grant recognized him as one of the less military appearing of the supply types. In an area where they had access to just about every service one would need to live a civilized existence, Specialist Rogers seemed to take special pride in being as unkempt as possible. Grant had heard First Sergeant Harrison complain that he was the one bane of his existence, a true Sad Sack and Beetle Bailey rolled into one. Callan described how Rogers was beginning to feel put out by Sullivan using him as his personal whipping boy. There was even a rumor that Sullivan had taken Rogers with him on a quick visit to his girl friend, and made Rogers drive around for an hour while he knocked off a quickie. He wouldn't even let Rogers go into the bar for a beer.

"He thinks Sullivan may be doing some illegal stuff when he's on his own. I've got some of the younger troops tag-teaming him whenever they can. Between him and everyone else who doesn't like Sullivan, I think I've got it covered."

"Good. While you're at it, I'm sure the First Sergeant would be grateful if you could talk Rogers into getting a decent haircut the next time they pass by a barber shop."

"I'll do my best."

The exiles, as they began calling themselves, settled on the southernmost bivouac site to spend their time out of sight and out of mind. It was out of the way enough to make it a pain in the ass for the casual visitor to get to, but still offered easy access to the limited road and trail network in that part of their sector. It was used as a staging area before teams rotated for their 72 hour tours on *el Indio*, and was almost in a direct line with the end of the *el Monumento* airstrip.

There had been a need for extra tenting to accommodate the newcomers, and Sergeant First Class Powell's troops soon had another GP medium up for the bulk of the troops, and a GP small for the NCOs. Bonneville was distressed because Lieutenant Powers offered space in her tent in lieu of forcing the NCOs into the medium tent. Other than looking like an arrogant bitch, she couldn't think of any way to turn down the offer. She saw her time alone with Grant, once again, vanishing in the wind. As she unpacked her rucksack and rolled out her sleeping bag Grant knocked on the tent pole.

"Are you going to be busy later?"

"I don't know," she smiled. "How much later?"

"There's a team rotation scheduled for the U-boat tonight. I haven't watched one yet and I want to see how it goes. It goes off after dark, and I thought you might like to come along. You'll need some special battle rattle and a full load of ammo."

"Just the kind of offer a girl wants to hear! What kind of special gear?" she said rather icily. Grant let the iciness pass. She was entitled. "I'll bring it by later. Then I'll have a treat for you."

"A treat? With field gear and a load of ammo?"

"That's for the official part of the program. Later on we can get in a little side trip. There's a spring a couple of miles back on the lower slopes on the US side of *el Indio*, about 20 minutes away. Powell tells me the off duty troops use it for a swimming hole, but there won't be anyone there tonight. Bring a bathing suit if you want to try it. I doubt the Kevlar makes a very good life jacket."

"Just the two of us? No radio operator, security element or old drinking buddies to keep us company?"

"Just you, me and whatever illegal immigrants are watching from the bushes."

"I would be happy to observe the operation, Sergeant Major."

At dusk the relief and their support team assembled outside the bivouac. SFC Powell explained the procedure. The convoy stopped at an assembly point about a mile from the border. The support group secured the route to the base of a gully that led up to the summit of *el Indio*, not too far in on the Mexican side. If everything was clear, the relief team made its way up to the OP. After a briefing and an orderly hand over of the position, they made a quick police for trash, then exfiltrated down the hill. Once they passed through the support team, everybody fell back to the US side, and made their way back to the assembly area. Barring any activity on or near the route, the change over usually took two hours. There had been some sheepherding activity on the lower eastern slopes, but they stayed well away from the route or the US position on the summit.

Grant could tell that the troops were very well practiced in what they were supposed to do. The pre-movement briefing was short and to the point. Contingencies, emergencies and reaction drills were all repeated. Every soldier verbally acknowledged he understood his role. Powell was not on either of the teams, Grant didn't want the senior NCOs isolated in Mexico for three days at a time, but Powell pointed out that when his soldiers were involved, he accompanied them as far out and back as he could. He didn't interfere, and he gave his squad leaders plenty of room to operate. Powell subscribed to Grants philosophy that you needed to let your junior leaders do their jobs. Train them, advise them, critique them and observe them, but stay out of their way and let them perform. A good leader will rise to the challenge. A poor one will stand out equally so. Powell didn't seem to have any weak ones. Bonneville watched everything with a combination of military interest and fascination. She usually avoided these scenes because it was usually Grant going out to where people would be shooting at him. She had never participated in the actual preparation. "Why are we wearing these uniforms?" She meant the Mexican style BDUs the group was wearing. "Those are mandatory for the OP team and their support group. It just worked out as part of the contingency operation that everybody wears the same thing. It's almost a given that somewhere along the trail they'll lose something. Other than a RFID chip they all have on their gear, everyone who's operating on the Mexican side of the line isn't carrying anything that could ID them as US troops."

"What about us?"

"I don't think we'll be going over unless you really want to."

"I think I really want to."

At the border the fence had been adapted for an easy passage: two fence posts were looped together with snap links. The links were removed to open a gate, and closed after passage had been made. One soldier was carrying, of all things, a straw broom to whisk away any footprints on either side of the border, a simple but effective technique.

Grant had hesitated at the border. He was mindful of his warnings to his NCOs about going over. Then again, he thought, he was the CSM. He asked Major Bonneville if she was certain she'd like to join in a brief invasion of Mexico.

"How far?"

"Just a couple of hundred meters. We'll be in and out in less than an hour. You're the XO now. If something happens to the CO you'll need to have an understanding of the operation."

"Has Colonel Kearney been here?"

"No, but I haven't asked him either."

He took Powell to the side and explained what he was going to do. Powell didn't like it. There were enough things to keep track of without tourists. Grant insisted. "She's the XO, and I'm the CSM. Remember, this was all my idea to begin with."

"OK, but it'll be on your head. You keep an eye on her and make sure she doesn't do anything stupid or leave anything behind."

Bonneville was game for the trip, and her field craft, not up to the standards of the soldiers who did this for a living, was adequate for what was asked of her, meaning Grant stayed right with her and didn't let her do anything dangerous. She followed instructions, and watched her sector while the relief was being made higher up. When the team came down the hill they all moved back to the US side, and then to the assembly area, in silence. Grant got an abridged briefing from the team leader. There had been little activity in the past twenty-four hours since the made-up raids. It looked like there were some sentries posted at the sites, but no overwhelming presence. With that accomplished, the support team returned to the border area for their 72 hour overwatch assignment, and Powell loaded up the rest of the troops and headed back to the bivouac and some cold beer. After cooking under camouflage nets for three days, they deserved it. Grant and Bonneville watched them drive off.

"Sergeant Powell didn't want me to go, did he?"

"Sergeant Powell was probably right, but I felt it was important enough for you to go. I planned on the Mexican uniforms and weapons in advance though. I shouldn't have sprung it on him at the last minute.

Hopefully I can make it up to him and his troops with beer and liquor."

What was a twenty minute trip in daylight took a little longer for Grant. He was in blackout drive and navigating by quick glances at his marked map. Linda Bonneville kept up an animated one sided conversation about what they had done tonight, and how she was looking forward to a chance to get rid of her uniform for a little while and have a nice relaxing swim. At the half hour mark he was almost ready to give up the quest, at the risk of disappointing her, when he saw the cleft rock that marked the turn. A couple of S-turns later and they were parked on the shore of a small pool. It was only about 30 meters across, with some low rock outcroppings on the far side. Because of the water source, there was heavier vegetation in this area, and even a couple of overhanging trees. Grant looked around the area with a set of night vision glasses. It looked clear, so he turned on his headlights to get a better look at the area.

"Are you going to leave the lights on?" He could hear the rustling of her getting out of her uniform.

"No. The light would attract anybody else who might be wandering around out here. Not to mention somebody might have a drone up tonight. Take a good look around and orient yourself. There's a box of chemlights on the floor over there. Take a couple and find a place to hang one on your suit."

"I've got a better idea."

Grant had no idea what she was talking about. He'd find out in a few minutes. He flipped off the lights and grabbed a bag out of the back. His idea of a bathing suit was an old pair of cut down BDU trousers. It wasn't the latest style, but one did have to make allowances for being in the field. He changed quickly then stepped out in front of the truck. Linda was already standing there, and he saw what her better idea was. She had cut open a chemlight and dabbed the liquid onto her bathing suit, outlining both sections. She turned around and Grant could see two hand prints on her bottom. Grant always thought she looked good in anything she wore, and she looked even better when she was almost not wearing anything. The skimpy suit accentuated what she already had. The glowing liquid highlighted the best parts. He could feel himself stirring. He had anticipated that they would make love out here by the pool, but seeing her standing in front of him like that just ramped up how bad he wanted her.

"You like it?"

"Well, it will be easy to find you in the dark."

"Think so?" and she splashed into the water. Grant finished spreading out his poncho liner by the water and placed a small Styrofoam cooler with a couple of iced beers next to it. Ever the cautious man, he also took an Argentine semi-automatic out of its holster and checked the chamber before he laid it on top of the cooler. He looked over the pool for Linda and saw her at the far end. He looked again: he couldn't see her. What he did see was her two piece suit hanging from separate branches of a low hanging tree. He could hear her laughing. "Can you see me now?" His eyes hadn't fully adjusted to the dark after the glare of the headlights, but he could see where she had spilled some of the luminous chemical on herself when she cut the stick. There was a small glow circling the pool, coming around to him from the left. He got into the water and dived under. He could see the diffraction of the small glow as it moved up and down out of the water. He worked his way around until she was between him and the shore, and waited. She was keeping low in the water, barely visible on the surface, and she stopped opposite the front of the truck, trying to spot Grant in the dark. When she couldn't, she raised herself up a little to look around.

"I've got a surprise for you if you can find me!"

Grant swam along the bottom until he was just a few feet from her, and waited until she had turned to face in his direction. He reached out and placed his hands on her hips and stood up. He could feel her shudder at the unexpected contact, and she stifled a little scream when his head broke the surface in front of her. She recovered quickly, and threw her arms around his neck. She pressed up against him and she snorted. "How come you're still wearing that damn bathing suit?" He could feel her hands loosening the buttons. When it was loose she pulled them down, and hooked them with her foot. Grant stepped out of them and pressed up against her. Her mouth was on his and she was guiding him into her. She gasped again as he filled her up and her legs went around his waist, moving up and down on him until her first orgasm exploded. She hung on him, gasping for breath. "I'm not done yet," he said. He walked her back to the shore, still wrapped around his waist, and laid her on the poncho liner, never breaking contact. He thrust slowly, building up his speed and power until he felt her start to shudder again, just as he reached his peak.

"God, I love it when you do that to me! Now lay still while I give you your prize for finding me. Her lips trailed off his and he could feel her moving down his body. She took him in her hand and squeezed gently, then he felt he mouth envelop him. He closed his eyes and tried to rock his hips to her rhythm. It took a few minutes to have the effect she wanted, but as soon as he was ready she mounted him again. She squeezed her muscles and rocked slowly, bringing them both to another climax.

She lay there with her head on his chest. Her breath was slow but he wasn't certain if she was sleeping. He squeezed and stroked her breast until he felt the nipple harden. "You keep doing that and I'm going to expect some more sex out of you."

"That was my plan."

When they were finished again, Grant took two beers out of the cooler and opened them. He passed one to her as she picked up the pistol and put it off to one side.

"Why do you carry these foreign guns? Don't you like the M-9?" The M-9 was the military designation for the Beretta 92 9mm pistol. Grant didn't like it.

"I want something that'll knock a bad guy down quick so I can move on to his buddies. The 9mm won't guarantee that. The .45 auto will, so I try to keep one handy wherever I am."

"How many do you have?"

"Right now I've got about ten left. Back in the 80's, when Sharp and I were in Central America in places we weren't supposed to be, I came across a case of these. Where they came from I've got no idea.

Our side was using US issue, and the other side was using Soviet Bloc. But they were handy and the price was right, so I brought them home with me."

"Just like that? You brought them home?"

"You have to remember it was a different time back 20 years or so ago. I flew in on a C-130 and flew out the same way. There weren't any civilian airports to deal with, and no customs inspectors going through the baggage. We got back to Bragg and there was a Colonel at the foot of the ramp when it dropped. He shook our hands, passed out some beers, and had a bus take us to Camp McCall, where we turned in our GI stuff, changed into real Army uniforms, and went home. Nobody cared what we brought back. We were professionals. That's how we acted, and that's how we were treated."

"You said you only have ten left?"

"Yeah, some I've given away, and some I've had to throw away. I thought about changing barrels to save the gun, but there are too many marks left on the head of the cartridge casing for that. There's no record of these weapons in the country, and, like I said, the price was right, so why take the chance." Grant looked at his watch. "It'll be dawn in another 90 minutes."

She was quiet for a while, then stirred and got up. She walked to the other side of the truck and started gathering up the uniform she had discarded earlier. The moon was out now, and Grant could see her clearly. He agreed with his earlier thought: she was a damn fine looking woman. What the hell was she doing with an old man like him? She walked back to the poncho liner and dropped her clothes in a pile.

"Where are you going?"

"My bikini is hanging from a tree over there, and your shorts are floating around somewhere. Unless you want to leave them for the next bunch, one of us better go back in and get them."

"No, you get dressed, I'll get them. I need a cold bath after watching you walk around like that."

"Why, Sergeant Major," she said coyly. "I'll bet you say that to all the girls!"

"Only the ones I have to salute, Ma'am."

She was dressed when he got back. She helped towel him off, making a mockery of his cold swim. He controlled himself and got his uniform on. She sat there watching him. "What do you think will happen to that Mexican Sharp saved?"

Grant had been thinking about that himself. "Probably nothing. Once the Mexicans get him back and realize he can't say anything, they'll probably pull the plug."

"So it's all for nothing?"

"I don't know about nothing, we learned a lot by what happened. I just hope the Mexicans aren't learning anything from it."

"What do you mean?"

He finished lacing up his boots and leaned on the drivers' seat. "The bad guys are three things, vicious, incompetent and impulsive. I hope they're stupid, too." She looked at him. He went on. "Montoya was pretty much fucked up when he took that shot to the head. The medic had him on a bag and was breathing for him by the time they got to the rally point."

"So?"

"Once their doctors look at him, they're gonna wonder how he crawled a couple of kilometers to our side of the fence."

"Maybe they'll think he was chasing whoever shot him."

"That would work if they didn't already know he was a prisoner and they executed him at the airfield. They didn't cut off his ropes until after they shot him. They know what condition he was in."

"Then how did he get to where Sharp was?"

"Exactly the question they'll be asking. I won't push Sharp on it, because he already feels bad enough about what he did, but there was no way Montoya crawled out of there."

"That means. . ."

"That means Sharp was in the building when the executions happened. He tried to save that guy because of the police vest."

"Sergeant Sharp is lying to you about what happened?"

"No. Sharp wouldn't do that. He told us everything that he saw, and everything that happened, except for Montoya."

"Is that going to be a problem," she asked.

"Only if the Mexicans figure it out."

He helped her up and watched admiringly as she moved about the area gathering up the debris of their night. In the half darkness she still had a figure to be admired. I'm one lucky son of a bitch he thought. The really amazing thing was that he hadn't screwed this up yet. Correction, he thought. I'm lucky I haven't been caught screwing this up yet. The sex he was having on the side with Major Sylvia Carson was pretty amazing, and she had few if any demands of him besides physical pleasure. At some point that could change and he had better make up his mind and decide which woman he was going to stick with.

The radio was quiet on the ride back. Grant checked his watch. At this hour of the morning he wasn't surprised. It was getting to that magic hour when the early morning activities hadn't started yet, and the night shift was getting drowsy and starting to lose focus. In other words, it was the perfect time for a raid or surprise attack. Hopefully, that wouldn't be something the Mexicans had in mind. The OP would give them ample warning, but there was always the possibility that Mexican army would remember that they were actually soldiers and not just drug thugs and apply sound military principles to their drug smuggling. It probably hadn't occurred to them that it would be relatively simple to overwhelm what was essentially a reinforced company trying to cover over 35 kilometers of border without any depth.

He kept going back to the thought that as inept as the Mexicans had been, they couldn't be as consistently stupid as they had been. At some point one of the up and coming over-achievers would start to consider all that had been happening and come to some logical conclusions, and one of those conclusions would be that the Americans had been getting up close and personal on their side of the border. Grant had given them suggestions, so they must realize he was the one who took the guns away from Homer and Gomer in *las Palomas.* Giving the serial numbers to the Mexican sergeant major at the Academy wasn't one of his smarter ideas, but it was too late to change history. At some point they would probably want to come after him, just to prove they were the top dogs in the alley. Somehow, he thought whatever they tried would have the subtlety of going after a fly with a nail gun.

He looked over at Bonneville. She was out like a light, and he was starting to feel pretty drowsy. He turned off the road and slowed for the gate guard to ID him. He reported it had been a quiet night and moved the barbed wire barrier to let him pass. After dark there was a dismount area where all vehicles were required to unload their passengers and have a ground guide lead them any further into the camp. Grant decided to just park off to one side and leave the truck there until morning. He reached over and shook Bonneville's shoulder. "Time to go, Major. We're back in the Army."

She looked over and smiled. "I want to go back to the pool."

"So do I, but it ain't gonna happen today. Leave all your gear here and I'll take care of it. Put that Mexican uniform in this," he handed her an empty sand bag, "and give it to me after you've gotten some sleep."

"Sure you don't want it now?"

"If I recall, and I'm sure I do, you don't have anything on under that. It might be a long walk back to your tent."

She just smiled and got out without another word. Grant broke down the gear and stowed it in a duffel bag with the weapons, and headed to his tent to change. His tent-mates were all asleep, so he tried to be quiet as he changed back into an ACU and stowed his BDUs. When he was done, Sharp was rolling out of bed and pulling on his pants. "If you're getting dressed I guess you don't intend to get any sleep tonight. How about we get some coffee?"

"You've been waiting for me?"

"No. I woke up when I heard the vehicle pull in. I figured it was you. When you and the Major didn't come back with the relief team I guessed the two of you were going AWOL for a few hours."

"Anybody else notice?"

"Just Price and Powell, but they don't give a shit. The troops cracked open a case of beer and were probably glad you weren't around."

"I wouldn't have cared."

"I know that, and you really believe that, but you're still the all mighty and all powerful Command Sergeant Major, and nothing you do or say will make them forget that. There is no fucking way in hell you can help putting a damper on their fun. Neither can I, and neither can Price, now that he's got his E-7 again."

"Jesus fucking Christ are you two going to start swapping spit?" Price was up and searching for his boots. "You think you'd have a little consideration for us poor bastards who weren't out getting laid all night!"

Sharp threw one of his own boots at him. "And then there are those among us who really aren't impressed by rank at all. Are you joining us for coffee, you fucking loser? Or are you just going to lay there and play with yourself?"

"Fuck you!"

"It'd be the best piece of ass you ever got. Hurry up. We'll wait outside."

Chapter 8

The clerk looked at the clock as the well tanned man walked up to the counter. At least he thought it was a tan, although the man's features hinted at a Mediterranean heritage. It was also very late, later than they normally checked in guests, but this one had specified a late arrival, so technically he had been paying for the room since 3PM the previous afternoon. "Welcome to the Mirador Hotel, Mister LeBlanc. We've been expecting you."

The man grunted and reached for the registration card as he slid his passport across. It was from Monte Carlo, of all places. The clerk noticed he was wearing what seemed to be expensive gloves. "Is my room on the east side on an upper floor as I requested?"

It had been an odd request, but not terribly strange. He had specified an east facing room because, he said, he was a Muslim, and when he prayed to Mecca he preferred to see the sky. That made sense to the clerk, although his experience with Muslims here on the Mexican border was very, very limited.

"Yes Sir, and as you requested there is no alcohol in the mini-bar, and a bowl of fresh fruit has been delivered." Another grunt before he asked about expedited check out. "I am expecting a call about some last minute travel arrangements and I may have to leave quickly. I don't want to have to delay while someone tries to tabulate my bill."

That was a rather routine request that didn't normally come with an explanation. "Early checkout is not a problem, Sir, as long as we have your credit card number on file."

LeBlanc slid an American Express card over, a Platinum card, no less. The clerk swiped it and handed it back. "Can I get someone to show you to your room?"

LeBlanc waved his hand, indicating no, and picked up his bag and headed for the elevator bank. The clerk turned away and didn't see him look over his shoulder to see if anyone was looking, then slid off the gloves to reveal purple nitrile gloves underneath. The expensive kid leather gloves were thrown into a trash receptacle. Before the cleaning crew came through in the morning, he would be gone. He rode the elevator to the sixth floor and moved in the direction the little wall tag indicated. He slid the key card in the lock and pushed the door open. He gave the room a cursory sweep, knowing he wouldn't be making any phone calls or speaking to anyone. He would simply sit in silence, waiting for a flash of light to come from the building across the way, from the third window from the north corner on the fourth floor. He opened his bag on the bed and removed the M-79 grenade launcher and an olive drab bandolier containing four gold tipped high explosive rounds. He placed it with the action open on the coffee table, and placed a small hammer next to it. He had hoped for operable windows, but he would just break what was there when the time came. The hotel could charge the damages to the real Mr. LeBlanc. He moved a chair over to face the building across the way and picked up the M-79. It was an older weapon, no longer in general use anywhere in the world, but he preferred it for its compactness and ease of use, unlike the bulky M-203 that the Americans devised to be hung under the barrels of their M-16 rifles. An experienced grenadier (and he preferred to call himself 'The Grenadier') could point and shoot a round into an open barrel at over 100 yards. He would be using the excellent leaf sight and firing at a larger target. It had been rumored that in Vietnam some grenadiers had perfected the art of using their M-79s as light weight mortars. They would mark the slings with range marks to help gauge the angle of fire, giving them excellent results into trenches and behind obstacles at ranges as close as 25 yards. LeBlanc had practiced it, and it was true, but he rarely travelled with a sling.

He took an apple from the bowl and bit into it. It wasn't as sweet as he would have expected for the price that no doubt would be charged to his account. He tossed the remains into his bag. Nothing would be left behind. He took an over priced bottle of water from the mini-bar and took several swallows before he saw the light in the window across the way. He looked at his watch: there was plenty of time. He finished the water, giving whoever it had been making the signal time to get out of the room and away from the area. He slipped the thong on the hammer around his wrist and gave the glass a hard smack. He was surprised that only a little hole broke out. The head of the hammer pulled back and enlarged the hole, bringing most of the broken glass into the room. When the opening suited his needs he casually tossed the hammer into his bag with the empty water bottle. Two rounds were removed from the bandolier, one resting on the window sill, the other into the chamber of the M-79. He carefully aimed and fired his first shot. The empty casing was ejected into the bag and the second round loaded before the explosion. Before the shock wave could reach him, he fired the second round and was closing his bag as the second explosion reached him.

He was down the stairs and out to his car without meeting another person.

The tent they were using as a dining facility had been simply equipped. Sergeant Moura, the intrepid Mess Sergeant, had begged, borrowed or stolen enough equipment so that every platoon could have a rudimentary kitchen. There was one major hot meal, supper, prepared every day at the headquarters location and distributed to all outlying units in Mermite cans. Breakfast was provided in tray packs, pre-cooked and shelf stable meals that could be quickly heated and served. It was the individual units' responsibility to assign people to do it. Lunch was always an MRE, which the troops genuinely enjoyed because of the variety. Sometimes the elements on patrol had to make do with an MRE for supper or breakfast, and the outpost teams ate them exclusively for 72 hours. There was also a generous issue of soup mix, drink mixes and coffee. By now, all the elements had acquired ice makers of varying efficiency, and pooled resources maintained an adequate supply of soft drinks and beer.

Mouras' section had expanded by bits and pieces as this deployment had gone on. He had the flexibility to give his cooks regular days off, as well as assign them on a rotating basis to each line platoon to make certain all the soldiers were well fed, and to handle any complaints that tend to spring up in the field. There had been some resistance to the practice at first, but the cooks grew to enjoy the two day trips out to the platoons that happened once a week and some were even beginning to request their favorite platoons. Moura was considering assigning each cook a platoon as their personal responsibility. It was all a matter of scheduling. He was here on this particular day because he also made it a point to include himself in the rotation and visit each platoon on a regular basis. He didn't enjoy it as much as his cooks did because it took him away from his own responsibilities, but it kept him current, and kept complaints to an absolute minimum.

He was testing the quality of the coffee from a new urn he had installed the day before when the flap was pulled aside and the Sergeant Major came in with Sergeant Sharp. They traded pleasantries as they got their coffee and sat down at a corner bench as Sergeant Price came in, boots unlaced, still pulling on his blouse. Moura liked working with them. It was the first time in his service in the Guard that he had been with a unit that included food service in their planning and training. They encouraged a 'work together' atmosphere that made everyone's job easier. Grant waved him over and asked him to sit. This Sergeant Major was always interested in what was going on in all sections. They spoke for a few moments and Moura excused himself to get his serving line set up. He was doing eggs to order and fresh bacon this morning. He had put the word out the night before and expected a heavy turn out.

Grant watched him putter at the far end of the tent. The unit was lucky to have a Mess Sergeant who always tried to go over and above. He said as much to Sharp and Price. Then he got down to business. "Dave, tell me about the Mexican." He said it conversationally, but there was an edge Sharp recognized. "I thought my story was simple enough."

"It would have been if your little buddy wasn't shot up so bad. As soon as the medics started working on him they knew he didn't crawl 10 feet, never mind a couple of hundred meters. Want to try again?"

"How long have you known?"

"As soon as Carson heard the story I saw her eyes light up. She didn't say anything to Kearney, but she told me she had her doubts." Grant didn't add that she also said she expected a weekend in either El Paso or *Cuidad Juarez* to keep it that way.

Sharp started to tell his story. He had originally planned to keep his distance after the hostages had been brought into the hanger, but there had been several women and what looked like a teenage boy in the group. That had bothered him. "I wanted to see if I could find a way out for them without getting myself in too deep. I worked my way over to a side door I had rigged a while back, but the shooting started almost as soon as I got in. This guy came running over to where I was and dived over a box I was behind. They shot him in mid-air before he landed on me. He started moaning and saying something that might have been anything. Before I could do anything somebody leaned over the box and started popping off with a little pistol. When my guy jerked up the Mexican saw me and started shooting at me."

Price interrupted, "Did he hit you?"

"Good question," Grant added. "Did he?"

Sharp nodded. "Yeah, he hit me in the left arm. Just a graze, really. I had my pistol out and I put a couple of rounds into him. He turned and started to run, so I put a couple more into his back."

"You were using that little Tokarev again, weren't you?"

"Yeah, that 7.62x25 has pretty good penetration, but sometimes it just keeps going."

"Get rid of it! I've told you that before. I don't give a fuck what you carry for a personal weapon on your own time, but when it starts to jeopardize people around you, it becomes everybody's business. Either get something bigger on your own or come see me for a 1911. That fucking little pistol is going to get you killed." Grant paused. "Get that arm taken care of as soon as possible."

"What are we going to do about the Mexican, Luke? I mean. What if the Mexicans figure it out?"

"For now I think I have it covered. I asked Doctor Carson to downplay the head wound. She said she'd try. She also said the chemical coma they put the guy in will keep everybody quiet for a bit, but at some point a good neurosurgeon will look at him and tell the world they've been lied to. I've got Mel Braga working on that."

"Who?"

"Local State Trooper. I explained there could be a problem without telling him what the problem was. Fortunately, he didn't ask. He said he'd try to leak a story they've brought the guy out of his coma and he gave them some information they're trying to run down."

"Will it work?"

"I don't know, but I can't keep making midnight phone calls to ask for favors without people asking for something back. Stop putting me in that position."

"Won't the Mexicans start worrying if they hear about the dead guy talking?" Price asked.

"He's not dead yet."

"You know what I mean."

Grant took a long drink of his coffee. "I know what you mean. I just hope nobody else figures it out before the Mexicans do start worrying."

"Then what?" This was from Sharp.

"Hopefully, our troubles go away."

"You mean the little fucks try to kill him again."

"No. I mean the little fucks kill him."

Price didn't say anything. Sharp looked at Grant over the top of his cup and raised his eyebrows. "That's pretty extreme, Luke, even for you."

"Yeah, but like Price says, he's a dead guy already. What we really need are the Mexicans to come over and make sure of it, and do a good enough job this time so the autopsy doesn't show he was already brain dead." Grant drained his cup and put it down. Sharp was staring at the table.

"Look at me!"

Sharp didn't move.

"I said look at me!" Sharp raised his eyes. "Remember this the next time you want to get humanitarian on me. As long as the Mexicans are killing each other, it makes our job easier."

"But, Luke..."

"But nothing. All this did was put our people at risk. Our job is to keep our side of the border safe. If we have to do it by operating on their side, so be it, as long as it all happens on their side."

"It won't happen again, Luke."

"And get rid of that fucking Tokarev."

Grant slept for a couple of fitful hours. While it could get to a comfortable temperature at night, the ground never really lost its surface heat. A couple of inches down, like in an animal burrow, would keep a steady level, but the surface was hot, and a tent in the desert was hotter. Operations in Iraq and Afghanistan had the luxury of air conditioning in base camp tentage. Operations in New Mexico got very few of them, and what they did get usually didn't get much below headquarters level. Grant woke and looked at his watch. It was still early in the morning, but he was baking in his sleeping bag. He threw off the bag and grabbed a bottle of water out of a cooler on the table in the center of the tent. There was still some ice floating around, so the water was cool. He took a long drink and poured some over his head. It felt good enough to entice him into a cold shower. He grabbed his gear and headed for the shower point. Being located by one of the scattered water points in the desert, the platoon had rigged rudimentary showers with running water. That was one of the geniuses of the American Army: there was a time and a place to be miserable, just not always and not everywhere. He let the water run over his body, then soaped up and let it run again. Not as refreshing as the swim in the spring the night before, but it was enough. A cold water shave, and he was ready for the rest of his day, or so he thought.

Grant was dressed and on his way to the Mess tent for another cup of coffee when duty NCO caught him. Headquarters was looking for him and the XO. Grant thanked him and directed him to Bonneville's tent. "Ask her to join me for coffee before we face the music. I'm sure she needs a cup as much as I do."

They were driving up the border road at patrol speed. Grant liked to do that in case the Mexicans had any trail watchers. An extra vehicle making a slow pass would interfere with any schedule they were trying to figure out, at least that was his theory. You couldn't always predict what the bad guys were trying to do, but that was no reason to stop trying. There was no reason to suspect they were trying to establish a schedule, but there was also no reason to suspect they weren't. Never underestimate what the other guy might be doing; he always manages to surprise you.

Bonneville had been quiet for most of the trip, her attention fixed on her laptop. Sergeant Callan and his crew had done a remarkable job establishing a secure computer network out here in the desert with little or no support from the rest of the Army. That was one of the little victories they could claim. The other one was that the intelligence folks at Bliss were still funneling real-time information to them, but even that seemed to have degraded in quality and quantity in the past few days. Grant suspected that General Vaughn could have something to do with it. All good things must come to an end.

"Sergeant Callan is sending me a live feed of something here, but my audio is screwed up. I can't hear the narration."

"What's it look like"

"Big white building with smoke coming out of an upper story window. It looks like a fire or something."

"Let me see." She leaned over with the computer screen facing Grant. The camera was panning across the front of a building. An ambulance filled the screen for a moment, then moved off to the left. Grant read the sign for the Columbus Hospital. It looked like the cartels might have found Montoya. He looked down at the corner of the screen. An icon told him what he was looking for.

"You have your speaker on mute."

Bonneville took the computer back and hit a few keys. The sound came up. The reporter was describing an explosion in one of the rooms on the intensive care ward. Initial reports had one patient dead and several staff injured. They speculated on the cause of the explosion, concentrating on the theory of a spark in an oxygen rich environment. In the corner of the frame Grant spotted a familiar face. Major Apuesta was surveying the scene with Homer and Gomer. They were all smiling. Grant knew what that meant; the story he had Mel Braga leak to the press about Montoya talking had worked. The Mexicans had silenced Montoya.

Grant told her to freeze the frame and zoom in on the group. He asked if she recognized any of them.

"Isn't that the Commander of the Mexican unit on the other side of the border?"

"Look closer. See who's with him?"

She looked closer. "Oh my God!" Aren't those the two you took the guns away from on our little trip? What are they doing there?"

"I ran into those two at one of the first shooting incidents we had not too far from here. They just happen to be Apuestas aides. Once they get a little further into the investigation they'll probably find out it wasn't an oxygen leak that blew out the room."

She watched as he took out his phone and scrolled through his speed dial list. When he found the one he wanted he hit the button and waited for an answer. Without preamble he asked whoever was at the far end if he was at the hospital and launched into a description of who was at the scene and where they were located. Looking over at the monitor he could see the trio still in the background, pointing off into the distance. Whatever they saw made them turn around and walk hurriedly out of the scene. A few seconds later another figure walked into the scene. This must be who Grant was speaking to. He listened for another minute, apparently as the man on the far end was looking for the Mexicans without success. There was an exchange of words, and what Bonneville could make out it wasn't a happy exchange, and an agreement to meet at the Headquarters bivouac later on in the day.

"Who was that?" she asked.

"New Mexico State Trooper I met in Columbus a while back. He works on the drug task force and has an interest in what Apuesta and company do in the States."

"Is he mad at you for something?"

"You could say that. I was the one who got him to release the story that Montoya was coming around and talking."

"You couldn't have known this was going to happen."

Grant shook his head. "Braga's right. This is what I thought would happen. I just didn't expect it to be so spectacular. I figured the Mexican Consulate would have arranged for someone to go in and overdose him or something."

"You wanted this to happen?"

"Yeah, I didn't want anybody to figure out what his condition really was. If they did they would have to know he couldn't have walked to the border. Then the cat would have been out of the bag and they would have known for sure we were operating inside their territory. With Montoya dead, they can only guess, and I'll bet that explosion fucked up any autopsy they might have planned."

"You gambled with his life?"

"It was no gamble. Montoya was a dead man before Sharp hoisted him over his shoulder. It was a stupid move on his part. This was just clearing up a loose end and protecting our people."

She was quiet for the next few miles, trying to control he temper. She was staring at her monitor screen when she felt the vehicle start to slow. She looked up to see Grant pick up his M-4 from the floor of the Blazer and lay it across his lap. He motioned for her to do the same thing, pointing down the road. She followed his arm to where it was pointing at a trio of armed, uniformed men who were leaning on the fence on the Mexican side.

"Get on the radio and see if any of the patrols are close enough to back us up, just in case." He slowed even more, coming to a stop about one hundred and fifty meters short of them. The answer came back that the nearest unit was a couple of miles ahead of them. They were turning around and headed their way. One of the men at the fence stepped through the wire, an obvious challenge to Grant's presence and authority. He accented it by waving Grant closer with his upraised weapon. Grant wasn't taking the bait. He pulled the Blazer across the road with the passenger door on the safe side. He told Bonneville to get her body armor on and keep an eye on the border to her right, just in case. Grant pulled his own armor on, cursing to himself for breaking his own rule and not wearing it when he left the bivouac, and thanking whoever the genius was that had come up with the idea of Velcro. Once he had it on he stepped out of the vehicle and took a position by the front tire. The Mexicans were laughing and pointing at him. He couldn't understand what they were saying, but he was pretty sure they were trying to have some fun at his expense. One of the Mexicans stepped back from the wire and disappeared for a moment or two into the brush. He came back out with another armed soldier, and three other figures. The last had their hands tied in front of them, and they all had sacks tied over their heads. Grant was pretty sure that one was a woman, and the other two were children. The Mexican on this side of the fence stepped back into Mexico, and the three prisoners were lined up at the fence. Bonneville called over to Grant.

"What are they doing?"

"I don't know. Keep an eye out for more of them."

The three prisoners had the bags taken off their heads. Grant could see they were indeed, a woman and two children. The soldiers took out some speed cuffs and fastened their tied hands to the top strand of the fence.

"What are they going to do?" Bonneville asked again.

Grant didn't know. They looked like bait. He remained silent. One of the soldiers spoke English, and he called to Grant. "Hey, *Gringo,* you want them? Montoya is dead now. We don't need them anymore."

"Luke, what are they going to do?"

Before Grant could answer the soldiers stepped back from the fence and raised their weapons and fired into the backs of the prisoners. Then they fired at the US vehicle. Grant dropped to one knee and returned fire as he heard his windshield being blown out. He could hear Bonneville screaming something as she began firing. Two of the Mexicans went down. The others tried to drag them off, but Grant, or Bonneville, exploded one of their heads. The others gave up the effort and faded back into the brush. They fired a few more bursts before Grant heard an engine. He remembered that this was the area where an access road came almost to the fence at a sharp angle for the last few yards.

"Watch the brush!" he cried out as he sprinted to where the prisoners were dangling by the speed cuffs from the top wire. He looked over them and fired off a long burst at where he thought the vehicle would be. As the engine sound faded into the distance he looked down at the bodies. The woman and two children were obviously dead. They had each taken a full burst of 7.62mm to the upper back and head. Two of the Mexicans were dead. One had been hit in the face and the other had his chest torn open. They must not have expected any return fire, or they would have worn their body armor. That was the price of overconfidence. The last one was moaning. Grant reached through the wire with his muzzle and pushed the man over. This one had been stitched up from his groin to his navel. The pain must have kicked in at that point, because he started screaming. Well, Grant thought that was just tough shit for him. He heard Bonneville come up. She gasped and quickly turned away. He could hear her retching. He gave her a few moments to get rid of breakfast, then led her back to the Blazer. He found a bottle of water and had her rinse out her mouth and take a few swallows. She recovered enough to ask what he was going to do about the wounded man.

"Not a fucking thing. With any luck, he'll take a long time to die."

The patrol vehicle pulled up and the occupants got out, forming a hasty perimeter. The team leader slowed as he passed the screaming Mexican. "Sergeant Major?" he called.

"Leave him!" Grant answered. The team leader just shrugged. Whoever he was, the Sergeant Major didn't think he was worth saving, and that was good enough for him.

"You OK, Sergeant Major?"

"Yeah, we're good. Help the Major while I call this in." Grant looked into the vehicle. It looked like the dash was pretty shot up, and the radio was too. He hoped Sergeant Mitchell wouldn't be too mad about losing this truck. After all, it was a junk yard salvage job. Commo would be pissed about losing another radio though. He walked over to the patrol HUMMV, stopping on the way to snake the three rifles from the far side of the fence. He didn't feel like he was violating Mexican territory. A fact that most people on both sides of the border are unaware of, is that the United States is so careful about border encroachment that the fence is placed several feet inside the United States, in effect giving up thousands of acres to Mexico.

The Mexican was back to moaning now, getting fainter by the second. The bastard didn't take long enough to die as far as Grant was concerned. Anybody who could shoot women and children in the back with an automatic weapon deserved to linger. He cleared the rifles and put them on 'Safe' and laid them on the side of the road. If anyone asked, he would tell them they fell on to the US side. It would be true, and explaining the location of the fence on the border would just take too much time. He made his report to the CP. Nobody was going to be happy about this. The big question was, were these really Montoya's wife and children? And how did they know to have them here? And what was the message they were trying to send?

Sharp heard the radio calls and decided to head north to backup his friend. He left the rest of his reconnaissance section unpacking the sniper rifles. He had located a small valley a few clicks to the west that would be ideal for a one thousand yard range. He had already measured out and staked one hundred yard markers. The enforced down time would be a perfect opportunity to hone their skills and familiarize themselves with the weapons. He had even obtained some .50 BMG rounds at his own expense, and it was an expense at over $2.50 a round. Once he was comfortable with his teams' skills, he'd submit a requisition with the pukes in the S-4 shop. He hated dealing with them, but sometimes you had to bite the bullet, pun intended.

His driver, Sinclair slowed up and pointed to the North. "Something going on at the fence up there, Sarge."

Sharp picked up his glasses and gave it a quick look. There was a group of what looked like Mexican police lined up at the fence. What the hell were they doing there? "Go slow, Danny. This doesn't look good." And it wasn't. As they got closer Sharp could see exactly what was going on. They were lined up shoulder to shoulder on the Mexican side. There were ten of them, all in Mexican Police uniforms. Their hands were tied behind their backs. Their feet were pointed toward Mexico. Their heads were mounted on stakes on the US side.

Sharp looked over at his driver, who was starting to gag. "If you're gonna puke, Danny, do it outside of my fucking truck."

He disappeared behind the Hummer, and Sharp could hear him revisiting the ghosts of breakfast past. He checked his M-4 to make sure there was a round in the chamber and scanned the far side of the fence. He couldn't see anything, but that didn't mean shit. Anybody could be hiding in the maze of trails he knew were just beyond the fence. "You got that out of your system yet, Danny?"

"I think I do, Sarge."

"Then call this in. Tell them these bodies are fresh."

"How do you know?"

"The XO and the Sergeant Major went by here a while ago. I think they would have mentioned it if these guys were laying here." He thought for a second. "And call back to the rest of the recon section. Get them up here. We'll have to put off range time until another day."

As soon as the recon team came up, which was remarkably quick in Sharp's opinion, he headed north to where Grant was. Traffic was already building up. Mitchell was there with his recovery truck, looking pissed off that another one of his junk yard treasures was down for multiple gun shot wounds. He walked over to where Grant was standing with Bonneville. Looking around, his first question was "Where's the CO?"

"Funny you should ask. Seems like he got invited to a commander's call at Fort Huachuca. He took Fisher and Gaston with him." Meaning Operations and Supply. "That's why we got summoned back this morning. I guess Captain Menklin felt he was a tad out of his element and needed someone else to blame."

Sharp looked from Grant to Bonneville. "Blame?"

Bonneville answered. "General Vaughn showed up just as Kearney was pulling out. He had a stack of folders under his arm and was looking for someone to give them to. Menklin mentioned my name."

Sharp looked up and down the road. There was a lot of traffic approaching from both directions, some looked official, but most of it didn't. He noticed that someone had organized traffic control points on either side. Sergeant Robinson was in charge, and in spite of his best efforts, the traffic was starting to overwhelm his small detail.

"Want me to take over site security?"

"Yeah, keep the tourists out. You'll know who they are. Any questions, just call me. I'll come and handle it."

"How about officers?"

Grant thought for a moment. "If any more show up, send them to the Major. Everyone else, keep back."

Robinson was glad to get the help. Sharp gave him some instructions, which he acknowledged and hustled off to do his job. He turned and saw Price at the south end of the cordon. He called to Robinson to let him in. "I get the feeling there's going to be a lot of tourist traffic here pretty quick. Think you can get a couple of guys to secure an LZ over on the access road?"

"No problem. And I've already got some of my people helping with traffic control." He pointed to where a bucket loader was pulling across the road. On the other side, a bulldozer was filling the same role. There was a Blazer trying to squeeze by. The dozer operator stepped in front of it and smacked his hand down on the hood. The driver popped out and started yelling at him. Price smiled. "Well, well, well. It looks like my old buddy Sullivan managed to drag his ass down to the border this morning." He started to walk back, but Sharp stopped him. "You and him got a history. Want me to handle it?"

"Naw, that's what the little fucker is counting on. He's gonna cry that we're picking on him no matter who kicks his ass out of here. He doesn't have the balls to handle it man to man. I got it."

Price slung his rifle and ambled over to where Sullivan was starting to poke his finger into the operator's chest. He was trying to pull rank. Price heard part of the exchange. "You can't stop me, Specialist. I'm from the S-4 and I got every right to be here. Now get your ass out of my way before I write you up for insubordination!"

Price put his hand on the operators shoulder. "I got it, Paul." Was all he said to the operator. Then he turned on Sullivan. "Sullivan, don't tell me your lazy ass hasn't got something better to do today than be a fucking ghoul?"

Sullivan turned his attention to Price. "Tell this moron to get this piece of shit out of my way. You can't stop me from going over there."

"Yes he can, Sergeant."

Sullivan turned around with his hand raised. "You just keep the fuck out of this, pal . . ." He stopped in mid-sentence when he recognized Major Bonneville and the CSM. Bonneville brushed past him saying "You handle this, Sergeant Major."

Grant did. "What are you supposed to be doing today, Sergeant Sullivan?"

"I'm checking on fuel requirements, Sergeant Major. We didn't get a report last night."

"Didn't you submit the paperwork, Price?"

Price smiled. "I sent it to the S-4 last night. Remember, Sergeant Major? You were talking to him about getting a couple of extra pioneer sets."

Sullivan's face started to redden. "Well, he didn't give it to me, and I need to know."

Grant smiled. "I'll inform the Major. I'm certain she'll want to take it up with the S-4 when she gets back to headquarters." He paused, then stepped back and looked Sullivan up and down. "By the way, Sullivan, weren't you aware that all personnel coming out to the AO were to be in full gear, pot, armor and weapon? Where's yours?"

"I don't usually carry it with me, Sergeant Major. I thought that only applied to the line platoons."

"Nice try. You know better than that. Now you hustle your ass back to the HQ area. You see anybody on your way, you stop them and tell them this area is off limits unless they're assigned out here." Sullivan turned and walked away. Grant called after him. "And, Sullivan, make sure the Motor Pool gets that vehicle back. SFC Mitchell has already gotten a report that it was stolen. You of all people should know better than to leave the area without a proper dispatch. Turn in those spare keys you keep on that ring of yours too. You're not authorized, got it?"

They watched as Sullivan backed the Blazer and sped back up the road.

"Everything that's going on and I have to deal with children."

"Careful, Luke. He'll probably go to the IG again."

"I don't doubt it. That little son of a bitch is rapidly turning into another Winder. I can imagine what he'll be like with another stripe or two." Grant turned around to give the area another quick sweep. "Have somebody drive the Major back to the CP. I don't want anyone traveling alone. Send an escort with her."

"What are you going to do?"

"The alphabet agencies will probably be here pretty soon. I'd rather have them fighting with the Mexicans over custody of the bodies. I'll stay long enough to take the blame for those three mutts."

"They all yours?"

"Linda got the one who was still moaning a few minutes ago."

"I think he finally died."

"Good for him." He paused as Bonneville drove off. He could tell she wasn't happy with an escort. "As soon as we get this place secured," he told Sharp, "I've got a one star who's really trying to fuck up the rest of my life."

Several kilometers up the road Sullivan was still stewing about the put down he got from Grant and Price, or 'those two fucking ass holes' as he referred to them to people he thought he kept in check. His partner was still snickering about it, despite Sullivan's repeated efforts to tell him to shut the fuck up. His influence among the junior enlisted in the Staff sections was starting to wane. Even the new piece of shit over in the S-3 shop, Callan, was constantly fucking with him, always telling him he wasn't authorized to go snooping through the briefing boards in the Ops tent or denying him access to the secure network.

The old bastards running the company were into all kinds of shit. He knew it, and everybody knew it. Even Rosie in Columbus was always asking about what they were doing, because they heard 'things' as she put it. She was starting to cool off a little because he couldn't come up with the war stories she liked to hear. Even the rest of the bar flies in that tavern weren't paying him as much attention, or fronting for his drinks, as they used to. They all used to hang on his every word, but now they seemed to know when he was just passing a load of bull shit. That would have to change, and he knew what it would take. A couple of the after action reports off the classified net would put him back in the limelight. He just had to convince Gaston to let him use one of the laptops the staff left behind when they went to Huachuca.

Chapter 9

The public reaction from Mexico on the killings was more subdued that anyone expected. That was in spite of the fact that there were several problems for Mexican spin doctors to overcome, and they lacked the sophistication to craft a believable story on short notice. First and foremost was the fact that the Montoya family had been kidnapped over 100 miles from the border after the premature notice of her husband dying on the police raid. Witnesses swore that the men who took the family were wearing military uniforms and had been driving military vehicles. There was a report that she called out to one of the neighbors that the Army was taking her to a safe location in Mexico City. They were having trouble explaining how the family ended up dead on the border, killed by her Mexican Army escorts.

Secondly, the *Federale* police detachment that had been butchered on the fence was also in the wrong place when they died. They were supposedly part of a larger force that was assigned to secure that sector after Montoya was reported dead. Their commander reported that he had sent them several kilometers to the north of where they were found. His report had been broadcast live on Mexican television, and they were having trouble with the retractions of that story.

The Mexican government did file an official, and public, protest with the US State Department, Department of Defense, Homeland Security and anyone else who would listen. The blame for the upsurge in violence, they claimed, was the provocative presence of the American Army on the border. These soldiers, they pointed out, were the very same ones who had committed so many criminal acts in Africa. There were American politicians who echoed the same sentiment. Bonneville felt the end of their mission wouldn't be long in coming. Grant wasn't so sure. "Everyone expects us to pull in our heads and lay low until this all blows over. This would be the time to finish the job." He went on to explain what he meant. "We've already done all the planning and recon. We know all the areas, we have our approaches laid out, and we have a pretty good tactical plan. All we need are some heavy weapons, a shit load of demo, and two nights to cache it all. Then we can go in and take it all out in a couple of hours."

"Aren't you assuming they won't be expecting you?"

General Vaughn interrupted. "After everything that's been happening, do you still think you can get in, wreck their infrastructure and get out without any casualties?"

"I'm hoping we can. You know as well as I do all the good intentions in the world are out the window as soon as the first round goes down range."

Bonneville was more realistic. "You know damn well if you go over there with the bulk of the company some of them are coming back injured, maybe worse. Do you think it's still worth the effort?"

Grant nodded. "I do, and deep down so do you. You were right there when the bastards killed that family. There was no hesitation, and it didn't look like they would have minded taking us out too. Yeah, I still think it's worth it, and so do those soldiers out there who have to keep policing up the guns, drugs and bodies they keep leaving all over the place."

Vaughn spoke up. "He's right. You've disrupted their operations and called a lot of attention to the area. This was a backwater before. They liked it quiet, and now they want it to go back to being quiet. The chatter we're picking up has them standing down and waiting to see what our government does. They'll be rebuilding their infrastructure and stockpiling product to move a lot in a hurry as soon as you're gone." He looked around the tent. "Grant is right. Now is the time. You said you need three things: time, heavy weapons and demo. How much of each will you need?"

"Before we get to that point, what about Kearney? He's still the commander."

"Kearney won't be back in time. I'll see to it." Grant and Bonneville exchanged looks. Cutting the commander out of an operation was a serious step. Vaughn continued. "When this all goes off, Major Bonneville, you will be the defacto commander of the 289th. It'll be up to you to supervise and approve the planning, and on a 'Go' order you will execute. Is that clear?"

Bonneville looked at Grant. He didn't look convinced. She had to make her own decision, and she did. "I can do this."

"I'm sure you can. Do you have anything to add before I close the subject, Sergeant Major?"

"Yeah. I wish she would have told you to let this cup pass."

"It sounds biblical, Sergeant Major. I didn't know you were a religious man."

"I'm not. It was what Christ said in the garden right after he figured out he was going to die the next day. He may have been committed to his cause, but I really think he would have taken an out if one were handed to him."

"I've already made up my mind." Bonneville said.

"In that case, Major, as your Command Sergeant Major it will be my pleasure to hang on the cross with you." He turned to Vaughn. "Here" and passed his lists over. "Once we get what we need, I want two nights to preposition the gear that'll be too heavy to haul in one night. We'll go the third night. I don't want the boots on the ground exhausted from heavy hauling before they light the candle." There was a pause as he fished out another list. "Here's what I want." Vaughn noted that he said 'want', not 'need'. He looked over the list and passed it on to a civilian sitting next to him. Grant watched the civilian's eyebrows raised, then he passed the list back to Vaughn. "I can handle this" he said to Vaughn. Then to Grant, "When do you want it?"

Grant looked over at Sharp. Sharp shrugged. "You give it to me tomorrow and we can start moving it across the border tomorrow night. Barring any problems, we can light the candle two nights later."

Vaughn conferred with the civilian in low tones. Most of it seemed to be a matter of fact discussion. He finally finished and gave them the go ahead. They could spend the day planning, and Sharp could pick up his supplies in Columbus the next morning.

"You've got all this shit available in Columbus?"

"Sergeant Sharp, you would be amazed at what the Border Patrol picks up quite by accident. We have all this and more." Grant and Sharp looked at each other and exchanged nods. Grant looked at Vaughn. "I want to add one more target."

"Which is?"

He walked to the large map that dominated one side of the tent. He pointed to the location of the *hacienda* with the lookout tower and armed guards. "This is Apuestas's local headquarters. There's a small motor pool located just a little ways behind it. We need to take this out. Otherwise, he has a base to use to rebuild his empire as soon as we're done."

"What will it take?"

Sharp answered for him. "Twenty men, a 60mm mortar, and all five sniper systems." He paused. "And a half hour head start."

"Why the head start?"

Sharp walked over to the map. "If we hit them up north and nothing is going on in the rest of the valley it'll pull any extra troops they've got off the other sites, making them softer targets for the elements."

"And what do you do with the troops moving north?"

Grant stepped in. He pointed to the long access road that angled away to the east from the border. "Just before Sharp starts his attack, we'll secure this road to here," he pointed to the second airstrip at *las Castillo*. "This is the natural choke point."

The civilian asked a question. "What will you use to secure it?"

"First, I'll use a dismounted squad, eight men with SAWs and M-203s. Then we'll bring up a couple of Hummers with mounted .50s to block the road."

Vaughn whistled. "You'll have most of your weight up north?"

"Yeah," Sharp answered, "the heaviest element of the whole op, but if we don't take out the hacienda they'll still have the organization and base to rebuild in a hurry. And if we don't take it out quick, every little rat in the valley will get called in to defend it. And if the Sergeant Major doesn't take *las Castillo*, they'll have time to get there. I need the weapons to take it out fast, and the troops to mop up or react to any countermove. Then we can use their own vehicles for our retrograde movement, or to move further south in a hurry to support the other elements."

"You've spent a lot of time thinking about this. How do you propose to make your approach in and out in one night? That's one hell of a hike."

Now Grant stepped in. "It's only a hike if we go from this side. Our plan is to go in from the north."

Vaughn considered the plan for a few minutes. "There are some problems with your plan, but on the whole it looks good. I'll just have to truncate your timeline. Two nights of prep before you go is too long. The most I'd authorize is one night before you go." Grant conferred with Sharp. They agreed it was doable with the tighter schedule.

"All right then. Do it. Show me all your planning elements later on tonight. Try to remember that this is just a raid. We don't intend to occupy any territory or overthrow the government."

"Too bad. I think Price would have made one hell of a *presidente*."

At the evening meeting Vaughn had approved the plans with very little revision. He had given them a bonus by arranging two medevac helicopters to be staged in their area in case of emergency. There were to be no American dead or wounded left on the Mexican side. The helicopters would start making regular runs in and out of the bivouac sites the next morning. Part of the deception plan would be several hours before the launch one would broadcast in the clear that it had an emergency and would be settling down in the southernmost LZ. The second would be dispatched with 'parts' and ordered to remain in the area, 'just in case.' Helicopters had periodically come and gone ferrying different civilian and military VIPs into the area, and it was well known that the Mexicans routinely monitored aircraft frequencies in the area, to the point of cutting in to warn pilots when they looked like they were getting too close to Mexican air space.

Grant and his NCOs were feeling pretty good about the plan, and held an impromptu question and answer session in Grant's tent to give everyone an opportunity to make suggestions, changes or point out potential problems. There were only small details to work out, and a bottle was eventually produced. Bonneville shared one drink with them. Before she got too caught up in their celebration she begged off. She said she was very tired. Grant stepped outside with her.

"Any last minute advice, Luke?"

"Take this cup from my lips?"

"You already said that."

"Best I can come up with. I really think Vaughn is setting us up to take a pretty big hit. Whatever we do is going to be traced right back to us in a big fucking hurry. And if it doesn't work I can see him disappearing into the woodwork and leaving your ass out on a limb."

"Aren't you the military genius who suggested most of this?"

"I am, and I hope it doesn't turn into another charge of the light brigade."

She smiled. "I know. I also believe you won't leave my ass hanging out."

"No, Ma'am. It's such a pretty ass. I've grown rather fond of it."

She turned and walked away. Over her shoulder she casually called, "And I'll be with the support vehicles."

Grant didn't know she was planning to go across the border with them. She was taking her leadership role seriously in all this. He caught up to her. "When did you decide to do that?"

"I've planned it all along. I've already briefed the General, and he agreed with me."

"Vaughn would agree to anything that gets us over the border. Trust me; he doesn't have your best interests at heart. That's why he got Kearney out of the way. He's got so much deniability built into this operation that we could all disappear into some Mexican prison and he'd still be in the clear."

"I'm still the commander. My place is with the troops. Captain Blackman and the First Sergeant can control the rear operations. My forward CP will be with the blocking force."

"I don't think that's a place you want to be."

"Where do you think I should be, back here? In the rear with the gear, as you like to say?"

"That's not what I meant. Set up a forward CP on the border. There's no need to come any further forward."

"Is that what you would have said to Kearney?"

That comment caught him off guard. She was right, and they both knew it. It was an argument he shouldn't have even tried to make. "No, you're right. You're the Commander, and your position is anywhere you damn well want it to be." He stood back and saluted. "I was thinking emotionally, and I stand corrected, Ma'am."

Harrison had stepped out and watched as they left, Grant walking her back to her tent. He saw the animated conversation going on, and could tell Grant was on the losing side. The salute confirmed it. When he came back the First Sergeant asked if everything was all right. "Yeah, Ralph. All of a sudden the burden of command sat its fat ass down on her shoulders, and all she did was shrug."

"Is she going to be OK?"

"She's doing better than I thought she would. The training is kicking in, and she's starting to add her own touches. The personal involvement wasn't letting me be objective." He told Harrison about her plan to go with the vehicles to the blocking position.

"That's not a good idea."

"It may not be, but I've already lost that argument."

"You may have created a monster, Luke. When this is over, she won't want to give the Group back to Kearney."

The next morning Grant planted himself in the operations tent to spend some time going over the plans before he headed out to the platoons to check on their preparations and rehearsals. All the platoons were operating a normal patrol schedule while they started to integrate their support people into the routine. The bulk of all the line platoons would be across the line, but the patrols had to be kept up until the assaults started so any Mexican watchers would believe that there had been no changes in the routine. As they got closer to the operation, a curious Mexican was a dangerous Mexican.

Bonneville joined him for a while, and they shared a cup of coffee before she was distracted by SFC Callan. Callan was usually on top of things, but he seemed to be having problems with some of the other staff this morning. Bonneville asked if she could do anything to smooth things over for him.

"With the CO, S-2 and S-3 gone, I figured this would be a good time to collect their laptops and do a security audit."

"What's the problem?"

"Well, the S-3 took his with him, and Colonel left his here in the CP. I haven't been able to locate the S-2's yet."

"Did he take his with him too?" Bonneville asked.

"No Ma'am. He left his with the S-4, but Captain Gaston says he can't seem to locate it right now."

"That's not an acceptable answer. Get Gaston over here, and tell him he better have that laptop." Callan made the call on his field phone. Grant looked up over the edge of his paperwork at the direction the one sided conversation seemed to be taking. Apparently, Captain Gaston didn't seem to recognize his new position in the universe now that Major Bonneville, the XO, was now the de facto commander. She took the phone from SFC Callan and refreshed his memory. Grant was proud of her. She was growing into her new position and responsibilities nicely, and proceeded to verbally make mince meat of Gaston over the phone. Her last word to him was "Now!" before she slammed down the phone. Grant dropped his head back down to his papers. He took a quick glance out the tent flap to see Gaston running over with a laptop in his hands. Grant could see the 'S-4' stencil on the lid. That was not the computer Bonneville wanted.

He had it opened as he walked in the door and put it on the desk. Bonneville fixed him with a cold stare. "Was that so hard, Captain Gaston?"

Before he could answer Grant coughed to catch Callan's attention. When the Operations NCO looked his way, Grant just shook his head.

Bonneville and Gaston both noticed it. "What's that supposed to mean, Sergeant Major?" Bonneville demanded.

"That's the wrong computer, Ma'am." And he went back to reading. Bonneville closed the screen and looked at the stencil. "And where, might I ask, is the computer I told you to bring?"

Gaston stammered. "I, I, I let Sergeant Sullivan use it to do some of his requisitions."

Callan cut in. "That's not possible, Ma'am. All the laptops are linked into the main network. They're all password protected. Only the users can get into them to access the net and any information on them."

"How is Sullivan using it then?" Bonneville demanded.

"Captain Menklin loans his computer out a lot, usually to the other staff officers. He has the password written on a piece of tape on the keyboard. I didn't think it would be a problem letting Sergeant Sullivan use it."

Grant stifled a derisive chuckle and tried to avoid dirty looks from both Bonneville and Gaston. Somehow he didn't think an innocent look would work, so he excused himself and decided to try to beg, borrow or steal a new vehicle from the Motor Pool. Sergeant Mitchell took it very personally every time the platoons got one of his trucks shot up, even if it was one of the obsolete Blazers he had rescued from the Fort Bliss bone yard.

Grant walked over to the maintenance tent, an oversized canvas Quonset hut. SFC Mitchell was standing next to a work bench, pieces of an instrument panel scattered about. It was probably the one from the truck Grant got shot up. Mitchell would have to rebuild it if he wanted to reuse it. There weren't any spares for a 30 year old Chevy in the system. He looked up to see Grant beckon, so he wiped his hands and walked over.

"What can I do for you today, Sergeant major?"

"I need a vehicle. It doesn't have to be anything special. I can use another one of the old Blazers if there's another one lying around."

Mitchell got a funny look on his face. Grant wondered what he had said that was so confusing. "Is there a problem with that, Sergeant Mitchell?"

"What was wrong with the one I gave you? You break it already?"

"I haven't been anywhere to break anything. When did I get it?"

"I left it for you two or three hours ago, out in your parking spot. All cleaned, fueled, 2404'd and dispatched, ready for any abuse you cared to give it."

Now it was Grant's turn to get a funny look on his face. "There's nothing out in my spot, and I haven't been anywhere." Mitchell walked past him and went outside. His head swiveled as he checked the compound. "It was parked right over there, Sergeant Major. I thought I saw you pull out with it a while ago. Somebody must have moved it." Grant went back inside and cranked the field phone.

"What was the bumper number?"

"Headquarters- 9. I thought you'd like the touch." The switch answered and he had them connect him to the front gate. Harrison had taken to keeping a sentry there to control vehicle flow in and out, and to keep track of where all the headquarters platoon people were disappearing to. He asked the sentry to check the log for his vehicle. He wasn't happy with the answer.

"It went out about an hour or so ago, Sergeant Major. Sergeant Sullivan said he was on his way to Bliss for supplies."

I should have known, Grant thought. "Did you check the trip ticket?"

"Roger that, Sergeant Major. I tried to bust his chops asking him what he had to promise you to get you to sign your dispatch over to him."

Grant threw the phone down and walked back to the operations tent. Bonneville was finishing up with Gaston and he was preparing to leave. Grant interrupted "We have another problem, Ma'am."

Gaston put on his hat to leave. "You don't need me for this."

Grant put his hand up to stop him. "Oh yes we do, Captain." He paused for effect. Bonneville had a puzzled, one step away from annoyed look. "Sergeant Sullivan has left the reservation, Major. And he probably has that laptop with him."

"Where did he go?"

"I'm not sure at this point. He probably went into Columbus to see his lady friend. He told the gate guard he was picking up supplies at Bliss."

"I thought vehicles were controlled through the Motor Pool and only issued with authorization. What did Sergeant Mitchell have to say about that?"

"Mitchell's off the hook on this one. Sullivan took my Blazer and forged my signature on the dispatch. Gate guard didn't think he would have to double check that."

Bonneville's face was getting redder. Grant had always wondered how long it would take her to go from zero to ballistic: now he knew. "Captain Gaston, you are his direct supervisor. I hold you responsible for his actions."

"That's not fair, Major! There are two NCOs in the chain between me and him. I have to rely on their judgment when it comes to supervising the section."

"That's not quite true." Everybody turned around to see First Sergeant Harrison standing in the tent doorway. "The Captain here has gone out of his way on several occasions to go to bat for Sullivan and let him get his way. Even his section NCOs have complained that they have little or no control over Sullivan because you protect him so much." He looked at Gaston. "I guess that's come home to bite you in the ass."

"You know what's going on, Top?"

"I heard. Now what are we going to do about it?"

Both NCOs looked towards Bonneville. Grant knew what he would do, but he figured he should let her make the call first. She was, after all, the acting Commander.

"Sergeant Sharp is in Columbus drawing equipment from the Border Patrol. Call him and have him stop Sullivan and recover that laptop."

"Do you want Sullivan back here?"

"I want that laptop. I don't care how Sergeant Sharp does it." That was exactly the idea Grant had. He gave her a big smile. "I'll let Sergeant Sharp know."

Sharp had gotten an early start to pick up the gear the Border Patrol guy had promised. He had gotten together with all the platoon Sergeants to make absolutely sure they got what they thought they would need, then the Sergeant Major and the First Sergeant reviewed it and added their own wish list. There was enough gear on it that Sharp felt justified bringing a 5 ton cargo truck along with the two Hummers. They'd be hauling quite a bit of weight back. The same guy who made the promise was waiting for them at the Immigration and Customs Enforcement compound near the border crossing in Columbus. He pointed them in the direction of a low slung storage building on the far side of the parking lot. It was surrounded by a barbed wire topped chain link fence, and there was an armed guard box by the vehicle gate. The two civilians exchanged words, and the gate was swung open. Sharp was directed to the second overhead door. He pointed back to the first one. "What's in there?"

"Drugs" was the answer, "lots and lots of drugs. We pick the shit up faster than we can move it out to be incinerated. The cartels are willing to risk some serious losses to get their product over here, and we try to oblige them."

The second door opened, and the 5 ton was directed to back in. Sharp looked around in awe. This section was filled with piles of weapons. There weren't any racks, and it didn't look like there was any effort to safeguard them from abuse or mishandling. They were just stacked in what looked like categories. "Holy shit! I'll bet you guys know how to throw a party!"

He ignored the comment. "You want to take your guys over to the left. That's the US military pile."

There were several piles, and behind them were stacks of ammo cans, wooden crates and cardboard boxes. "What's in the boxes?"

"That's ammo. We'll get to that later."

"This is all stuff you pick up on the border?"

"All this, and a lot more. Anything that remotely resembles US Military gear, old or new, gets returned to the Army. That includes old Springfield rifles, M-1s, BARs, you name it. The rest we offer to other agencies, which shall remain nameless, and what's left goes to the chopper."

"Chopper?"

"Yeah. Captain Crunch, a 25 ton hydraulic chopper makes little pieces out of it."

Gunrunning from the US into Mexico was one of the great myths of the Mexican drug war. The most convenient scapegoat to be found was the United States Constitution's 2nd Amendment, and, by extension the US National Rifle Association and American gun owners in general. Mexican politicians used the myth to avoid their responsibility for the tremendous amount of smuggling coming into their country from all over the Caribbean basin. US politicians jumped on it as another opportunity to show how evil and degenerate American gun owners were. The truth was almost at polar opposites of what everyone would have the world believing.

The military grade weapons the cartels were using weren't generally available in the US. Sure, they could be had, but the process was drawn out, heavily regulated and expensive. Gun runners couldn't walk into a gun show and walk out with several hundred fully automatic weapons, and semi-auto rifles aren't that easy to convert into fully automatic weapons without an investment in parts and machining. Cost was prohibitive, too, even for an organization awash in illegal money. A semi-auto AR-15 cost an average of $900 to $1200 on the open market, even more on the black market, in the United States. A fully automatic M-16, the military version, costs anywhere from $8,000 and up. There was a cheaper source. The United States has sold or given hundreds of thousands of weapons to various countries in Central and South America. The former Eastern Bloc of Europe, as well as Cuba, Nicaragua and Venezuela, have also provided hundreds of thousands of weapons to friendly states or insurgencies. These are the weapons that have been captured, stolen or diverted into the same drug smuggling routes that reach into Mexico. An honest appraisal of weapons seized by law enforcement in Mexico would reveal a weapon that might have been made in the United States, but was sold to a legitimate foreign government law enforcement agency or military. This is an incredibly inconvenient truth that politicians on both sides of the border would rather keep hidden.

These weapons are needed by the drug cartels to protect their territories, their inventories, and their trafficking routes, or to wage a campaign of terror against the government or average citizens who get in their way. They are regularly included, along with ammunition, in the shipments that move north of the border to protect their wholesale and retail hubs in the border states and beyond. Large amounts of weapons and ammunition are regularly seized by the Border Patrol, sometimes with drug shipments, and sometimes on their own. Like the confiscated narcotics, they occupy and impressive amount of warehouse space. Every US made weapon can be traced back to its point of origin, and then on to all subsequent users until it drops out of legitimate use. The last owner is most likely the agency responsible for the weapon entering the illicit stream, and in almost every case, that last owner was a Latin American agency or military.

Sharp went through and picked out what he wanted. He got his .50 caliber MGs and mounts, Squad automatic weapons and M-16s with under slung grenade launchers. He even found two complete 60mm mortars. There was a pile of M1911A1 pistols to one side. Sharp picked out a half dozen that looked to be in pristine condition, all marked 'U.S. Property' and grabbed a box of new looking magazines. These were much better than the Argentine clones Grant was fond of using. Sharp would keep one for himself to replace the Tokarev and give the rest to Grant as a peace offering. They all went on the trucks. He mentally totaled up ammo requirements and handed them to the civilian. "Can you fill that?"

"Sure, and I'll even make it easy on you. I'll have a forklift run it out into the parking lot. The 40mm grenades and the 60mm rounds are kept in a separate shed. I'll have that brought out too."

On the way out he looked at a crate full of sub-machine guns he had never seen before. He stopped to pick one up and examine it. "What the hell is this supposed to be?"

The agent took it from him, dropped the magazine and worked the bolt. This particular piece of crap is called a 'Mendoza'. The Mexicans make them in a backyard plant in Mexico City. They tried to sell them to the army, kind of on the lines of the Uzi, but the army didn't want any part of them. The government ended up pushing them off to the local police forces."

Sharp took the weapon back and manipulated the controls and worked the bolt. It seemed to be fairly well built and robust. It was a simple blowback operated weapon, more like a Sten gun than an Uzi, although they were similar. "How does it run?"

"From what I've heard it's pretty reliable, but I don't know anybody who's ever had to use one."

"Why is it a piece of crap?"

"Mainly because of the caliber. They could have been had in .45 ACP, 9 Luger, or .38 auto. All three magazines are different enough to cause problems with the wrong gun. Their supply services being what they are, the guns, ammo and mags sometimes got mixed up at the wrong time. Once they straightened that out, it was still a pistol caliber. It's good for clearing a house, but it's not something you'd want to take against a rifle out in the open. This batch is all in .38 auto."

Sharp turned it over in his hands a few times. "Could I get a few of these?"

The agent looked at is paperwork. "I guess so. These haven't been logged in on any inventory yet, so there's no paper trail. Throw the box on your truck. The spare magazines are in that box next to it. I'll see if I can find some ammo for you too."

The ammo was waiting at the Border Patrol station as the civilian had promised. There was even a cardboard box marked '.38 A.C.P.' There were a lot of sideways glances and double-checking of documents as the military truck was passed through the checkpoint and into the parking area. There were more strange looks as the cargo was wordlessly brought and placed onto the trucks. Sharp signed for thousands of rounds of mixed ammo. He was glad he had brought three trucks. This was an overload.

Sharp gave their contact at the station a looked worried. "Are you sure this is legal? I've never heard of anything like this before. How are you going to account for it?"

"Same way I always do. I transfer it to the US Army. You're the US Army. Everybody will be happy. Just sign here."

"My own name?"

"I don't even care about that. See that camera" he pointed to a pole in the corner of the lot, "and this letter here?" He indicated a sheet of paper at the bottom of the pile on his clip board. "I'm covered. Besides, you think I used my real name? I've been in this business way too long."

Sharp grunted. Paperwork and cameras, a record that would last forever. They should have just picked a spot on the border, backed up two trucks and swapped loads. Fewer prying eyes, fewer questions. "Paperwork's signed by enough people on both sides to start another country. If it ain't legal, I don't know what is." What was left unsaid was that like the names they were using, most of the names weren't of real people.

"That's a lot of ammo, Sergeant," the agent volunteered as they finished stacking it. "It ought to get you through a few bad days."

"Not hardly. A full platoon, thirty guys, with M-4s and SAWs firing one magazine or belt, is into the second can in less than a minute. A basic load for a company is about a quarter of this, not counting grenades, 40mm, and 7.62." He paused for effect. "I don't know too many grunts that carry a basic load after the first time out." The agent was impressed.

Sharp radioed in before they headed out to give the head shed an ETA. He checked his crews to make certain they were all locked and loaded. This was a lot of firepower. He was surprised when Grant came up on the net. "Dave, turn on your phone. I don't want this over the air."

Sharp did what he was told and got the word to be on the lookout for Sullivan. He muttered a few choice words and told Grant he'd take care of it. He already knew where the Mexican bar was.

"Who's that?" he heard Robinson ask.

"That was the Sergeant Major. We've got another little errand to run."

"No, I didn't mean who was on the phone. I meant up there." He pointed towards the town. "A Blazer just pulled off the border road." Sharp lifted his field glasses to try to catch sight of the bumper numbers. He couldn't make them out, but he recognized the castle painted on the rear fender. It was Kearney's way of identifying all the vehicles in the Group. That had to be the little weasel Sullivan. His timing couldn't have been better. He hopped out of his truck and called to the border agent.

"Hey, can I get one more favor from you guys?"

They were in a three vehicle column of unmarked white Toyota trucks watching the Blazer pull up in front of run down looking bar. A uniform got out, looked around, and disappeared in the front door. Sharp could see the laptop in his grubby little hands.

"Son of a bitch!"

"Friend of yours?"

"Yeah, an old buddy." It was Sullivan. "You know anything about that place?"

"Mexican bar. Local cops keep an eye on it for drugs and gangs. What's he doing in there?"

"That's what I'm going to find out." Sharp started to strip off his MOLLE gear, but the agent stopped him. ""They'll probably notice the uniform. Let me go." The agent crossed the street and walked by the front of the building, leaning in to look through the window, then he went inside. He was back out in a few minutes, holding onto two beers. He passed one to Sharp as he got into the truck. Sharp looked down at the beer. "You can drink on duty?"

"I'm not drinking it." Sharp nodded and took the other beer.

"What's going on?"

"It looks like your buddy is into selling off surplus computer equipment. He was demonstrating the new and improved functions to one of the head honcho Mexicans. It appeared to satisfy their requirements."

Sharp looked at him. "You always talk like that?"

"Only when I haven't got the slightest fucking idea what I'm talking about."

Inside the bar, Sullivan was sweating as he waited for Cardozo to come out. The Mexicans had slapped him around a bit before he could convince them that they needed to see what he had brought them. When Cardozo finally emerged Sullivan fired up the laptop and typed in the password. He was streaming through the directories when someone walked in the front door. When he just indicated to the bartender that he wanted two beers to go, they ignored him.

"This is everything they have planned, *Jefe*, I swear. This is a classified computer. You can even access their network."

Cardozo didn't understand everything he was looking at, but that didn't matter. There were others who would know what it meant, and he would leave it to them to be happy or mad. He put his hand on Sullivan's shoulder. "You did good, *gringo.* You better go back now."

"I can't go back! They know I took this. It'll only be a matter of time before they come looking for me. Can I stay here for a while until the heat is off me?"

Cardozo didn't think that was a good idea. The *gringos* might know this is where Sullivan might come. "No, *Gringo.* That's not a good idea. I'll have *Rosalita* take you some place safe. He went out back and spoke quickly to the Mexican whore. He handed her a set of car keys. "Take this *gringo* to the migrant house. Keep him quiet, make him happy if you want, and kill him." He handed her a little plastic bag. "There'll be more of this when you get back."

Sharp saw Sullivan come out with the Mexican woman in tow. Christ, she looked like a handful. They got into an old sedan and drove off. Sharp called back to the second truck in line. "Follow the little fucker. If I can't get the computer back, I'll take it out on his sorry ass!" After he pulled out he called to the third truck. "After I go in one of you grab the Blazer and bring it back to the weapons truck. Stay there until we get back."

The agent looked at him. "Are you going in there?"

"Not if you've got a better idea."

"Sure. There's your computer coming out now. Grab it on the street and let's get the fuck out of here!" The agent pointed to a Mexican who was walking across the street towards the truck parked in front of them. Sharp waited until he was getting in the cab when he jumped out and ran between the vehicles, his rifle coming up. He reached for the handle and pulled the door open, the muzzle of his M-4 jamming into the Mexican's neck, just below his jaw. He heard the agent coming up behind him. "What the fuck are you doing? Grab the laptop and go!"

"Can you speak Spanish? Translate for me."

The Mexican tilted his head and slowly spoke. "I speak English, *gringo*. You know who I am?"

"I don't give a fuck who you are, *amigo*. What did the little fuck give you in there?"

"*Nada*."

"Bullshit!" Sharp yanked him out of the truck and threw him to the ground, his rifle still in his neck. People on the street were starting to notice the commotion. Some did the sensible thing and ignored it and walked away. Some stopped and watched. One went into the bar.

"You've got about thirty seconds before it gets ugly out here! Let's go!"

Sharp flipped the Mexican over and jammed his muzzle into his mouth. The eyes went wide, and Sharp could tell his *amigo* had lost control of his bodily functions. Sharp leaned the barrel in a little harder and reached into the cab and grabbed the laptop. A quick glance told him it was Army issued, a big 'S-2" stenciled on it, so he assumed it was the one he wanted. He looked some more, and came up with a stainless steel Berretta tucked into the Mexicans waistband. He dropped it into his cargo pocket, then found and took the spare magazines. There was some shouting coming from the direction of the bar. Sharp looked up towards the noise and back down at his prisoner. He pulled the Mexican to his feet. "What's your name, *amigo*?"

"*Esteban*"

"Well, Little Stevie, tell your friends everything is fine and they should go back in."

"A word from me and they will kill you!"

"Yeah, but guess who gets dead first? Tell them!" He emphasized it with more pressure on the rifle barrel. Little Stevie said something to his friends. They backed up on the sidewalk, but didn't go in the bar. Sharp grunted. "Close enough." He looked into the cab of the truck and spotted the tail end of a folding stock AK-47 sticking out from under the seat. When he pulled it out, there was a bandoleer of spare magazines wrapped around the barrel. He threw it over his shoulder, and told the agent, "Drop your tailgate, and turn the truck around so we can get in."

"What are you going to do?"

"I'll be right with you." He backed the Mexican up and out into the middle of the street, keeping his rifle stuck in his neck. The agent pulled the truck around and Sharp backed up and sat on the tailgate. "Tell your *amigos* if they move before we reach the corner, I shoot you, then them."

"I'll see you again, *gringo*!"

"I'm sure you will, but if you're smart, you'll forget this ever happened." He called over his shoulder, "Drive slow and stop at the corner." The agent did as he was told. When they got there Sharp pushed the Mexican to the ground. "The next time we meet I may not have to be as courteous, so you might want to take some pains to avoid that." He kept his rifle on him as the agent drove away.

Back at the Border station he waited for a report on Sullivan. When he got the information he gave it to the Border agent. "Think you can have the local PD pick up a deserter for me?"

"Would they be interested in him?"

"Tell them he stole a weapon and is trying to move some drugs. They might be interested." He shook hands with the agent and got back in his Hummer.

"What about that shit back at the bar?"

"Listen, Pal, I was just following orders, so my boss isn't going to have me filling out paperwork for the next three days. If that's how you want to spend your time, that's fine with me, but somebody might decide to ask you what you were thinking about when you came with me and didn't interfere. I'll bet they don't want you walking into drug bars without backup either." Sharp convinced him that his best course of action was to pretend none of this happened. "You're wearing a hat, dark glasses and an unmarked uniform. The trucks were impounds with Mexican plates, and the gate was hanging over it. You're either in the clear, or you're in deeper shit than me."

"What about the guns?" He meant the AK and the Berretta.

"These are easier for me to explain than you. I can get rid of them in Mexico some dark night and nobody will be the wiser. You walk into the office with them, and you have to come up with a story and three days of report writing. The best you come out is aiding and abetting or conspiracy. As it stands, I'll swear to Christ you took me into town to grab a quick beer. My people will believe that. I have a history." The agent though about it and didn't respond. He knew his job security rested with going along with Sharp.

"Where'd you get the AK, Sarge?" Robinson asked.

"I took it off a drunk Mexican. Now shut up and forget you saw it."

Robinson just put up his hands, dropped the truck in gear, and drove off. Even a simple errand with Sergeant Sharp was always an adventure.

Across the street, in the Braga family café, the State Police Drug Task Force was monitoring their listening devices inside. No one suspected anything out of the ordinary when Sullivan pulled up. He was a regular visitor, and the Mexicans were using Rosie the prostitute to turn him into their mole. What did raise a few eyebrows was the small convoy of trucks that seemed to follow him up the street.

"Somebody better get Braga up here. I think something is about to go down over there."

Before Braga came they listened as Sullivan described the laptop he had brought them. The two State Troopers looked at each other, realizing that this could be serious. They heard a voice give Rosie her instructions to kill the American soldier. Braga was just coming in when Sullivan and the girl came out and drove off with one of the white Toyotas following.

"You better get the local PD to stop them someplace and hold them for us. Don't let them make any phone calls. That Army Sergeant Major doesn't have much use for that little fucker, but I don't think he wants him killed."

The Mexican known as Cardozo exited the bar and went to his truck. The State Police watched as Sergeant Sharp ran up to Cardozo and their little drama played out.

"You want me to call in some help, Mel?"

Braga shook his head. "Just watch. I don't want to fuck up two years of surveillance because some GI decided to take out a drug smuggler. Besides, he seems to have the situation under control."

And Sharp did. They watched as he recovered the laptop and several guns, as well as arrange his own escape.

"What do you think, Mel? Should we report this?"

"Yeah, call it in, but try not to panic anyone. Tell them it looks like the Army was trying to get one of their own back. It sure as hell wasn't legal, but I doubt that Cardozo is going to file a complaint with the Columbus Police Department."

"Can you tell if they accessed anything important?" Grant was concerned the Mexicans may have been able to access the network. Sharp had just dropped the laptop off and went to start his equipment breakdown. There was a place on the map called Tank #7 South, where he would be staging from and he was in a hurry to get to it. It was located almost due north of the *hacienda* and a fairly easy hike in. The Border Patrol maintained a small station that was manned 24 hours a day that could serve as a secure equipment dump, bivouac area and, if need be, rally point if the whole operation went bad. Once he broke the loads down and issued it to the other platoons there would be a quick briefing update from Grant. After that his entire assault team would be at this remote location, getting updates by phone or e-mail.

Callan had one of his section computer geeks going over the internal logs to see what files had been opened. He assured Grant that once the computer had been discovered missing it had been locked out from connecting to the network. He verified that and showed Grant. It meant nothing to the Sergeant Major. This kid was calling up pages on the computer screen that Grant would never be able to find again. He finally got to the last page.

"Here you go, Sergeant Major. You can tell Major Bonneville that everything is secure. All Sergeant Sullivan did after he got his hands on this thing was to open up the directory. He looked at the folder titles, but he didn't go any deeper. Sergeant Sharp must have gotten it back before anybody could have tried."

Grant was happy with the report, but needed to make certain there were no more compromises. Callan was ordered to limit all access to tactical planning. If anyone besides the CO needed to get in they would have to come to the Tactical Operations Center and justify their need, and there was a very limited access roster.

"Some of the officers aren't going to like being kept out of the loop."

"They'll have to live with it. If anybody really wants to know what's going on I'll make room for them in one of the platoons."

"There any word on Sullivan?"

"Nothing since Sharp's boys lost him in traffic. I do have a rather pissed off New Mexico State Trooper on his way out to see me. I'll see if I can't get some help from local law enforcement."

Sharp was waiting by his truck for Grant to come out. Once he pulled out they wouldn't see each other until the operation was over. Grant handed him some updated satellite photos Harrison had gotten from his sources at Bliss.

"Sorry I couldn't get Sullivan back."

"Don't worry about it. The object of the exercise was the computer. Callan says nothing was accessed, so we're probably still in good shape. Just make sure you keep your eyes open when you start caching your gear. If you even think you've been compromised, get the fuck out of there. Leave the gear, just get out."

"I will be the soul of discretion, Boss. That *hacienda* isn't going anywhere. There will always be other opportunities." Grant looked at the boxes he had stacked up. "What's all this?" Sharp got a broad grin and opened the top box. "I thought you could use something a little better than that South American shit you usually carry."

Grant pulled out what was a fine example of a 1911A1. "The Border Patrol gave you these?"

"Sure did. I grabbed one and a couple of magazines to replace the Tokarev you love so much. Now you can stop worrying about me."

Grant picked through a couple more. "You did good, Dave, but it'll be hard to toss one of these away like I do with the Ballesters. I'm going to have to start swapping out barrels. What's in the other boxes?" Sharp showed him the Mendozas. "I held on to a couple. I figured you could spread them around the other platoons. The guy I talked to said only the local *policias* carry them. I figure if we salt the area with a few it'll add to the confusion."

"That's a good idea. I'll make sure it happens."

They shook hands and Grant watched him drive out the gate, passing a police SUV that was coming in. Mel Braga had arrived. Grant went over to the Mess tent to wait for him. There was a lot in the operations section he didn't want the State Trooper to see, and there were too many casual conversations he didn't want him to hear. Hell, there was too much in his own sleeping tent that he didn't need anyone to see either. His life was getting complicated. He gave his watch a quick glance. His original plan had been to visit the three platoons that would be running the cross border operation before night fall. That fucking Sullivan and the computer had altered his plans. He was still going to hit the road today, even if he had to spend the night with one of the platoons while they pre-positioned their equipment. It wasn't an ideal plan, but he didn't want to bother the platoons at the last minute. They would have enough to do without entertaining him. Bonneville was planning her visits on the last day. He had thought about making it a joint trip before he realized if he did he would just be overshadowing her. The platoon leaders would just keep looking over to him every time she said something.

Braga wasn't smiling when he came in the tent. Grant waved him over to the coffee pot and waited for him to join him. He plopped himself down heavily on the far side of the table and glared at Grant as he took a long drink from his cup. He paused to swallow, then started in.

"Do you have any more plans to fuck with the Mexicans in Columbus?"

"That wasn't planned or intentional. I needed that laptop back."

"What was so important? There are two people dead because of it."

That was news to Grant. Sharp hadn't said a word about any shooting. "My guys didn't kill anybody."

"No, your guys didn't, but we found your AWOL Sergeant and his piece of Mexican pussy dead in a rest area north of Columbus."

"The cartel?"

"Indirectly. I've got the bar wired for sound. We heard one of the greasers tell the little whore to kill Sullivan. We think he gave her some laced coke at the same time."

"How'd he die?"

"My guy at the scene says it looks like he thought he was going to get a roadside blow job. His pants were down and his head was back. It looks like she snorted her coke, killed him and died herself, although she may have killed him first and snorted the coke second. The only thing we are sure of is she died last. You can have his body after the autopsy. What was so important about the laptop?"

"I can't say. It's classified."

"What can be so classified about watching a road and a barbed wire fence?"

Grant didn't answer him directly. "Give me three days, Mel."

"Why three days?"

"In three days we'll have wrapped up what we came here to do. I need you to give me the time and not tell anyone."

"What did you come here to do?"

"All I can say is that none of it will happen in your jurisdiction."

Braga's eyes narrowed. He knew what that meant, but he didn't say anything. He looked at his coffee cup and put it down. He rose and walked to the door of the tent. Major Bonneville was standing there.

Can I have a moment of your time?" Braga stepped back into the tent.

Bonneville kept her voice low and started talking. "What would happen if the Army cartel was run out of this area? Would that make your life easier?"

"Not really. Whatever gang beat up on them would just take over the routes and it would be business as usual, with maybe a little extra violence to demonstrate that there was a new guy running the show."

"What if it wasn't another cartel? What if the Army lost to someone who had no interest in picking up their business?"

Braga thought for a moment. "I can't see that happening, but if it did, there would be a power vacuum that somebody would have to fill. Either the government or another cartel would try to take over."

"If that happened, how much time would it take?"

Again he thought. "Maybe four to six weeks, longer if the government was winning."

"Would that be worth two or three days?"

He didn't respond.

Bonneville took a step in. "Give us the three days he asked for, and maybe you'll get that four to six weeks." Braga still didn't say anything. He stepped around her and walked to the door. He looked back and started to say something, but changed his mind. He turned again and just said "Okay," then walked to his vehicle. Bonneville didn't say any more, and she left. Grant finished his coffee and listened as the SUV started up and drove out of the compound. When the sound died he went to gather his things for his own road trip.

Chapter 10

Grant tossed his pack and sleeping bag into the Blazer and walked over to the commo tent to pick up a fresh radio battery. When he came back Major Carson was standing by his truck with her nurse, Lieutenant Robles. There was a small stack of packs that Grant took to be Aid kits. They probably wanted him to deliver them on his rounds. If only life could be that simple for him.

Bonneville was walking up from the CP "I've got one more job for you."

When she got closer Grant could see she had some papers in her hand. "In all your planning you left out the Medical Support annex. I had the Major write one up and give it to Vaughn to approve. I want you to take her and Lieutenant Robles around to the sites and brief the platoons."

"I wasn't planning on coming back until the morning, Ma'am. I can take all this and do the briefing for them."

Carson interrupted. "It's not that simple, Sergeant Major. Lieutenant Robles will be setting up a triage at the other helicopter site, plus she'll be monitoring the radio to make sure any serious casualties get air evacuation."

"Can't the medic on site do that?"

"Multiple medical evacuations will require someone to prioritize. That'll be Maria's job. I'll be doing that at this site."

Grant knew that further argument would be pointless. At least having a third party present would keep temptation out of the picture.

He told the women they would need their armored vests and weapons. Carson said she would be coming back in the morning.

"Doesn't matter, Major. Everyone going out on the road needs all their gear. Look what happened the other day. Major Bonneville didn't expect to be in a gun fight either."

Both women were back in a few minutes. By then Grant had loaded all the medical gear into the back and was strapping himself into his own armor. Lieutenant Robles had hers all rigged and was ready to go. The doctor seemed to be having some difficulty with hers. She asked for some help. She turned her back to Robles and held out her arms so Grant could rearrange her load. As he was working she kept her eyes fixed on his face. He could feel her take a couple of heavy breaths. He could tell she was making plans for him tonight.

Because of the way they had organized the work on the border, the platoons displaced as the heavy equipment work moved south. In the planning stages it had been agreed to use the same basic layout for all the bivouacs so that the platoons could just uproot and move without having to rebuild their living quarters from scratch. The first move had brought Price and the heavy equipment into the central area. That would be the site of the helicopter pad, simply because the heavy equipment was able to carve one out in less than an hour. Grant had wanted it further to the south, but that bivouac had some terrain features that would make it more difficult for aviation operations after dark.

Grant sat down with the NCOs briefly, not wanting to interrupt their preparations for the night moves. It only took a few minutes to cover the new medical annex. Everyone hoped they wouldn't need it, but everyone was glad somebody had thought of it. Carson and Robles gathered the assigned medics and went their own way, scouting out and setting up a location for a primary care area. All the platoons had dedicated medics. The working relationships they had developed went a long way to ensuring a safe work area, not to mention Price's on again off again relationship with Sergeant Elko, the senior medic assigned to the heavy equipment platoon. Elko had been a good matchup for Price. She was gutsy and liked to go places that a female soldier would not normally be allowed. As a result, she had already been decorated for valor on two separate occasions, in the Sudan and again in Moldova.

Price and Lieutenant Stanley had their operation well in hand. Grant reviewed it with them, knowing in advance there would be nothing for him to criticize. Price produced a bottle of tequila and a set of shot glasses. Lieutenant Stanley did the honors and poured, and they had a quick toast to luck. "I'll see you when this is over, Jonah. Don't go and do anything stupid."

"Don't worry, Sergeant Major. I'll keep him out of trouble." Stanley said.

"I'm sure you will, Ma'am. Just remember he tends to be a bullet magnet. If you hang around him, make sure you've got the extra trauma plates in your vest."

Price and Stanley excused themselves to finish their preparations. Grant wandered over to where his truck was parked. His vest and helmet were piled on the tailgate with Major Carson's gear. There was no requirement to stay suited up in the bivouac areas, only on the road. He noticed her blouse was there too. Well, it was hot, and she was as entitled to a little comfort as the soldiers working in the area. He opened an old bottle of water that was laying there and poured some of it over his head. In the distance he could see where the sun was. There were probably four hours of daylight left, plenty of time to get to the next platoon, and maybe head back out to the last area, up north. If he could work that out he could avoid having to spend the night out here alone with Major Carson. He thought about that for a minute. In spite of the relationship they had, she had never used it to leverage him. When the opportunity arose and she wanted sex with him, there were no promises, no commitments, just sex. Okay, there had been one promise she had eked out of him for a night in a hotel in El Paso, and Grant actually thought that would be good. He didn't want to jeopardize his relationship with Linda Bonneville, but Sylvia Carson didn't seem to have a problem with it. All in all, Grant thought, the situation could be a lot worse. Sometimes his conscience acted up, but he knew he was going to hell anyway. Maybe a night out here with her wouldn't be such a bad idea. He thought about the night she had surprised him in his sleeping bag. That had been a memorable night.

"Deep in thought, Sergeant Major? That is an awfully wicked smile you've got going there." She had walked around the side of the truck as he was thinking about how she had looked sitting up on his bunk. He still had that image of her as he looked at her, and she must have recognized it. She looked around quickly for anybody within earshot. "The only times I recall you looking at me like that I don't think we were in uniform, Sergeant Major. I hope that's a promise for this evening."

"Well, Ma'am, I may be guilty of some immoral thoughts right now, but it's not a promise. Tonight's going to be busy for the troops going over the border, and I think I'd rather pay attention to what's going on with them for the moment. I'll have to get one of those rain checks you've talked about in the past."

"Oh, I'll give you one of those," she said as she walked past, her hand brushing his crotch, "but you better not wait too long before you cash it in." She started to put on her body armor before she got into the Blazer but stopped. "Do I need my blouse? It's awfully hot with all this stuff on."

Grant looked at her. She was sweating heavily. "Don't you have one of the combat shirts?" That was a new addition to the clothing bag. It was a long sleeve t-shirt that had ACU sleeves. It was designed for wearing under the combat load.

"I never think about bringing that with me. I'm one of those rear people, remember? I only wear this crap when I absolutely have to."

Grant sympathized with her. The gear was hot and uncomfortable, and it took some acclimatization before you could function comfortably and efficiently in it. He carried a spare in his day pack and he offered it to her. "Here, it might be a little big for you, but it'll do the job."

"Sergeant Major, you are a knight in shining armor." She took the shirt and got into the truck. Grant couldn't resist looking in from the rear. The Blazer had high back bucket seats with a wide, flat space in between. She was sitting sideways with her back to the passenger door. Her t-shirt was coming up over her head. The sports bra she was wearing was damp from sweat and he could see her dark nipples through the fabric. He felt that old stirring. She was making it hard to keep the promise he had made to himself just a few minutes earlier. She caught him looking at her chest and smiled. "Still want that rain check, or are you having second thoughts?"

"Get dressed, Ma'am. I'm not the only one who would appreciate the view."

She smiled again and slid the combat shirt on. It wasn't as big on her as Grant thought it would be. She got out of the truck and came back around and grabbed her vest off the tail gate. "I still need a hand getting this on straight." She had said that for any stray ears that might be in the area. As soon as Grant got close and tried to adjust the side opening she turned ever so slightly so that his hand went under the vest and came to rest on her breast. "Why, Sergeant Major! Are trying to cop a feel?" She said with a sly grin and the tip of her tongue between her lips. Grant pulled his hand away, slower than he probably should, letting his fingertips linger.

"No promises, Major. These soldiers are going where they don't belong tonight. I want to make damn sure they all get the support they need and get back safe. They'll have even more to worry about tomorrow night. I'm not even going to think about any recreational activities until they're safe."

"I don't want to interfere with your sense of duty, but we both know this won't take your every waking moment. I just want to claim some of that time you give to every soldier in the unit. You're my Sergeant Major too." She picked up her rifle and got into the Blazer. "I'm ready to go any time you are."

Grant got behind the wheel, cursing silently to himself. She was determined they were having sex, and she knew he was weakening. "Are you saying something, Sergeant Major?"

"Just that I'm going to hell."

"I know that," she said with the same sly grin on her lips, "and I'll be happy to do anything I can to help."

The drive down to the southernmost bivouac site didn't take long, and it could have been all in silence if she hadn't kept up a running routine of questions about what the troops were doing that night and more about the next night. All of this had been covered in the briefings that had been given in order for her to plan her medical response, but Grant recognized it for what it was, an effort to bring the intensity back down. It worked, and Grants mind was back on operational matters by the time he pulled through the gate.

SFC Powell and his Platoon leader, Lieutenant Powers, were waiting for them. Price had probably called ahead to give them an ETA, something Grant would have done himself if he hadn't been distracted. Major Carson excused herself to go talk with her medics while he followed them into a tent that had been set up for a quick pre-operation briefing session. There was a large scale map of their area pinned to a sheet of plywood, heavily annotated. Grant looked closely at the notes and smiled. The notes were in several different hands, indicating that the Lieutenant and all her NCOs had input to their plan. He could see where areas for caching supplies and routes in and out had been marked, erased and relocated. Without physically walking the same ground Grant was willing to trust their judgment. They were the ones who would be carrying out the mission, so they had the biggest stake in the planning. Lieutenant Powers led off, followed by SFC Powell and then by each of the NCOs. There was a give and take as questions were asked and answered. Grant could tell they had been through this before, as there was very little tweaking of the plan. Grant made a comment or two, but really couldn't find any flaws with it.

"Do you plan to go through this exercise again before you go out tomorrow night?" Grant asked at the end. Powers was quick to answer. "We plan to use the same model tomorrow afternoon, Sergeant Major. There shouldn't be too many variables we can encounter tonight, but just in case there are we'll revisit every aspect of the plan. We don't want surprises any more than you do."

Grant was satisfied. He was ready to grab a quick nap before the units started moving out, and he questioned whether the troops would have the same opportunity.

"We've been trying to rotate them in and out of their racks for the last 48 hours to make sure they're as fresh as they can be."

"Did that rotation include you and your Lieutenant?"

"Sure did, Sergeant Major, although the good Lieutenant did take a little extra convincing that she needed as much sleep as the troops did."

"How did you do it?"

"I finally got the medic to make up a flow chart to show her how degraded her thinking would be for every hour she stayed up past 24. The medic was good. She had all the figures ready. I'll never turn down any medical support from here on out, even if it is a female." Powell had initially been reluctant to have any females assigned to his platoon when they were first mobilized to go to Sudan. He had also become an early convert.

Powell showed him where he could unroll his sleeping bag. It was the same tent he had shared with the other NCOs several nights before. The bunks were still set up. One of them had another ruck sack and sleeping bag piled on it. He knew without asking whose it was, but he figured he'd ask anyway. The answer didn't surprise him. The gear belonged to Major Carlson. "Why don't you move her in with Lieutenant Powers for the night, and you bunk in here with me?"

"Already thought about that, Sergeant Major, but she said she didn't want to disrupt anybody this close to an operation. She said she'd tolerate being in here."

"Tolerate? Is that the word she used?"

"Sure was, Sergeant Major. I guess she's been around long enough to know how to put up with unpleasant tent mates for a night."

Yeah, Grant thought to himself, if only you knew.

They woke Grant for a late dinner before night fall. He looked over and noticed Carson's gear hadn't been disturbed. It was a small blessing, but one he was grateful for. She was already in the mess tent, sitting with her assigned medics. When she saw Grant come in she excused herself and indicated a table for him to join her at. The mess section had laid on a simple hot meal for them, along with plenty of hot coffee. They were also filling insulated containers with hot and cold drinks for later. Grant made a mental note to pass on a good word to Sergeant Moura.

His people continued to go over and above for the line platoons. Carson joined him, bringing two cups of coffee. He thanked her and took a few sips. "Did you manage to get any sleep this afternoon? Your gear didn't look like it had been touched."

She was pleased he had asked. "When I came back you were dead to the world, so I just let you sleep. You're getting a little congestion in your lungs. I could hear it when you were sleeping. Come see me when we get back and I'll give you something to clear that up."

"So you didn't get any rest?"

"I couldn't sleep in there with all that noise. I went back to the aid station and borrowed a litter for a while. Tonight, though, you better sleep on your side, because if you keep me awake with that noise, you won't get any sleep either." She concentrated on her coffee for a few minutes, letting Grant think about what she had just said. Just in case it was slipping his mind she occasionally pressed her thigh up against his.

"Stop that!" he said to her under his breath. I still have to stand up and walk out of here!"

She smiled at that and changed the subject. "I understand you plan to observe the activities from an observation post on the border tonight. Do you mind if I join you? You can explain things to me as they develop."

"Are you going to behave?"

"Right up until you get the word that everyone's back. After that, we'll see."

"I'm going to hold you to that."

The caching operations went smoother than Grant had expected them to go. Between phone contacts, monitored radios and updates from SFC Callan in the TOC, Grant was able to monitor all the operations in almost real time. There were some delays in relaying information from the smaller elements that had shorter range radios, but it was anticipated that it would be easy to correct the following night.

Grant and Carson had set up in one of the dummy OPs that SFC Powell had established early on in the exercise. It had been a neat little deception operation, placing teams in at last light and picking them up again after dark. It gave the illusion that the border was being patrolled at a higher density than it actually was. Powell's plan had been to steer any border crossers away from this area to minimize the chance they would stumble on anything related to the observation post on top of *el Indio*. From the lack of contacts they were having this far south, it seemed to work. Of course, there was also the possibility that the Mexicans tried to keep prying eyes away from their airstrip operations at *el Monumento*. Whichever it was, Grant didn't care. The less foot traffic meant less of a chance for his men to be observed or intercepted as they lugged a couple of hundred pounds of equipment to caches around their targets.

Major Carson watched the comings and goings with interest. Grant had rigged an extension to his headset so she could hear what was being said. Most of the traffic was coming from Callan or the rear support sites. The teams in Mexico were keeping up a very tight radio discipline.

"Explain to me why this is happening over two nights. Why couldn't they just go in and take everything out in one swoop?" She asked. Grant deferred to SFC Powell, who was with them for the first half of the exercise. He had split up responsibility with his Lieutenant. There was a need for both of them to be familiar with the ground in the target area, but there was no need for both of them to risk the exposure on that side tonight. Powell gave a brief but thorough explanation of the plan. There was a lot of demolition that would have to be carried out in order to neutralize the airstrip and other targets for long enough to make the trip worth while. They needed the extra time to haul all the explosives, plus the heavier support weapons into place. It would take several trips to get it into place, but it would shorten the work load when the time came.

"It still seems like a long way to go from point A to B."

Grant answered that. "It is, but we don't have the luxury of air support or using vehicles to make a high speed run in and out. All the powers that be, meaning Vaughn, want this to look as much like a family squabble as possible. That means we have to make it look like it was another cartel barging in on their territory."

"And you expect it to all go off without a hitch?"

Grant sucked in his breath. "I hope so, but no battle plan ever survives the first shot. We just hope it doesn't change so much that we can't improvise around it."

Powell left them with the announcement that Lieutenant Powers was back on the US side. Her report was that all had gone well, and they had been able to haul more weight than they had thought. This part of the operation would be done a lot sooner than they had planned.

"What about activity?" Grant asked.

"There seemed to be a few people around, probably a reinforced squad or more. Their security was pretty lax, and it looks like most of them suck down a few beers and some *tequila* before they do anything else. They do the same thing tomorrow and we'll roll right over them."

"How much longer tonight?"

"I think Sergeant Powell should be done in about ninety minutes or so. The troops have a good rhythm going."

"Well, that's nice to hear," Carson said as soon as they were alone.

"Don't get your hopes up yet. There are still more teams working out tonight, and I want them all back."

She leaned back against the berm and brought her night vision goggles up to her eyes. "Spoil sport."

In the center, Price and his people were making good progress too. Thanks to the heavy reconnaissance they had been doing, he had a good idea of exactly what would be needed. Their targets were lighter than what Powell and Mason had in the south, and far less challenging than what Sharp would have in the north. As a result he had taken on four of the targets out of a total of eight, Powell had one, the large air strip facilities, and Mason had two, the smaller abandoned village at the northwest end of the strip and a smaller site just to the north of that. Sharp had the *hacienda*, which was expected to be a tough nut to crack. Bonneville and Grant were between Sharp and Price. They would be securing the choke point at the auxiliary strip and providing support and rapid reinforcement if anyone else needed it. They would bring a couple of vehicles mounting heavy weapons, but the route they had to follow was rather indirect. It would take them longer to drive than it would for Price to walk to his closest target.

Price had calculated he would need less demo to knock everything down. He had been in and out of every building in the area, and not one of them was built to last. He was surprised some of them were still standing. There had been a lot of hurried maintenance applied to them, but it was just that, hurried. One would think that with all the money the cartels had to burn they would have hired a good contractor to fix the place up.

His eastern most target area, *Las Aguilas*, was close to the edge of the dry lake. After a quick check to determine if there were any stay behind guards he climbed on the roof to scan the area. Out in the dry lake, about seven or eight kilometers out, he could barely make out some activity. There were vehicles, in black-out drive, heading away. It could have meant anything, but he wrote it off to the Mexican Army going home for the night.

The choke point was considered to be a fairly easy objective. There was a small cluster of three buildings with good, covered approaches from all directions. Grant had decided to let the Robinson twins handle the ground approach. It was only about four kilometers in a straight line from the border, but almost three times that by the road. It was also an area that had different levels of occupancy, although they hadn't been able to determine why. Tonight had been one of those nights when there seemed to be a party going on. There was a generator roaring, plenty of lights, and a radio playing loud salsa music. It made it easy to get close, but the noise also masked any activity that might have been in the brush. Edward Robinson, who, by an alphabetical quirk on the promotion orders was senior, had them move in their equipment as close as he dared, then sent the teams back for another load while he kept watch. The party gradually got louder, before somebody took charge and made them settle down. The site was quiet by the time the next load of equipment had arrived, and Eddie had fixed the only sentry that had been posted. Sentry was probably a poor term to use. The man sat down on a chair leaning against one of the buildings. There was no field of view from where he had positioned himself. After relieving himself on a bush, he sat down, had a smoke, and now was snoring every bit as loudly as some of the other Mexicans in the buildings. Robinson checked his watch. In less than 24 hours this place would be secured. He hoped that tomorrow's party, if there was one, would end earlier.

Sharp had planned his operation just a bit differently. His initial assault would be with the suppressed rifles, followed by a quick mortar barrage. Between Squad Automatic Weapons and grenade launchers, he planned to make a short brutal assault, and then clean out the motor pool and head south. He had plenty of people to carry the gear in, and only half of them had to make a second trip. He used his extra time positioning explosives and ammo caches as close as he dared, then marked his primary targets for the 60mm mortar. The low wall around the compound gave him an unobstructed view all the way through. A scout on some high ground was able to tell him that the sentry on the tower was curled up and sleeping. Sharp was able to make two complete circuits of the compound and motor pool and refine his plan. The motor pool was almost empty, a good sign. The compound itself was mostly in the dark. He resisted an urge to get closer and look in some of the buildings. He would assume they were empty, but a 40mm grenade round or two would go a long way to insuring a lack of response. He mentally went over his approach and fire plans, adjusting them for the possibility that there could be more vehicles the next night, meaning more troops present. He tried to keep it simple. Improvisation in the dark sucked.

The signal came in that all the equipment was in place and everyone was gathering at the rally point. Sharp took a quick look around and made his way back. His people were all accounted for, and he dispatched them in small groups along their exfiltration routes. His group would be the last to go, and they were heading out when the lookout called Sharp's attention to the far horizon.

"What have you got, Bobby?"

"I don't know, Sarge. There were lights out there for a couple of seconds. It looked like someone was driving around in blackout drive."

"Which way were they going?"

"South to north, and then they turned away. I can't tell if there's a road there or not. My map doesn't cover out that far."

Sharp looked through the night vision glasses for a long minute. Whatever had been out there was gone, and it could have been anything. "Don't worry about it, Bobby; it probably wasn't anything we need to worry about. This time tomorrow we'll be back in the US and this will all be just a fond memory."

Lieutenant Powers and her driver were breaking down the equipment in the OP and preparing to head back to the bivouac for a couple of hours sleep. Sharp and his group had been the last to check in. Both he and Price had reported the blackout lights to the east, but neither thought they were significant, or even close enough to be an issue. Callan relayed the info to Grant, who asked if he could get some photos out that far, just in case. Callan said he'd work on it. "Are you headed back in to the barn now?"

Grant looked at Carson before he replied. "No, I don't think so. There are a few more things I want to check out on this side, just in case."

Carson heard him say he wanted to 'check out a few things' and noticed the way he was looking at her. She went to the far side of the Blazer. Callan was back on the air. "Okay, Sergeant Major. If you don't need anything more from me I'm going to turn it over to the night shift. I'll see you when you get back." With that the frequency went dead. The regular internal radio net would be enough to handle any communications for the rest of the night.

Grant watched Powers drive out of the hidden gully on the back side of the OP they had used for a vehicle park while pulling at the Velcro that secured his vest. Carson was in the dark on the far side of the Blazer. Grant could hear the rustling as she took off her helmet and vest and put it on the back seat. She walked around rubbing her hair with her fingers, trying to shake it out. "I don't think I've ever sweat so much, and my head feels like a bale of hay. This girl needs a shower and a shampoo to feel human again." She saw that Grant had his vest off too, and slipped her arms around him and snaked her tongue out in between his lips as she kissed him. "There! I was a good girl all night. I think that entitles me to a little reward."

Grant ran his arms around her and slid his hands down to cup her butt. He didn't know why he did that: it was a reflex at having her pressed into him like that, "Didn't I just hear you say you wanted a shower?" She turned around and ground her butt into him, taking his hands and pressing them into her breasts. She was still wearing Grant's combat shirt, but somewhere during the course of the evening she had discarded her bra. He could feel her nipples harden under his palms.

She wiggled a little. "I won't complain about you being all sweaty if you don't complain about me."

Grant could feel himself responding to her ass pressed against his groin. She could feel it too, and reached back to grab him. There was a list of noble intentions running through his mind, but none of them seemed very important at the moment. There were no two ways about it: he was getting laid tonight. He had another idea; this time about the spring fed pool he had taken Bonneville to a few nights back. I should feel like a son of a bitch, he thought to himself, but I'm going to hell anyway, whether we get naked here in the dirt or over in the pool. We might as well be comfortable.

"Can you wait ten minutes? I might have a surprise for you." He told her about the pool.

"My medics told me about that. I didn't know you'd been down there too."

"Just once, in another life. You want to go and clean up or stay here for a while? I kind of like the idea of a quick swim."

"Let's go!"

She had been able to wait the ten minutes, but only just. She had started to undress in the truck. Grant could make out her body in the moon light, and it made it hard to concentrate on the road. At one point she knelt between the seats and started to undo his pants, but he made her stop. It was bad enough driving without headlights without having that happening to him. When they got to the pool she helped him undress. Grant, by this point, was glad he had zippers put on his boots. She briefly teased him with her mouth before pulling him into the water. She laid him on his back in the shallow water, and mounted him, guiding him in with her fingers. She shuddered as he thrust up into her, and she began rocking up and down on him almost in a frenzy. He thought she would stop after her first orgasm, but all she did was open her eyes, smile at him, and start pumping again. Her movements were slower, and her muscles were tighter. Grant held his own explosion back as long as he could, but she leaned back and reached down to manipulate him with her fingers. It was too much for Grant, and his own climax was explosive.

They were lying on a poncho liner at the edge of the water. She had one leg thrown over his thighs, her hand stroking him. He was playing with her breasts, amazed at how big and hard her nipples could get.

"I like it when you do that," she said. He squeezed and she gave a little whimper. "I know, that's why I like to do it. You have magnificent nipples." He leaned his head forward and nipped one, then the other. She held the back of his head while he did it. "Don't stop. Can you rub me while you're doing that?"

Grant did. She was wet and kept having little spasms. She pushed him away and rolled him on his back and slid herself over his manhood. She pushed down hard, trying to get him as deep inside her as she could. Her breath was ragged and she was biting her lower lip. Suddenly she tensed up and let out a long low moan. When she stopped she lay down on top of him, holding him inside with her muscles, slowly squeezing him. When he came again she let out another low moan and kissed him, then slid off, keeping an arm and a leg thrown across him.

He let her sleep for a while. It was starting to get light in the east when he woke her. They made love again, this time slower. She wanted to feel him on top of her. When they were done they took another swim, and he helped her get back into her gear,

She kept smiling at him, but on the ride back she never said a word about what they had done. She just smiled.

Back at Powell's platoon bivouac she went right to the tent and crawled into her sleeping bag. Grant headed over to the local CP to check the message log. He found a message from Callan waiting for him. Major Bonneville was concerned he was checking something out and wanted to know if there were any problems. Grant hadn't anticipated this. He tried to bluff it out. "It was just a hunch. I wanted to get up a little higher to see if there were any lights down this end like Price and Sharp saw."

"Were there?"

"None that I could see. Tell the Major it was probably nothing, but get some overhead images of the area from the time period if you can. It'll be better to be safe than sorry." He knew that Sharp or Price, probably both, had already requested them in their after action report. It wouldn't hurt to reinforce the request. "Is the Major still up and about?"

"Negative. She turned in right after your last transmission. She said something about you being a big boy and being able to make the call if there was a problem. I'll leave the note for when she wakes up. Somebody let me sleep late in the morning."

Grant looked at the clock on the tent wall. It was a little after 0400. Nobody was getting any sleep tonight. He wandered by the mess tent to grab a quick coffee, and thought better of it. He went to his sleeping tent to get as much of a rest as he could. Carson was already sleeping. He could hear her heavy breathing in the dark. He dropped his boots and was asleep in a few minutes. It was a fitful sleep. Even unconscious the thought of the lights in the distance came back to haunt him. It meant something. Blackout lights at night in the desert wasn't something the Mexican Army did with any regularity. They controlled all the smuggling in the area, so there was no need to be stealthy. In all the time the 289th had been on the border, this was the first time anyone had reported blackout drive being used on the Mexican side. It definitely meant something. The idea was enough that it seemed to keep him awake, but checking his watch showed that he had been sleeping, or something like that, for over two hours. He got up and put his boots back on, again grateful for the zippers he had put in. The sun was up and it was light enough to see Carson in her bunk. She was on her back, sleeping bag unzipped. Somewhere along the way she had changed back into a regular t-shirt. Grant's combat shirt was neatly folded and laying on the foot of his bunk. He picked it up and held it to his nose. He could still smell her on it. He rolled it up and put it in his stuff sack and added his own dirty combat shirt, just in case.

There was a low level of activity in the compound. The leaders were not overstressing their troops in the daylight. In a normal world, they would have started reverse cycle training, that is, sleeping during the day and training at night, to prepare for this operation. Reality never seemed to cooperate with plans.

There were only a few soldiers in the mess tent. Grant nodded to them and went through the serving line. There were leftovers from breakfast still in the insulated containers. The bacon wasn't bad, but cold, runny scrambled eggs never managed to endear themselves to him. He grabbed a couple of slices of cold toast and made himself a sandwich. With a cup of coffee it was more than adequate for his needs.

He was finishing up when Major Carson came in with one of her medics. She nodded to the Sergeant Major, and made herself an equally unappetizing breakfast. She added the scrambled eggs to her sandwich. Grant motioned her over and asked if she was ready to hit the road.

"I am, but did you get any sleep last night?"

"I got a little, enough to keep me going. I'll get another couple of hours this afternoon, and I'll be all set for the night." He got up and tossed his trash in a barrel. "I'll meet you at the truck."

Chapter 11

If one were to look at their Area of Operations from end to end, one would realize that in spite of the length, which would be longer than a company sized unit would normally cover, it had no depth, and a very straight access road that everything fed off. Once it was broken up into local platoon areas, nothing was all that far away. The trip back to the headquarters area could be as slow or as quick as a driver wanted it to be. Grant chose to make it a quick trip. Not from any sense of guilty conscience or post-coital embarrassment with Major Carson, as she always clicked right back to business mode after she had gotten what she wanted out of him. Grant was more interested in getting back to the business at hand and monitoring any and all intelligence that could have an effect on the coming operation. The current lack of a level of activity was as important as if there had been a lot going on. It bothered Grant that it had been so quiet. Even the independent *coyotes* were avoiding this area. Apuesta's men must have put out some kind of word that was being obeyed. That could only mean they had plans that they didn't want disrupted either. Grant wanted to make absolutely certain that the two plans didn't collide that night in the middle of the Mexican desert.

He was deep in thought and missed what Carson had said to him. He asked her to repeat it.

"Do you expect any casualties?"

"I'm hoping there are none, but when the shooting starts you never know when something is going where you hoped it wouldn't.

That being the case, I'm hoping that anything that does happen will be minor."

She laughed at that. "Who'll be the judge of 'minor'? A term like that doesn't have much meaning if you're the one laying in the dirt wondering what the hell just happened to you."

Grant had to agree. A minor bullet wound can be very traumatic, especially if it hits a nerve bundle, causes a lot of bleeding, or it's just your first time. Not that anyone really builds up a lot of tolerance for getting shot. If anything, it makes you just a little more cautious the next time out. She did, however, have a point. They would be across the border trying really hard not to let everyone know where they came from. When it comes to making the call for a helicopter evacuation, the difference between major and minor will be very thin.

"That, Major, will have to be the call of the medic on the spot. All of yours are pretty experienced, and they have a pretty good rapport with the platoons they've been assigned to. Everybody's going to have to trust them."

"And if they don't?"

Grant thought about that. "It'll be kind of hard to second guess the medic on the spot. I guess if there's a decision to be made they'll have to kick it up to you. It'll either be you or Lieutenant Robles flying in, so you better have a pretty clear understanding of what the situation on the ground is."

"How will I do that?"

"Stay on the radio. When we get back go see the commo people. Lieutenant Johnson has worked magic with the equipment we've got. He can run a remote station out to the helipad so you can monitor what's happening on the ground."

She was quiet until they were turning in to the compound. "I notice you all do a lot with cell phones. Are you sure I'll get the situation reports?"

"You'll get them. If things are going that bad, nobody will have time to scroll through a speed dial menu." He looked past his parking spot to the visitors parking area. It was full. Grant threw his gear over his shoulder and walked over to the Operations tent. He saw Vaughn sitting inside with another strange face. This was getting to be a bad habit of his. He kept bringing people into the loop that nobody knew. It had a potential for a lot of leaked information.

He could hear his name being bandied about. "Here he comes now."

Vaughn had a sheaf of papers in his hand. Grant could tell that some of them were intercepts. Vaughn didn't usually bring those out with him. He handed them to Grant, who looked around the room before he sat down. Bonneville and Callan were there, as well as the rest of the duty shift. For a change they hadn't sent out all the bystanders. Grant greeted the Major and asked who the new guy was.

"That's not important right now," was the General's answer.

"Bullshit," said Grant. "We're hours away from launching and now we've got another strange face listening in. I want to know who he is or I'll throw his ass out."

Vaughn looked over at Bonneville, who shook her head. "See? I'm not the only one. We need a little more trust from your side."

"Major, you and the Sergeant Major here aren't in any position to try to dictate terms to me. You're only the acting commander, and I'm still a General."

"That may be true, General," she stretched the word out like it left a bad taste in her mouth, "but we still seem to be operating under some pretty questionable instructions. Sergeant Major Grant keeps telling me he doesn't think you're for real. I'm starting to agree with him" Vaughn looked at Grant, who just smiled at him. He was glad Bonneville was pushing the point. It was her ass on the line. There still hadn't been anything put in writing about what they were about to do.

The civilian tossed an ID folder into the middle of the table. Grant slid it over to Bonneville, who looked it over and slid it back to Grant. The new guy was the Deputy Director for Southeastern Operations (DDSO), Drug Enforcement Agency. The ID card was embellished like an old hundred dollar bill. Grant flipped it closed and handed it back.

"That's very nice, but I still don't think Vaughn is real."

"You want to see my ID?"

"It'd be nice, but if you work for the same people, I'm sure yours would be just as pretty."

"Relax, Sergeant Major," said the DDSO. "I'm for real, but I agree with you about him. He's probably CIA." Vaughn made no response. The DDSO launched into a quick recap of the situation on the border on both flanks, and reiterating what needed to be done in this area. The Mexican army had pretty much stayed out of the drug wars in Mexico, being content to stay on the sidelines, making money where they could, and reigning in excesses when they occurred. This was the first area they had actually taken control of security, smuggling and distribution on both sides of the border. It was felt that if they could be successful here, there would be a widespread move to take over the entire operation, even if it meant a savage, no holds barred civil war. The Mexican government was very afraid that was about to happen.

"The Mexicans have asked for covert assistance in this area. The 289th has made a significant impact on their operations, but the government wants more. They are actually asking for a limited incursion, sort of like what Blackjack Pershing did in 1916, only this time with Special Forces troops."

Grant sat back in his chair. "So you're calling us off?"

That was not to be the case. Somehow, Apuesta had discovered the request and was planning on ramping up his operations in the next few days. "He anticipates any Spec Ops buildup in this area will be centered out of Fort Bliss, and he has enough sources there to tell him when that would happen."

"What does he think we're doing?"

"That's where our sources come in. Apuesta has done his homework carefully. He knows that the striking force in the 289th rests with you and a few other NCOs. He also thinks Lieutenant Colonel Kearney has been sent here specifically to pave the way for any Special Operations, but not to participate in anything that involves cross border operations. We've encouraged that kind of thinking."

Bonneville interrupted. "What does he think of our operations so far? He must have some idea we're responsible for some of the stuff that's gone on."

"At first he did, Major, and he had prepared some nasty plans to discourage you, as you noticed over the past few days on the border. However, Mexico being what it is, there are several other players in the area who were making noise."

"Like the *federales?*" Grant asked.

"For one, but they really don't have the resources to take on the Army. We came up with a better idea: Mexican Marines."

"Is that what's been going on out in the desert to the east?"

"Absolutely not. Do you realize where we are? This corner of Mexico is about as far away from any ocean as you can get. Their Marines don't want any part of this. They're content to wander around on the coast, watching the tourist girls in their bikinis. What do you think has been going on?"

Grant told him about the blackout lights.

"Those were my guys. I've had some of my local assets driving around at night, flashing their lights and dropping bits of uniform and gear. It's got Apuesta watching the area between *Cuidad Juarez* and here, making sure his rear area is secure. As soon as he is, he's planning a big blitz on the border. He's been stock piling drug shipments in your target areas. He plans to come over hard and roll over your bivouacs, then move his merchandise. We've identified a couple of *rancheros* a couple of miles from here that he's been herding migrants to use as mules. We plan to let the *federales* know about them so they can execute some raids about the time he pulls his security off to reinforce the border after you hit him tonight. Hopefully, that'll break his back."

"And if it doesn't?"

"That, Sergeant Major, is not something we're planning on."

Outside Vaughn was upset with his partner. "Why did you tell him I was with the CIA? I could have just as easily shown him my ID to prove who I was. And why did you say those lights were from your people? You know damn well there were really Marines, and they got spotted last night."

"Relax. I just told him what he wanted to hear. As far as they're concerned, they're working for the CIA now, rooting out the evil in the world that lies at their doorstep. And if they knew the Mexicans were complaining about them being over the border they might have pulled back and re-thought this for another day or two. We don't have that kind of time. Kearney will be back tomorrow. He's been fighting this operation since it was handed to him. And the Mexicans aren't going to wait forever either. They as much as said they were moving against Apuesta in the next few days. We have to do it now."

Vaughn wasn't convinced. "All they have to do is go to an Army website and do a search for my name. My whole fucking biography is posted there. There's no need for this kind of deception. And what happens if the Marines move early?"

The DDSO grabbed Vaughn by the sleeve and gave his arm a good squeeze. "All we have to do is get through tonight. Let them do what they have to, and we'll be gone. Everybody wants Apuesta and his men taken out of the picture. If we let the Mexicans do it with their fucking Marines like they want to, they'll probably be the next ones filling the vacuum. If we take out Apuesta maybe they'll think twice about letting the situation get out of hand again. They'll know what we're capable of."

Grant was listening from inside the tent. He put down the parabolic microphone and took off the ear piece. Bonneville was looking at him intently. "Well, what did you hear?"

"Not much more than we did before. It looks like the operation is sanctioned by somebody high up, but everybody between them and us is looking to cover their ass, even Kearney."

"So what do we do?"

"Fuck it," said Grant. We're in this too deep to back out gracefully. Vaughn's still a general officer, and even if there's nothing in writing, I'll bet there's an audio or paper trail somewhere. We don't go, we're refusing an order, legal or not. If we do go, and it turns to shit, we exceeded our mission parameters."

Callan asked, "What parameters? We haven't seen any yet."

"Callan, I've been getting beat up by the Army long enough to know that A, there are parameters, and B, they can prove we know what they are."

Bonneville chimed in. "And what if everything goes according to plan and nothing gets screwed up? Are we off the hook?"

"Maybe yes, maybe no, it all depends on the politicians and diplomats making the noise tomorrow morning. I think if the Mexicans can take credit for it, we'll be fine. We better make damn sure we only leave the right kind of evidence behind." He looked at the two Mendozas that were on the back table. "I may have to kiss Sharp for grabbing the Mendozas. We'll have to leave them in the right places."

"How about shell casings? They'll probably be a shit load of them scattered all over the place." Callan was thinking out loud.

Grant laughed. "That'll be something else I owe Sharp for. Every fucking round of ammo he picked up has Russian or European head stamps."

The sun was high in the sky by the time Grant decided there was nothing else he could do to guarantee success tonight. He had Callan call around to all units to make certain that the maximum amount of rest could be gotten by the raiding parties, then he decided he would try to get a couple of hours himself. His tent was like an oven, but he didn't care. He had slept in worse conditions before, and he'd rather sleep in the heat of the day than freeze his ass off in an arctic sleeping bag somewhere in a snow drift.

As he pulled off his boots he looked down at his running shoes poking out from under the bunk. It had been a long time since he had pounded a few miles in them. He kicked them out of sight so he wouldn't be reminded. He laid his head back and closed his eyes. Sleep usually came easy to him, and it did today. He was able to shut out all worries about the operation and relax.

He didn't hear the rustle as the tent flap was pulled back, or the squeak of someone walking across the plywood floor. The first he was aware of anyone in the tent with him was when he felt somebody sit on the edge of his cot. Before he opened his eyes he caught the scent of his visitor. It was Linda Bonneville.

"I couldn't sleep."

He pulled her down wordlessly to lie beside him. Army cots weren't built for two, but there was enough room to squeeze close together. They wrapped their arms around each other and lay there in silence. Grant could feel her breathing slow as she relaxed. He could feel the tenseness leaving her back and arms as she slowly settled in. It didn't take as long as Grant thought it would before she fell asleep. He buried his nose in her hair to enjoy her scent for a few minutes, then he drifted back to sleep. They would both have a few hours of peace this afternoon.

All along the border soldiers were making preparations or trying to rest. For some it came easy, as it did for Grant. Some of the younger or less experienced slept only fitfully, or not at all. In the north, Sharp had the added advantage of being in the Border Patrol station. There was no requirement for him to maintain a sentry or any of the other duties he would have in a tactical bivouac. Unlike the rest of the unit, he had the added advantage of having an air conditioned building. His men would be the freshest when they hit the *hacienda* later tonight.

Sharp slept quietly. His plans were made, and, although he was very adept at improvising on the fly if he had to, he preferred not to. His plans, as grand as they might seem, were very simple to execute. Let the other guy keep to a detailed schedule or intricate movement plans. Sharp believed in KISS: keep it simple, stupid. The fewer steps, the fewer opportunities to miss one. His designated riflemen would take out the sentries at the gates, the motor pool and on the tower. If there was any opposition as the assault teams moved in, it would be dealt with by a mortar barrage and a liberal application of SAW fire and 40mm grenades. Anybody that resisted would be crushed; anyone who surrendered would be disarmed and sent out into the desert to wait for rescue in the morning. Any vehicles he couldn't use would be destroyed, as well as all the buildings. He had plenty of demolitions for that. After that he had the option of moving back north across the border, which he planned to have most of his men do, or head south to reinforce the rest, which he planned to do with a small section. That was his plan, and he wanted to stick to it. As far as evidence that they were anything but Americans, he had enough FN-FALs, G-3s, AKs and Mendozas to leave lying around to make it look like a United Nations operation.

Price slept fitfully in his bivouac. He had agreed to the largest target load, and he kept going over in his mind the dispositions he had made. He kept telling himself he was satisfied, but the half hour head start Sharp was getting bothered him. It was one thing to draw off enemy forces from the southern end, but if his targets were alerted by the extended firing, it could pose problems for him. There had been an absence of Mexicans the night before, but the U-boat had reported some activity during the early morning. Price planned on getting into position as close as he could to his targets. If they were unoccupied, he would take them immediately and start prepping them for demolition. If they weren't, at the first sign of firing from Sharp he would take them down. He had kept that modification of the plan to himself. If everything went according to the master plan, it would not make any difference. And if the plan went to shit right away, as plans were sometimes known to do, he would already have his improvisations in place.

Price kept tossing and turning, but now it was because of the heat. He had the plan settled in his mind.

Powell and Mason were cooperating in their area, only because the drain on them for people to reinforce Sharp, maintain the U-boat and keep up with patrols on the border had left them shorter of manpower than anyone would have liked. That situation was allowed to stand only because it was expected that once Sharp started making noise up north at what was believed to be Apuesta's headquarters, reinforcements would be called for from their location, and their assaults would be easier. That, and the promise of rapid reinforcement if there were too many Mexicans left in their area to handle. The ambush that the Sergeant Major would organize at the choke point should take care of the bulk of the Mexican army, and scatter the rest into the brush, hopefully to hide out until daylight. Their biggest target, the airfield and buildings at *El Monumento*, were mainly wood structures and would take less demolition material than the stucco and brick in the other areas. That big hanger would light up the night sky all the way to *Cuidad Juarez* when it burned. A last minute change had allowed them to bring up a couple of vehicles after the shooting started. It would let them get out faster and not be illuminated for as long. To help with hiding their wheel tracks, SFC Mitchell and his mechanics had rigged up a couple of sections of scrap chain link fence to drag behind each vehicle. They were rolled and attached to the back bumpers. When the time came, a couple of snips with some wire cutters and they would drag out any tread marks they might leave, and raise one hell of a dust cloud.

They had been faced with the problem of maintaining site security before the mission, but the assigned mechanics and the rotating cooks volunteered to help out. Mason and Powell would have the maximum of their troops rested before they moved out after dark.

The two men were in uniform. The older one kept staring out of the window from the very well appointed *Comandancia*. The younger, but senior in rank, sat on the leather couch set against the far wall, under a heroic but historically inaccurate mural of *Pancho Villa* y *Emiliano Zapata* riding roughshod over what appeared to be American cavalrymen during the early part of the 20th century.

"*Jefe,* we are leaving too much product unattended by the border. Please, let me send another company to help guard it." Cardozo was speaking about the drugs that had been stockpiled ahead of the big push Major Apuesta was planning for in the next few days. Initially, half of the battalion had been slated to pull the security and escort the shipments to pick-up sites on the United States side. The other half would remain in the *Cuidad Juarez* area and conduct operations against rival cartels and, when necessary, against overly ambitious *Policia Federale* agents, the fucking cops. Every so often another ambitious little cocksucker would decide it was time to make a name and a career, and he would plan and lead some raids that had the potential to be embarrassing. It would not be good for too many of his soldiers to be taken into custody.

Eventually, it would be public knowledge that the Army was a major player in the trafficking, and not a player on the good side.

There was the added problem of these fucking Marines moving into the area. They should content themselves with strolling the beaches and the docks over on the sea coast, stealing what they could over there and chasing drugged up American *tourista* girls for a little free sex. They hadn't even had the decency to check in with Army headquarters. Instead they went right to the local prosecutors office and arranged a 'shared responsibility' that didn't provide many details. Even now they were starting to patrol the desert out to the west, getting very close to his operation on the border. Just last night his men had reported that they had seen some of those fucking Marines in between his stations and the *gringos*. It was only a matter of time before they decided they would like to use the airfields out in the desert. Then there would be major problems. Instead, Apuesta had been planning a few 'interventions' with some of his cartel allies to discourage the Marines from sticking their noses too far into their bag. For that he needed to partially strip his forces from the border. The *gringos* had been very cautious, almost cowardly, in the way they performed their denial operations. Other than a few ground sensors that the late Sergeant Sullivan had told them about, there was only the very occasional foray to follow a back trail of some migrant group. There was nothing at all to worry about.

"Relax, *Esteban*, relax. We need to take care of our little business in *Juarez* before we get back to our shipments. If we don't discourage the Marines from getting too aggressive they will just try to move in on us as we did on the *Zetas* and the other cartels."

"I would rather we move that material first so we didn't have to worry about it. There are too many millions of *gringo* dollars sitting out there almost alone."

"Again, relax. So little of that was paid for by our own money we wouldn't suffer any loss. The other players in *Juarez* need to see that we are willing to resist any new interlopers into our little republic of cocaine and methamphetamine. If they could sense our weakness it would only be a matter of time before they tried to form new alliances. We still need to build up our strength in the area."

It was something that Apuesta had been worrying more about lately. His battalion, normally 525 soldiers strong, was down to little more than half strength. The constant street battles and raids had been sapping his strength for several months, and the General Staff in Mexico City had been giving one excuse after another when he asked for replacements. Their loudest cry was for soldiers in the south to keep a lid on the potential peasant revolt. They had been rising up more and more since the mid 90's. Apuesta had cut his teeth and earned his first company command putting down the rebels. He had little sympathy for a commander who was having trouble controlling his district with the superior firepower they had. The peasants were not as savage or well armed as the cartels, nor the control of millions of dollars of drug trade to show for their efforts. A good infantry sweep with some free fire tactics and the *campesinos* quickly realized that their one room shacks and miserable subsistence garden plots weren't worth dying for.

"A couple of days and we will be back in business. Have faith."

Cardozo wasn't convinced. "At least let me send an extra squad to your *hacienda.* If there are any problems they will be in a position to respond."

"Do you really think the Marines would be that audacious to try to take on our operations before they have their entire strength here? We need every man to deal with their movements as they come in piecemeal. They won't be expecting any trouble when their convoy comes in from the south tomorrow. A well placed tractor trailer on the *Calle de Revolucion* and we will have them bottled up on the bridge. Our cartel allies will make short work of them, and we can move in and 'rescue' them."

"I am not worried about the Marines, *Jefe.* I think the *gringos* may be the ones our men saw to the west last night. That one that insulted me in Columbus shouldn't have been there. They were watching our *cantina.* I think they know more about our operations than we realize."

Apuesta got up and walked over to his Sergeant Major. He put his hand on the older man's shoulder and squeezed. "We take care of the Marines first. The Americans aren't going to do anything until their Colonel Kearney gets back with his new orders. We'll be on the move before he leaves his conference. Then I promise you, I'll make a present of any Americans we capture to you" Apuesta walked back to the couch and sat down. "Maybe we can catch that big breasted *puta* they put in charge while Kearney is away. You can kill her slowly while you take your pleasure on her, just like that little *gringo* girl I found for you in El Paso."

Cardozo smiled at his reflection in the glass as he thought back to that night, not so long ago. For the promise of a little cocaine she had gone back to the safe house with them. She had never gotten any drugs. Cardozo liked his women to feel all the pain as he alternately fucked and tortured them. That one had been remarkably long lasting. He thought the *puta* Major would last even longer.

Somewhere south of *Juarez* there was a military column pulled over to the side of the road, preparing to bivouac for the night. It was only an advance party, less than a company's worth of Mexican Marines preparing the way for the rest of their battalion under the command of the executive officer, a long serving major who had spent most of his career fighting bandits and smugglers in the southern provinces. He was fond of answering the question of when would he retire by looking at his watch. He had no intention of retiring any time soon, but it sent the message that he had put in his time and could be gone at any moment he desired. Few people realized, as he did, that he had nothing outside of the Marines, and he considered retirement as the same as a death sentence. He would prefer it if his life were to end while he was still serving on active duty, so he could have a proper military funeral, and not be laid to rest in some forgotten little cemetery behind a village church. Not that he was looking to dying soon. He hoped he still had a long and healthy life ahead. But there are worse ways to die than surrounded by fellow soldiers.

The men were clustered around in their assigned areas, waiting for the word to pitch their tents, roll out their sleeping bags and have their evening meal. The officers, and for some reason there were a lot of them with this little advance party, were clustered around the Major's

HUMMV. The Marines were joking that it wouldn't be a movement unless the officers were somewhere fucking it up.

Major Fuentes was listening to arguments from the two Captains in the group. The rest were junior lieutenants who followed the rule that it was better to keep quiet and look ignorant than to open your mouth and prove it. At this moment they could only look back and forth between the seniors, because they truly did not know what was going on. Their training had left out quite a bit about these operations in urban areas. For now, they were content to listen and learn.

"Again, Major, tell me why we are marching right up this road into the city. Everyone knows Apuesta doesn't want us here, and he'll probably do something to prove it."

The Major sighed again. He had his orders, but these young Captains were proving they had studied their lessons well and were asking all the right questions. He really didn't have any answers for them.

"Do you really think that Major Apuesta would be foolish enough to challenge us openly? It would only bring the weight of the government down on him."

"Apuesta doesn't care about the government. He's allied himself to the cartels and he's taken over this whole sector. He doesn't have to challenge us. He can have his friends do the dirty work and at the last moment come to our rescue, making himself look like a fucking hero. Going into the city over that bridge is suicide. Change the route of march and let us come in from over here," he pointed to the map, "by the airfield. Once we secure it we'll have a base to bring everyone else in on. It's one of our objectives anyway, and I'm pretty sure the Colonel won't mind if we secure it first. He doesn't even want to be here. And, as a bonus, we won't have to depend on the Army to quarter and support us." The word 'Army' came out like a dirty word. This Captain was very loyal to his branch.

The Major was growing tired of this young officer and his incessant demands to change the plan, but he had several good points: the battalion commander didn't want to be here, nobody trusted Apuesta, and he was the one who had drawn up the plans for their entry into *Cuidad Juarez.* He looked at his watch. They had several hours of daylight left, and there was no hard and fast schedule. They had agreed on the arrival time for the advance as a matter of courtesy, but they had no real deadline, since the main body of Marines wouldn't even be leaving the coast for another two days. He decided to indulge his subordinate. If he was wrong, there would be no big problem, other than his soldiers would lose a night of sleep. But if he was correct, they would avoid the ambush that everyone secretly expected and have an airfield for their helicopter support, and they would have outflanked Apuesta and his narco-soldiers, a small victory to begin this shitty campaign. He held up his hand to stop the back and forth bickering and regain control of his leaders meeting.

"Very well, Captain Nunez, here's what you are going to do. Break out a platoon and secure that airfield. Drive all night if you have to, and have it secured before daylight. We won't move from here until we have that word from you."

"It will be done."

Ambition and arrogance: two characteristics of either a good officer or a complete fool. The Major attempted to moderate his ardor. "Don't get involved in anything you can't handle. I don't imagine Apuesta leaves his main smuggling asset unprotected. If there is too much strength in the area fall back and radio me for instructions. We don't have the men to get involved in a heavy battle." He moved his finger over to the south west of the map and rested it on an elevation marked *el Indio*. It did not escape the attention of the assembled officers that they were conducting their operations based on an American printed and issued map. "If things are going well for you, send a squad up here to establish an observation post. This seems to be the best place in the valley for it, and it will probably serve as a good communications relay point." That should teach the young officer a lesson. If he wanted to go change the plan, the Major would give him more to do than he had planned on.

The group stepped back as the meeting broke up and gave the Major a perfunctory salute. As the officers started drifting away he called them back. "One more thing, Captain." He pointed to a baby faced Lieutenant whose name he hadn't bothered to learn. "Take this officer with you. If there's any shooting, make sure he's in it. He looks like he needs some seasoning."

The Lieutenant smiled at the opportunity to see action, but his Captain wasn't so sure. It was just like the Major to saddle him with an untried officer when there were other, better Lieutenants he could have chosen, but he knew it would be pointless to argue. He gave the Major another, wordless, salute and led the Lieutenant away. "Don't get too excited, my young friend. If things go to shit tonight I can promise you that you will be the one to wipe its ass!"

Chapter 12

"Are you good to go, Ralph?' Grant asked his old friend as they walked around the compound. The sun was getting low in the west, thinking about dropping beyond the continental divide. All around them was the quiet activity of men and women getting ready to go into harm's way.

"I don't suppose I'd get another day or two if I said I wasn't?" First Sergeant Harrison was a worrier. He never seemed to have enough time, but he was always ready. Grant knew he would be tonight. "All you have to do is watch the back door, and make sure nobody tries to close it on us. I expect you're going to have a very boring night."

Harrison wasn't convinced. "Luke, I still think you're going in too soon with too little intelligence and no support. Your buddy Vaughn may talk a good game, but I really don't think he has your best interests at heart."

"Ralph, in all my years, I don't think I've ever met any officer over the grade of Major who's sent me anywhere with my best interests at heart. And I only exempt the lower ranking officers on the condition that they're coming with me."

"You know that, and yet you still go. I think a good psychiatrist would tell you it's a sign of insanity."

"Yeah, I was abused as a child. I'm always looking for attention." Grant asked a few general questions that he already knew the answers to. Harrison and Blackman had come up with a division of labor for the rear detachment. Blackman would stay back and monitor the commo nets with Callan, and he would direct the last of the palace guard if there was a need for additional troops. That would definitely be a worst case scenario, because there really wasn't anything left that would qualify as a combat force. The ones that might qualify would already be just short of the border in a staging area with Harrison, and Grant hoped the hell they wouldn't need them either, because they were just shy of the bottom of the barrel. All Grant wanted them to do was secure the border crossing. Nothing more, nothing less. Both men knew that if Harrison had to take his scratch force over into Mexico to reinforce anyone, the situation was probably already beyond salvaging. Grant decided to change the subject.

"What's the good word on the Witch?" The Witch was the Wicked Witch, the crashed B-17 they had salvaged in the African desert and had somehow managed to get all the way home. Harrison's wife Willa had recognized the value in the pile of junk and had established a non-profit organization to restore it. The extra parts, manuals and supplies Price had found in the Quonset hut had been shipped to the hanger it was stored in and had been put to good use by the volunteer restorers. Harrison perked up at the question. He was looking forward to the day when he'd see it again, and he was planning on getting his multi-engine pilots rating so he would be able to fly it.

"Last time I talked to Willa she said they had the fuselage back together and were working on the wings. They're having trouble finding another engine stand, so they can only work on one at a time, but they've already tested one and it runs good."

"Do they really think it'll fly again?"

Harrison broke into a broad smile. "You bet your ass they do, and I'm going to fly it. Those schematics and spools of control cable Price found are making all the difference in the world. He found some other parts that just don't exist in the world any more, and now we don't have to try to re-invent them."

They walked over to the Mess tent where SFC Moura had put out a buffet for the evening meal. There was something for everyone and they could eat as much or as little as they liked. At least two thirds of the soldiers going out tonight had been on similar outings in Africa and Europe. The remaining third had joined the unit at Fort Bliss, and had yet to come under fire. They were scattered throughout the platoons, so nobody had to worry about too many new guys being together in the same place, but Grant and Harrison worried anyway.

"How come Vaughn isn't here? You'd think he'd want to be right up front to take credit for all this."

Grant shook his head. "Vaughn doesn't want to be any closer to this than the press conference if it all goes well. He's probably someplace establishing his alibi right now." He glanced at his watch. "Ralph, I've got to start thinking about getting into position. I'll talk to you later."

"I thought you were letting the Robinson boys handle securing the choke point?"

"I am, but I'm still going to be close."

"Can't leave it alone, can you?"

"I'm going to try. I keep telling myself I'll only interfere if I see a problem they're not addressing."

"You know you're a fucking liar?"

"I'm going to hell for much bigger things than that." They shook hands and went their separate ways. Harrison already had his little scratch force briefed and rehearsed, and was confident that, if the situation went to hell in a hand basket, his people would be up to the task. He had included in his briefing that if they did have to go into action, it would be a last ditch effort.

"Hell, First Sergeant, if things are that bad we'd rather be with our buddies anyway." The rest of his small group responded with a loud "Hooah!" Harrison wasn't worried about them. He got them formed up and waited for the word. He would route march them to their staging area in a small hollow just short of the border road. Then they would wait, maybe the hardest part of all.

Sergeant Sharp moved his people out before dark. He was confident that they would make better time and get into position without being observed. He had been correct, and all his elements were in place and settled in to watch and wait as the other assault units got into place. He would be starting twenty minutes before everyone else, the idea being that an attack on their headquarters would bring reinforcements from the other sites. Those reinforcements would have to pass through the chokepoint that the Robinson twins, under the close supervision of Sergeant Major Grant, would secure before Major Bonneville brought up her vehicles and heavy weapons. Soldiers in convoy on a road are easier to kill than soldiers deployed in the brush, and Grant preferred killing them easy rather than the other way around.

The hours passed slowly, the moon making a slow arc in the sky until it went down just after midnight, shortly after the last unit had reported getting into position. That was SFC Powell, who had to maneuver across a lot of open territory around the *el Monumento* airfield. Sharp's troops had kept a close eye on the *hacienda* and had what he thought was an accurate head count of all the Mexicans in the compound. There were far less than he had expected. It didn't appear as if any command elements were present, only a duty officer and NCO, and he had modified his plans to take advantage of it.

There would probably be no need for the 60mm mortar to go into action as he had planned. It looked as if his assault elements would be able to take out individual Mexicans with the help of the suppressed weapons. The only tough nut could possibly be the headquarters building where there should be a 24 hour radio watch set up. If those people had anything on the ball they could be alert and respond to any unusual activity by reporting it to higher headquarters. But one of his men worked his way up to the rear of the building and was able to report that the young Lieutenant, the Duty Officer, was otherwise occupied with his Mexican sweetheart, and the only man left on duty had dimmed the lights and was reading a skin magazine. So much for the tough nut to crack.

Back at the motor pool there was but one soldier on duty. The team covering it watched as the man made one cursory check of the area after dark, then went back into his guard station and appeared to be sleeping at his dispatch desk. He would not present a problem when the time came. That left the tower, where a two man crew was equipped with a field telephone, scoped rifle, binoculars, a searchlight and a radio. They had been on their feet and keeping a 360 degree sweep of the area until after the Lieutenant made his rounds. As soon as he left they concentrated on watching his movements, paying attention to the lights in the headquarters building. About the same time Sharp's man was reporting the Duty Officer had retired with his woman, the tower crew got a call on the field phone, probably telling them that the officer was down for the night, or at least the foreseeable future. The tower crew relaxed and pulled a bottle from under the radio bench. Their dedication to duty only extended as far as the amount of supervision they got. Sharp considered the situation. Unless this was an elaborate set-up to draw them in, it looked like the first string players had the night off, or were otherwise gainfully employed. These were the guys who got the shit details, and the way they performed their duties, they earned every one of them.

He listened in on the Group net for reports from the other elements. They were all quiet, so he started flipping through the platoon frequencies. All up and down the border he listened to fragmentary reports from the other platoons, catching snips of conversation from each of them. The stories were all the same: there was some security, but not much. More of the planned objectives than they had planned appeared to be deserted. Others had fewer soldiers on duty than they had the night before. Something had drawn off the Mexicans. It would make operations easier than they had planned, but they would need a modification of the opening move. Instead of an early start, Sharp calculated that it would be just as well if all elements went in at once. It was time to call in to Grant and Bonneville and let them know that things were changing.

Price had moved his troops according to schedule. He would have rather gone earlier, but he had more objectives to cover, and a more involved movement plan. He had to make sure that there were never too many patrol vehicles in his area, in case there had been observers, as he felt there must be, even though they never found any evidence of them. What kind of a fucking army ran the type of operations they did and didn't pay any attention to what the opposition might be doing? These Mexicans were way too used to fucking over each other. At some point they would realize that the Americans preferred not to play by their rules.

The approach phase went smoothly, and the moon was just going down when he had all his people in position. The situation reports they were sending in to him at his *ad hoc* CP were both encouraging and confusing. There were fewer Mexicans on duty tonight than there had been the previous evening, when they were prepositioning their equipment. One target, where there were a number of black plastic wrapped drug bundles, had no security at all. It was a puzzle Price didn't want to have to solve tonight. There was obviously something going on somewhere else to draw all the strength off. Price just hoped whatever it was would keep the Mexicans occupied until they were safely back on the US side.

Farther to the south, Powell and Mason had moved their soldiers in closer to the airstrip. They secured a small built up area less than a kilometer from the border known as *el Mirador* and rapidly moved east. A small detail remained behind to open up the track they would be using to bring up vehicles for the withdrawal. The outlying objective, closer to the border, also marked as *el Monumento* on the map, appeared to be unoccupied. Powell led a fire team to check it out and secure it if possible. Unlike the night before, it was completely deserted. The only sign of recent activity was a pile of black plastic wrapped backpacks, each weighing 40 to 50 pounds. It didn't take a genius to realize they were full of narcotics waiting for their human porters. Powell called over his demolitions specialist and told him what he wanted. The demo specialist knitted his eyebrows in thought before he said he could do it. He and his assistant went to work rearranging the bags around a small charge of C4 and slicing them open to spill the powder. This first charge would 'energize' the narcotics and create a good sized cloud of dust. The second charge, more C4 and a gas can, would ignite the powder and create a spectacular fireball. That would be the opening to his attack.

SFC Mason was positioning his soldiers in a loose arc on the northern side of the hanger. His intent was to use a maximum volume of fire to neutralize any guards that would be left behind when Sergeant Sharp's action at the hacienda drew off any reinforcements. He was making a second circuit when one of his squad leaders stopped him.

"What's up?"

"Sarge, something isn't right here. Last night this place was swarming with the greasers. Tonight, I don't think there are a dozen, and only two trucks. Where the fuck did they all go?"

Mason checked the area with his night vision goggles and was able to roughly confirm what he had been told. He could see the cots set up in the open hanger, but only a few of them held a lumpy form. The lights were on in some of the offices that lined one side, and he could see some movement. There was way too much noise for anybody in there to be getting a good nights' sleep. It was puzzling, but the fewer Mexicans meant they would have less exposure to return fire and be able to get back to the US side earlier than they had planned. "I don't know, Mike, but the plan stays the same. As soon as that fireball goes up, put as much automatic fire in there at about knee level. We want to get them down and out fast!"

The Robinson brothers moved across the border and closed rapidly on the area now known only as 'the choke point' under the watchful eye of Sergeant Major Grant. The younger NCOs had their soldiers under control and they were moving out and taking positions almost exactly as they had been briefed and had rehearsed. Grant almost felt like excess baggage. The objective was at the upper end of a southwest to northeast running auxiliary airstrip. The few buildings didn't amount to much, but it was here that they had found the Border Patrol vehicle in an out building and torched it. The charred remains were still visible in the fading moon light. There was another surprise in store for them. This area also seemed to be deserted. One of the adobe shacks had a small pile of the black plastic back packs, but there were no sentries in sight. Instead of waiting, Grant signaled the team in to secure the area ahead of schedule. He called a radio operator over and called back to Major Bonneville, who was waiting with her vehicles in a small depression to the west of the border. The original plan was to have her stage at a small speck of nothing called *los Moscos* that was also in the process of being cleared. There didn't seem to be any point to that now, so he signaled her to pick up the advance and drive straight on through to the choke point. While he was waiting, he called back to Callan in the CP for any updates he might have.

"Only thing I have, Sergeant Major, is that there's a lack of Mexicans in the area. Seems to be something going on over in *Juarez*."

"What would that be?"

"Damned if I can figure it out. I'm monitoring a couple of Mexican stations and they all have a different story. One says that the Army is cleaning out some areas jointly with a Marine task force, another one says that there's some gang on gang action at some of the drug hotspots. The most interesting one is that the *federales* are attacking the Army. All I am sure of is that they're piling up the body count in the old town tonight!"

Grant didn't know what to make of it either. "Anything from the U-boat?"

"Nothing so far, but wait one and I'll check again." There was silence on the handset until Callan came back.

"This is interesting. U-boat says there seems to be some vehicle traffic way down to the south east. Looks like a couple of vehicles coming up from the river crossing." Grant was familiar with that crossing: it was where he and Bonneville had stopped for their picnic lunch on his recon some time ago.

"OK, have the U-boat keep an eye on them and let Mason know. He should have enough people to throw an ambush across the road if he needs to."

"Roger that," and the handset went quiet. Grant made a quick change of frequency and uttered one word: "Go!"

Apuesta was reading the reports coming in from around the city. His units were reporting attacks on their positions from both the drug gangs and in some areas, the *federales*. That didn't make any sense to him. While the non-aligned cartels occasionally tried to flex their muscles, they usually kept it to one or two major operations, not these little pin pricks all over the city. And those fucking *federales*! They never were so bold as to take on his men toe to toe. This had to be something else, maybe another bunch of drug thugs in stolen uniforms. This could all interfere with the reception he had planned for the Marines in the morning. His people would take longer to get into position, and the upswing in violence would have the Marines on alert, not the sitting ducks he had expected. He briefly considered sending someone down to where they were bivouacking and instruct them to delay their entry until noon. He threw the messages down on his desk. Timetables, he thought. He might have planned everything too closely. It would all bear watching for several hours.

Cardozo came in with a worried look on his face. "What is it now, Esteban? Is somebody else throwing grenades in the hotel zone?"

"No, *mi Commandante.* I have word from our watchers to the south. The Marines have split up. One element has been dispatched to the north west of their position. It looks like they may be sending troops to secure *el Monumento.*"

Apuesta looked at his map on the wall. It was also an American printed and issued map. He pondered for a moment. "That makes sense. At some point they would want their own logistics area, and *el Monumento* would be perfect. We can't let that happen. Have you taken any steps?"

"*Si, Commandante.* I have give orders for a platoon to be sent to reinforce the airfield. There is only a squad there now, under Ponce. Unfortunately, it may take a little time for them to disengage in the eastern neighborhoods and move across town. In the meanwhile I have given Ponce orders to send an ambush to meet the Marines in case that is where they are going."

"Very good, Esteban, I knew there was a reason I kept you around. Is there anything else?"

"One more thing, *Commandante,* I would like to send more men to your *hacienda,* just in case." Apuesta looked at the map again, measuring the distance from *el Monumento* to his *hacienda.* The Marines didn't seem to have the strength to sweep up the valley, and Ponce's ambush would hold them up long enough to put his own reinforcements in their rear. "I don't think that will be necessary." He looked at the pained expression on Cardozo's face and knew he was about to get an argument. He put up his hand to forestall it. "I'll compromise with you.

Have the duty officer prepare a squad and keep them on standby. If the situation changes, you can feel free to dispatch them."

Cardozo wasn't satisfied, but he knew he was getting all there was to get out of Apuesta for now. He saluted and backed out of the room.

The word came into the airfield just after midnight. Ponce was not the most ambitious of soldiers, and it showed by the assignments he received. Being a caretaker here instead of leading combat troops against the cartels in *Juarez* was an example of how his skills were regarded, and it bothered him. When the Sergeant Major, his high and mighty self, called to warn him about the approaching Marines and to order him to send out an ambush patrol against them, Ponce was of two minds. The first was that he had only a small scratch force, hardly enough to secure the airfield against any attacks by the *gringos* and repel an attack by Marines at the same time. His other side told him that *el Commandante* had made the assignments tonight. Ponce was aware of his low opinion of him, and if he thought the situation was such that Ponce was the man to be in charge, then there must not be much of a threat from the *gringos* tonight. He saw an opportunity to prove to *el Commandante* and his pig of a Sergeant Major that he was worthy of more responsibility, and, naturally, a bigger cut of the profits. He decided he would lead the ambush himself.

He roused all his men and told them what was going on. Several of them knew exactly what should be done, but Ponce wasn't taking any suggestions. He selected half a dozen of what he would consider his supporters and told them to get the vehicle and mount a machine gun on it. They would leave in a few minutes. One of the soldiers staying behind wasn't so sure it was a good idea.

"Ponce, you haven't even done a reconnaissance, and your men have no experience with setting up an ambush at night. Let me take this. I swear I'll let you have the credit for it."

Ponce sneered at the man. "Sure you will. Apuesta may not have much faith in me, *amigo*, but he put me in charge, and you serve me tonight. Keep your fucking opinions to yourself and try not to let anyone get hurt while I'm gone!"

The truck was ready and they were off. Ponce knew the man was right about his lack of experience, but all he had to do was find a good place and set his men up on either side of the road and wait for the Marines to come through. They wouldn't expect anything in the dark. He had his driver use parking lights to steer by and told the men in the back to keep an eye out for headlights in the distance. That would be his element of surprise. Once they spotted something in the distance, and he expected that at night he would be able to see the Marines coming a long way off, he would stop and set his ambush. It would be as easy as beating a *piñata*.

Sharp heard the word and signaled his riflemen. They would open the attack with their silenced rifles, taking out the sentries in the tower, any visible soldiers at the gates or in the compound, and whoever was to be seen in the motor pool. He held off on the mortars. The lack of soldiers in the south meant he wouldn't have to draw off reinforcements. He would take this place out at a more leisurely pace, neutralizing the survivors of the first volleys with grenades and automatic weapons fire. They would be able to gather whatever intelligence material that was here before they set their explosives and leveled the place.

With his night vision goggles, Sharp could see the entire compound. As far as he could tell, all the targets went down at once. He gave the order for the ground assault to move in. He watched two men go to the front of where the radio room was. Before they could kick in the door there was a burst of fire coming from the base of the tower. One of his men went down with wounds to the leg. The other soldier sought cover and returned fire, while another element maneuvered for position to direct some 40mm grenade fire at the unexpected resistance. While they were doing that, the team pulling outside security was redirected to the back of the radio room to neutralize it before any warning could be broadcast. They got to the window and glance in to see the operator yelling into a handset. One soldier lifted his M-4 and fired a burst into the radio operators back, then put another burst through the radio on the table. He shifted his aim to try to cover the room where the Lieutenant had been seen with his evening's entertainment. The door was open and a semi nude woman was standing there holding a sheet around her waist, screaming as she watched the radio operator die. The Lieutenant had run out the front door in his underwear, pistol in hand to see what the shooting was about. He looked down at one uniformed figure lying on the steps, crawling for cover. He could see the man had been shot in the legs. He quickly fired two rounds into the prone figures' back and turned to look for other threats. He saw two more men running towards the tower building and he fired at them. They went to ground, and as he was lining up his pistol for a better shot, the partner of the man he shot in the back emptied the rest of his M-4 magazine into his stomach and chest. The Lieutenant was thrown back into the building. Another burst from across the compound pinged into the wall over the partners head. A ricochet slammed into the back of his helmet and drove him to the ground. As he lost consciousness he heard the explosion as a 40mm grenade took out the threat. He didn't hear the second explosion as the team finished their job.

Sharp was on the ridge with one sniper team and the medic when the call came in that he had soldiers down. He got a quick situation report and started redeploying his teams as he grabbed the medic and started running down the hill to the *hacienda.* The perimeter team was sent into the radio room via the back window. Sharp realized he was breathing heavy as he shouted out the commands. He could feel every ounce of the load he was carrying on his knees and ankles.

The half naked woman screamed as the perimeter team dropped into the room. She disappeared back into the bedroom. The soldiers elected to ignore her while they secured the rest of the building. They were civilized enough to believe they should give the woman a moment of privacy to get some clothes on before they went charging in after her. It almost got them killed. She came back out of the room, sheet wrapped around her waist and breasts exposed, with a small handgun blasting away. She was a lousy shot, and the soldiers recovered from their shock (and embarrassment) at the same time and sprayed in her direction. The .223 caliber bullets tore her up and drove her back into the bedroom. They exchanged glances at each other, and continued their search.

Sharp reached the casualties a few seconds after the medic. She did a quick assessment with her tactical LED flashlight, reaching under the first soldiers' vest when she saw the shredding from the 9mm rounds. She felt the backside of the vest for any penetrations. When she didn't find any she went to work on his legs while she peppered questions at the soldier who had been hit in the back of the helmet. She had to tell him several times to take off his Kevlar pot and turn the back of his head to her so she could check for bleeding with her light. There was none, so she told him to sit quietly and not move around. Her initial guess was that he could have a concussion, and she had to keep him quiet, otherwise this macho guy would try to shake it off and do more damage to himself. Sharp knelt besides her and listened to her talk as she treated the leg wounds. When she paused he interrupted with a question. "How bad is he?"

She spouted off a few long words that Sharp was only vaguely familiar with. He had to stop her and ask for an easier answer. "Both legs got hit through and through. He's not bleeding too badly, so I don't think the artery is hit, but his left leg is pretty bad. He ain't walking out of here."

"Do we need the Medevac?"

"Call it in."

Out in the motor pool the team was checking vehicles, selecting the ones they could use and preparing the rest for demolition. The sentry in the guard shack had been alone and died slumped over his desk masturbating to a skin magazine. The Americans pushed him over onto the floor and rolled him over on his stomach. They didn't need to look at that as they torched the shack.

In the compound Sharp was gathering his men and mentally checking off his list of things to do. As the teams finished hauling their satchel charges and getting them placed he sent them out to the motor pool to bring up the vehicles they were taking with them, all American built HUMMVs. The only thing bothering him was the radio warning that might have been sent. He warned Grant about it and called back to Callan to see if he had monitored that frequency. He hadn't. It was one of those things that he didn't have any information on. It must have been a new frequency.

He could hear the UH-60 coming in from the west and had his men illuminate the far end of the compound for an LZ. The chopper flared in and Major Carson leaped out and ran to the approaching stretcher. She asked the medic a few questions and examined both patients. The man with the concussion insisted he was good to go, but Carson ordered him on to the chopper anyway. He continued to argue, but Sharp came up and cut him off. He and Sinclair had hauled down the .50 caliber rifle and the mortar, and were piling them in the cargo bay. The head injury was ordered to shut up and take care of the gear. Then he turned to the Major. "Welcome to Mexico, Ma'am!" he called over the rotor wash.

She instructed the litter bearers to load the patient before she turned to Sharp. "This wasn't how I planned to spend my vacation, Sergeant. I thought this was supposed to be a quick in and out operation."

"Shit happens, Ma'am. The bad guys either didn't get or chose to ignore the 'No casualties allowed' memo." He gestured to the dead Mexicans sprawled at the far end of the compound. "They have been duly reprimanded."

She shook her head and pushed past him to get on the UH-60. The crew chief pulled the door shut and lifted off, staying low as it headed back to the west, trying to stay under any radar that might have been active in the valley. Sharp didn't bother to watch it go. He had other things to worry about.

He had his men line up the vehicles and collected the detonators. Half his force he dispatched south to reinforce Grant, if need be. The rest were sent back up to the north. They could bring two HUMMVs back to the Border Patrol station, where a maintenance bay had been set aside for them to repaint the vehicles with American markings. SFC Mitchell wasn't going to keep them. He was planning to strip them for all the spare parts he could get and burn the hulks somewhere up in the mountains. He felt the Mexicans owed him that for all the equipment they had damaged. Sharp gave them the order to leave one of the suppressed rifles with him and move out.

"What about you, Sarge, you planning to freelance?" Sinclair asked.

"Don't worry about me. Tell the Sergeant Major I stayed behind just in case that warning went out. I'll keep them occupied until the rest of you are out of here."

"Maybe somebody should stay with you, you know, to watch your back and help haul your gear out?"

"If there's a problem I'll dump everything I don't need and start running. The only thing Uncle Sam cares about is the part with the serial number, and I plan to take good care of it." Sinclair looked at him blankly until he realized Sharp was referring to his own serial number. "Get going. I'll be fine."

He watched as his men drove off. When they were out of sight he walked back into the compound and went to the flag pole. He lowered the Mexican flag and threw it on the ground. The he took the stainless steel 9mm he had taken from his new best buddy *Esteban* in Columbus and tied it to the lanyard. It would be bait for any relief force that arrived and it would send a message to the ugly fucking Mexican he had taken it from.

"Commandante, the radio room reports there was a brief call from your *hacienda*. They couldn't make out the message, and now they don't answer. Can I dispatch the relief squad?"

Apuesta sat at his desk and stared at his Sergeant Major. There were too many things happening all of a sudden. "Are you certain the *hacienda* isn't answering?" Could it be an equipment problem? The radio out there is old."

"No, *mi Commandante*," he answered. "I had them try both the land lines and cellulars. There was no answer, and there are several phones out there."

"Very well. Have the squad assemble in the courtyard. As soon as things quiet down a little we will send them out. You will lead them." Apuesta looked up at his map and the little yellow pieces of paper that were stuck to it. "We had those reports of vehicles the last few nights. It's probably those fucking Marines fucking with us." Cardozo knew his *Commandante* was bothered by all this. The man rarely swore, and here he did twice in the same sentence. He saluted and went to his own quarters to get into his combat gear. If there were Marines out there, he would teach them a lesson. And if it was the Americans, that would be all the better.

Far to the south Captain Nunez called a halt and instructed his men to stay alert. He positioned them on the trucks in what he considered the best possible arrangement and walked back to his HUMMV. His driver was standing on his seat looking to the north with a pair of binoculars. "There's a vehicle headed our way, Captain." Nunez climbed on to his seat and took the glasses. His driver pointed to where he had seen the lights. "They come and go, but every so often you can make them out." Nunez was about to give up when there was a flash of light on the edge of his field of view. He had been looking just off to the side.

"OK. Black out drive. Let's see who's coming to welcome us to this little patch of heaven."

Chapter 13

Grant had his area secured, or rather, the Robinsons had the area secured. It took a mighty effort, but Grant had managed to avoid taking over from them. He did exercise his authority as soon as they gave the 'all clear' and gave instructions for them to redeploy and provide a security screen to the south. As soon as the vehicles arrived he placed them in their best protected positions to cover as many approaches as possible. Bonneville dismounted and walked over to where he was standing on a low wall, scanning with his field glasses. He jumped down when he noticed her standing there.

"Sharp had some casualties. He called for the helicopter."

That was news to Grant, but he wasn't monitoring all the frequencies all the time.

"Serious?"

"The medic doesn't think so, but there were broken bones. She felt it would be better if they flew out. The other one seems to be a concussion."

Two casualties, Grant thought. That wasn't so bad. Sharp was taking the largest group in against what could have been the most heavily fortified target. They got off easy. He was about to say as much to Bonneville, who was clearly upset about any casualties, when a huge flash of light erupted to the south, followed by a low rumble of thunder.

"It would seem, Major, that Powell and Mason have opened their part of this little affair."

Nunez had just called another halt and cautioned his men to be alert. He had the drivers turn off their lights and engines. He cursed the powers that be for not authorizing them any night vision equipment, "You are only an advance party," they had been told. "We do not expect you to conduct any night operations!" The vehicle approaching seemed to be unaware of their presence until the last minute. They came around the last curve in the road and screeched to a halt as their parking lights dimly illuminated the military vehicles parked on the side of the road. Both sides sat there, looking at one another, trying to formulate a plan of action, when a huge fireball erupted to the north. Nunez looked at it, any night vision he had ruined, and thought to himself that the sound of the blast was less than what he would have expected for such a large column of light.

Ponce was surprised by the explosion also. He turned to look over his shoulder and came to the immediate conclusion that he was the one who had been ambushed on this dark road. He convinced himself that he had stumbled onto their vehicle park. There was a low staccato of gunfire building up too, and that made up his mind. The fucking Marines had slipped past him and were attacking the airfield. He could see figures moving around the parked trucks, and gave the order to fire at them. Nunez and his driver, who had both stood to look at the fireball, were the first targets. Both men went down, the driver dead and Nunez with several bullets to his left side. He fell out of his vehicle trying to bring his weapon with him, calling out for his own Marines to return fire. He was trying to bring his weapon into action as the Battalion Commanders words echoed in his brain: "We do not expect you to conduct any night operations!" The joke was on somebody, but Nunez wasn't sure who.

The explosion brought the rest of the Mexicans out of the hanger to see what was going on. The building that exploded was at the far end of the strip, about two and a half kilometers away, but they could feel the shock wave and the heat from the explosion. Several of them started firing in the direction of the blast, prompting others to believe they had seen something. They started spraying bullets in every direction. The immediate result was that Sergeant Mason, who had stood up to see the blast column when it went off, was immediately cut down, along with his radio operator. Both survived because of their body armor, but they were hit in the arms, removing them from any further participation. The medic, had remained on the ground but turned to see where the firing was coming from and took a round under the rim of her helmet, killing her instantly. Mason tried to crawl over to her to get her to start rendering first aid, thinking she had frozen under fire. When she didn't respond to his cries for help, he painfully fished an LED flashlight out of an equipment pouch. Her dead eyes were staring back at him. He crawled back to his radio operator, who seemed to be either unconscious or in shock and tried to raise somebody, anybody, on the radio. He made several calls, but got no response. The effort wore him out, and Mason found himself drifting off. He lay back to try to regain his focus, and promptly passed out.

The wild firing was returned by the rest of the hidden assault force, laid out in an arc that covered the hanger and two other buildings from the north and west. Both those buildings were a combination of wood and adobe, and had been targeted by 40mm grenade launchers, M-203s. The grenadiers, surprised by the volume of fire from the hanger, sent their first couple of salvos wide. By then, return fire from the rest of the Americans had forced the surviving Mexicans back into the hanger to try to find some protection, and the grenadiers were able to score hits on their targets.

Powell was trying to raise Mason on the radio. He finally sent a runner over to try to find him. At the last minute, Mason had changed his position for a better vantage point, and hadn't told anyone where his new position was. For the time being, he could not be located. There was still firing coming from the hanger, and Powell wanted an immediate end to it. He called out for any and all grenadiers to start lobbing grenades into the hanger, and not stop until the return firing ceased, or the fucking place collapsed. The muzzle flashes from inside the building made convenient aiming points, and the firing soon ceased. Powell ordered his men to move in and mop up and start preparing all the structures for demolition. He got on the radio to try to find the medic. He had another man wounded in the wild firing. When his efforts were unsuccessful he called for a combat lifesaver. Several of his men had additional first aid training, and now would be the time for them to demonstrate they had paid attention in the classes.

Ponce's men had concentrated all their fire on the lead vehicle, giving the rest of the Marines a chance to deploy on both sides of the road and make short work of the soldiers. An NCO checked on Nunez and his driver. He pulled Nunez off to the side of the road and called for a medic, which they didn't have. Nunez sent him to look at the driver. When he reported the man was dead Nunez roared that he wanted any survivors from the opposing force brought to him. There were sounds of explosions to the north while the Marines checked the bodies. They found Ponce cowering on the floor of his vehicle. They pulled him out and dragged him to where Captain Nunez was propped up against the wheel of his vehicle. The Marines threw Ponce to the ground in front of Nunez. All Ponce could do was beg for forgiveness and plead his ignorance of what just happened.

"We are all on the same side. This was just a terrible accident!"

Nunez lashed out with his boot. "You fucking pig! You're trying to tell me a soldier doesn't recognize military vehicles when he sees them?"

Ponce was sobbing now. "Please, Senor. I have a family!"

"So did my driver!" Nunez called his NCO over. "Take this piece of shit over to his friends and let him join them." The sergeant grunted his response and dragged Ponce away. He continued to blubber until a single shot quieted him. Nobody else said a word. The NCO came back and inspected his wounds. Nunez winced under his probing fingers, especially when he touched around the shoulder. The NCO winced with him. "I don't think you're too bad, Captain, but your shoulder is fucked. I'll try not to hurt you when I immobilize it. Nunez laughed at that statement. Here they were in the heart of drug smuggling territory, and they didn't have any morphine for his wounds. He was patient while he was bandaged, then told his men to help him to his feet. He looked into his HUMMV and could see that the radio was useless.

The faceplate had been blown off. There was still firing and explosions coming from the airfield. He was asked for orders.

"Load the men up and move up a little closer to the shooting up there. Let's try to see what's going on."

"What about him?" the NCO asked, pointing to the body of the driver.

"Wrap him up in a poncho and take him with us. The rest you can leave for the scavengers."

Price pulled his people back to their rally point and called for instructions. He was prepared to go either north or south as needed, but Bonneville, after consulting with Grant, told him to get a good headcount and take his people back to the friendly side of the border. While he was assembling his men, vehicles came down from the north. He threw his men out in a screen and switched to Sharp's frequency. He was relieved when they flashed their lights as requested and passed them through. Price thought it was odd that Sharp hadn't slowed down and conferred with him, but everyone had their own orders. He reassembled his troops and started the hike home.

Powell had radioed in that Mason was missing, and delayed blowing up the rest of his targets until he found them. Bonneville was growing impatient with the delay. There had been reports of more vehicles coming up from the south, but they had stopped short of what Powell termed 'engagement range' and seemed to be content with observing what they could in the dark. As soon as Sharp's element pulled into the chokepoint, Bonneville started splitting them up, some to take their captured vehicles back to the border, and others to go south and help in the search for Mason. She stopped issuing orders when she realized Sergeant Sharp wasn't there.

"Where the hell is he?"

There was a collective shuffling of feet and down turned faces until one soldier told her that Sharp had taken a scoped rifle and stayed behind. Grant heard the last part and came over to find out why.

"He didn't really say, Sergeant Major. He just wanted us to tell you that he was hanging back in case any warnings got out, and he'd watch out backs."

"Okay, Sinclair. Get your people ready to move out."

Bonneville was getting ready to boil over. "He's not answering his radio. The last thing we need is another MIA."

"We don't have another one. At least Sharp told them he was doing something. Mason just vanished. There's a difference."

She didn't agree. "We don't have him, and he's not talking to us. That makes him MIA."

"Yes, Ma'am. Can I suggest we find Mason first? At least we know that Sharp, as of a few minutes ago, still had all his parts working." Grant was trying to calm her down. He didn't know what Sharp was planning, but he had faith that he would only do something marginally stupid. "Once we get the situation down south stabilized, I'll handle finding my prodigal."

"You better, Sergeant Major. I have no intention of leaving anyone on this side of the border when we go."

Grant was about to respond almost as heatedly when Bonneville's RTO interrupted with news that Mason had been found. He and his RTO were shot up, and the Medic was dead. One other soldier had been slightly injured. "Sergeant Powell says he's calling the Medevac. As soon as it's clear he'll blow the hanger and then get the fuck out of Dodge!"

Powell had his men bring the casualties in close to the side of the runway and had his men lay out light sticks to mark an LZ. The night air was still enough so that they could hear the UH-60 bearing in on them before they could see the navigation lights. To the south, Nunez had slumped into unconsciousness, and his NCO was worried about him. One of his soldiers pointed out the helicopter coming in. "More fucking trouble."

The NCO looked over at it and realized where it was coming from. He looked around for the young Lieutenant, whose name nobody bothered to learn. He was sitting back in the cargo truck, trying to ignore everything that was going on around him. The NCO wasn't the sharpest tool in the drawer, and he knew it, but he was savvy enough to realize his Captain was in a bad way, and somebody needed to make a decision.

"He's coming in from the *Estados Unidos*! With all those lights on he's not trying to hide."

"What do you think?"

The Sergeant rubbed his face. "I don't think. I hope it means they have some casualties too, and that's a medical evacuation helicopter."

"You hope?"

"Yeah. Shut up and help me with the Captain. Make sure he doesn't fall out." He told the driver to get out and took his place. He started the engine and called to his men to stay right where they were. "I'll be back." With that he put his headlights on high beam and turned on his emergency flashers. If the *gringos* could see him coming like this, maybe they wouldn't shoot.

"Hey, Sarge, that fucking Mexican is coming up with all lights blazing. What should I do?"

Powell looked south and could see the lights coming up. He turned back to the west and saw the chopper was almost there. He clicked his handset. "Hold him up and see what he wants. If the fuckers want a fight, waste 'em!"

The UH-60 flared and Lieutenant Robles jumped out. She was visibly upset to see that the KIA was Sergeant Abbott, one of her medics. She shook it off and moved to the other two casualties. A quick glance and she started giving them orders to load them. Powell's radio came to life again. "Sarge, the Mexican here says he's a Marine and he has a badly shot up officer. He wants to know if we have a medic who can look at him."

"Stand by." He consulted with Robles. "I don't have time to look at him. Tell them to bring him up here and we'll take him out with our wounded!"

"Is that a good idea?"

"It's my call, Sergeant. Get it done."

Bonneville had been monitoring Powell's frequency and heard what was happening. She started to tell them to leave the Marine behind, but Grant interrupted her. "The Mexicans already know we're here. Might as well go for some good will."

"They can't prove anything yet."

"We don't know what they can prove. Keeping this guy alive might tone down how pissed off they are at us." She looked at him with hard eyes. No two ways about it, she was seriously pissed off. "All right. As soon as the chopper is gone have Powell blow everything up and get out of there."

"Cardozo! Get your relief squad ready. I've lost contact with the airfield too."

Cardozo was ready with his gear. If Apuesta had listened to him earlier he would already have the troops he needed out in the desert and things probably wouldn't be going to shit the way they are.

"I'll follow you out in my helicopter. I'll do a fly by to see what going on and we can meet up before you enter the compound."

The vehicles were lined up and heading back towards the border. Grant had pulled the last Mexican HUMMV out of line and sent the soldiers over to another vehicle. He had them leave one of the scoped rifles for him.

"Are you going for Sergeant Sharp, Sergeant Major?"

"Son, all you have to remember is that I was in the last vehicle and you lost track of me. Don't say anything to anyone unless you're asked, got it?"

"Can we go with you?"

"Get in your vehicle, and get the fuck out of here. This part of Mexico is not the place you're gonna want to be when the sun comes up."

He watched as the last vehicle turned down the trail to the border, then he kept to the right and headed back up to the *hacienda*. There had been no tell tale flash in the sky to the north, so he was pretty sure Sharp hadn't touched anything off yet. He was keeping it intact for bait, but

Grant couldn't figure out for what. He snapped his headlights on and drove north as quickly as he dared. A quick glance at his watch told him he'd be running out of night pretty soon.

Sharp lay in a little depression just below the ridge to the west of the *hacienda*. He had been lying still for almost an hour now, and his kidneys were starting to scream at him. He had several reasons for not emptying his bladder right now and one of them was only about 50 yards above him. The other was about four hundred yards down slope, just to the left of the main building. It was a rather simple equation: he could take out one, but not both, and whichever one he left would have his position and the advantage, so he continued to wait for one of them to make a mistake. The far horizon was starting to lighten, but the sky to the east looked overcast. At least he wouldn't have the sun in his eyes. He lifted his head slightly and glance towards the sound of a vehicle coming up on the right. It couldn't be good, because by now there wouldn't be any friendlies left in Mexico. That made three problems.

It was one of the Mexican HUMMVs his men had taken south several hours ago. He recognized it by the baby puke green canvas rolled up on the tail gate. He shifted his scope to see the driver. What the fuck was Grant doing up here?

"Is that my loveable Sergeant Major I see where he's not supposed to be?"

The HUMMV slowed and there was a response. "Where are you?"

"About four hundred meters up, say 11 o'clock from your front bumper."

"Are you coming down?"

"Not yet. I've got a couple of problems here I should probably tell you about. Stop in front of the two story building. There's a gomer on the other side of the compound." Grant did as he was told. "Stay on the far side of the vehicle; he's got a buddy up here."

Grant walked around the HUMMV and took the scoped rifle out of the rear. He sat down against the back tire and took it out of its case. Then he crawled under the vehicle and started scanning the slope through his scope.

"I didn't know you had any ghillie suits with you." A ghillie was a head to toe camouflaged suit that snipers and Scottish game keepers preferred. They were also popular with wannabe paint-ballers.

"If I had the ghillie you wouldn't have seen me so fast. That's the other problem I was telling you about. Him and his buddy started stalking me about an hour ago. They're not very good, but they're lucky."

"How lucky?"

"Small hole, nothing to worry about."

"You bastard. It's your turn to carry me out."

"We can argue that point later, if you don't mind. Have you got a shot? I rerally need to take a leak."

"Fire on three?"

"One... two...three!" Both rifles cracked at once. Grant saw his target slump ever so slightly. He put another round into him for insurance. Sharp did the same.

"Can we go home now?" Grant asked, scanning the rest of the hill side before he crawled out from under the HUMMV.

"Nah, not yet. There might be somebody else coming to the party. Why don't you park that hippie wagon of yours closer to the building so you're not blocking the road, then come on up here. But make it quick, I've got vehicles a couple of klicks out."

Grant got up and moved the vehicle up against the building. As he was taking his gear out, he got another call from Sharp. "You might want to crawl back under there."

"Now what?"

"Looks like a Loach coming up." A loach was a light observation helicopter. He probably wants to see why no one is answering the phone."

"You know, fuck head, if you had just blown this place like you were supposed to, we wouldn't be having this problem!"

There was no answer from Sharp, but Grant could hear the chopper now. It was coming on fast and low. He crawled back under the HUMMV and tried to stay as close as he could under the engine block. Its bulk would offer a little protection if whoever was coming in decided to give the place a quick strafing. The chopper made a couple of high speed passes, probably trying to draw fire. When he didn't, he made a couple of slow passes around the compound, slowing over any bodies he saw. Then he flew slowly around the area, looking for signs on the ground. He didn't fly out far enough to pass over Sharp's position. As he flew off and the engine noise started to recede, Sharp called for him to come up in a hurry. Grant unloaded his equipment and trotted up the hill. The slope wasn't too bad, but Grant was wearing body armor, a hydration pack and a double load of ammo. Plus he had the scoped rifle in its case and a bandolier of spare magazines for it. It didn't take long for him to start feeling every day of his age.

"You can slow down old man. The chopper landed next to the convoy."

Major Bonneville got her small convoy back to the border and shepherded everyone back to their assembly area. Her first order of business was to get a good head count. Anything else was secondary and could wait. She was not leaving anyone unaccounted for in Mexico. One by one the platoon and section leaders came back with their tallies. Everyone was accounted for except SFC Sharp and CSM Grant. Bonneville choked on the water she was drinking. "How long has he been missing?"

"Sergeant Major grabbed the last vehicle and sent us ahead, Ma'am. He told us he'd be OK alone," was Sinclair's' response. Grant had never informed her he was staying behind.

"When did the Sergeant Major get separated from us?"

Again Sinclair had the answer. "I don't know for sure, Ma'am. He took one of the Mexican vehicles and had the rest of us go ahead. I thought he was tail end Charlie on the trip back. He must not have made the turn."

Bonneville knew instinctively that Grant hadn't missed any turn. He never got lost. The bastard must have gone up to hunt for his friend. She felt a knot in her stomach and wanted to throw up.

Price heard the news and came up to her. "You want me to take a few guys and go back and get them?"

"Sergeant Price, do you really think those two want someone to go back and get them?"

"No, Ma'am, but they might need a little hand."

Bonneville shook her head. They wouldn't want anyone else coming back for them, that's why Grant arranged it so no one would know until they were back on the US side of the border. "No, have Callan see if he can put up a drone and look for them. I don't want anyone else wandering around in the dark over there."

"Ma'am, I'm pretty sure I'll be able to find them up around the *hacienda*."

"I'm certain that's where you'd find them, but I said no. They're big boys. They know what they're doing."

Price nodded and walked away. Bonneville sat in her command vehicle and thought to herself. They're not big boys. They're little fucking kids going out on one more big adventure, and they're going to get themselves killed this time. She buried her face in her hands and cried.

Apuesta had flown in on his personal observation helicopter. The situation in *Juarez* had quieted with the coming of daylight, as he had expected. Arrangements had been made to ambush, then rescue, the Marines coming up from the south, but they didn't seem to be in any hurry to move from their night laager. To compound everything, his communications officer was unable to raise anybody in the border region. The day was not starting on a promising note. The only thing he could think of was that the Marines had lied to him about their intentions and had moved into the border in some strength. He would have to take steps to resolve his problems.

As he flew to his *hacienda* he could see the smoke plumes rising from the damage done to the south. He fought the urge to survey the damage. There was nothing he could do about it until he had more strength on the ground. He directed his pilot to make a couple of passes around his compound to try and draw fire. When they got none he had him make a slow, hovering circuit. There were bodies scattered around the compound and on the roof of the tower, his motor pool had been emptied of all but a few of his commercial vehicles. The military trucks were gone, except for one parked in the shadow of the tower. He knew it was his from the ugly green tarp it carried. It didn't belong where it was, but he would determine why later.

"Do you want me to land, *Senor*?"

"No. Check the land outside the compound. See if the bastards left any observers behind." There was nothing to be seen. "Go back to Cardozo." The pilot did as he was told, then zipped back to where the convoy was parked. Cardozo was waiting for him, binoculars in hand. Apuesta bounded out of the chopper and went to him for a report. The Sergeant Major told him there was nothing. He had sent a sniper team ahead of the main body. They reported a movement in the brush and shot it, but didn't find anything. Since then they had been quiet.

"I didn't see them, Cardozo."

"My men are very good, *Commandante.* You weren't supposed to see them."

Apuesta grunted. All his 'very good' men had let him down so far today. He directed Cardozo to take his men into the compound and secure it. Apuesta would wait here with the helicopter. When all was clear, he would come up. Cardozo saluted and issued the necessary orders. Apuesta noticed there was an officer with the convoy who seemed to be content to let Cardozo give the orders. A man like that was one of the reasons things had gone to shit for him overnight. He made a mental note to get rid of the man as soon as he could. It was a death sentence for the officer, because Apuesta could not afford to transfer out anyone who knew what the battalions' true operations were.

Cardozo made a high speed approach to the compound and slowed at the motor pool. He dispatched men to check the area and secure it. He walked into the guard shack and found the sentry lying on the floor in a pool of blood. The flies were already gathering. There was a pornographic magazine open on the desk. Cardozo lifted the body with the toe of his boot and saw his penis was hanging out of his open fly. If he wasn't already dead, Cardozo would have shot him. These pigs were paid to be on guard, not masturbate all night.

He left a couple of soldiers behind and drove on to the compound. He stopped his vehicles outside and sent his soldiers in on foot to clear the buildings. He walked around the compound examining the bodies while waiting for the reports. It looked as though at least some of his soldiers had fought back. There was evidence at least one of the attackers had been wounded and carried off. The remains of the bandage wrappings were on the porch of the main building, next to the body of a young lieutenant who was wearing nothing but his boxer shorts, but had a pistol clutched in his hand. Cardozo took it and checked the magazine. There were rounds missing, and there were shell casings on the ground.

The teams were reporting the buildings were clear. He called for Apuesta and went inside the big house. He could see the dead radio operator at the far end of the living room. He glanced into a side room and saw the naked body of a woman. She was lying on her side on a crumpled sheet. The front of the body was marked with small bloody entrance wounds. The back looked like hamburger. She had a small caliber handgun gripped in her hand. Sometimes even the whores fought back, but now he knew why the lieutenant was in his underwear. Even the one in charge of the guard detail had been fucking off.

He walked back outside when he heard the helicopter land at the far end of the compound. The prop wash created a small dust storm, and Cardozo could hear the soft rhythmic clang of metal on metal. As the helicopter powered down he traced the origin of the sound to the flagpole. He changed direction and walked towards it. Apuesta walked towards him as he got to the base of the pole and grabbed the stainless steel Beretta that was tied to the lanyard. He recognized it as his pistol, the one taken from him by that fucking *gringo* in Columbus.

"What's that Cardozo?" Apuesta asked.

Cardozo's eyes were wide as he looked at his *Commandante*, and turned to look towards the rising ground outside the compound. Apuesta looked at the pistol in his Sergeant's hand, not registering what he was seeing. Then he realized what he was looking at.

Grant was breathing hard when he got to Sharp.

While he was waiting for his Sergeant Major, Sharp had gone over to the dead sniper and recovered his weapon and part of the ghillie suit. It was a commercial hunting rifle with a cheap scope. The ghillie wasn't even custom made. It looked like something bought out of a paint ball catalogue. The idiot hadn't even bothered to use hunting ammo, just military surplus full metal jacket. No wonder it hurt so much going through his calf, but didn't do too much damage. He was re-bandaging it as Grant came up to his position. "Can you walk on that?"

"I don't have to walk, Luke. When we're done we'll ride out in that pretty truck you brought."

"It's going to be that easy?"

"I sure as hell hope so."

Both men settled in and concealed themselves as best they could. Sharp took his knife to the ghillie and passed half to Grant, who used it as a drape for his rifle.

"What's the plan?"

Sharp rambled on about placement of explosives and maximum damage. "I figured this was important to somebody, and he'd want to see what we did. I hadn't counted on the sniper team or the helicopter, but if they showed up, I guess whoever comes next is pretty important."

They were quiet for a few moments, both watching the activity in the distance, when Sharp spoke again. "I hear they hauled another Mexican out of here on one of the Medevacs. Isn't that what got everybody pissed at me?"

"Yeah, they did. Every time I think we have people trained, somebody else wants to be a humanitarian."

Sharp laughed. "Is that what I am now, a fucking humanitarian?"

"Not the legacy you were looking for, is it, Dave?"

"Well, I have to admit I was kind of looking forward to being the town drunk somewhere. This could screw up my retirement plan."

They watched as the convoy stopped at the motor pool, and then continued to the main compound. Sharp watched one figure in particular. "Know who that is?"

Grant had been following him too. "That's Apuesta's Sergeant Major, an ugly fuck named Cardozo. I met him at the academy a while back. I don't think he likes me."

Sharp stifled a laugh. "He's the guy I got the laptop back from. That's his *pistola* dangling from the flag pole. I know he don't like me."

"Fine, Shoot him, blow the place up, and lets get out of here before the rest of the fucking Mexican Army shows up looking for us."

"Okay, Luke. Just as soon as I see who's in the chopper."

They both watched as soldiers scurried around the compound, darting in and out of buildings and reporting back to Cardozo. Finally, they seemed to be satisfied and the helicopter was called in. They watched as it settled in at the far end of the compound and powered down. They both recognized who got out.

"Which one do you want, Dave?"

They watched both men walk over to the flag pole. "I'm kind of partial to that ugly fucking Sergeant Major, if you don't mind."

"As long as it doesn't become a habit. Say when."

They watched as both men looked at the pistol, and turned to look at the hill side.

"When."

Sharp fired a split second before Grant. Apuesta heard the impact of the round into Cardozo's' head. He looked as his Sergeant Major snapped back at the same time he heard the sonic crack of the round. He looked for the source as everything went blank for him. Seconds later, the placed charges started detonating. When the first one went off the pilot looked for Apuesta and saw him on the ground at the foot of the flag pole. His next impulse was to power up and get out of the area. He was pleased with himself as he lifted off and skimmed across the compound, gaining altitude. As he crossed over the top of the two story building the blast came up from under him and rocked his chopper on its side. He tried to regain control as the ground rushed up and he could see the rotors digging into the dirt. That was his last memory.

Grant and Sharp watched as the dust settled in the compound.

There were a few figures left moving around, but they quickly ran back to where the vehicles were parked and headed back east. Grant said to let them go. They didn't stop to check for any wounded. The two Americans watched a short while longer, and when they were satisfied they were no remaining threats they collected their gear and moved down the hill. They stopped at the HUMMV Sharp had thought they'd be driving out on. Part of the building had collapsed on it.

"I told you I wasn't carrying you out." Grant said. Sharp looked sheepish as he glanced around the compound to where the other vehicles were parked.

"Want to try one of those?"

They walked through the compound, weapons at the ready. It was like the end of "The Wild Bunch", only they were still alive. They paused at the flag pole to look at the bodies of Apuesta and Cardozo. Sharp cut the pistol from the lanyard and put it inside his vest. Grant didn't say anything. Sharp had earned it.

If there had been any Mexicans left, they elected not to bother the two men walking through the compound. One of the Mexican HUMMVs looked to be in good shape, and Grant motioned for Sharp to get behind the wheel.

"North or west, Sergeant Major?"

"Whichever is quicker. I have the feeling that Major Bonneville is miles beyond pissed at us right now."

Chapter 14

Grant and Harrison sat in their vehicle on the border road, waiting for the convoy to come up from the south. It would be the last of the line platoons leaving the Area of Operations and heading back to the barracks at Fort Bliss. A new unit had moved in and taken over in response to 'concerns' of the Mexican government. Their ambassador in Washington had presented a public letter thanking the 289th for saving the life of Captain Nunez of the Mexican Marine Corps, and for 'assisting' in blocking actions that led to the destruction of human and drug trafficking routes in the border area.

It had been a masterful work of diplomatic bullshit. There was a brief section mourning the death of Major Apuesta and much of his command staff in a pitched battle at his forward command post in the desert. His valiant efforts to fight the cartels and cooperate with the Americans would remain a model of international cooperation for years to come. He was a national hero, and they were planning to name a plaza after him in *Cuidad Juarez*. There would be a ceremony, but, regrettably, they requested no *Norte Americanos* attend. There was still some sensitivity that Mexican soldiers had died protecting American interests.

There had been a second, secret message from Mexico that was far less eloquent in its praise for American cooperation. It was a strongly worded, yet highly classified formal complaint about the 'Acts of Aggression' committed by United States soldiers on Mexican soil that resulted in the deaths of many Mexican nationals and the destruction of millions of dollars in property. Left unsaid was that the dead were predominantly criminal elements of their own armed forces, most notably Major Apuesta and his command staff, and that the millions in destroyed property included unspecified amounts of illegal drugs about to be smuggled across the border. The Secretary of State, in a less than stellar performance in front of the Mexican Ambassador in the privacy of her office, apologized profusely and offered reimbursement, plus an indemnity for each dead soldier. It was graciously accepted by the ambassador, on behalf of the victimized.

Certain members of Congress, sensing a political opportunity at the expense of the secure borders crowd, began calling for secret hearings on the excesses of the military, particularly the 289th Engineers, who had spread so much havoc across three continents. Secret hearings would get out the juiciest of details, which would be all the better to leak to friendly press outlets.

Several investigators immediately appeared at the headquarters of the 289th demanding full access to all records and reports. Much to their dismay, they were provided them.

The political appointees at the top of the food chain may have been anxious to float the blame on somebody else's pond, but the people close to the problem had other ideas. The DEA and ICE provided a wealth of documentation about the players on the Mexican side. The file on Apuesta and his staff, plus a comparison of the names on DEA wanted lists to the reported dead Mexican soldiers painted a grim and embarrassing story. The New Mexican State Police had hours of surveillance tape and recordings from Mexican owned businesses in Columbus that had long been identified with the drug trade. Elements of the Mexican Justice Department, learning of the investigation, fell back on old memos instructing them to cooperate with the Americans and provided copies of documents that had linked Apuesta with the cartels. Staff Sergeant Gordon, Major Bonneville's very talented and efficient NCO, quickly sorted through the megabytes of information provided and extracted copies of reports to prominent politicians, some of whom were calling for the hearings that not only outlined the problems, but identified the players. There were also documents financially linking some of those players with some of those politicians.

The Mexican government soon got wind of what was percolating and panicked. The story they were circulating publicly would be an embarrassment if the true story were revealed. This called for another visit to the Secretary of State from the Mexican Ambassador, and yet another apology for any thought that there would be any embarrassment to the Mexican government. To make certain there were no misunderstandings, she promptly doubled the restitution for damaged goods.

The resulting tsunami went unreported by the press, and there were efforts to have everything classified and removed from the files of the 289th. Operational computers and laptops were ordered confiscated, to be properly safeguarded. Again, unfortunately for the attempted cover-up, somebody requested a list of files so that each could be examined and have 'the appropriate level of classification assigned'. SFC Callan had never seen a request like that before and quickly realized someone was giving him a heads up. He made the list, and then burned several sets of CD-ROMs and distributed them to the people in the unit who would know what to do with them.

"Here they come now." Harrison pointed to the south. They both got out and stood by the side of the road. SFC Powell pulled his vehicle out of line and joined them.

Together they returned the salutes of the vehicles as they drove by. It shouldn't have been a long convoy, but Grant noticed they had a few extra vehicles in line, mostly sporting a Mexican camouflage pattern.

"Where is Lieutenant Powers?" She had been the platoon leader designated as the property transfer officer for the new unit coming in.

"She's not done with them yet. Somebody thought they could just waltz in and take whatever gear we had that they liked. Not that we had a lot, but some of the comfort items are near and dear to the troops." The 289th had a history of living well when they could. "She's nit-picking them over the last hand receipts. We may have stolen it, but they'll have to sign."

"They didn't want the vehicles?"

"Well, they did, until we explained what they were."

"What's going to happen to them?"

Powell laughed. "As soon as we get to Bliss, Mitchell's going to strip them of every useable nut and bolt."

Harrison cocked his head at that. "Why? We'll be out of here in 30 days. He sure as hell can't take it with him."

"No, but there seems to be a huge spare parts shortage army wide. He figures he can swap this stuff out to make up for losses, and use the amnesty program to get credit on the excess he can take back to home station." The Army had a policy of giving credit for spare parts turn in, no questions asked. They established it to try to stop units from hoarding short supply items. Mitchell was one NCO who knew how to make it work for his unit.

Powell waved and followed the convoy up the trail.

"30 days?" Grant asked. "I hadn't heard that."

"It's not official yet. It could be as long as forty five days. I don't think the Army is done fucking with us yet. We may be a bad taste in their mouth, but they always have been masochists."

They drove back to the headquarters area, or what was left of it. The New Mexico National Guard had moved in and taken over the area. The first unit in was an armored infantry battalion equipped with Strykers. They were to train up on the new equipment, qualify and turn it over to the next battalion when they moved to their own deployment in Afghanistan. This had been declared a safe area for training, now that the cartel problem had been absorbed by the Mexican Marines.

These soldiers came in with all the new equipment. It was a far cry from the old and obsolete gear the 289th had been issued. With trainers and support elements, the area that housed less than 150 soldiers now had to handle over one thousand. Price and his heavy equipment spent their last days clearing new bivouacs and motor parks, and the vertical construction platoons got to string barbed wire around their perimeters. Then the newcomers absorbed the heavy equipment platoon. Somehow, Price managed to get absorbed with his equipment. He had said goodbye the day before.

"Are you sure you want to do this, Jonah?" Grant asked, using Price's first name on a very rare occasion.

"What else am I going to do, Luke? I sure as hell don't want to go back to the fishing boat, and I don't think I could handle being a part-time soldier."

"You don't need to do any of that. Go back to being a retired puke and work for Harrison's wife. It's not like you need the money."

Price shook his head." It's not about the money, Luke. It's about this. As fucked up as it gets, I need this. Besides, it won't be like I'll be alone."

He was right, he wouldn't be among strangers. The soldiers of Delta Company, 4th Battalion, 711th Infantry Regiment who had joined them so long ago at Fort Bliss were nowhere near their release from active duty date. They too had been absorbed into the Stryker Battalion. Callan even managed to keep his position in the operations section. He did give Harrison the Guidon they had carried to that first formation. "It'll look good crossed with the red one behind your desk," meaning the engineer flag. Before they left Grant had Callan collect the 711th into one last formation. It was a brief goodbye. Grant promised that if the awards the unit had put in for were approved he would make certain each one of them got theirs. Other than that, he wanted to give them each one of the challenge coins he had minted. "Someday, all this shit will be public. One of you might even write a book about it. After that happens, some loud mouth in a bar somewhere will brag about these past few weeks and tell everybody how hard it was. Ask him for his coin and smack yours down on the bar. When he doesn't show you one, kick his ass. If you need bail money, give me a call. I'll be easy to find."

Sharp was waiting for them when they pulled into the parking area. There was a packed duffel bag at his feet. Grant groaned when he saw it.

"Give me a fucking break, Dave. Don't tell me you're staying here too!"

Sharp looked puzzled. "What are you talking about? There's no fucking way I'm staying here."

Harrison asked. "What's with the bag?"

Sharp looked down at his feet. "This? This is a lot of shit we don't want anybody to see at Bliss. I've been collecting it for three days. Price just brought this load in from the boys in the 711th. There are three bags just like it in your tent." He kicked the bag again. It had a heavy metallic sound. "Why would you even think I'd want to stay?"

"We thought you might miss Price."

"That shit head? Its worse being around him than it is being around you. I think this is the first time he didn't get shot at and hit and he misses it. He wants to go fuck with some rag head in Kabul." He paused and smiled. "You know he's not too fucking bright."

They all laughed. Grant agreed. "None of us are, Dave. None of us are."

That evening after supper, Grant was taking a slow run around the perimeter of the expanded bivouac. It had been a while since he ran like this and his legs were sore, but he kept running, just to prove to himself he could. He was soaked in sweat when he got back to his tent, but he had made the three laps and he was pleased with himself. He sat his ass down in his lawn chair and spread his legs out. A good shower and a beer would go great right about now. He glanced over his shoulder at his cooler. The beer would come first. As he got up he saw Major Bonneville coming his way. He pulled out another chair and set it besides his. "And how is the Executive Officer this fine evening?" Kearney had returned after the uproar had settled down. Bonneville had gladly relinquished command back to him. She was tired of being mad all the time and not knowing why.

"I saw you coming around the motor pool. Want some company?"

She sat besides him and he offered her a beer. "The new commander says he wants a dry bivouac."

"And he's welcome to it. This area, however, is still the property of the 289th Engineers. Once we do the hand over he can enforce any rules his pointy little head desires." She took the beer from him. "Kearney just told me we'll be pulling out in a couple of days. Once we get everything turned in at Bliss we'll be sent back to home station to be released from active duty."

He didn't respond. The cold bottle felt good in his hand and he drained half of it.

"Will you be released from active duty with us?"

"Probably not. I was assigned from the Active Army, remember? They'll still have a claim on me." She was quiet, thinking about what to say next. He didn't give her a chance. "As I recall, my orders assigned me to the staff of the Adjutant General. It's up to him if I get discharged or not."

Her hand slid over and rested on his. "So what do you want to do?"

"I don't know. I've never really liked the son of a bitch." It was true. When the State AG was a young Second Lieutenant he was responsible for Grant's first Purple Heart and his Medal of Honor. "I have to decide if staying would piss him off more than leaving."

"Wouldn't he have a say?"

"He'd like to, but that little blue ribbon with all the stars trumps most of what he has to say." He pulled his hand out and put it on top of hers. "I will be around to complicate your life, whatever happens. That is, if that's what you want. I know I'm a crotchety old bastard."

She turned to look at him. "Do you think Powell showed the new people where the spring is?"

"I don't think Powell got along with the new people well enough to tell them where air is." Grant finished his beer. "However, if you'd like, I'd be happy to go down there and check and post it off limits, if that's all right with you, Ma'am."

"Would you like some company, Sergeant Major?"